Best wishes.

Bob.

Retrogenesis 2

Retrogenesis 2

The Journey

Robert Swann

Library of Congress Control Number:		2012921046
ISBN:	Hardcover	978-1-4797-4699-6
	Softcover	978-1-4797-4698-9
	Ebook	978-1-4797-4700-9

To order additional copies of this book, contact:
Xlibris Corporation
0-800-644-6988
www.xlibrispublishing.co.uk
Orders@xlibrispublishing.co.uk
304904

Also by Robert Swann

Retrogenesis 1
The Anomaly

A miraculous new technology is discovered which can be of greater benefit to the whole of world society than any previous innovation. The advantages it offers will make the world a better place, but there is a dark side to this fantastic technology which, in the wrong hands, can destroy civilisation—*completely*.

The challenge that its creators face is to introduce the technology for the humanitarian benefits it promises and to have it made available to all nations rich or poor without favour. Their search of the world for a judicious keeper of the technology does not meet with success. The bitter experience of their dealings with powerful governments and a particular megalomaniac politician tells them that ultimately the value their technology offers will be eclipsed by its more unsavoury capabilities.

Eventually, after investigating and rejecting all possible contenders, they believe they have no alternative but to create a completely new nation and society where none had previously existed, using the phenomenal power of the new technology.

Their mission is to protect their innovation from exploitation by the superpowers which demonstrate an unhealthy interest in the dark supremacy that this powerful tool will give them. This is a battle between grasping governments and rogues and the will of those who care deeply for humanity.

What Julia Ann Charpentier of ForeWord Reviews *has to say*

With this, the author has a gem in the making . . .
Formidable and strange . . .
A mesmerising concept . . .
Intriguing . . .
Sinister . . .
Sophisticated . . .

About the Author

Born and educated in the London borough of Hillingdon, I started my professional life as a student civil engineer in the Atomic Power Division of a major British Engineering Company. After three years in this environment, I decided that the constraints of formal engineering were not for me and opted for the more open arena of logistics, which, at that time, was virtually unexplored—except by the military establishments.

Progressing through general management and directorships along my chosen path I ventured into the field of logistics management consultancy, first, with a British company and then as vice president of an American consulting group in their London office. Ultimately, I bought out the London practice and formed a close friendship and a joint working agreement with an American business entrepreneur, and we have worked together collectively and separately in around forty different countries.

I feel eternal gratitude for the opportunities that I have been fortunate enough to enjoy through the extensive world travel my professional life has enabled. This literary work is populated by a selected amalgam of many of the fascinating people with whom I have had the privilege to meet both socially and professionally and the truly wonderful and, sometimes, extremely challenging countries it has been my great fortune to visit.

Acknowledgements

The portrayal of something that has not yet happened, but conceivably will, is by its very nature challenging in its illustration, and it is with this in mind that my thanks go to those who undertook to comment on the many early, intermediate, and final drafts of this work, and who offered their invaluable advice on matters of style, perception, and substance. My eternal gratitude goes to my wife Jenefer for her dogged determination in enhancing the prose by reading and re-reading so many drafts and offering the, oh so invaluable intuitive female perspective.

Help was gratefully received from Marty and Debbi Buchalski from the USA and from Terry Thurston, Tony Bungey, and Emma Thompson and Val Strutt, from the UK, who gave generously their time and their invaluable insights, which helped to supplement new perspectives fermenting within my imagination. They gave not only their time but also their intellect, and I will be forever grateful for their unstinting help and their sharing of ideas. Special thanks go to Cornelius Graham, my English tutor, from long ago, who introduced me to the subtle beauty of language and the magic of words. I am also grateful for the professionalism of Levi Grimm, my publishing consultant, copy editors—James Calonia and his team, Rhea Villacarlos—and the publisher's production team, all of whom worked so hard to ensure the quality and presentation of the books and who displayed their skill and dedication in a market which is hugely subscribed and in which recognition can be, and often is, elusive.

1   Thus the heavens and the earth were finished and all the host of them.
2   And by the seventh day God ended his work which he had made; and he rested from all his work which he had made.

(Gen. 2: 1, 2)

Humanity neither creates nor destroys anything; it merely rearranges what nature provides but not always to the benefit of mankind.

(An observation)

For Jenefer, Manda and Kriss

Prologue

*I*n the hallowed precincts of 10, Downing Street, in the bustling heart of London a shadowy figure slid silently into the otherwise empty private study of the Prime Minister. It was obvious from his posture that his presence there was illicit; it was equally obvious that he was familiar with the office and its layout. Despite there being no window illumination to light his way, he was able to navigate the many obstacles from the dim illumination, which seeped in from the partially open door, giving access to the world's most famous cabinet room.

The interloper made his way to a bookshelf filled with the latest copies of *Hansard* in week-by-week red leather binders, each of which was carefully numbered and dated in gold embossed characters. He selected a three-month old copy, which he knew with reasonable certainty would not be accessed for some time, and withdrew it from the shelf. Placing it on the old and battered, walnut writing desk favoured by the Prime Minister, he opened the binder and laid it flat on the desk; his hands shook with the acute tension of the moment. The bottom of the pages were short of the bottom of the binder by some two-fingers width which was adequate for his purpose of concealment.

Pausing in his endeavours, he took and held a deep breath before listening carefully for any sounds which would alert him to impending discovery; there were none. From his formal and quaintly old-fashioned morning coat pocket, he withdrew a long, flat box, slender enough and short enough to fit into the cavity at the bottom of the selected file and when closed, it would still allow the file to sit, level, on its shelf. He placed the file back into its location and looked, as best he could with the available light, to ensure that the file was indistinguishable from its counterparts. All was well, but still his hands shook.

Pressing the on button on a small remote controller, he gently tapped three times on the desktop and then, pressing the button again, switched the device off. Removing the leather binder from its shelf, he extracted the box he had placed within it and switched the unit back on using the remote controller once more. Three distinct taps could be heard with sharp clarity from the tiny speaker at one end of the box. Satisfied with the success of his work, he replaced the binder with the recording device back on to the shelf. He had undertaken this task without illumination, not only out of fear of the light being seen, but also because he knew that had he switched the light on, it would have activated the room's silent security system and a damning record of his presence would have been made.

His face was pale as he exited the study; what he had just done was tantamount to treason. He had abused the position of trust which gave him access to this part of number10, and what he had just done was totally alien to his normal character. Wiping the cold sweat of fear from his brow, he quietly closed the study door behind him and entered the unlit cabinet room. He had succeeded in his task, but he was in mortal fear of its consequences. His actions could radically change not only his life, but also that of the Prime Minister of Great Britain. His trepidation was acute.

One

The evening was sultry and the palm trees silhouetted against the afterglow of the setting sun, black against fiery orange. Several friends sharing the comfort of close companionship lounged in comfortable rattan chairs on the terrace of one of the cafes on the lower slopes of Recovery Island's Central Mountain. Conversation among them flowed easily as in the mellow of evening as they relaxed after a busy and rewarding day.

They mulled over events, sometimes dramatic, which had occurred since they had created and now occupied their new homeland. Chester Gilliland smiled lazily as he saw the easy harmony between the members of their group. He had a special smile for Penny Caine with her dark hair and golden tan all of which gave her a languid almost ethereal beauty; he watched intently as she entered wholeheartedly into the conversation. She was such an important part of his life, and without her vibrant personality, he would not have had the courage to make the truly staggering decisions which had provided them with their remarkable, much coveted, new lifestyle.

Bruce Crook laughed at something Penny Caine had said; she was one of the rare people who could make him laugh out loud and transform the intensity of his usual dour manner. He shared Penny's humour with

Silas Pettit, who was normally as taciturn as Bruce, maybe even more so, and his reaction was a sardonic smile.

Gilliland, a marine biologist, Crook, a particle physicist, and Caine, a psychologist had all graduated with doctorates from Hinckley University in Colorado (HUC) in the USA where their deep bonds of friendship had begun, and again later, with post-graduate work at Cambridge University in England. Unlike them, Silas Pettit was not an academic but had been a soldier of fortune in the power of Colin Wilson, a rogue British politician, who had been his boss until he had been instrumental in rescuing not only Gilliland and Crook, but also himself from one of Wilson's vindictive self-serving plans.

Juilietta Gray slid into the remaining empty chair, smiling greetings to the others as she settled next to Silas Pettit and leaning towards him, planted a kiss on his cheek. Juilietta had been the last to join the inner circle, and with her background in personnel management, had fitted in instantly and effortlessly into their group. Now working closely with Silas Pettit with whom she had formed a special and close relationship she had drawn him out of his shell of remoteness in much the same way as Penny Caine rescued Bruce Crook from his occasional darkness. Gilliland observed his friends and felt a sense of well-being as they reminisced over their recent history.

Several traumatic, but on the whole rewarding, years had passed since Gilliland and Crook had discovered an amazing anomaly during an experiment in enhanced radar detection for the British Ministry of Defence (MoD). The anomaly they uncovered during the experiments could, in the right hands, do many things to help mankind but in the wrong hands could destroy it in its entirety. Gilliland recalled with a chill how close he and Crook had come, unwittingly, to killing themselves during the early stages of their fantastic discovery.

They had kept their find a secret from their unprincipled boss, Colin Wilson, the DDP (Director of Defence Projects), who was an adviser to the British MoD, knowing that they could not trust him with this revolutionary technology while continuing with the development of the original research, which had produced the anomaly. They had realised early in their association with Wilson that he could not be trusted with anything important, let alone something so potentially destructive. The anomaly unquestionably had many powerfully destructive applications.

Despite scouring the world for a benign partner, they were unable to identify a single alternative government or country which could be trusted with the power of this technology. Further problems evolved when the characteristically unprincipled actions of the DDP forced the abandonment of their research project just as it was about to reach its initial conclusion. They soon recognised by his irrational behaviour that his intention was to steal the technology for personal use and recognised that it was down to them and them alone to prevent him from realising and stealing the full power of their discovery.

They were thankful that he was, at least initially, unaware of the existence and value of the anomaly, which was an adjunct to the original experiment with which they had been charged. They remonstrated with him about the untimely cancellation of the original radar-based project, code named Broken Arrow, and in response, he dishonestly terminated their contracts and promised with relish to ruin their professional reputations.

Being a vindictive man and wanting their original technology, to further his lofty ambitions, he endeavoured to have the scientists branded as traitors and, actually, had them imprisoned without just cause, with the intent of their being spirited away and eliminated. After a nerve-wracking escape, aided by Silas Pettit, who had been originally charged with capturing them, but who had defected to them after a contretemps with Wilson, they all eventually reached Gilliland's bolthole on the Azores island of Flores.

From this location, the three men, joined by Penny Caine, Gilliland's childhood sweetheart, and now his constant companion and now also a close friend of Bruce Crook, developed what had been until then an embryonic plan for constructing an island base which enabled them to create the alternative society which would ensure the safe use of their technology. The original three had spent their years at HUC, and as post-graduates at Cambridge University, exchanged their thoughts and studiously idealistic passions about man's inhumanity to man as is the accustomed habit of the developing young.

The opportunity for them to fulfil their dreams came when they realised that they could harness the anomaly's extraordinary power and use it to create and form a new land mass from the seabed in the middle of the Atlantic away from prying eyes and interference. They had realised this dream and had begun the task of populating it with carefully chosen specialists for whom, should they wish to stay after completing their specific tasks, a totally new way of life was offered. To allow breathing space to develop their plans unhampered by the interference that they knew instinctively would come from Wilson, they feigned their collective demise in a maritime accident and successfully leaked the misinformation to Wilson. This move had enabled them to construct and populate their new Island without initial interference from him. The technology giving them this incredible ability was known as "BAM2", an acronym for Broken Arrow Mark 2, the adjunct to their initial radar-research project, and was truly revolutionary in concept. Its anomalous nature enabled them, among many other things, to create and control volcanic activity which empowered them to form their Island home in the shape that they had jointly agreed. In creating their Island home, they found, on the seabed from which the Island was to be formed, the remnants of what was probably an Iron Age settlement which long ago had sunk below the waves of the Atlantic in a cataclysmic geological event. Recovery Island, aptly named because it was recovered from the seabed into which it originally sank hundreds of years ago. The location of the original island is recorded on the seventeenth century maps of Moses Pitt and also that of Gerardus Mercator and Ludocus Hodius and was originally named as Las Maidas by Mercator and Hodius. The new Island of Recovery, perceived by world powers to be a threat to their supremacy, was placed under siege and it was only by using the power of BAM2, this time as a means of defence, that the Islanders were able to prevent being invaded and overrun by their much more powerful adversaries.

Recalling the tribulations of their chosen path, the conversation became a little more sombre and the laughter a little less frequent. Even though, they had used all means at their disposal to keep the technology secret, it soon became apparent to the rest of the world that something very unusual was happening in this newly formed, man-made, mid-Atlantic Island. This was inevitably brought to the attention of a new superpower, the Federation of Nations, which had emerged following the sudden and dramatic collapse of world finances, and they were not slow to realise that commandeering the power of the anomaly would give them the opportunity to take control of the rest of the world. The Federation was dominated by China, by far the largest national population in the world. The newly formed dictatorship in China, which replaced the previously more inclusive democratic government, had reverted to the unyielding totalitarian state of the old pre-enlightenment regime.

Much to the annoyance of the UK DDP Wilson, who was in cahoots with the Federation of Nations, the newly formed embryonic Island nation, quickly and firmly established its independence despite the Federation's best efforts to frustrate their rapid development. To impose their will, the Federation placed the Island under siege, and it was only by using the power of BAM2 as a means of defence that the Islanders were able to frustrate the ambitions of their much-more powerful adversaries and prevent being invaded and overrun by force of numbers.

The siege of the Island was imposed by the Federation when they had grown weary of the resistance of these few puny Islanders against the magnificence of their superpower status. Discord was escalated when the Federation of Nations used its military might to prevent the cargo ship *Ironman* from delivering vital freight by tightening a ring of naval might around the Island. Justification for the escalation of the siege by the Federation was that *Ironman*, a man line freighter, was carrying munitions and other strategic materials which posed a threat to the "free" world. This was, of course, untrue, but there was no mechanism for the Islanders to refute the gross fabrication.

The attempt to prevent *Ironman* from completing its task, much to the frustration of the Federation had, yet again, been repulsed by the use of the Island's technology, and *Ironman* was escorted into the protection of the Island's dock by *Wallow V*, the sole vessel of the Recovery Island's "Navy", which was in truth the Island's maintenance vessel fitted with BAM2 defence capabilities that operated both above and below the water in the form of an impregnable protective bubble that would destroy anything and everything which tried to pass through it by guarding against attack from, on, above, or below the sea's surface.

Defeating the might of the Federation of Nations' Navy with its aircraft carriers, cruisers, and battleships was a humiliation too far for the pompous Federation demagogues, and they were seething with impotent rage at the ludicrous sight of the tiny motorised *rowing boat* protecting an unarmed merchant vessel against the full force of the might of the Federation.

The BAM2 system allowed for the defence of the Island and its sea craft as well as the visiting vessel, and it had the potential for the destruction of other sea and air transport although it would never be used by the Islanders for destructive purposes. That the might of the Federation had once more been thwarted by the puny Island state, made them more determined to use any means to crush the Islanders and all they represented and made the Islanders more determined to resist them by all ethical means at their disposal which was only made possible by their absolute technological superiority.

The mood of the four founders and Juilietta Gray lightened again when they finished their reminiscences and concluded that notwithstanding the traumas they had encountered they were free to follow their lifestyle at least at home but not on a worldwide basis in which they had been branded, entirely without foundation, as terrorists. They would discover in the fullness of time, and in many different ways, that life would not always deliver the results they had a right to expect.

T W O

*I*onman, the flagship of the Man Cargo Corporation, which had been the catalyst leading to the dramatic siege of the Island when the Federation Navy had tried unsuccessfully to prevent a delivery of vital freight was now, thanks to the Island's powerful defence capabilities, a frequent visitor bringing much-needed goods to sustain life: goods which the Island, during this early stage of its development, was unable to produce from within its own boundaries. This freedom of movement, which the Federation's siege was intended to prevent, was made possible by the threat of remote protection of the vessel, using the capabilities of the Island's unique BAM2 and NRT radar technologies against which the Federation had no counter measures. Being held at bay in this way did not sit easily on the shoulders of the Federation, and they strove continuously to invent ways to disarm the Island without destroying the resident technology which they were so desperate to commandeer intact.

Consideration had been given by the Islanders to fit a BAM2 projector on to the *Ironman* to provide it with an on-board defence from attack both above and below the water but having a mobile unit travelling freely about the world would leave the technology vulnerable to capture. It could also lead to the instant destruction of *Ironman* and all on board if it were mishandled by uninitiated operators.

The valuable incoming cargo was unloaded and stored in the Island's dockside warehouses. Freight was moved from ship to the warehouses by automated surface transporters, which were the only surface transport allowed on the Island. All other mass movements were accomplished underground by means of automatically controlled transfer cars (TCs), the network for which covered the whole Island and was freely used for both people and freight.

As soon as the unloading was completed, *Ironman* was reloaded with sacks of maize, which had been received as payment for work undertaken by the Islanders in South Africa, a country which had braved the wrath of the Federation in return for technical aid from the Island. The maize would be sent back to Nematasulu, a newly emerged West African country, which had been, until the intervention of Island technology, an unwanted fever-ridden swamp. Nematasulu was the richest of the new African states and was in all but name a protectorate of Recovery Island.

The maize was payment for the superfast growing organic material from Nematasulu which comprised the bulk of the *Ironman*'s cargo and would be used to supplement the increasing volume of organic medium forming the basis of the Island's growing agricultural infrastructure.

The rest of the incoming cargo was tiny in volume but made up greater than 98 per cent of its value. It comprised of uncut diamonds, their commission from the joint mining venture in Nematasulu. The diamond mine had been opened up using BAM2 technology—turning the country from desperate poverty to previously unimagined wealth. Tembo Mbunani, a minister in the Nematasulan Government and personal friend of Chester Gilliland, was as good as his word; the payment in Nematasulu diamonds was continuous and, at a commission rate of 10 per cent of the diamonds mined, substantial. Apart from the commission agreement, the two countries had established a system of bartering which was also a great success. Additionally, the Recovery Island administration received goods from many other countries, mostly in Africa, as a reward for the mining and other civil works carried out for them; this income enabled the Islanders to live and develop their society. Nematasulu was used as a staging point for all African-generated products, much to the anger of the Federation of Nations.

When reloading was completed, *Ironman* departed the shelter of the harbour and headed south-east for the West African coast. Recovery Island communications operation advised the Federation siege force that *Ironman* was leaving port bound for Nematasulu with a cargo of maize and that the vessel contained only non-military goods and should be accorded free passage from the Island. They also advised that the vessel was not being escorted but that any attempt to delay the vessel in international waters would elicit a protective response from the Island's security resources.

No reply was received from the Federation; the forces of which were entirely frustrated by the Island's ability to protect *Ironman* remotely by using the resources of BAM2. A close watch was kept on the radar screens to check on any interference from the Federation or any other vessels. None were detected, but there was an increase in air activity from helicopters initially and then as *Ironman* became more distant from longer-range aircraft.

Pettit watched the recently upgraded Holographic Map Tables (HMT) as *Ironman* was tracked over the horizon, using the original Nano Receptor Transmitter (NRT) radar-bending technology which the MOD, under Wilson's guidance, had abandoned as not being value for money. He radioed the Federation flagship once more to reinforce their undertaking to protect *Ironman* wherever on the ocean she might be.

Urgent message for the C-in-C Federation Fleet. Recovery Island defences continue to track Ironman *by radar using NRT. The Federation is free to fly over international waters completely*

unhindered, provided they do not threaten Ironman *in anyway.*
Message ends.

The HMT operatives watched land, sea, sub-sea, and air transport movements which hovered, dome-shaped to represent the shape of the earth, in layers over the viewing table. They tracked the movements of two Federation submarines, an aircraft carrier, assorted other surface vessels, and patrolling aircraft from their carrier base. *Ironman* continued on its course to Nematasulu unhindered but with an armada of accompaniment at arm's length. Each holographic layer was a different colour so that low-flying aircraft could not be confused with surface vessels and the surface vessels with the shallow sub-surface vessels. They would continue tracking the activity all the way to the Nematasulu coast and, if necessary, beyond.

There was no immediate response from the Federation. Pettit assumed that they were digesting, with continuing ill humour, the information about NRT, which they knew was very embarrassing to the UK MOD and to Wilson, whose illicit actions had deprived the UK and, therefore, Europe and also the Federation of NRT ownership. Because radar tracking was in operation twenty-four hours a day, radar being operable both day and night, the progress of *Ironman* and the attendant Federation vessels were so closely monitored that Federation intervention could be reacted to immediately, and they would realise, definitively. Pettit sent a further message to the fleet, warning that the protection offered by Recovery Island included Federation air and surface vessels from whatever location. His radar observers advised him of the number of "bogies" they had detected, and he passed this information on to the fleet, indicating to them by deduction that NRT was functioning and not just a bluff.

Subsequent to the earlier friction between the Islanders and the Federation, the Island's radar capabilities had been improved to enable a more complete picture of possible threats from off Island. The holographic images were projected above the radar tables, and at full projection that could reveal the whole of the earth's globe or in larger detail or just a part of it. Nano Receptor Transmitter (NRT) technology had enabled them to see a complete image of their adversary's assets. Commercial aircrafts crossing the Atlantic were also clearly visible and were at a greater altitude than the military aircraft and were flying specific routes. Also commercial merchantmen were equally easily recognised but were still tracked carefully to ensure that they were what they seemed to be. The watchers had become accustomed to seeing the miracle of holographic global-layered transmission but were not immune to the wonder of what they could see. A surface vessel began closing in on the freighter, and the watcher switched to another HMT to take a look at what was happening in closer proximity. He selected a segment of the dome which covered the activity in which he was interested and magnified it. The magnified image showed *Ironman* and was detailed enough to be able to recognise the outline of the vessel and to see the surface interference the wake was causing. The closing vessel was much smaller but did not appear to be military.

"*RI control to* Ironman. *Are you receiving me? Over.*" The watcher spoke calmly into the communicator.

After a brief delay the response came. "*This is* Ironman. *We are receiving you in sunshine clarity, over.*"

"*We read a close proximity vessel converging. Are you aware? Over.*"

"*We have the vessel on radar, and we have a visual. It looks like a deep-sea fisher, probably Russian, but we're keeping an eye on it, and let you know if anything develops. The captain thanks you for your vigilance, over and out.*"

"*Over and out.*"

*

With no further incursions into the Island's twelve-mile exclusion zone and no other communications from any part of the Federation, the Islanders settled down once more to the waiting game but did not relax their vigilance. The defensive domes over the Island, which prevented the ingress of any solid matter, had been switched off allowing rain and wildlife through, but as this left the Island vulnerable to attack, an extra vigilant watch was being kept. It was assumed that the Federation had deduced that their defence system comprising the dome, which was otherwise invisible, had been outlined by rain interaction and, later, by the Federation helicopter formation, spraying water which would indicate to them whether the defence domes were inactive.

Silence and inactivity prevailed for three days. It was broken by the surprise launching from the fleet of an Unmanned Aerial Vehicle (UAV) which headed straight for the centre of the Island. The estimated flight time to the Island was seven minutes from the time of detection, which gave the Islanders only limited time to react. Crook was on duty in the radar room when the incident occurred, and he immediately activated the inner Island's defence dome and contacted Gilliland and Petit.

Pettit crashed through the radar room doors at the run and was shortly followed by Gilliland. Caine followed some three minutes later at a much more sedate and ladylike pace. She looked at all the occupants of the room and saw varying stages of shock and agitation from Gilliland, Crook, and the radar observers; she also saw that Petit was calm, collected, and calculating. She listened to the gabbled debriefing and watched as the UAV crossed the middle of the Island and continued on to the north coast.

"What is the purpose?" She tilted her had towards Pettit.

"Among other possibilities, it's probably a photographic reconnaissance flight," Pettit answered in a slightly flat, almost disinterested voice. "But we can only watch and wait."

"And how do you propose we respond, after we've watched and waited?"

"Well, they can take photographs from space so that isn't primary, although they will get much better resolution close-up. They probably want to see how we will react to their probing."

"As I said, how do we respond?"

"Easy", he said, picking up a radio phone *"Federation fleet, this is the Recovery Island's Director of Defence. One of your UAVs is obviously off course and is over-flying the Island without clearance from our air traffic control. This contravenes our aviation laws. Please recall the UAV immediately and do not fly back over the Island. Make a right turn and fly east out of the twelve-mile zone."*

"Recovery Island," the C-in-C answered personally; he had clearly been waiting for a response. *"Your assumed rights in this matter are not valid. You are not recognised by the international community and, therefore, the stated laws do not apply."* There was a pause and some angry indistinct exchanges in the background before the C-in-C continued, *"By international law, you are required to desist from interfering with the lawful activities of the Federation which are supported by the international community."*

"So! International law only applies when you want it to. Interesting, if you fly over the Island, again the UAV will be destroyed." Gilliland took over the radiophone from Pettit. *"And tell Wilson that if he has something to say to us to come out in person, instead of hiding behind a stooge."*

There was a pregnant pause followed by expletives in the background and then the connection went dead.

"Just as we thought," Crook said dejectedly. "Wilson's back in the frame. That's going to make life so much more unpredictable."

"The UAV has changed course and is still heading towards us." The senior radar observer announced in a deadpan voice.

The air in the radio room of HMS *Foxhound* was blue. Wilson was snarling and spitting, angry that, he thought irrationally, somebody had told the treacherous Islanders that he was on board rather than accepting that his irrational behaviour had given him away. He berated anybody who was within hearing about the inability of sailors to keep their mouths shut. He had thought that with the demise of Gilliland, Crook, and Pettit, which was the misinformation he had been fed, he would meet with less stringent opposition. Clearly, their required capitulation was not evident. The C-in-C sighed in resignation and wondered why it was he who had been selected to work with the maniac seething and bubbling before him.

The C-in-C had rightly surmised that "the treacherous Islanders" as he referred to them could tell by the politically motivated ranting that he had been prompted to espouse sentiments which were totally out of character for a naval officer of his rank. He thought it prudent not to voice his opinion, knowing the boiling rage it would promote, although he was sorely tempted to wind up this silly little man.

"Turn that thing around and fly it back over the Island and do it now!" Wilson shouted in frustration.

His orders were followed, and the UAV was turned in a wide sweep to the east and then back round to over fly the Island. They watched the video link which showed the UAV approaching the Island's coast; the picture definition was excellent, and they could see all buildings, installations, and people in absolute detail as it flew over the coastline. With startling abruptness, the picture disappeared.

"Get that damn picture back," Wilson screeched. "What is the matter with you people, can't you do anything right?"

The C-in-C picked up his ringing telephone and listened intently. He put it down slowly and looked at Wilson as he fumed and continued to be thoroughly unpleasant.

"Director". he drawled urbanely, "we can't get the picture back."

"Why the hell not?" Wilson was once more beside himself.

"The UAV has disappeared without trace. One minute it was there on our radar, and the next minute it was gone."

An unnatural quiet settled over the room, and its occupants froze as they, and that included Wilson, realised the significance of what the C-in-C had said.

Three

Wilson was depressed; the UAV sortie had been to no avail. Even the good news trickling in from his many international informants failed to lift the darkness of his mood. He learned that people in the United States were close to rising up against the administration of President Klastheim. It had finally been recognised that Klastheim was being manipulated by the Chinese to support Federation aims.

Europeans were also dissatisfied with the subservience shown by the various presidents and prime ministers of most of the more senior member nations which were influential enough to make a difference. Several of the thirty regrouped European country members were beginning to demonstrate against the tightening hold of the Federation, and anti-Chinese and anti-Federation feelings were gaining momentum.

The situation was looked upon by Wilson as being an opportunity for him to consolidate his plans for expanding his personal power base while the destabilising influences were occupying the various national security agencies. Their ability to frustrate his goal of influencing their countries' courses of events was diverted by their need to suppress insurrection. This also, paradoxically, included the very heart of China where, Wilson's informants advised him, there was a strong hint of resistance among the proletariat which threatened to burgeon into a full-scale popular uprising against their unyielding dictatorship.

But his other frustrations were not being reduced. He was permanently agonising over how he could get control of BAM2 technology, but the knowledge that all his past efforts had been successfully repulsed continued to haunt him. There must, he thought, be another way; if it was not possible to steal it, then there would have to be another avenue of approach. He looked over the findings of the scientists who had failed to progress the Broken Arrow Project after he had chased Gilliland and Crook from the Isles of Scilly.

Pouring over the notes of the scientists that he had employed to complete the originally interrupted work of Gilliland and Crook and which his renegade scientists had failed dismally to conclude, he was unable to make head or tail of the hieroglyphics and jargon. Terms that they used were alien to him, and he idly looked at the notes on which his scientists formed their failed conclusions. Looking at the document on which they had based their continuing experiments, he was suddenly jolted out of his lethargy. His replacement scientists had not used the original documents which Gilliland and Crook had submitted to the then MoD. They had used the version that Wilson had intercepted and doctored before passing them on to his then boss, the MoD.

Being a senior UK Government advisor with a special portfolio enabling him to undertake covert operations which were kept secret even from cabinet ministers, he did not appear to require authorisations from anybody. Using the sole electronic key to a secure communications room which had been provided for his personal use by the Federation of Nations on board the Federation flagship HMS *Foxhound* he set about implementing his new plan to access BAM2 technology.

The lateness of the hour did not deter him from immediately contacting fringe scientists whom he knew to be good at what they did, but who were also unscrupulous, perhaps almost as unscrupulous as he was himself—but not quite. He did not allow his inability to speak their language to deter him. After an hour of scrambled telephone discussions and being shunted from person to person, he finally found somebody who spoke enough English for him to be understood.

Several hours later, he had secured the services of three top, but definitely under-the-counter scientists and a technical translator. These people could not, of course, be allowed to know who he was, but the amount of money he was talking about ensured their cooperation and their complete silence. They would be unlikely to enjoy the benefits of their promised wealth because their unexpected disappearance would be sudden and terminal just as it had been for the unsuccessful team of scientists he had employed after dispensing with the services of Gilliland and Crook.

Wilson's mood continued to be mercurial, he see-sawed between elation and manic depression as the thoughts in his head conflicted with each other. He used the telephone conferencing facilities in his security suite on-board *Foxhound* to set up the BAM2 experiments in Nuovostan. This new country, located in Eastern Russia near the Manchurian-Mongolian borders, had stumbled out of the chaos of the worldwide financial crisis that had momentarily laid Russia low and was run by the remnants of the Russian Mafia who had taken advantage of the disarray caused by the economic collapse. These were people whom Wilson could understand and deal with.

At long range, Wilson's arrangements were not without their difficulties. First, in accordance with the previously suppressed notes of Gilliland and Crook, he needed to acquire a large quantity of small diamonds to construct the active transmitting dome required for the experiment. This was followed by programming the NRT to transmit for a pre-determined distance so that the NRT wave would travel the chosen distance before returning to the transmitter dome, the intention being to register any obstructions within its field of travel as it did so. This was the element that had been missing from the attempts previously made by the first set of scientists whom Wilson had bribed to work for him and then disposed of after their failure to deliver.

Next had been the task of locating and acquiring a site where the experiments could be carried out without discovery or interference. The scientists were nationals of the newly independent Nuovostan, and its remoteness in the far wastes of what had been Eastern Russia was ideal for the work to be done secretly. Its distance from his current location on-board *Foxhound* and his London base made Wilson anxious, but the security offered by Nuovostan's remoteness outweighed the disadvantages of the lack of instant personal access. As technology developed, the need for people to meet physically was required less and less, but Wilson found it more difficult under these circumstances to terrify people using these methods.

Finally, misusing military intelligence sources in the MoD, Wilson settled for setting up his research establishment in the virtually unpopulated centre of the Nuovostan Mountains on an Island within the shores of a high-altitude lake that had a network of natural dry caves and caverns which extended below the waters of the lake from a small uninhabited rocky Island. Prompted by the promise of generous cash payments from Wilson's slush fund, the laboratories were fast tracked to be equipped with the simple needs of the experiment and the original Broken Arrow Project notes which he had kept to himself. They were translated into technical Russian by groups of specialists each of which only ever had part of the notes. They would mysteriously disappear after they had completed the critical translation and their disparate works had been joined together by the chosen scientific team. Normally, the setting up of such a facility would have taken months, even years, but with Wilson's persuasive guidance it took only a matter of weeks.

There were high hopes, from Wilson's perspective, that the previously overlooked more up-to-date experiment notes would yield the final success that had become the focus of his existence. All the replacement scientists had to do was to put themselves in the shoes of Gilliland and Crook and follow their experiments through to a logical conclusion; *surely, that wouldn't be too difficult?*

From the notes, it was obvious that the originators of the experiment had decided that the transmission of the curved radar signals which would go on forever around the globe had no practical purpose. And worse, if the radar energy beams were set by NRT on a course to travel around the world with unlimited distance parameters, and they would continue to circulate ad infinitum. Such an operational feature would lead to a complete scrambling and an endless duplication of overlapping images, making the whole system unworkable.

The notes would enable them to programme the transmission distance of the carrier waves, and they would establish that the directional programme algorithm could be rewritten to give the transmission a finite travel distance which could be instructed to return to the transmitter and would indicate whether there was an object to be detected or there was nothing there to detect. This was a concept which Wilson could just understand, but he was unable to progress in this unaided.

Nuovostani physicists were satisfied that they could emulate the thought and method processes of Gilliland and Crook, and their intentions were to plough on, carefully recording the progress of their efforts. The achievement of their objectives was expected, by them, to be imminent. The reports that Wilson would receive would give him a great deal of satisfaction but not necessarily the whole story. The new scientists need for ever-increasing funds would need to be handled delicately while taking advantage of the fact that Wilson would not be diverted, focussed as he was on the success of the project. They did not know or care that the whole project would be funded, unknowingly, by the British taxpayers through Wilson's double-dealing.

From their underground laboratory, the scientists were prepared to work tirelessly in pursuit of this Holy Grail. They would have neither the time nor the inclination to completely share the results of their work with Wilson or with anybody outside their immediate group. They would also fail to recognise that they were working for a past master in the art of deception and that Wilson would expect them to withhold information. Wilson was quite willing to bide his time, and when the moment was right, the scientists would be eliminated, at which time, Wilson would be on record as being a long way away from the scene of their elimination, yet another advantage of the remoteness of his chosen location in a lawless country.

Four

James Creswell, in his capacity as UK Prime Minister, headed the delegation of presidents that comprised Klastheim of the USA, Savollard of France, and Van der Linde of the European Union, and they were jointly charged by the Federation, who felt it prudent not to be at the meeting, in case, it failed, to negotiate terms for a settlement with the Island's Ruling Council.

Not having been on the Island before, the delegates were fascinated by what they saw. No report or photographs could prepare them for the alien nature of the architecture and the infrastructure. The buildings they saw were functional, almost child-like in their simplicity. The boulevards were wide, uncluttered, and clean; juvenile tropical trees and other plants broke up the plainness of the architecture, and they were all struck by the lack of vehicles or even places where they could park.

They were led to a transfer car station, marked with a discreet TC, and escorted aboard one of the cars by two guides. They watched in fascination as one of the guides pressed icons on a location board which mimicked the layout of the TC network. The ride from the dock where they had disembarked from their naval cutter was short and smooth with just the vaguest hint of a sucking sound from the pneumatic tyres. Because there were no windows, there was no sensation of speed, acceleration and deceleration were smooth and the clearest sign that they had actually stopped was that the barely discernible sound of the tyres gradually diminished to complete silence.

They were all profoundly impressed when they exited the TC station inside the council building the Island-side windows of which gave way to a sizeable Piazza flanked by colourful restaurants and cafes. The atrium into which they walked was four stories high, and the vast chamber was lit by a soft glow, which did not appear to have a focal source. The three upper stories had access walkways which opened directly on to the atrium and were strung between three lift towers which were also open to the atrium. There was a lot of activity on the walkways, which grew as word reached others about the arrival of the off-Island visitors. The visitors were easily identified by their mode of dress; without exception, they wore standard business suits with formal shirts and old-fashioned ties.

The delegates were led to the central lift tower where they boarded the glass-sided cage and ascended to the fourth floor. Exiting the lifts, they were ushered along a softly lit corridor to a conference room with windows on each of the long sides, one of which looked out over the atrium and the other to the centre of the Island with views over the central mountain and beyond to the sea and on to the melting blues of the horizon.

"We don't have a guard of honour for you to inspect." The voice of Gilliland broke their contemplations. They all jumped at the sound and spun round to see him as he otherwise silently entered the room through a barely discernible door, "my apologies, I didn't mean to startle you." He smiled benevolently and swept his arm towards the conference table on which was a large tray containing coffee, tea, and carafes of water. "Please help yourselves to beverages, and if you require other than what is on the tray, please ask."

The four-man delegation each carried identical document cases, which they deposited on the conference table at the positions displaying their names. On the opposite side of the table, there were three places with

ID tags which simply read: Chairman, Chief Executive, and Head of Security, facing the visitors. They had not used their actual names because to all intents and purposes they were no longer living, having supposedly disappeared at sea. an act which they had faked with the intention of getting Wilson off their backs.

Gilliland and Crook were nervous about the uncovering of their deception because they had, many years before, briefly met Creswell the UK Prime Minister when he was Minister of Defence, and it was he who had sanctioned the original research which led to the discovery of NRT and, later, BAM2. Their single meeting had been brief and one of many hundreds which Creswell had had as a minister of the crown, so it was unlikely that he would remember them. Creswell's steady gaze when they greeted their visitors gave no sign of recognition.

"Gentlemen," Gilliland addressed the small group, "I don't think introductions are really necessary even though we have not formally met before. I suggest that we address each other by title rather than name." He smiled at the visitors, spreading his arms wide he continued, "I haven't welcomed you to Recovery Island. So on behalf of all Islanders, I welcome you to our midst in the hope that we can overcome our differences and establish a basis for peaceful co-operation. It is also my hope that this small delegation has the support of the rest of the Federation without which the fruitfulness of our discussions will be limited." He left the barb that the Chinese were not represented, hanging in the air and looked expectantly across the table.

"Err," Van der Linde had been appointed by the Federation as spokesman and had taken on-board the meaning of the barbed expression. "Thank you for accepting the position of hosts in our forthcoming discussions, and thank you for your welcome."

The three Islanders looked on blankly at his attempt to distance himself from the defeat of their choice of venue on which the Islanders had refused to cooperate. "What we have to discuss is a matter of some delicacy, and we would like to be assured that all issues raised will remain absolutely confidential."

"Confidentiality on our part is absolutely assured," Pettit advised. "I should tell you, however, that all official meetings held on the Island are recorded so that there is no need to keep minutes of the meeting as such. This is an official meeting, and it is being recorded. You will have an opportunity after the meeting to listen to any of the proceedings and to offer any clarification that you may feel necessary." Noting the look of alarm on the faces of the Federation delegates added, "This is not a point of negotiation that is written into the law of the Island." He was aware of the looks of confusion which was being exchanged. "Gentlemen, if you wish to debate this point among yourselves, we will leave you alone to do so. If it helps, there is no way that the recordings of our meeting will be heard by other that those present and the Ruling Council of our Island."

"I don't think that will be necessary," Creswell spoke up and looked meaningfully towards his three colleagues who were obviously ready to have a closed discussion on the point. "The matters at hand must be discussed without delay, and we must, as guests, observe the customs of the Island." He raised his hand to stop Van der Linde from objecting and looked directly at him. "The rights and wrongs of the legitimacy of Island laws are not part of this discussion, Jan. There is much more at stake."

Thankful for Creswell's intervention Gilliland decided to officially declare the meeting open. "Very well, gentlemen, then I suggest we proceed with the purpose of our gathering. As this meeting is at your request, I suggest that you start the ball rolling by outlining your agenda. We have no specific agenda of our own."

The Islanders listened for half an hour to Van der Linde's diatribe covering old ground. They made no comment but did not hide their boredom and irritation at the rehashing of what they considered to be yet another unacceptable attempt to gain access to NRT and BAM2 technology which they had previously rejected out of hand.

"Jan," Creswell interrupted him, "our hosts don't want to hear this old stuff. You know it's unacceptable to them. They've already made that clear."

Van der Linde gave Creswell a withering look and turned to Klastheim and Savollard for their support. They both avoided his gaze; he shrugged and looked ill at ease.

"May I suggest, gentlemen," Creswell addressed the meeting, "that we really get to the crux of the matter and say what's on our minds?" His three colleagues said nothing but looked relieved to pass the task to Creswell. "Okay." He accepted the challenge. "We have a problem. As you know, the press has whipped up a lot of bad feelings about what you are doing and the potential threat your technology poses for the rest of the world. I'm sure you understand that." He looked at the Islanders enquiringly.

"We do understand," Crook took up the offer of comment. "But you must also understand that we previously allowed journalists and observers on to the Island to explain the peaceful nature of our pursuits and that our openness was abused by some very disreputable journalism, all of which I might add emanated from the United Kingdom." He looked meaningfully at Creswell. "But, yes, we understand that there is a lot of apprehension which needs to be allayed. Having said that, you promoted the apprehension so, it is up to you to stop it."

"Think about that for a moment," Creswell said in a placatory voice. "You have just destroyed a Federation UAV, and that will be looked upon by the whole world as an overt act of aggression."

"Depends on how you present it." Pettit joined in. "You could always admit that you violated our air space despite several warnings and gave us no alternative."

"It was an unarmed device which posed no threat. That's how it will be remembered and promoted. Forget the rights and wrongs, it's perception that counts."

"So what do you propose that we do to counter that perception?" Pettit enquired.

"My suggestion is that you open up to the possibility of sharing the technology." Creswell said evenly.

"Not on my watch." Crook was vehement and unyielding.

"Slow down," Gilliland raised his hand to prevent the discussion from becoming too heated. "Maybe the Prime Minister has a point." He gave Crook a smile which told him that what he had said could be interpreted in another way. "Prime Minister, we need to give worldwide perception time to turn around. These feelings, history tells us, can always be reversed over time. We could agree that talks could take place so that we can be assured that opening up the technology will not lead to its misuse." He looked at Crook who was looking at him with horror.

"How can you possibly say that? It goes against everything that we stand for." Crook had soon forgotten Gilliland's indication that all was not as it sounded and his voice quivered with indignation. Pettit remained silent.

"It does not mean to say that such discussions will ultimately be fruitful," Gilliland said to a confused looking meeting. "It could be that in the end we would agree to disagree."

"What the hell would be the point of that?" Klastheim blustered.

"The point," Gilliland said to him as though talking to a child, "would be that the delay would give you the time to stop the Chinese from doing whatever it is they are proposing to do and with which you all disagree— hence, there is no Chinese delegate in attendance." The Federation delegation looked startled by his simple logic. "And it absolutely reinforces our reasons for not trusting you with the technology."

Gilliland sat back in his chair and watched a variety of expressions from shock to indignation to resignation. He smiled inwardly; Penny Caine had been absolutely right during their pre-meeting discussions about the reason for the Chinese not being represented. A four-tone bell sounded, and the Federation delegation looked at their hosts expectantly.

"Meeting concludes." Crook explained to them, "we have a ruling here that the maximum length of a general meeting should not extend much beyond the hour and a half mark. The idea is that short meetings remain focussed and that the meeting should not be resumed on the same day."

"I suggest that our guests be given the opportunity to freshen up before we give them a whistle-stop tour of some of the more interesting facilities and then have dinner. You are all welcome to take up our offer of accommodation." Gilliland smiled ruefully, "That is, providing you don't want to spend the night on board the Federation cutter in the harbour?"

The offer of accommodation was taken up with alacrity by all the four delegates, and arrangements were made for their overnight bags to be delivered to the ground floor block of four double apartments within the Council Chamber complex which had been allocated to them. The crewmen on the cutter were likewise offered accommodation, but in their case, two people to a double apartment in the Western Island complex. They accepted without hesitation.

Five

Ceswell entered his designated apartment, which was spacious without being opulent. The decor was somewhat plain for his taste, the predominant colour being pale butterscotch. He would learn later that all ground floor apartments were decorated in this colour and that each of the subsequent floors throughout the whole Island was of a different colour. Being designed by engineers, the interior was as functional as the exterior and quite clearly lacked the feminine touch.

He unpacked his toilet kit and placed the contents on a shelf above the hand basin in the bathroom in specific location order, a legacy of the officer cadet training in his youth. On reflection, he admired the functional simplicity of the bathroom and of the other rooms, wondering if this were a standard apartment or a visitor's deluxe version; he made a mental note to find out later.

Some unfamiliar items on the bathroom shelf intrigued him. There was a lower face mask of pliable material which the instructions advised him was for facial depilation. The whole of the mask was of a pliable soft compound, and he was able to fit it on to his face, following the written instructions and adjust the sides so that it extended up as far as his sideburns. With the mask fitted snugly to his lower face and jaw, he pressed the operating button and felt the mask tighten into the contours of his face. There was a faint buzz and a tingling sensation which lasted for a few seconds after which the contraption switched off. He waited and when nothing further happened, he removed the mask. His chin when he stroked it was completely smooth and hairless. He stroked the smoothness in wonder and realised with a certainty that the Island had a great deal of innovation to offer the world, and it gave every indication to be willing to do so.

There was also a sonic teeth hygiene device, which comprised a U-shaped gel pad, the shape of which was workable to the touch. Again, following the instructions, he placed the pad into his mouth and bit down on it. His teeth sank into the soft material until it encased his upper and lower teeth from tip to gum. Following the instructions, he pressed a plunger which protruded from between his closed lips and felt a flow of cool fluid which he was unable to taste because of the tight fit of the pad with his teeth. After a second of delay, the sonic vibrator activated and hummed for ten seconds before the liquid that had been dispensed was reabsorbed into the pad, and the vibration stopped. The pad then reinflated, pushing his teeth apart; he removed the device from his mouth and ran his tongue over his teeth which were now smooth and free of surface irregularities.

Moving from the bathroom out to the living area, his fascination with the accommodation was further piqued by the Information Portal, which he had read of in the newspaper accounts of some visiting journalists. It was two of the visiting British journalists, he now believed, who had been entirely responsible for misrepresentation and the distorted accounts of life on the Island. He was not particularly surprised by the sensational treatment by Julia Hammond, a tabloid journalist, but he was taken aback by the similar vein of articles by D. K. Valerie, a revered broadsheet journalist. He made a mental note to talk to them both on his return to the United Kingdom.

The information portal (IP) was mounted on one wall of the living space; it had a simple on/off card slot operated by the Recocard he had been given on arrival and which to all intents and purposes was a credit card with the advantage that he did not have to pay it off. There were no other manual controls. A remote control handset was in a holster on the wall at the side of the screen. As with the rest of what he observed, simplicity was the byword, there were four buttons each with a label: menu, forward, back, and select. He pressed the menu and selected the newsflash option, the screen darkened for a moment and then resolved into a recording of the arrival of the delegation showing them being escorted to the TC station. Their arrival at the council chambers was also recorded, and a voiceover informed that the delegation was on the Island to attempt to resolve differences of ideology which had arisen. There was no recording of the conference room itself, and the piece concluded with an optimistic expression concerning the outcome of the meeting.

Creswell was both fascinated and worried by the piece; he had not been aware of any cameras being present, and he wondered if their private internal discussions when they thought they were alone had been recorded and whether he was now being recorded. Putting aside his concerns, there was little he could do about them; he continued scrolling through the menu. He was struck by two things: the openness with which the Island's issues were divulged and the complete lack of information of any kind about NRT or BAM2 technologies. The conflict concerning the expressed openness of information, coupled with the total lack of information about the two technologies struck a discordant note with him, although it came as no surprise on reflection.

At random, he selected another item from the miscellaneous menu because of its title "Drug Freedom". The screen was filled with photographs and words positioned in such a way as to make the reading of an otherwise dull scientific paper easier to digest. The introduction was simple and to the point:

> *Drugs are given to counteract the symptoms and causes of an illness. They do so by either supplying something that the body lacks or by prompting the body to produce a reaction which will help to counter the ailment.*
>
> *This research defines what the drug does to the body and then by the application of autonomic stimulation techniques persuades the body to emulate these affects. Put simply if the cure of an ailment is the introduction of penicillin; autonomic stimulation can be used to have the body simulate the effects of penicillin, without actually taking it.*
>
> *Application of this technique started with a simple experiment using aspirin for the control of headaches. Subjects were selected and placebos given to those subjected to the appropriate autonomic stimulation; the remainder were given aspirin and did not receive the stimulation. Of those taking aspirin, 85 per cent were relieved of the headache and 87 per cent of those given the placebo, with stimulation, also recovered. Similar experiments were carried out using other drugs and ailments. In all cases, the placebo users were as or more successful than the drug users. One of the initial conclusions is that the new therapy is effective for most people but not all.*
>
> *There is still a lot of research being undertaken to understand more of the techniques and their long-term results, but there is significant optimism among the researchers that it will be possible to treat patients without there being any physical or mental side effects. There is also a programme in place to consider the possibility*

of the regeneration of body parts and perhaps in the long term even the regenerating lost limbs.

This research is being carried out under the guidance of Dr Carlina Tarrentelli our medical director who is also running a number of other experiments which can be found by accessing "Medical and other research" from the main menu.

Creswell accessed and scanned twenty pages of the text and photographs without reading any detail. He switched off the images and watched the blank screen with a far away thoughtful look. After a few moments, he shook his head as if to clear it and his vision and reached for his telephone and keyed in VA for visitor apartments, and the numbers of the apartments occupied by his colleagues were displayed. He spoke to his three companions in turn and asked them to look up the article on the view screen.

As he had arranged with his companions, Creswell met them an hour before they were due to congregate with Island dignitaries for a formal diner. They met in the anteroom annexed to the dining hall which comprised of comfortable seating around tables of various sizes seating from two to twelve people. They found a table for four tucked away in one of the corners, next to windows offering views of the ocean to the west and Central Mountain to the north. None of the four showed any real interest in the view which, as the sun was setting, was spectacular.

"Did you all take the opportunity to look at the "Drug Free" item on the view screens?" Creswell asked of them collectively.

"Yes" or "I have" was the unanimous assent.

"Good. What did you think, Jan?" he turned to the president of the Federation of Nations.

"My first thought," he said in perfect English, "is that the implications of this are too great to allow them to develop the technique alone. We should take over the programme and direct it ethically and properly."

"Kurt, what do you think?" Creswell turned to the president of the United States of America.

"Potentially—dangerous," Klastheim grunted. "This is a kind of hypnotism which could be used for all sorts of nefarious objectives. We ought to stop them in their tracks. We would also get a lot of opposition from the drug companies." His response was jerky as reasons to object popped into his mind at random.

"Pierre," Creswell arched an eyebrow as he looked at the French President, "your thoughts?"

"This thing is too big for such an insignificant little Island. In France, we have facilities and qualified scientists who can truly develop this if it really works, which I doubt."

"Interesting," Creswell said with a far-away look.

"And your thoughts would be?" Van der Linde turned to face Creswell.

"My thoughts?" He smiled a distant smile. "The first time I met the two who discovered this technology a civil servant whom you all know, but I will not name, asked me the same question about what they were developing all those years ago. My answer then was the same as it is now. I said they should be given the time and space to develop their idea because this idea, like the original one, was so off the wall as to be bordering on the genius and that none of our existing researchers were equipped to cope with the concept and develop it. The first idea was taken up and development began funded by the UK MoD. For reasons I have never understood, and to my knowledge has never been explained even in principle, a halt was called before the project's completion. The, now unconvincing, reason given was that the two scientists could not be trusted to complete the task in the interest of the MOD and that they were a danger to security. There is no evidence to support this supposition. So," he sighed heavily, "if you will forgive me, I cannot support any of your initial thoughts of taking over the project in one way or another or of assuming that they have an ulterior motive against the wishes and security of the Federation."

"You are proposing we do nothing?" Van der Linde said tersely.

"I propose, Jan, that we allow them to develop this technique without our interference. After all," he smiled at them ruefully, "if they had any ulterior motive they would not have left this information lying around on their public information system for us to find, as we did."

Their discourse was interrupted by the appearance of their three hosts accompanied by a strikingly beautiful dark-haired woman in her early thirties.

"Gentlemen," Pettit waved his arm towards their companion, "may I now inform you that this is actually our personnel and promotions director, not exactly as she was first introduced to you in our first meeting with the Federation in the Azores which was our first attempt at settling our differences and which concluded so disastrously in stalemate."

The four men stood, and they all chose to linger over the handshakes.

"You are four of the most influential men in the modern world, and it is a great honour to meet you in my true position," she said this with a twinkle in her eye and all four were struck by her relaxed self-confidence.

"What pray," Creswell inclined his head to one side and looked at her almost coquettishly, "does a personnel and promotions director do?"

"I don't know what they do in general, but this one looks after Islanders' interests and promotes their future well-being." She held his candid gaze and wondered to herself what would have developed with this urbanely handsome man had he been thirty-five years younger.

"I'm sure you do it extremely well, my dear," he muttered this softly so that only she might hear. As he spoke, his grey eyes slid slowly and candidly over her from head to foot.

"What did the lovely, old reprobate say to you?" Pettit asked her with a smile as he, later, guided her into the dining room.

"What he said was not remarkable. What he meant though was very clear. His intentions leaned more towards the bedroom than the dining room." She squeezed his arm against the softness of her body. "It's quite exciting to be ogled by one so powerful. It could turn a girl's head."

"Don't get so excited, it'll never happen. After all, he is the Prime Minister of the United Kingdom."

"Yes"—her tinkling laughter made the others turn their heads—"but mostly he is a man,' she said this softly so that only Pettit could hear, "and I hope that when you grow older, you will be as desirable as he is."

He realised with a tingle of anticipation that for the first time in his life that somebody was offering him a relationship that would endure—and one that he wanted.

"All you need to do is give me the chance," he said slightly breathlessly.

Dinner was as successful as a business dinner could be. They didn't talk specific issues, but they did gain personal impressions which would be stored away for future consideration. It was unlikely that they would have the opportunity again to meet under such relaxed and confidential conditions. They also knew that in future meetings with others present there would not be the camaraderie that they engendered here.

The relationships developed had differing basis. With Pierre Savollard, the relationship was sophisticated and based on the likelihood of trade in the future if their differences were ironed out. With Jan van der Linde, the interaction was businesslike and he continually represented the interests of the Federation, to the exclusion of all else. Kurt Klastheim wanted to further Island/USA relationships by having Island's specialists visit the USA to give specialist lectures. James Creswell's interests were cultural and sporting links with the United Kingdom. When he discussed this with Juilietta Gray, he winked and said that there were certain sports that he would like to explore with her personally. She neither repulsed nor overtly embraced his insinuations.

On the morning following the first meeting, a tour of the Island and its facilities took place. The tour was brief and intense and left the four visitors reeling with information overload. After a brief, light lunch, they once more sat across the table in the meeting room.

"I hope you enjoyed your tour," Gilliland opened up the meeting. The four guests nodded their assent. "Good," he looked serious. "The time has now come to get down to brass tacks." He smiled at the visitors collectively. "You are clearly looking for a way out of this impasse without resorting to physical conflict such as that proposed by the Chinese element," he continued, ignoring the dark looks from their guests, "I can only reiterate our position. We have no evil intent but do not think that we will not use any moral means at our disposal to resist physical intervention from any source."

"You think it was moral to shoot down a very valuable unarmed unmanned aerial vehicle." Van der Linde said forcefully.

"Yes." Gilliland offered no further information. There was a momentary silence at his curt reply.

"Yes, doesn't do it for me," Klastheim rasped, "we need more than just yes."

"If you want more, Mr President, perhaps you would like to justify the UAV being over the Island in the first place?"

"It was there getting legit information gathering on behalf of the Federation."

"The information "legit" or otherwise is not the issue, you were asked not to fly over our sovereign territory and you ignored the request. We warned you, but you insisted on deliberately bating us and pushing us to test our resolve and limits."

"You sure showed a lack of control," Klastheim grimaced and shook his head.

"Kurt, this isn't going to get us anywhere, we're looking for solutions not conflict," Creswell attempted to defuse the situation, and he looked towards Gilliland. "What can you suggest we do to alleviate this difficulty?"

"There is no difficulty as far as we are concerned. We simply want to be left alone to live our lives in the way we choose. We are an Island with a twelve-mile territorial limit in the middle of the Atlantic Ocean, we are, through the application of our technology, self-sufficient, and we can offer to you and others some of the huge benefits of our research."

"What about your technology?" Van der Linde asked hopefully.

"Like the twelve-mile limit that's not up for discussion but as far as the rest of the world is concerned, we could enter into what appears to be discussions about possible future sharing. As we said yesterday, that will give you the opportunity to reach some sort of peaceful agreement with the Chinese."

"But this is not a negotiation, you have not moved from your original position." Savollard gave an exaggerated Gallic shrug of his shoulders.

"Maybe you would like to tell me how you have varied from your original position?" Gilliland addressed his question to the meeting as a whole. The request was met with silence, and the faces of all present took on glum look.

"What makes you think the Chinese are not behind us in our endeavours?" Van der Linde ignored the flash of irritation on Creswell's face.

"The experience we had in Beijing," Pettit broke his silence. "We had a joint agreement which they tried to break. From what happened, there they obviously consider themselves to be the senior partner in this alliance, and they took it upon themselves to take unilateral action.

We rebuffed that action and were not aware of any protests or support from any of you. In addition as our Chairman said, yesterday the lack of Chinese representation at this meeting speaks volumes. The Chinese also owe us for a wrecked BAM2 unit which they destroyed after we had fulfilled our part of the bargain with them by drilling for oil in China using BAM2—we sent them a bill but still haven't had the courtesy of an acknowledgement."

"So," Creswell said after a long pause, "we take away with us only the smoke and mirrors of quasi discussions about some future sharing that will not actually take place."

"Succinctly put," Gilliland shrugged, "what did you expect?"

"We expected a little give and take. We offered an olive branch," Klastheim responded.

"I understand what you want to take, but I don't recall what you intend to give."

"You will have the protection of the Federation, and under their patronage, you will be entitled to protection through the armed forces of the Federation," Van der Linde toed the party line.

"That," Pettit said with some exasperation, "is exactly what we don't want. We have, I believe, demonstrated the ability to look after ourselves."

"Our engagement so far has been very limited, and we have chosen to use no military might at this time, but it does not mean to say that we can't."

"The only way we can interpret that comment," Gilliland said gravely, "is as a threat. If that is so, then this meeting is terminated."

"One moment," Creswell interjected, "let us not overreact, and there is no ultimatum here." He looked meaningfully towards van der Linde. Van der Linde would not meet Creswell's eyes; he stared doggedly at the table and refused to say anything.

"Well, well," Pettit laughed humourlessly, "you three think that the Chinese are not represented at this meeting but the President of the Federation knows differently don't you, Mr President?"

The other three representatives stared at Van der Linde in disbelief. He remained silent staring morosely at the table.

Creswell looked pale and pinched and behind his grey eyes was a red hot fury which he could barely control. He stood up and put his shoulders back and looked candidly at his hosts. "Thank you, for your hospitality and for your patience. Under the circumstances, this meeting was bound to fail in its primary objective. I must apologise to you for our tardiness, and I ask you not to be overly influenced against the good intentions of some of us by this deception." He beckoned to his companions as he walked towards the door, "It is time for us to go."

"Mr European President," Gilliland called out to the departing president "I detect the hand of Wilson the DDP in this, are you acting under his influence?"

The look of shock on van der Linde's face spoke volumes and Creswell's reaction showed barely contained fury; they left in silence.

Silence was the watchword during the journey back to the dock and the uncomfortable journey in the cutter which took them back to *Foxhound*. Their mutually agreed silence was broken as soon as they were, all four, alone in the senior ward room.

"What in the name of all that is holy were you thinking of, Jan?" Creswell thundered. "I presume"—he turned to the other two—"you knew nothing of this debacle?" They remained silent.

"I must remind you," Van der Linde blustered, "that you are addressing the president of the Federation, and you should show respect for my position."

"Respect, respect," Creswell's shout resounded around the ward room. "I've got more respect for a cart horse's compost end than I have for you." The two presidents looked on askance; they had never before heard Creswell use such undiplomatic language and his cultured tones added weight to his outburst. "How can you have let Wilson know about our intentions you must have known that he would run straight to the Chinese." He paused for a moment as a thought struck him "The Chinese will make things very difficult for us now that they know we went behind their backs. What the hell were you thinking?"

"I had no choice with Wilson." He betrayed his subservience. "There are things about Wilson that you don't know. Things that make it impossible for me to resist his demands."

"Time for you to make amends," Creswell pointed a quivering finger at van der Linde, "you will report back to Wilson that we have persuaded the Islanders to enter into negotiations about sharing technology. You will not, and I repeat not tell him that it is a sham."

"I don't know that I can," Van der Linde cringed, "you don't understand he really will know if I am lying, and if he finds out, I'll be a dead man . . . politically speaking," he added in haste.

"You will do this, or I will make sure that you're a dead man," politically speaking "that is", he added sarcastically. "You will do it, and we will engineer you off the delegation so that we can meet with the Islanders without endangering your political life and our aims of a peaceful settlement"

"How can you do that? Wilson will insist on my being at those meetings, and I can't resist him."

"When do you next chair the Federation Council meeting in Beijing?"

"As usual on the last Friday of the month." He looked puzzled.

"Good, I'll set up another meeting on the Island on the last Friday of the month."

"Just so that you know," Van der Linde whispered to Creswell when the other two were out of hearing, "I was not really talking about my political death. I mean my corporeal death." He left the wardroom and would have found Creswell's open-mouthed look of horror amusing, had he not been in fear of his life.

Six

On his return from the Island to *Foxhound*, which was anchored ten miles outside the Island's imposed exclusion zone, Creswell scoured the ship finally locating Wilson who was alone in his secured radio room. Wilson had his back to the door and was talking animatedly into a handset; he paused when he realised that someone had entered the room and said without turning around. "I told you this was a confidential call and not to come back until I called you. Get out!"

Creswell remained silent; Wilson turned around irritated at the lack of response and froze when he saw who the intruder was. "Call you back." He looked at Creswell with irritation as he replaced the handset on its cradle. "I thought you were the radio operator." He did not offer an apology. "What do you want?"

"Have I missed something of significance here? I thought it was I who was Prime Minister, and you who were the advisor."

"What do you mean?"

"What I mean is as Prime Minister I am the one more entitled to ask the questions and my question is, what are you doing on board HMS *Foxhound*?"

"As director of defence projects, I have every right to be here, and I am involved in a black operation which it is best you don't know about. You know the drill."

"Yes, I know the drill, but I'm beginning to think that the drill is something we should reappraise."

"How are you going to handle these unsatisfactory technology disclosure meetings?" Wilson asked tersely, forgetting Creswell's warning.

"Oh, so you know about those already, very interesting."

Wilson realised he had slipped up and tried to cover his tracks. "I happened to bump into Van der Linde on my way here, and I overheard him discussing it with Klastheim. When is the next progress meeting to be held with the Islanders?"

"It's fixed for the last Friday of the month."

"It'll have to be changed," Wilson said dismissively. "That's the same day that the Federation General Meeting starts in Beijing."

"True, but I won't be going to that meeting—I don't, as usual, have an invitation," Creswell said pointedly.

"Maybe, but Van der Linde will be, and he can't be in two places at once."

"His attendance is of no consequence. He can contribute very little to the meeting and anyway having the big chief attend the exploratory meetings seems hardly appropriate. It could be seen as a sign of weakness."

"Nonsense, his attendance is vital." the statement was curt and brooked no interference.

"When you are put in charge of this operation, you may have a say in its structure but until that time your opinion is of little interest. Stick to being involved in matters that deserve your interference."

"Your attitude is unacceptable," Wilson snarled. "This is an MoD matter."

"In that case, I'll take it up directly with the MOD," Creswell said facetiously. "Where are you due back in London?" Creswell's sudden change of tack threw Wilson.

"Don't know," Wilson said sulkily. "I have a lot of most sensitive work to do."

Creswell took a small black book out of his pocket and scrutinised it. "Be in my private office at No. 10 on the twentieth of the month immediately after lunch at 1.30 p.m. Allow an hour for discussion about your role as a cabinet adviser."

"I can't make it back to London by that time," Wilson said frostily.

"This isn't a request." Creswell turned and left the radio room without waiting for a reply, as he did so he replaced the small black address book back in his pocket and made a mental note to have his secretary clear his diary for the time of the meeting with Wilson.

Wilson fumed following Creswell's departure from the radio room. After an outbreak of shouting rage, he calmed himself sufficiently to think more rationally and began to accelerate his plan of campaign to take Creswell out of the picture. The more he thought about it the less morose he became. By the time, he had thought through his idea he was as close as he could ever become to being happy.

His first task was to finish the telephone call that Creswell had interrupted. He did so but changed its content slightly to further his vendetta against his newly confirmed enemy. A second telephone call was made, and the person at the other end of the line who sounded bright until he realised the identity of his caller after which he adopted a monotone. "I've got something that I want you to do for me, and if you do it right, I will conclude our little arrangement." Wilson said menacingly. "Now listen to me very carefully . . ."

✕

Creswell broke his journey from *Foxhound* back to London by detouring back to the Island to further develop his discussions with the Island's chairman, chief executive, and security director to pass on the disquieting news about the activity of the Chinese in their guise as representing the Federation. He looked out of the window of the Recovery Island's executive jet, which had been sent to shuttle him from Lisbon. As it swung round to the east before turning to land at the Recovery Island's air terminal, he admired the symmetry of the construction and the clinical lines of its simple uncluttered architecture which also epitomised the Islanders simple way of life.

He was looking forward to being on the Island without the encumbrance of his Federation associates. The meeting he had requested was below the radar and only he Gilliland, Crook, and Pettit knew it was taking place.

"You obviously have something you want to say to us," Gilliland opened when they were together.

"Yes, I have. What I have to say, however, is not sanctioned by the Federation and I am laying myself open to serious censure and even imprisonment if what I say were ever to leave this room."

"Whether or not it leaves the room depends on what it is you have to say." Gilliland turned to Pettit. "This is rather like the conversation we had on Wave Walker just before you joined us."

"A carbon copy, and I remember it vividly," Pettit concurred, thinking back to the time when he had first been invited to join their team as a full member, without being told the ultimate plans.

"I don't know what that means." Creswell looked slightly mystified. "But I don't wish to defect to you if that's what you're thinking. I'm too ensconced in my British way of life to want that. Maybe if I were younger," he mused, "but I'm not—so that's that. It's just that I have personal standards which will not allow me to remain quiet about something which I believe to be morally indefensible." He paused and seemed to be trying to resolve some inner conflict. The room remained silent as he cogitated. "But," he expelled air through pursed lips, "I'll just have to trust you."

"Are you sure you want to go through with this?" Pettit asked with a frown of concern.

"Actually no, I am not sure." Creswell sat back in his chair and looked pained. "Tell me something before I go on. What is it between the Island and Wilson? He goes into a blue funk whenever it's mentioned to him?"

The three exchanged meaningful looks until Crook broke the silence. "Actually you were in at the beginning of the saga, but you don't appear to remember it or us."

The dawning of realisation showed almost comically on Creswell's face. "You are Gilliland and Crook." Creswell pointed to both of them. "And you must be Pettit. Well, I'll be damned you are supposed to be dead, all three of you. I met the two of you a long time ago and very briefly. I suppose that believing you were dead inhibited me from identifying you."

"I guess our being thought of as dead does make recognising us illogical." Crook looked impassive. "If you remember you recruited us after Chester's flat was broken into and you found our documentation on the Broken Arrow Project. I presume that was Wilson's doing?" He waited and Creswell nodded imperceptibly, "You were Minister of Defence at that time, and as you know, we formed a team and began to develop NRT on the Isles of Scilly. We were very close to being finished when Wilson pulled the plug without warning and ditched the whole project. We never did understand why he did it, and we still don't, although we can conjecture that it would be to do with his own interests. What Wilson didn't know until later was that we had discovered something quite accidentally which enables us to lead a life with no outside interference. You now know the anomaly we discovered as BAM2," he continued slowly and carefully.

"BAM2 is such a powerful tool that can, and has, done so many good things that we would not even consider letting it loose on a self-serving moron like Wilson." Creswell smiled tiredly. "The analogy we drew relates to nuclear fission. The atom bomb was developed for the evil purposes of war and later became a force for good with the development of nuclear power as an energy source. NRT or rather BAM2 is developed for the good of mankind but could become a devastating weapon of unbelievable mass destruction which would make the atom bomb look like a damp squib in comparison."

"I can believe that from the demonstrations I've already witnessed," Creswell said. "And I can't help thinking that you're absolutely right about it being a danger in Wilson's hands. Or anybody else's," he added as a mournful afterthought.

"You're his boss," Crook observed, "so why don't you sack him?"

"It's not as easy as that. Wilson seems to have many fingers in many pies and many friends in high places, and he makes major mischief at the drop of a hat. Wilson has no friends at all, and he seems to have a hold over people, and he can get serious things done with extraordinary speed. I have a meeting with him later this month, in London, and I'm going to get to the bottom of his relationships, and it is my intention to exclude him from the Government team, provided I can do so without ruffling too many feathers."

"Good luck with that. I can tell you from personal experience that he's a twisted little weasel, and he has an uncanny knack of wriggling his way out of trouble and causing monumental collateral damage."

"So I am beginning to learn," Creswell said ruefully.

"Knowing about this side of his nature is why Wilson doesn't like us. We can expose him for what he really is," Gilliland said. "And you will understand why we don't like him. We were forced to go to the lengths of faking our own deaths just to get him off our backs. Even now I find it difficult to believe that we had to do that." His expression changed as he pulled himself back to the matter in hand. "So, James, we have shown ourselves willing by divulging a secret to you, are you ready to divulge your secret to us?"

"It goes against all my principles to do so, but I feel I must." He was still struggling with his conscience and felt he had to set the scene a little more. "Two years ago the Federation was formed. The chairman of the Republic of China, before the global crash, was a man of vision who was beginning to embrace the ways of Western civilisation and had come to terms with capitalism and the moral need for human rights. At the time of the crash even the Chinese, the biggest in the world in terms of population and monetary volume went into a nose dive, and there was acute civil unrest. The visionary chairman was ousted and replaced by diktat with the present incumbent, Chung Ho Chen, who is a tyrant of the old school. He is a totalitarian, and the only reason he joined up with the Federation was that as the member country with the greatest population and, although diminished, the greatest residual wealth he would make China numero uno. The USA and Europe could not survive the crash on their own and have become, although they won't admit it, subservient to China. The United Kingdom and our economy are too insignificant for us to hold any sway over what the Federation does." He took a deep breath, stood up, and began pacing the floor. "China has made a unilateral decision. If we do not get agreement from you to share the technology, they will use their nuclear weapons against you."

There was a shocked silence.

Seven

Ceswell returned to London, to attend to accumulating prime ministerial matters and to prepare, with many misgivings, for the fraught face-off with Wilson.

After Creswell had departed from the Island, the three founders of the Island sat in one of the strictly private rooms in the Atlantean Club which is situated on the southern slopes of Central Mountain. They were all completely wrapped up in the machinations of the shocking discussions with Creswell and were oblivious to the beauty of the views from its expansive windows, which looked out across the shimmering Atlantic to the blue melt of its Western horizon. This venue was usually chosen for its relaxing atmosphere and was officially designated as a place safe for sensitive discussions among Ruling Council members. Gilliland and Crook sat quietly but were obviously not being influenced by the supposedly relaxing atmosphere.

After the simple debriefing, Pettit was reflective, and thanks to Creswell, they had been forewarned of the possible Chinese action and could take precautions, should precautions be required. He opened his mouth to start the debriefing when Gilliland placed his right index finger over his lips in a gesture of silence.

Pettit watched Gilliland walk to a control panel on the wall and open it with an electronic key card. He adjusted something that Pettit could not see and returned to the table. Pettit looked puzzled but said nothing, safe in the knowledge that Gilliland would reveal all.

"As long as the switch is disabled and the panel door is left open," Gilliland said as he resumed his seat, "the automatic recorder will be switched off but the memory will continue to run and record elapsed time as though the room were silent."

"Hey," Pettit said gruffly but in good humour, "I'm supposed to be the security chief. Why didn't I know about that?"

"Sorry, Silas," Crook apologised, "that little bit of subterfuge is a leftover from the Wilson days in the Scilly Isles. He used it when he talked in confidence to us, but he didn't realise we knew. In view of what we're about to say, it's just as well we do know."

"I don't think I like the sound of this, and I'm not too keen on the way you two are looking"—Pettit sat forward in his chair—"but give it to me, no holds barred."

"We might have the heads-up on the possibility of hostile action from either the Federation or the Chinese, or both, but there is something we haven't shared with you. BAM2 has one significant weakness as a defence mechanism that we obviously do not want to share with anybody."

Gilliland interrupted and took up the task. "BAM2 is good at dismantling solids but doesn't handle gasses in the same way. For reasons we don't understand yet, radiation can get through unscathed. The problem we have is that in a nuclear attack the physical bomb will be destroyed if it tries to pass through the shield but the radiation in the molecular breakdown will get through, and if the nuclear device is detonated outside the force field, it is likely that the resultant magnified radiation will seep through. We are vulnerable to radiation, laser, and any other energy beam. It's a weakness we haven't yet been able to counter."

"If the Federation, the Chinese and, especially, Wilson ever got to know this there is no doubt they would use it, and it would be curtains for us. One day, they might wake up to the fact that radio waves get through, and if they think about it hard enough, they will understand that they have an opportunity to achieve their wishes." Pettit was no longer reflective, if anything he was more agitated than his two companions. "It's a weakness we must attend to."

His companions nodded morosely but did not have the heart to tell him that there was no known scientific possibility within the shields make up for defence against radiation.

*

Sir Lionel Wentworth was a happy man. Reacting to the telephone call from Wilson, he had been able to finish the task set with surprising speed—for a bureaucratic dinosaur. The accounts had been manipulated to show that large sums of money had been transferred, from the slush fund, to a private account offshore over the past six months. The account was in the name of John Connaught an imaginary person with, of course, no tax records and whose domicile was shrouded in mystery.

As Wentworth sat congratulating himself in his Whitehall office, Chung Yi, a covert official of the Chinese Peoples' Republic, who had also received an interesting telephone call from Wilson, was in his office in Beijing doing what he liked most "destroying the life of a decadent Westerner—especially the Prime Minister," by inventing a trail of deception. He finished his task and hoped that he would be given more opportunities to indulge himself with there being no possibility of recrimination.

Wentworth was beginning to feel Wilson's grip on his personal life weaken because of the actions he had taken in furthering Wilson's nefarious aims. His regret was that he was destroying the life of somebody he had known for many years and who thought of him as a close friend. He wondered if he was becoming as unprincipled as Wilson by doing so and determined that he would find some way to redress the situation.

Eight

During the days immediately following Creswell's return from the clandestine visit to Recovery Island, life was one continuous and wearing round of cabinet and committee meetings which fortunately kept him from dwelling on his plight. It seemed to him that since becoming the Prime Minister, he was less in control and less influential than he had been as Minister of Defence, a situation to which Wilson had made a significant contribution by misusing the many favours he had manufactured to manipulate others to his own selfish advantage.

Creswell's diary was filled for him, his travel arrangements made by the staff of his permanent secretary and his speeches and thoughts scripted by his personal speech writer. He had become a puppet with his strings being pulled and severed by a dozen people in a dozen departments.

Two days before the ad hoc meeting he had forced upon Wilson, he was summoned, rather than invited, to the Second House—the revitalisation of the old House of Lords—for a meeting with the recently reintroduced Lord Chancellor, Lord Roland Clearman. Clearman always looked harassed, but today, he looked positively manic, his tie was awry and his expensive but ill-fitting suit rumpled and his wispy hair was in chaotic disarray.

"James"—he was very agitated—"what the hell have you been doing?"

"Would you like to be a little more specific, Roland?" Creswell endeavoured to calm him down with his most gentle voice.

"Very well," Clearman kept his eyes averted. "Who is John Connaught?"

"Who is John Connaught?" Creswell repeated thoughtfully. "All right, I'll play your game. I give up who *is* John Connaught?"

"He is, as you must know a Brit who is a non-dom living in a tax haven with a large sterling deposit there."

"For God's sake, Roland, will you get to the point? What is this all about?"

"We will have to inform the police about this. It's much too big, and if it leaks out, it will be worse for you." He looked as if he were about to cry.

"The worse for me? Roland, pull yourself together, take a deep breath, and start again."

"I don't know what to do, I just don't know."

"Roland, we've known each other for what, forty years? Don't do this to me, don't do this to yourself, for goodness' sake. Just say what you've got to say."

"I really shouldn't do this." Clearman pushed a manila folder marked STRICTLY CONFIDENTIAL—EYES ONLY. His face was a mirror of fear, and he looked as if he were going to be physically ill.

The actions of Creswell's old friend caused him great alarm; he turned the folder and opened it. It was an MI5 document and the first of two A4 pages, dated a week previously, was signed at the bottom by Trevor Coniston, the head of MI5, whom Creswell had only recently proposed for the honours' list. The document was succinct:

Information has come to the notice of the firm concerning significant money laundering between the United Kingdom and an offshore tax haven. To date there is a paper trail which accounts for six million sterling, in three equal instalments. The first was deposited in February of this year in an account under the name of John Connaught.

Seeing the date of the first transfer made Creswell blanch uncomfortably, the record of this deception had been started shortly after his inauguration as the Prime Minister; whatever it was, it had happened, unfortunately, on his watch.

Connaught is known to be an alias and tracing him through the usual channels has proved to be inconclusive. We have been advised by a, believed to be, reliable contact in the Chinese Embassy in Paris, in one of his regular updates from Beijing, that the name John Connaught is on a covert file, and that he is a highly placed mole in Whitehall.

Our sleeper mole in the intelligence service in Beijing has been activated and instructed to ascertain the true identity of or determine a method of contacting Connaught. This information is expected to be made available within the next ten days.

Coniston

"This is most unfortunate, Roland, but I don't understand why you're so agitated by it. It's regrettable but hardly the end of the world."

"Read the next page, and you will understand why I'm so nervous." Clearman was shaking visibly.

ADDENDUM (Information received—China Intelligence contact)

Connaught is understood to be high up in the British Government and goes by the code named Topman. He has direct access to the British Black Ops fund and can sanction fund transfers. The transfers which took place were not connected to Topman's work with Chinese Intelligence, and CI is not happy that Topman is receiving funds from the British as well as themselves.

TC

"This is bad." Creswell nodded sagely at Clearman. "Do we have any further information about Topman or Connaught?"

"Look at the last page."

The last page was handwritten at the top and signed by Sir Lionel Wentworth:

As requested, I've looked into the fund with the aid of the Assistant DDP and have ascertained that there are four fund transfer signatories: the DDP and his deputy, the PM, the Deputy PM. Neither of the deputies has signed off any transfers, and of the other two, the DDP has signed in excess of four hundred transfers for special operations over the last two years and the PM has sanctioned three.

Wentworth.

A handwritten note initialled by the Lord Chancellor:

Using my right, as Lord Chancellor, to access non-critical operations information I have determined the following in relation to transfers in the last three months. They are underlined

Signatory	Destination	Sum (£mio)
DDP	*CO/SA*	*£0.5*
DDP	*CO/NIC*	*£1.7*
PM	*SP/CHI*	*£2.0*
DDP	*CO/US*	*$5.0*
DDP	*CO/SA*	*£2.3*
DDP	*SP/ARG*	*£4.8*
PM	*SP/CHI*	*£2.0*
DDP	*CO/FRA*	*£3.7*
DDP	*SP/NIC*	*£1.3*
PM	*SP/CHI*	*£2.0*
DDP	*SP/US*	*$7.3*
DDP	*CO/CHI*	*$6.0*

Legend:CO = Covert Operation
       SP   = Special Project
       /AAA = hree Alpha country or destination identification.

'This can't be right" Creswell said in alarm, "I haven't sanctioned any Black Ops funds. I didn't even know I was a signatory." He turned to face Clearman "Get me the documentation, Roland, and let's sort this thing out."

"I can't," Clearman said dejectedly "It's in the hands of MI5. You're going to be in so much trouble, James." He buried his face in his hands. "Your three transfers of two million each coincide with the transfers made to Connaught's offshore account. You'd better have a damn good reason for that having happened or the natural conclusion of others will be that John Connaught is your undercover name and that you are Topman."

"This can't be happening," Creswell now looked as alarmed as Clearman had at the beginning of the meeting, "I know absolutely nothing about this. Who apart from you knows about it?"

"Nobody else knows about the three payments sanctioned by you coinciding with the payments to Connaught, but it's only a matter of time before they find out."

"Roland, keep a lid on this for as long as you can and inform me if it begins to get loose. And, Roland," Creswell paused and looked at Clearman and waited until he looked up, "Thank you for giving the early warning—you are a good friend."

"James." Clearman smiled shyly. "I know you didn't do it, and I trust you implicitly but the evidence against you is damning. Take great care, somebody is out to get at you."

"If that's the case, I know who it is but knowing who it is doesn't make getting out of the mire any easier." Creswell's worst nightmares were haunting him and cold fear gripped him. He had no idea how he could counter these lies, and there was nobody to whom he could turn for help.

Nine

Wilson gathered up his documents and belongings and walked to the Lynx helicopter sitting on the sun-washed deck of HMS *Foxhound,* presently cruising the Atlantic Ocean between Portugal and the Azores. Disgruntled as he was about having to interrupt carefully crafted plans to further his ambitions he was still euphoric about having gained possible access to the secrets of BAM2, and in addition, he looked forward with vicarious pleasure to the destruction of Creswell.

The metaphoric tide was moving in his direction, all of his hard and devious work in securing the cooperation of key people in government and Whitehall was beginning to pay off. He felt omnipotent, and he even impressed himself with his ability to manipulate the destinies of senior world leaders. He made use of the unwieldy bureaucracy of the Chinese-dominated Federation of Nations permeating the new brutal junta which had wrested control of China from its previous more enlightened leadership.

He went over in his mind, as he had several times recently, how he would handle Prime Minister Creswell in their meeting set for the following week. He had come to terms in his own mind with the time and venue being set by Creswell, rather than being dictated by himself, by planning an even more vicious attack than was his original intention.

He had lined up the press with an offer of a spectacular revelation that would rock British politics and leave the rest of the world gasping.

These thoughts sustained him during the boring flight from *Foxhound* to Lisbon where a very special jet of His Majesty's Flight waited to whisk him to London. Being the Director of Defence Projects, and not really being answerable to anybody, certainly had its privileges, and he took every advantage available and then some that weren't, like using the King's Flight as a taxi when it wasn't required by the Royal Family. He had learned early in his quasi, non-elected, political life that representing constituent's interests was not for him and that almost anything was possible with the requisite degree of assumed authority free from the inconvenience of being voted into power.

Once in London, Wilson entered his ground floor office in Whitehall amid the scurrying of some of his minions whom he castigated for not having been ready for his arrival. He conveniently overlooked the fact that he had not informed them that he had changed his schedule and was arriving three days earlier than his originally stated intention. Among those who were in attendance at the time of his arrival, there were no friends. In his paranoia, he was aware of this, but it was overridden by his euphoria at having succeeded in identifying the route to BAM2.

*

Creswell had hastily set up a security scrambled video meeting, from his bunker in Downing Street, with Gilliland and Crook to discuss the tip off he had been given by Clearman. Gilliland introduced Creswell to Caine and could not help noticing the old roué's predatory interest in her even through the poor definition of the two-way communications screen. They observed the customary "How do you do's" and Gilliland and Crook grinned at each other as they saw the sultry look on Creswell's face as he lingered over the introductions, just as he had with Juilietta Gray at their first meeting.

"Delighted to meet you, my dear," Creswell smiled at the screen.

"I can see I'm going to have to watch you." Caine laughed musically.

"Even more charming," Creswell said softly, "you are American."

"Take care," Caine said equally softly, "I am the resident psychologist, and I can deduce exactly what you're thinking."

"I doubt that, If you could, you would certainly be blushing." Creswell laughed dismissively.

"I stopped blushing when I became a fully enriched woman." She raised a satanic eyebrow.

"I don't often wish I were younger, youth can be so boring, but this is one of those times." Creswell smiled sardonically and left the sentence in the air.

It was as if he didn't realise that the other two Islanders could hear and see their conversation; actually, he didn't care.

Then they settled to the business of their talks; as they did so, Creswell's demeanour changed, he became very brusque and business like. The exchanges lasting over an hour was intense. At its culmination, Creswell switched off his screen and disengaged the scrambler with a grim look on his face and went to the printer to pick up a sheaf of documents marked BA Interim which had been sent to him directly from the Island, which he put into a manila folder. He locked the new document securely in his briefcase together with other notes pertaining to his forthcoming meeting with Wilson. The file contained the original un-doctored report which was sent to Creswell as Minister of Defence but which he had only received after it had been tampered with, it was now clear to him, by Wilson.

*

It was late into the night before Wilson let his people go to their homes. He had returned to his office unexpectedly, not having advised his department that his plans had been changed, particularly because he had not been the architect of the changes. He vented his spite and frustration on each member of staff in loud, open office discussions.

Pale faced, cowed, and worn out by his tide of invective, they left one by one, each receiving a final word of disapproval from Wilson. When the last one had left his office, he stood up and stretched, arching the small of his back. His sleep of late had been poor quality, and he should have felt tired, but he did not, the adrenalin coursing through his veins kept him alert. He looked at the notes before him on the desk they set out, chapter and verse, the downfall of Creswell. He had a look of evil satisfaction on his face as he placed the notes into his document case finally spinning the combination locks to secure the contents. He was ready for, and had the scent of, victory.

*

Wilson, once more in the grip of ever more frequently present pent-up rage, walked unannounced into Creswell's day office which was annexed to the cabinet room in 10, Downing Street. He looked around plotting his next moves among which were that he would appropriate this office as his own when Creswell was finally disgraced and gone. After achieving that aim he would engineer another more manageable candidate into the PM's position and that, he thought smugly, would be very soon. He arrived fifteen minutes early and did not feel the need to knock on the door; he simply entered and stared with hostility at Creswell.

"Good afternoon, Wilson," Creswell said mildly without looking up from the documents he was reading.

"Yeah," Wilson said dryly with no greetings preamble. "I'm busy, so let's get right down to business."

"You are early. Come back in ten minutes or so, or better still wait outside, and I'll call you when I'm ready. I've not quite finished with these documents before we have our little chat."

"You obviously have no idea just how much trouble you're in, otherwise, you wouldn't be so dismissive. Let me read out your death sentence to you." Wilson quivered with unstable indignation spurred on by Creswell's dismissive attitude.

"In ten minutes, Wilson, and shut the door on the way out, as I said, I'll call you when I'm ready."

Wilson spluttered and went white breathlessly unable, in his overwhelming rage, to speak.

"Just go and get yourself some coffee and come back at the agreed time."

Creswell smiled to himself as he reviewed in his mind the advice that Caine, the psychologist, had given him during his video conference with the Islanders. She had advised him to belittle Wilson by making him recognise his subservience to him as Prime Minister and by having to obey whimsical orders from his established superior. The fury this would engender in him would, Caine had assured him, make him careless in the prosecution of his case against Creswell, whatever it may be. The first objective had been met and much more simply than he had envisioned.

Five minutes after the appointed time, Creswell switched on the intercom that was linked to the secretary's desk outside the office. "You can come in now, Wilson. Oh and my secretary has the afternoon off.

Be a good fellow and bring me a cup of coffee from the machine. Black no sugar."

The door burst open and slammed against the stop on the wall; the glass panel rattled but did not shatter. "I'm not a damn servant," Wilson hissed. "If you want coffee, get it yourself." He was shaking with fury.

"No coffee?" Creswell said easily, making no comment about Wilson's outburst.

"Never mind, I'll get some later."

"Enough!" Wilson's voice was thick with fury "You're a dead man. I've got enough dirt on you to sink your miserable career forever."

"I called the meeting, so let's deal with my bit first, and once, we've done with that I'll listen to whatever it is you want to say," He didn't wait for a reply but simply continued, "To put it mildly, as I probably indicated to you on-board *Foxhound*, I am most disappointed with your attitude. Your interpersonal skills are somewhat lacking, and you seem to think that you are a free agent and as such you can do whatever you like. You also seem to be using the Dark Ops fund as a personal unaccounted expense opportunity. That has to stop. You are as accountable as any other member of this team, my team." He appeared both dismissive and distracted, "Yes, my team . . . hmm." Surreptitiously he reached under his desk and switched on the security-recording device without alerting Wilson.

"My God!" Wilson rose to his feet, knocking his chair over as he did so, "just listen to yourself. I'm telling you that your career is about to be destroyed, and you're harping on about my not being over kind to idiots and moaning about my expenses." He was whipping himself up into a fury, "You're a damn dinosaur, an inbred upper class misnomer. You have no idea what's going on around you. God knows why I chose to support you as Prime Minister. I don't make many errors, but in your case, I did. But now I'm going to undo my mistake."

"Really and how do you propose to do that?" Creswell's voice was soft and his look unnaturally benign. He could sense that Caine's predictions about Wilson's reactions were coming true. Wilson was unravelling before his eyes.

"I could have been diplomatic about this, but you're so stupid, I don't think I'll bother. I have irrefutable evidence that you are a crook and that you've been duping the country and stealing money from a covert account to feather your own nest." He opened his document case and extracted a number of papers, selecting one of the papers he flung it on the desk in front of Creswell.

Creswell picked up the document and scanned it. It contained three columns the first of which designated the initiator of the fund transfer. It was a similar list to the one he had been shown by Lord Clearman, the Lord Chancellor, but on Wilson's document only three references were left visible, the ones attributable to the PM the others had been blanked out. They amounted to six million pounds sterling.

"I have no knowledge of this particular document," Creswell said in a version of the truth. The document Clearman had shown him was handwritten and complete; this one was computer generated and incomplete.

"I have authorisations of the transactions bearing your signature." He flung three further documents on to the desk.

Creswell looked at the documents of authorisation and saw what looked like his signature at the bottom. "I have no knowledge of these documents. They are obviously forgeries."

"Not only are they not forgeries, but I have a witness to your signing them." Wilson shouted triumphantly.

"And who might that be?" Creswell asked in a quiet icy whisper.

"Never mind who it is. That person will be called at the appropriate time. Not so cocky now, are you?" Wilson's eyes glimmered with intense naked hatred.

"Your not being prepared to tell me who it is makes me think that the person is a figment of your imagination or that they are unreliable or have no credibility." Creswell's voice remained controlled and calm.

"Wouldn't you just like to know?" Wilson's voice was neither controlled nor calm.

"Not really," he said with a disinterested shake of his head.

"Not really?" Wilson mimicked. "You think I'm some kind of novice or something?"

"I think you're definitely a something—and by that I mean you're an idiot."

"Idiot," he repeated in disbelief, "idiot—I'll show you, idiot. Take a look at that." He threw a further sheaf of papers on to the desk. "This links the payments you made to Connaught, and it attaches Connaught to you, in fact, it shows that you are John Connaught, and you've been caught with your snout in the trough, not bad for an idiot, huh?"

"You could have written this proof yourself. In fact, you probably did. It won't stand scrutiny without independent corroboration," his voice was softly mocking.

"Okay, loser." Wilson grimaced. "I've got independent corroboration. This is a report from an agent in our embassy in Beijing who got it from a mole in the Chinese diplomatic corps. It proves that you and Connaught are the same person in the pay of the Chinese."

Creswell sat back in his chair and regarded Wilson with distaste. "None of this is true, but I must congratulate you on the skill with which you have compiled this tissue of lies."

"You say its lies, and I say it isn't. You have enough enemies, in your position as PM, who will believe the worst of you, and I won't be the one to contradict them. Don't you see I am above reproach. Don't you remember I'm the one who championed your cause as PM as everybody knows. I am seen as your ally, so why would I try to do you down. My words against you will be another and probably the final nail in your coffin," he concluded his diatribe with a smirk of satisfaction.

"Your own words will condemn you." Creswell nodded towards the ceiling where a microphone could be discerned if one knew where to look.

"Please," Wilson said with a pained expression "Don't take me for a fool. I look after security in this building. I disabled this sound system last night."

"Just as I said before—I congratulate you on your skilful manipulation of this fabrication." Creswell looked rueful. "Before you start patting yourself on the back on your masterpiece of deception which I presume you have also worked on other people, for example, van der Linde, let me just run through another scenario with you. I have some files for you to look at." He slid a thick folder across the desk.

Wilson opened it with some trepidation. He had not expected Creswell to produce any documentation. He scanned the front page and then opened pages at random. "So what?" he scowled. "This is old stuff. It's the reports from the two traitors, Gilliland and Crook, about how their invention would never work. They're just the reports I passed on to you, big deal."

"Try this one." Creswell slid over another similar file.

Wilson repeated the task, "Another copy of the same thing, what's the point?"

"Read on."

He began to do so. "So what, it's the same report?"

"Not quite, how many pages in the first report on the first file I gave you?"

Wilson opened the first file and flicked through the first report "Twenty-three," he said, mystified.

"Now compare it with the same report in the second file."

Wilson repeated the exercise. "Twenty-seven," as he said it, he frowned. "What are you getting at and what does it have to do with me?"

"The first file contains the reports that you passed on to me when I was your minister," he paused for effect, "the second file contains the original reports submitted by the two scientists and the difference is that you edited the reports and took out the findings and comments that would have justified the continuation of project Broken Arrow."

"Lies," Wilson shouted angrily, "you doctored the reports and, anyway, those original drafts were never kept." He realised with a jolt of fear that he had actually given the game away by saying that the original reports had never been kept but Creswell appeared not to notice his slip up. He also had no idea how Creswell had secured copies of the original reports, his paranoia quotient increased exponentially.

"They weren't kept on file because you had another use for them. What that use is I don't know, but I can dig. The answer to that question will be out there somewhere, and unlike you, I won't have to fabricate the evidence, my findings will be real." Although he had not reacted to Wilson's slip of the tongue, he smiled inwardly and gave silent thanks for having been given copies of the true reports by Gilliland during the course of their last video conference.

"It's your word against mine," Wilson smirked again. "Who will believe a discredited and traitorous Prime Minister?" He still held electronic un-doctored copies of the original reports under lock and key, wondering with alarm how Creswell had acquired his copy.

"And who would believe the ravings of a crook like you, one who denied the United Kingdom the unrestricted use of BAM2 technology which would have made us the most powerful nation on earth because he wanted, but failed miserably, to keep it for himself?" Creswell's voice was heavy with loathing.

Wilson picked up his papers and stormed out of the office without another word.

In the darkness of the cabinet office, Wilson failed to see Sir Lionel Wentworth, Chief of the Civil Service, sitting, statue-like, in a shadowed alcove. Wentworth watched the DDP scurry out into the corridor, clutching his document case to his chest, his face a frozen mask of murderous hatred.

*

Wentworth had sat patiently in the, otherwise, empty cabinet room off which the Creswell and Wilson meeting had been held; he was all but invisible in the unlit room which had no external windows. Although he had been unable to hear what was being said, the buzz of conversation did seep through to the cabinet room sufficiently for him to distinguish between Wilson's screaming invective and the calm responses from the PM.

The civil servant's bubble of happiness at being told by Wilson that the hold over him would be released, had been shattered on the previous evening when Wilson had told him that despite his promises the DDP had decided to retain the salacious and damaging information he had about him, in case his services should be needed again—despite his many promises to release Wentworth from his enforced bondage. Wentworth had fulfilled his part of the bargain by fabricating the fund transfer information and producing documentary evidence to back it up. He had even got the PM's signatures on the damning authorisation documents by slipping them in between official papers which required multiple copy signatures. Still Wilson held the all-important photographs and letters which could destroy him. Wentworth's conscience pricked him; he was throwing a man of principle like Creswell to the lions while supporting a miscreant like Wilson. Once again, he mollified himself by dreaming up possible means of retribution.

*

Creswell sat for a while in silence after Wilson's departure and closed his eyes. Caine had been quite correct. When Wilson was goaded, his need for immediate retaliation led him to be careless with information that he would otherwise have kept closer to his chest. He had divulged or alluded to sources of information which he intended to use to crucify him. There was a witness to his signing the documents which he hadn't signed and there were contacts in the British Embassy and the Chinese Ministry of Information in Beijing.

He sorted the papers on his desk and began returning them to his briefcase. It was only then he realised that his file containing the undoctored reports was missing. Wilson had appropriated the reports which were damning to him with the intention of weakening Creswell's case against him. He buried his face in his hands and shook his head; he realised that the actual outcome of the meeting was a Mexican stand-off. There was still more he had to do; a lot more. He was self-absorbed and failed to see Wentworth sitting in the unlit cabinet office as he left.

Wentworth watched the PM disappear through the same door that Wilson had used earlier. When he was sure that the PM had gone, he crossed over in the darkness and entered the PM's day office by keying an unauthorised code into the keypad. The look on his face was that of a deeply troubled and very frightened man.

Ten

The confrontation with Wilson was not something Creswell had been exactly looking forward to, but he had at least expected to nullify the threat Wilson posed and to commence the removal of Wilson from his position of power. Creswell sat, morosely, in his club nursing a third large brandy. The look on his face was that of a worried man. He had felt so sure that he would have been able to counter any of Wilson's lies and that it would now be over but events had proved otherwise, and he was still very much on the hook and uncomfortably at the whim of a maniac who demonstrated that he was losing touch with reality.

His ace in the hole was to have got Wilson to be indiscreet and then to produce the evidence of the security tape that ran constantly in his office and to use the evidence to counter Wilson's duplicity. The first part had gone to plan, although on reflection, he should have realised that it had been made too easy for him. The damning words had poured out from Wilson because he was safe in the knowledge that, as security advisor to the PM, he had been able to disable the security recording and fill the time slot with silence. Wilson had also been able, by sleight of hand, to purloin the original files submitted by Gilliland and Crook which he, Wilson, had doctored, and this was the main plank of Creswell's rebuttal. His means of defence against Wilson's fabricated evidence was considerably weakened, and he could only rely on the strength of his word against that of Wilson's; he had been told by more than one person that Wilson could garner support, from apparently impeccable sources, by his own devious means.

He sat for a long time in the comfortable club chair and consumed two further brandies, deciding against a further libation when the head steward gave him a disdainful look after serving the last round. Morosely, he rose from the seat and walked towards the exit where his two bodyguards attached themselves quietly to his shadow. Even in this desperate personal situation, he was unable to grieve alone. Such was the lot of a Prime Minister.

*

Wilson was puzzled about how Creswell had accessed the original Broken Arrow interim files. He, Wilson, had the doctored copies, from which the positive results had been removed, before passing them on to Creswell who was Minister of Defence at that time. But how had he gained access to the actual original documents? He had checked his safe again and located the digital storage devices containing electronic copies of the original reports. They were in their usual hiding place in a disc box titled Obsolete Statistical Analyses among other files which were low grade and unlikely to court any interest. He had put the data storage devices (DSDs) into his CPU and opened to the contents page, the password protected security file showed that he had been the last person to access the information which he had passed on to his newly employed scientists. The unauthorised access data file was empty; trying more of the suite of storage devices yielded the same result.

He considered the implications of his search. Creswell had copies of all the reports, but he had not accessed them through the DSDs. His trail of logic continued, the paper copies that he, Wilson, had used were disposed of so unless somebody had had the forethought to access the DSDs when they were first recorded which was extremely unlikely, there had to be another source. He thought back over the events of the disbandment of the project. He reached no definitive conclusion.

Pettit may have been a thorn in his side, but he had been chosen by Wilson because he was reliable, taciturn, and thorough. As soon as they had rounded up all the technicians in the Scilly Island's facility, where the original radar experiments had been carried out, Pettit had raided and secured all the confidential files. Wilson himself had overseen the destruction of the files one by one. Only he had an electronic copy of all the files and except for their being accessed by his tame, but ultimately useless scientists, who were singularly unable to complete the project as was his original intention, nobody else had had access. Recalling the inability of his original renegade scientists to conclude the technology research, he became unstable and furious once more. Their inability to complete had cost him earlier access to the technology he had so desperately wanted. He conveniently overlooked the fact the he had provided them with faulty information on which to base their findings.

He had personally taken charge of the security during the abortive attempts of the scientists to complete the project. No electronically recorded document could leave his department's complex because it would be wiped clean by the electromagnetic (EM) scanners when any personnel exited the building. There were no mobile telephones or computers which would allow the discs to be copied or emailed from within the complex. He felt sure that there had been no leaks from that source, but just to make sure he would put the frighteners on the scientists concerned and see what came to the surface.

At a loss to find the source of the leak, he abandoned that avenue of enquiry and focussed on what he could do to counter the moves that Creswell had used in his own defence. His protestations of having no knowledge of the authorisation of the transfer would, to any other observer, sound pathetically weak. There were documents with his genuine signature albeit obtained by deception. Application of the right kind of pressure on the witness of the signings would, because of his seniority, carry considerable weight. The information coming out of China was presented by a British agent, who believed it to be true because it came from an impeccable source in the Chinese Ministry. The Chinese source believed it to be true because he had unearthed the information from files that should only have been accessed by the minister himself. The minister was unaware that one of his own trusted officers had fabricated the misinformation and skilfully woven it into the files.

All he had to do now was to work on discrediting Creswell's evidence and strengthen his own so that he could finish off Creswell once and for all. Until then, he would bide his time; there was, after all, no rush. Their next meeting would be very different; he would not only reinforce his position, he would find out or fabricate more evidence and deliver the killer blow. His next move would be to set his tame bloodhounds on to Creswell's trail and find something that would suit his purposes. One way or another, he would get him, and the way he was currently feeling one of the options which was definitely on was assassination.

Eleven

The Islanders were unaware of the recent increase in tensions between their community and the Federation and of that between their interests and those of Wilson. The Ruling Council were very much aware of the former but not so much of the latter, they assumed that Wilson's former takeover attempts having failed dismally meant that he was out of the running. There was a buzz of speculation running around the Island at the visit from the UK Prime Minister. It was assumed that some sort of deal was being worked on with the UK Government, and that was looked upon as a move in the right direction, especially by the British contingent which made up some 20 per cent of the Island's population.

By now, the population had grown considerably, and there were representatives of many countries and all continents. The predominant contingent, in the region of 80 per cent, was from the northern hemisphere. The remaining 20 or so per cent hailed from a broad selection of southern hemisphere countries.

Creswell's visit to the Island was at his own instigation. As he arrived at the airport, he was beginning to feel a comfortable familiarity with the simplicity and lack of bureaucracy he encountered. There was no red carpet, no troops to be inspected, and definitely no insincere public speeches to be made.

Creswell was again impressed by the relaxed attitude of the Islanders and of the quality of the facilities offered to him with no cost attached. At the airport, he was greeted by a group of young immigration personnel all wearing the one piece Air Force blue uniform adopted by the Immigration Department. They were relaxed and smiling, and on his arrival broke off talking to each other in a language he had not heard before. It was peppered with single syllable English-sounding words but all interconnecting words were unintelligible to him. A senior officer addressed him in English and welcomed him to Recovery Island, his accent was strange sometimes flowing easily and sometimes staccato and uneven, almost hesitant.

There was familiarity too when he entered the council chambers. His discussion on this occasion was with Caine, whom he was delighted to actually meet in person; Gilliland, Crook, and Pettit were engaged elsewhere. Rather than use the formal meeting room for their discussion, they adjourned to Gilliland's private office which, apart from the usual accoutrements' had a small round conference table set for three but which could, at a pinch seat five.

Before starting the meeting with Caine, Creswell questioned her about the language being spoken at the airport which was unintelligible and then about the strange accent. At first, she looked puzzled and then realisation dawned on her. "I think I can answer that." She looked at him with her head enquiringly tilted to one side, "I am going to presume that the officers you are speaking of were very young." She accepted his nod of consent. "They are teenagers in training. They were all born on the Island, and this is the only life they know. Growing up here is like growing up anywhere. They feel the need of a language which they alone understand to give them some independence from the adult world. I'm sure that it was also practiced in your youth."

"I haven't really thought about it for so long. Youth is but a distant memory, but you're right, and it applied to my parents too." He assumed a look of fond recollection.

"You may remember something called, for some reason, Dog Latin. Kids used it as a code to say things in secret. What they did was to transpose words by removing the first letter or syllable from a word and adding it to the end of the word and adding ay to the end of that. For example, Hello becomes Ellohay and goodbye becomes oodbyegay."

"That I remember from my school days, and I spoke it quite fluently, but that is not what they were speaking."

"You're right." She laughed. "These kids have gone a stage further. They take each syllable of the word and reverse it so that hello becomes leho and goodbye becomes doogeyb."

"Bizarre, and I get it, but what about the strange accent when they use the English language—where does that come from?"

"Again, it's simple if you think about it. Speaking a language backwards means you have to employ oral gymnastics of a new kind. If you try and get your tongue around speaking backwards, and you do so frequently, speaking English round the right way becomes difficult. That's the accent you hear. This generation looks upon English as a second language. They are not concerned that their language cannot be understood in the rest of the world. They've never been there and, generally, do not see it as a serious consideration. An interesting anthropomorphic development is that second-generation users of "Gneshil", as they translate English, being taught English by the first generation have the accent built in naturally, so an accent is borne. What has taken many generations in other cultures to develop has been compressed down to just one or at most two generations."

"Why don't I hear this accent all over the Island, it was only the group at the airport that I heard speaking in this way?"

"That's another condensed social development issue. The east side of Main Island is occupied by people who have chosen to live with people with whom they share outlooks and attitudes. They tend to be the people who volunteer work with a given range of skills, and they have, as has happened throughout history, become tribal about their chosen way of life. These people seldom venture into the west of the Island, which is inhabited by a different group of people who, likewise, seldom venture into the east side of the Island. The accent adopted by the east Islanders is influenced by the "Gneshil" language, whereas the accents of those in the west are influenced by their origins. These accents are modifying but slowly and will die out to become Standard English or a slight modification of it as happened in the development of American, Australian, or South African English, for example." She shrugged her shoulders. "We are doing our best to stop this polarisation from happening, but it seems to be a trend of popular choice and we don't want to force the introduction of any social homogenisation, it would be better achieved by collective choice. The question we are pondering is, how we can promote harmonisation without passing a law, which would be counter-productive?"

"Fascinating, every time I come here I learn something new, a rarity at my age but truly fascinating." Creswell's wonderment was open and obvious.

He had enjoyed the diversion but got down to the business in hand by apprising her of the uncomfortable confrontation he had with Wilson and the stalemate that ensued. Caine, who had advised him, during their earlier video conference, of the best psychological approach to the meeting with Wilson, quizzed him in detail about the structure of the discussion, trying to ascertain the exact phraseology. She was disturbed that Wilson had been able to neutralise the recording of the meeting but also looked on it as a potential positive. That Wilson did not want the conversation to be available to any third party in its true form indicated that he knew that he was on contestable ground in some way that they did not yet understand. Suppression of the recording by Wilson could be used to counter his accusations, maybe.

She was amused when he told her that Wilson had stolen his file of the original reports and began to look a little more comfortable about the tenor of the discussion.

"Why do you find his stealing the reports amusing?" Creswell frowned.

"Because he obviously has no idea where you got the copies from, and he doesn't realise that we have made them available to you and that you can get duplicates from us." She paused and suddenly looked less comfortable again. "Does he know that you've come here to talk to us?"

"No, would it matter if he did?"

"Well, yes, I think it would. Given the opportunity, he would use that knowledge to his own advantage. He's likely to say that you were having covert meetings with what he calls a nest of traitors and plotting against the country and the Federation."

"Um," Creswell said thoughtfully, "as far as my office is concerned, I am on holiday, and I left my bodyguards at the airport. They don't know I'm here—and I had better make sure that Wilson doesn't find out."

"Where did we fly you here from?" Caine enquired.

"Northolt."

"That's a bit too high profile," she thought for a moment, "how about we fly you back to Bessingford, that's our Angam Oil airfield at our refinery on the Thames Estuary, and then we'll arrange a car to take you to your home."

"Suits me fine," Creswell said easily.

"I think I'll join you on that flight," Caine said, "I'll just need a moment alone to talk to Chester."

On the journey to Bessingford, Caine and Creswell talked easily. They were joined after two and a half hours by the captain who took a seat next to Caine, facing across the table to where Creswell sat.

"Everything okay here in first class."

"First class?" Creswell, who had his back to the flight deck, looked along the length of the fuselage at the identical tables and leather chairs that stretched all the way to the back of the cabin. "First class?" he repeated with a puzzled look.

"Yes, first class," the captain repeated with a straight face, "these first two table sets are first class, the next two are club, and the rest are economy."

"I can't see any difference." Creswell still looked puzzled.

"There isn't any difference." Captain Cox laughed delightedly. "Apart from their position in the cabin, they're all the same. It's what we Islanders call democracy. For us, everything is first class."

"How long have you been saving that up?" Caine laughed. "It's a good line."

"It feels like forever," he chuckled. "This is the first time I've had the opportunity to talk with an off Islander. It would fall rather flat on one of our own."

Creswell was struck once more by the lack of formality among the Islanders; from the chairman and chief executive down, they were all generally on first name terms. The captain's words had also made him acknowledge what he had not before realised. In his limited movements about the Island's hierarchic, preference was not apparent in the facilities they all shared. Offices were all of the same functional quality from clerk to director, living accommodation was the same for all as were the restaurants and other facilities. This was a one class society and the one class was first class.

"You look as if you have just had an epiphany, James." Caine looked at him with her head on one side.

"Do you know—I think I actually have." He had just realised that the Island structure was truly and actively democratic even if it was, paradoxically, a dictatorship. As a conservative by persuasion, he found it hard to believe that what had developed met with his absolute approval and was a pure form of communism not that which was tainted by political corruption. He had previously thought that, as somebody had once said, in communism, the practice was "everybody is equal—except me and I am a little more equal than everybody else." He did not enlighten Caine about his epiphany; he was still struggling with the concept in his own mind and found his approval of it whimsically amusing.

The captain returned to the flight deck after advising them that they would be landing in thirty minutes. Caine rechecked her lap strap and began gathering her belongings in a heap on the seat beside her.

"James, we will be leaving the airfield in separate cars at separate times. Should we meet at any time during my brief stay in England please act as though you don't know me."

"But why?" Creswell interrupted her.

"Maybe we can discuss it in the fullness of time, but it is imperative that you do as I ask. I'm not assuming that we will bump into each other but if we should . . ." She allowed her sentence to tail off.

"Reluctantly, I agree. It would be churlish of me not to do so."

Creswell left the confines of the airfield in the back seat of a four-wheel drive vehicle. He had been cleared through the Anglo American customs station which recorded the comings and goings of Angam personnel whether they were en route for some other destination or staying in England. He smiled as he sat back in the comfortable rear seat; there would be no record of his arrival back into the country unless Angam decided to inform HM Customs. His smile would not have been so apparent had he noticed the occupant of a black cab taking photographs of him as he was swept out through the gates. The photographer began talking rapidly into his satellite phone.

Twelve

Cine left Bessingford Field which is owned and run entirely by the Angam Oil Corporation, an influential private oil company, based in Colorado which was owned in its entirety by the joint families of Caine and Gilliland. They were both major shareholders in the company which was the source of their ability to spend the billions that the Island enterprise had so far cost. As a private airfield, with its own customs post, it afforded them access in and out of the country without the usual records and red tape.

She left the private airfield an hour after Creswell, dressed down in nondescript tourist clothes and drove herself in a British-built Ford that was almost old enough to be a classic and which had no recorded affiliation with Angam Oil. The black cab from which Creswell had been photographed was no longer in its former position, and her departure from the airfield went unnoticed.

Her journey into central London was uneventful even to being able to find a parking space in the underground car park at Marble Arch. From there, she took a cab along the Edgware Road into Paddington to a hotel off Praed Street at which she had reserved a room. The Beaufort Hotel was owned and operated by an American Government intelligence agency with which she had strong, generally unknown, family connections. Ownership of the hotel was almost impossible to trace, and its use by the secret service was not known to the British Government; a fact that sat uncomfortably with Caine. It irked her that her home country was being so underhand with their greatest ally. She ultimately reasoned that the Brits were probably doing the same in the USA, so it was tit for tat. Travelling, as she was, incognito suited her current purposes admirably.

Nondescript on the outside, there was a permanent no vacancies sign in the window, and the reception area was barren and unclean. A notice at the reception desk informed that the establishment was not open to non-residents and that no Social Security residents would be accepted and no guests were allowed in the rooms at any time. At some time in the past, the notice had been adorned with an illiterate graffiti message that had not been entirely removed it was faint but still visible *"Fashest Pigs"*.

A scruffy unshaven receptionist emerged from a curtained off office and looked her up and down disinterestedly "Wadjerwan?" He muttered around the cigarette clamped between his lips. His Eastern European accent was heavy, and he had obviously picked up his brand of English in the more colourful areas of the East End of London.

"I have a reservation," she said as she watched fascinated by the long worm of ash at the end of his cigarette; it remained firmly in place although it looked as if it would fall off at any moment. She handed him a card with a reservation number on it.

He took the card and shuffled over to a registration book. He compared the number on the card with an entry in the book, nodded sagely, and took a key from its scarred wooden pigeonhole rack and gave it to her. "Number 8 on a 'grahnd' floor." His cigarette moved up and down and still the ash remained, fascinatingly, in place. He picked up a grubby rotary telephone which had, in a previous incarnation, been white but which now had taken on a yellowy brown mottled patina except where greasy hands and fingers had prevented the patina from taking hold. "Bird 'ere's got a booking. Room 8." He listened for a moment "Okay," he put the phone down. "Fru there," he pointed at a double door. "Pressa button an' go fru when it buzz." His accent was as indeterminate as his appearance was scruffy.

She pressed the button at the side of the door, wrinkling her nose in disgust at the grime and the sour odours; only just resisting the urge to wipe her fingers on her jeans and hold her nose. The door opened on to a small vestibule which matched the insanitary decor of the reception area. Opposite the door, she had just entered there was another door next to which was an alcove. She had to wait until the first door she had entered closed before she could open the second, an in-built security precaution, but it was not the obvious door that she opened it was one disguised at the back of the alcove by a tired and desiccated-looking potted fern. The other two doors were interlinked so that they could not be opened while the third, secret, door was being used. Passing through the concealed door she entered an office which contained a secretary's desk and a table with computer printers and fax machines and a tray of various stationery items. Turning, she looked at the door behind her; it could not be seen as a door, the panel in which it was located was a floor-to-ceiling map of the world. The outline of the door was camouflaged by the longitude and latitude lines of the map.

The secretary sitting at the desk grinned. "Hi, Penny, it's good to see you again. Here for a couple of weeks?" Lin Carter was about the same age as Caine and obviously American.

"Hi, Lin." Caine returned the grin. "Yes, I am. Don't you ever take time off? Every time I visit you're here waiting."

"It's a plot. Whenever you're coming, they let me know, and I take over the office so I can meet up with you and catch up on the gossip. Nearly missed you this time. You didn't give us much notice." She rose from the chair and picked up Caine's single battered suitcase and marched out into the corridor with Caine in her wake.

They entered Room 8, which turned out to be a suite comprising of two double bedrooms with en suite bathrooms, a sitting room, and a dining room. On the table was a message from the manager welcoming her to the Lynden Hotel.

"Where did you find the gem of a receptionist in the Beaufort? He's the best yet."

"He's perfect for the job. He's of no fixed abode and certainly no fixed intelligence. He has no interest in what goes on at the Beaufort and doesn't ask any questions, some of the rooms that are paid for are often not used. We've put your dummy luggage in their Room 8 and we'll get somebody to muss up the bed there from time to time to keep what passes for housekeeping satisfied. Most of the other rooms are legit permanent residents. That keeps the hotel watchdogs off our backs."

*

Looking self-satisfied, Wilson replaced the phone on its cradle. It was all beginning to come together; the further dossier he was beginning to build on Creswell was filling out more quickly than he had thought possible. His quest for the destruction of the PM was ever active, and his watching man at the Angam airfield had provided a windfall bonus of having identified Creswell leaving the airfield in an Angam car. Further investigation through air traffic control identified the only flight in over the last two days was a direct flight from Recovery Island, the case against Creswell continued to build but this time the information was legitimate.

He dry washed his hands as he savoured the early signs of a complete victory over Creswell. Telephone calls to Creswell's secretary revealed that he was taking a few days holiday for private reasons but that the secretary could contact the PM if really necessary. Wilson wondered how Creswell would handle the leak to the press, that he had made an elicit visit to the land of the traitors when he was supposed to be on holiday. Such a leak would surely set the malicious bloodhounds on his trail and that would just be the beginning.

His gloating was interrupted by his PA advising him that his 4.30 appointment was waiting. With some irritation, he told the PA to send the visitor in. He was pleasantly surprised when a very attractive young woman was ushered into his office.

"Come in, come in." He waved her towards a guest chair and glanced down at his notes to remind himself of the name of his visitor. "How can I be of assistance to you . . . Ms DeLaney?" His smile which was intended to be inviting was, in reality, sickly, it was that of a man who was clearly unaccustomed to smiling.

"Thank you, sir." Caine, using her middle name which was actually her mother's maiden name, as her family name, smiled a genuine looking smile at him.

"You are here to . . ." he looked down at his notes again which he had clearly not read before.

"I'm here to do research into ethical security in democratic governance as part of my post-graduate studies," she helped him out.

"Ah, yes, and I see that your sponsor is the American Secretary of State. Most impressive . . . um . . . most impressive. What exactly does it mean? Ethical security?"

"My studies are post-graduate," she explained easily. "I am looking into the civilised way that our free democracies handle the difficult issues arising from having to restrict freedom and movement of individuals and groups suspected of undertaking terrorist activities." She looked at him wide-eyed as if in awe of his exulted position. "The Secretary of State told me that you look after these matters for the British Government and that you are a leading exponent of ethics in this field."

"He is very well informed." Wilson did not bother to fain modesty in the face of a blatant, but complementary lie. "So how can I help you?" He looked pointedly at his wrist watch. "Look I have a very busy afternoon, and I would like to go through these issues with you without time pressures. Perhaps the best way of dealing with this would be for us to meet for dinner this evening."

"You are very kind to give your time to me. I would find dinner most acceptable." Beneath her smile she was cringing.

*

Trevor Coniston, the head of MI5, frowned as he looked over the dossier that had just landed on his desk. The photographs were of poor quality but were not so poor that the face of the Prime Minister could not be recognised as he exited the gates of the Angam airfield in an official Angam car. The photos and notes about the time of the photographs were contained in a brief report based on information received from a regular, if low level, contributor. It was all very low key, and he wondered in passing why any gravity was placed on such an occurrence, and why it had found its way to his desk.

Later, he received other information which was, to him, also inconsequential. The report was brief and informed him that Creswell had taken a few days leave and had left the country covertly. He placed the file in the "don't do anything yet" tray which it shared with a dozen other snippets of information. It was accompanied by another unrelated file concerning the illegal transfer of funds to a mysterious figure by the name of John Connaught. The transfer was believed to have been facilitated by a senior figure in the British Government.

The Connaught file was heavyweight and was not transferred to the "don't do anything yet" tray and was placed to be dealt with immediately.

He looked at the files provenance and found that it emanated from a reliable "diplomat" in the British Embassy in Beijing. The agent's information source was a ten digit alpha numerical reference; he accessed an eyes only index on his computer and found the identity of the person through whom the information was researched was Chung Yi. "My old friend Mr Chung." He smiled wryly. "Our paths cross yet again!"

That evening, from his Belgravia flat, Coniston telephoned the embassy in Beijing and spoke to the author of the report on John Connaught. He was advised by the agent that his reason for researching Connaught was that he had been given an unsolicited tip from Chung Yi that they had information regarding the transfer of six million sterling into the Beijing branch of the Bank of Samurai. The Chinese ministry of information had been alerted by the size of the component transfers and that they came via a number of tax haven accounts across the world, and Chung Yi had thought that, because Connaught was obviously British, that the embassy would be interested.

Coniston replaced the telephone thoughtfully. It was not like Mr Chung to offer information without expecting something in return. As he had not asked the agent for anything, he could only presume that payment was being received from another source, if so he mused, what or more pointedly—who—was the source? Clearly, the information had been passed on to elicit a response of some kind, but without knowing what response was expected, he could only wait and watch.

*

Caine's dinner with Wilson had been painful. He had clearly been more interested in her than the project she professed to be pursuing. She had managed to fend him off with a promise of more dinner meetings to accommodate his busy work schedule. Having explained to him that

Great Britain was the pilot for the scheme to compare notes with other European countries, she asked if she could sit in with his staff as they handled the processing of suspect individuals. She emphasised that she had no wish to be involved in any sensitive matters which might impact on national security. He agreed to her joining this offshoot section of his department on a temporary and unpaid basis without hesitation; after all she was sponsored by no less than the American Secretary of State, a person of considerable standing who could be beneficial to Wilson's ever-expanding plans.

Being a cautious man, Wilson set his bloodhounds on her trail to make sure that she was not a threat. As she spent her first morning being taught the ropes, her contacts were being analysed. The Secretary of State's office in Washington confirmed that Penelope Delaney had been recommended by him to make a study of ethical security as practiced by others in order that the USA did not fall again into the trap that they had at "Gitmo" all those years ago and which had ultimately become extremely embarrassing. They also confirmed that she was funding the research herself having refused any government aid.

Research by the team found that her recommendation by the Secretary of State was actually facilitated through the Professor Emeritus at the Hinckley University of Colorado, which she was attending as a post-graduate, who was also a close friend of the Secretary of State.

Via immigration his team of investigators obtained her temporary London address as the Beaufort Hotel in Paddington. Further investigation of the hotel revealed that it had never even applied for a star rating and had it done so would never have been granted. Most of the clientele appeared to be back packers and immigrants on the way to looking for more acceptable accommodation With a very modest bribe paid to the desk clerk, they had gained access to her room and described it as a cockroach-infested rat hole.

Wilson thought he might turn her frugal life to his advantage by offering to help her with improved accommodation which his slush reserve would fund and which might give him an "in". He resolved that he would approach the subject during their next scheduled dinner meeting. He failed to recognise that such a well-connected girl would be unlikely to use such a "down at heel" hotel. His mind, concerning her, was on physically gratifying areas of her torso.

His uncharacteristic overlooking of the obvious was a by-product of his frustration at not being able to fit in a visit to Nuovostan to collect the working BAM2 unit before the scientists realised that they had actually achieved his objectives. His lone nature once more delayed the achievement of one of his primary objectives and having to delay the visit to deal with Creswell made him hate Creswell more than ever.

Thirteen

Coniston compiled the dossier which connected John Connaught to the six million and to the bank account in Beijing. Further investigation, which had pointed to a senior politician being closely involved with Connaught, was pursued relentlessly but reached a full stop when the suspect was traced to the cabinet and the trail went cold. He had no alternative but to approach the PM whose signature was appended to the appropriation documents to further the case. The thought of approaching Creswell on such a circumstantial perplexing matter filled him with dread. If Creswell were to be implicated, the repercussions throughout the world would be extremely harmful at a time of high vulnerability. A major part of his job was to prevent that happening.

A highly confidential meeting between the two was hastily, and secretively, convened and Coniston's opening gambit was hesitant. As senior as he was confronting the PM and accusing him of complicity in a crime did not sit easily especially as he was of the belief that Creswell's integrity was beyond reproach.

"Prime Minister," Coniston looked distinctly uncomfortable, "information has come into my possession that you have signed documents appropriating six million sterling for a project or projects not recognised by the black ops team. What is more, the funds have ended up in a bank in Beijing in the name of one John Connaught of whom we have no tangible knowledge."

"Trevor," Creswell said with a great feeling of unease "first, since when have you started calling me Prime Minister? For the last twelve years, we have been on first name terms, and I see no reason to change that. Second, why would you be involved with this matter and who is it that involved you?"

"James, I'm sorry, but I can't answer your second question. I have been approached through formal independent channels with a view to ascertaining the facts of this issue to find out who John Connaught is and to what purpose the six million was sequestered by you."

"Okay." He looked at Coniston levelly and unflinchingly. "I have no idea what the money was used for. I have never requested any such sum of money, and I do not know anybody by the name of John Connaught. So where do we go from here, and as I outrank you, by whose authority are you investigating this?"

"James, you're making life very difficult for me. You must be aware that even the Prime Minister is not above the law, and the Department of Justice is required by parliamentary act to investigate any suspicion of wrongdoing." He slid a file over the table. "These are the transfer documents and this," he stabbed his finger at the bottom of the first document, "is your signature, is it not?"

"It certainly looks like it."

"Help me out here, James. Tell me this is not your signature and give me a chance to rubbish these accusations."

"It looks like my signature, but I have no knowledge of ever having signed these documents."

"James," he exclaimed with a pained expression, "that really is not good enough." Leaning forward earnestly in his chair he continued, "If this is proven, the police will become involved and all hell will be let loose. You have to give me more than that. Don't tie my hands."

Creswell remained silent as he thought through his options. He could stone wall so that the investigation would stall, but he was sure that Wilson would not allow that to happen for long. He could play the NRT report card against Wilson but that would be like firing all his ammunition prematurely. His eyes quivered left to right rapidly as he hurriedly summed up his options. "I'd like to help you all I can, Trevor, but I haven't got all my ducks in a row yet. Give me a little more time, and I'm sure I can convince you that someone is trying to destroy me. Don't let Wilson's accusations get to you. The man's a pathological liar." He smiled humourlessly at Coniston's look of surprise.

"I wouldn't give Wilson the time of day in a matter like this. You're right, he is a pathological liar and that's one of his more acceptable traits. The accusation didn't come from him, and it is from a far more informed source and anybody listening to him would be convinced by what he says. I can give you a week but no more, and I'll struggle with that amount of time. After that, I will have no alternative but to turn this over to the authorities, and if that happens, your political career will be over."

Creswell was stunned by the revelation that it was not Wilson who had set MI5 on to him; as the bottom fell out of his defence, he was too much a politician to let it show on his face. He had hoped to be able to rubbish anything that Wilson said by revealing his part in the NRT debacle, but if it wasn't Wilson, then who was it? He left the meeting with no idea of how he could extricate himself from the tangled mess that had been created for him.

*

Delaney's second dinner with Wilson was even more painful than the first. He was smarmy, and the dark fringe of straggly hair partly surrounding his bald pate, glistened unattractively with sweat. He chastised her for staying at the Beaufort Hotel, insisting that it was unsuitable for a beautiful young lady like her. He assured her that she would feel more comfortable if she were to move to more suitable accommodation; perhaps to a nice little hotel quite close to the club in Chelsea at which he stayed while in London.

She fended off his overtures with a convincing mixture of unsophisticated gaucheness like a breathless star-struck college girl, saying that she was determined to fund the exercise herself so that it could not be said that she was beholden to any person or association, even her family, in the compilation of her report. He suggested that she should think again about his offer while he was away on state business for a few days, and they could come to a more amenable solution on his return. She made no comment about his suggestion.

When he realised that he would make no further progress with his intended conquest at this time, he offered to have his driver take her to her hotel. Initially, she declined but ultimately gave way to at least that suggestion. The Jaguar parked outside the hotel looked incongruous as did Wilson when he accompanied her into the impoverished reception area. The same porter emerged through the same grubby curtained doorway and looked suspiciously at Wilson.

"The key to eight," she asked politely.

"No guests," he stuck his chin out and pointed to the faded graffiti garlanded notice, "no guest's is allowed. This aint a knockin' shop," he grumbled to himself as he reached for the key "an' there's a bill to be paid, otherwise, yerout."

Wilson bustled up to the counter and snatched the handwritten bill from the porter. "You fellow," he shook his fist at the man, "get the manager, and I'll have him fire you on the spot."

"Ent a manager jus' me," he said completely unfazed by Wilson's anger.

"Please, sir, just let me settle the check. After all, I do actually owe the hotel this money," she said plaintively.

"All right, my dear," he patted her shoulder and whispered confidentially to her, "but, remember what I said earlier, don't call me, sir, when we're alone. Sir should be reserved for when we're with people like this." He looked disdainfully at the creature behind the desk.

She took the key to her room and, after she had persuaded Wilson to leave, entered into the Lynden Hotel through the concealed door. Lin Carter was behind the secretary's desk once more when she entered the office.

"What are you doing here again, Lin, just how long is your day?" She looked surprised.

"I waited for you because there's something you ought to see." She held up a DSD. "This came from the covert security cameras in the Beaufort earlier today." She slotted the disc into a player and switched on the view screen and pushed the fast forward until the clock read 10.34 a.m.

The screen had four segments each serving a different surveillance camera. On the one showing reception, two men entered and walked to the reception desk. There was no sound, but it was obvious that one of the men shouted for service, and when he did not get an immediate response, he pounded the counter with his huge fist. The desk clerk moved into position with a speed that she had not realised he was capable. The definition was not sufficient for her to see the look of anger on the desk clerk's face, but his body language suggested it.

The bigger of the two visitors reached across the counter and clutched the desk clerk's shirt front, bunching it up and pulled him halfway across the counter so that their noses were almost touching. There ensued a rapid discussion which was terminated when the desk clerk was released; he took a key from the pigeon hole and handed it to his antagonist. Reaching over, he pressed the button that released the door into the hotels interior.

Both men appeared on a second segment of the screen as they came through one door and disappeared through the other where they appeared on the third segment. They walked along the corridor and using the key supplied they entered Room 8. Ten minutes later, they exited the room and retraced their steps to reception where a very attentive desk clerk was waiting for them. The big man threw the key down on the counter and then placed what looked like a number of bank notes beside it. He reached across the counter and grasped the desk clerk's shirt again, but this time, he did not drag him across the counter, he spoke very earnestly to him, released his shirt, and then drew his index finger across his own throat. The same index finger was wagged in warning as the two men left.

"What are you up to, Penny? They looked like very dangerous men." Carter looked concerned.

"I can't tell you that, Lin, but don't worry about the two thugs, they were sent by somebody who's checking up on my bona fides. They weren't out to harm me." She looked at the DSD which was still running with all four segments showing no activity. "Can you let me have a copy of the disc? I'd like to email it to some friends."

Fourteen

Sir Lionel Wentworth had been attending to mundane matters that he thought, as head of the civil service should be done by others; it was irksome but necessary he supposed. His trance-like look was interrupted by the soft buzzing of his secure telephone. "Wentworth."

"This is a secure line. Is there anybody with you?"

"I am quite alone." Wentworth spoke despondently as he recognised Wilson's voice.

"Good, now listen carefully, this is very important. Are you awake? Is my voice registering with you?"

"You are loud and clear," Wentworth muttered, "unfortunately", under his breath. "What do you want this time?"

"That sounds hostile, Wentworth. Don't be hostile, or I won't be nice to you."

"That would be a first," he retorted softly at just below audible level.

"I've got good news for you, Wentworth. News that will make you very happy."

"I can hardly wait," he said in a soft mournful monotone.

"I am prepared to release to you the information and photos of your little dalliances in exchange for one more little thing."

"Is this the same little thing that you promised would be the final task last time?"

"Well, there has been a further development which requires just a little something . . . it's no more than a simple telephone call."

"To whom, and about what?"

"A simple call to Coniston at MI 5, saying that you've been thinking about the Creswell business a bit more deeply, and now you are even more concerned about some unorthodoxy in the dealings of the PM and that you hadn't mentioned before, but you saw the PM sign money transfer documents for a Mr Connaught."

"You mean, you want me to compound a felony with perjury? Haven't I already done enough by getting the signatures for you. Will you ever leave me alone?"

"It's for the last time, Sir Lionel," he wheedled sickeningly, "after that you will be free."

"Will I be any freer than the last promise you made?"

"This is part of the same promise, and after you make the call, I will personally hand all the documents, original and copies, to you."

"This is a nightmare." Wentworth buried his head in his hands and shook it dejectedly. "This is positively the last time I will have any dealings with you to support your dirty tricks."

"I am a man of my word," Wilson said piously in the firm belief that he was a man of ethics and integrity, just like the persona Penelope Delaney had intimated was essentially him.

*

Penelope Delaney began her bogus research into Wilson's "ethical treatment of potentially hostile foreign nationals". It meant working closely with Wilson's secretary who was an ambitious career girl and saw her current position as a stepping stone to working with senior elected officials of the government; perhaps even the Prime Minister. She also worked with the senior civil servant in charge of internal department affairs.

Delaney played her role very carefully, giving the impression that she was awestruck by the powerful people around her in the department. She had access to non-classified files relating to the hundreds of individuals currently under investigation. Innocent questions were asked by her of her two main contacts in the department about the methods of interrogation which they preferred to call fact-finding enquiries. She had no doubts that they both believed they were acting with complete integrity; she also had no doubts that Wilson only gave them access to information which would reinforce their misguided beliefs.

After a few days, she was able to research her subject without being continually scrutinised, and she was able to start early and finish late, having been given her own temporary pass. The pass was restricted to non-secure areas, but gave her access to general files and desk diaries. Through these media she was able to track the supposed whereabouts of Wilson over the last six months although not the content of any of the assignations he had.

She talked to the department's senior civil servant and expressed an interest in meeting the head of the civil service to talk with "the man at the top" about the exemplary performance of the department in the matter of ethics. Sir Lionel Wentworth was not an easy man to see, but in the interest of his career, he was able to arrange a brief interview.

The meeting with Wentworth proved to be very interesting; her praise for the senior civil servant went down very well with him because it reflected on his own ability to choose civil servants for specific posts. Her praise of Wilson was received quite differently; Wentworth was cool about the subject and made no overt signs of agreeing with her appraisal.

She discussed the matter of ethics and the actions of the government and the civil service and concluded that she felt honour bound not to divulge the way in which it differed from the American model but indicated that she approved of what she had researched in London.

She pressed Wentworth on the role played by Wilson, but he continued to resist making any comment. She continued pressing until Wentworth became irritated and said that he really had no dealings with Wilson in this matter, and that they did not attend the same meetings. She stopped pressing and continued with praise for the way the civil service intervened in the interests of fair play and justice. Their meeting concluded with Wentworth basking in the glory of praise. He didn't know who this young lady was, but he was impressed that she had been recommended by the American Secretary of State. She was so pleasant that he wished, for a fleeting moment, that his sexuality had not taken the path it had and that he were thirty or more years younger.

Fifteen

Creswell was lost and nervously unsettled; he had no idea who would have been a witness to the signatures that he had not knowingly made on the documents that were alien to him. As long as he thought that it was Wilson who was making the running in this battle, he felt he had enough to throw any attack into reasonable doubt and forestall it by threatening Wilson with exposure, but Coniston's revelation had scuppered that avenue of recovery.

Try as he might, he was unable to guess who the witness was, so he decided to change his line of attack and try to find out about John Connaught. His first port of call in the search was to discuss the matter with one of the few he knew he could trust—his old friend Lord Roland Clearman. They met in his small office in the Second House of Lords. Clearman was as nervous as on their previous meeting, and he sat uneasily fiddling with files and papers on his desk.

"I need your help, Roland," Creswell tried by his tone to instil calm into his jittery friend. "I have to find out who this fellow John Connaught is. I'm sorry if this distresses you, but it's very important . . . No . . . , it's vital to me."

"I've told you as much as I can." He kept his eyes fixed firmly on the desktop.

"Roland, I am now going to be very unreasonable. I demand to know who it was that linked Connaught's name to the six million and to me. If you tell me again that you don't know, it could come to light that you were the source of a classified information leak."

"James," he looked truly horrified, "you wouldn't. Not after we've been friends for so long."

"You're right, Roland . . . I wouldn't . . . because you are truly a friend, and if you are my friend, you will tell me what you know, and I know you know because you would never have advised me about such an accusation unless you had proof of its provenance."

"Oh God," he groaned, "what I'm about to do goes against all my parliamentary ethics, and I do it with the greatest reluctance. All I can say to you is beware people who appear to be friends. They may not have your best interests at heart."

*

It was all coming together more satisfactorily than Wilson had dared hope. The signature "witness", the transfer of funds to the bank in Beijing, the onward transfer to the offshore account at which point traceability was lost of the connection between Creswell and Connaught and the link between Creswell and the Chinese secret service. All in all a well thought out strategy, he thought immodestly, which tied together, otherwise, unrelated events by judicious leaking of titbits of information to the right authority. Even if he failed to fabricate that Creswell and Connaught were one and the same person, there would be a natural assumption that Creswell was at least in cahoots with the imaginary Connaught; Connaught, being non-existent, could tell no tales.

His thoughts turned to Penelope Delaney; with her, he was torn between the desire for a sexual liaison with her and the desire to develop links with somebody as influential as the US Secretary of State by demonstrating that he had aided his protégé and one good turn would deserve another. His diary was full, necessitating him being out of the country for the next five days, and he decided to pursue either or both of his desires on his return. In the meantime, he would make sure that she had access to all non-confidential information she required, and this he presumed would soften her and make her bend more readily to his will.

As far as he was concerned, Creswell would be exposed by the time of his return from his overseas duty as DDP by further leaking hints, this time, to the media. He would not, of course, dispense the leaks himself neither would he tell Sir Lionel to do so; that could be risky, and in any case, Sir Lionel had been led to the brink once too often and was showing signs of rebellion. He would get one of the lesser mortals who were beholden to him to do the deed.

Before departing for his five-day trip, he returned to his office and had a last discussion with Delaney. He allowed her to use his office when he was not using it himself with the intention of flattering her and in the hope that she would warm to him rather than being in awe. She made as if to leave his office when he arrived, but he waved her back into the chair at the guest table that she used in his absence.

"I will be leaving in a few minutes, just some papers to pick up before I go." He busied himself stuffing papers into his double briefcase. The telephone rang, and he snatched it from its cradle. "Wilson." He listened for a moment. "Yes, she is and she's in my office right now compiling her report." Listening for another brief moment, he turned away from her, lowering his voice as he did so. "Just get on with it," he whispered. "Don't argue. Just be ready for when I get back and do it. Don't be a wimp." He put the phone down without bothering to say goodbye and sighed deeply.

"Was that something to do with me?" she asked with a hint of false panic in her voice.

"It was that old duffer Wentworth," he said offhandedly.

"Oh," she said with feigned panic. "I hope I didn't upset him when I went to see him."

"No, my dear," he gave another of his hallmark sickly grins, "he was just saying that you had been to see him unexpectedly, and he wanted to make sure that I was okay with that. He said he thought you were charming. Which coming from him," he added as an afterthought, "is a rare sentiment. Even more rare than you might imagine."

"That is so nice of him. Actually, I was rather taken with his old-world English charm. He reminded me in many ways of my grandfather."

"Progeny is absolutely out in his case." Wilson's nasty side emerged briefly and just as quickly subsided.

*

"Delaney" arranged another short notice meeting with Sir Lionel; he agreed to see her at the end of his working day in his Whitehall office where he welcomed her with grace and charm, and they exchanged pleasantries for a few moments.

"Delightful as it is to see you, I'm sure you're not here to please an old man you have a question or questions to ask?"

"Yes, I have," she wore a slightly embarrassed look. "It is Mr Wilson. He confuses me a little. He is most charming to me, and it may be disloyal, but I'm not sure that he is being absolutely truthful with me."

"What do you mean? He hasn't done anything that makes you feel threatened I hope."

"Oh no, nothing like that, it's just that . . . Well, I don't know how to say this without being overly suspicious, but . . . he talks to me about his ethics being beyond reproach, but when I see him addressing people who work for him his ethics are, to put it politely, highly questionable."

"I don't know what it is you want me to reassure you about." He smiled, but it was not his usual avuncular smile, it was one of suppressed pleasure.

"Well," she said, continuing with her little girl lost look, "I trust you even if we have only met once before briefly. What I want to know is can I use what he is telling me and be sure of its veracity?"

"You must make your own mind up about that," he said. "All I can say to you is, if you have any suspicions about what he tells you, you must go with your instincts."

"Are you saying I should distrust him?" she pressed her question.

"I'm simply saying to you that if you have any doubts at all about the impressions he is giving you, you must discount the information concerned and seek another source. It would be imprudent of me to tell you that he has been misleading you."

Their discussion was interrupted by a brief knock on the door and a swirl of air as it was pushed open hastily. She spun round in her chair to see Creswell standing in the open door. For a fraction of a second his face registered recognition, and then it resumed a blank expression.

"Forgive me, Sir Lionel." He looked truly apologetic and turned his gaze on her.

"Please excuse me." He dipped his head towards her. "It is very rude of me to interrupt your conversation, my apologies, Lionel, for not waiting for your response to my knock, I thought at this hour, you would be alone."

"Oh," she said as if she had just realised who he was. She added nothing else and sat looking uncomfortably embarrassed.

"I'm James Creswell." He reached his hand forward.

"Yes, of course, I know who you are." She took his hand and shook it. "How do you do? I am Penelope Delaney."

"You're American," he said, crinkling his handsome face in a genuine smile.

"What can I do for you, James?" Wentworth enquired with his grey eyebrows raised.

"I was just passing, and there are a couple of things I wanted to run by you, but they'll wait until tomorrow."

"Are we almost done, young lady?" Sir Lionel turned to her.

"There are a few more questions I would like to ask, but they can wait for another time."

"I was going to suggest that we share a dinner, Lionel. We haven't done so for some time, and we can catch up with the gossip." Creswell allowed his words to hang in the air.

"Well . . . , I should eat soon." Wentworth looked at his watch. "Perhaps, we could go to my club. The beef there is the best in London." It occurred to Wentworth that he might use time over dinner to mitigate some of the damage Wilson was forcing him to commit and about which he was feeling pangs of deep regret which were only mitigated by his need for self-preservation.

"Excellent, but," Creswell turned to Caine, "I rudely interrupted your discussions, young lady," he hesitated and assumed his flirtatious face, "perhaps you would like to join us? Please say you will or our talk over dinner will be limited to boring matters of state which will be no fun at all."

She paused briefly gathering her thoughts, assessing the wisdom of such a public meeting. Clearly, Creswell had something in mind. "If I won't get in the way, I'd love to." She added as an afterthought, "Don't your clubs in London ban women from entry?"

"When you are in the company of the head of the civil service and the Prime Minister, it's amazing how the club rules can change."

"James," Wentworth feigned shock, "don't be so self-important. The club changed the rules years ago. We allow the ladies into the dining room . . . but not into the rest of the club, of course. We haven't modernised that far." He laughed and the other two joined in with him. The matter was settled.

Over dinner, she watched the two men talking; sometimes about minor matters of state and sometimes about mundane and personal things. She went into psychology major mode and assessed the meanings of their interactions. Creswell was transparent and open without showing any signs of reticence, whereas Wentworth while free flowing in his conversation, generally, had difficulty with some of the subject matter which showed most clearly when he tried to steer the conversation away from a selection of subjects. To any other onlooker, he would be seen to be sheering away from areas that should not be discussed in front of a non-government person, but there was something about the array of topics that piqued her interest but which she could not clearly define.

After dinner, they remained at the table, the two men nursing balloons of very expensive brandy; their guest having a fine dessert wine and the conversation turned to her project and the progress she was making. Wentworth indicated with a stern look that she should not broach the subject of Wilson's integrity, and she respected his wishes.

A waiter approached them and bent to whisper in Wentworth's ear. Wentworth excused himself to take a telephone call.

"I thought you said you didn't want me to know you if we bumped into each other," she whispered to Creswell, taking care that only he could hear her words.

"It occurred to me that if we were introduced by a third party, and at some time during our stay we needed to discuss anything at all, having been introduced, we could do so without raising any suspicions."

"Talking about raising suspicions what happens if somebody sees the Prime Minister having dinner with a female post-graduate from the USA?"

"They will expect it of me I have a certain, um, reputation for dining with young ladies, and I have no difficulty with that perception. I am unmarried, and so is Lionel, so it's more likely that the gossips would have a go if they saw Lionel and me having dinner together without a female companion. We've been friends since university days, but the gossips will still gossip."

"Beware of Sir Lionel," she whispered as she saw him returning to the table, "there's something not quite right about his discussions with you, but I don't know what it is yet."

Creswell blanched at her words; they uncannily echoed the intent expressed by Lord Roland Clearman during their very recent discussion.

Sixteen

The pseudo technology sharing meeting was held on Recovery Island by the same group of Federation collaborators as the first meeting, with the exception of Van der Linde, together with the Islanders. It was dissolved after an hour without any decision on Federation access to the Island being reached. This was duly reported back to the Federation president who was in Beijing.

When Van der Linde, having been briefed by his colleagues, advised Wilson of their failure to even agree on the next meeting, to discuss access to the Island, he exploded. His first action on learning of the failure was to telephone President Chung Ho Chen and advise him of the failure. He blamed Creswell for the lack of progress and said that he had information that Creswell had had covert meetings with the Islanders and that he, Wilson, suspected that Creswell was trying to reach a separate deal in his own exclusive interests. President Chung grudgingly thanked Wilson for passing on the information and said that he was going to call an extraordinary meeting of the senior members of the Federation but would naturally exclude Creswell.

The summit was called in haste and each of those invited was instructed not to make any contact with Creswell, concerning the meeting. Without expressing reservations the premiers and presidents of the major nations made their way swiftly and unquestioningly to Beijing. They had no doubts in their minds that to resist the summons to attend or to communicate with Creswell would lead to serious repercussions.

The meeting in the president's suite at the Ministry of Information in Beijing was called to order. The twenty-seven premiers and presidents fell quiet as Chairman Chung entered the room and assumed his seat at the head table which comprised, apart from himself and his bodyguards, a plethora of translators. He opened the meeting in Mandarin, and the interpreters sprang immediately into action. The cacophony was not a distraction to the listening politicians; they were wearing large acoustic headphones.

The address lasted two hours, and at its conclusion, when the translations had stopped, they all removed their headphones and sat in absolute stunned silence. The meeting which they had expected to be a discussion of the next moves in managing the Island situation turned out to be an instruction to them all to support the Chinese military in the complete overthrow of the Island and the capture and detention, if they still lived, of the three rulers of the Island. The people of the Island were expendable, it was only necessary to secure absolute ownership of their technology.

*

A telephone call from Creswell told Gilliland that something was seriously wrong. Creswell had learned from his own covert sources—too late to do anything about it—that a general meeting of the Federation had been called and that he had not been invited. Chung Ho Chen had instructed unequivocally they should all meet and that short of death, no excuses would be tolerated. He was unable to find out the subject of the meeting and all enquiries had led to promises of calls back which had not materialised. So much, he thought sadly, for friends. He was soon to discover that his foes were not limited to other politicians, they extended to the ranks of those professing to be on his side.

A telephone call from Wilson to Coniston, for example, set a course of action in motion to finally destroy the ambitions of Creswell. He said rather convincingly, even to himself, that he had reason to believe that Creswell was leaking information to the Chinese and that he and Connaught were one and the same person.

Satisfied that he had well and truly started the final demise of Creswell, he did the same for the traitors of Recovery Island by placing a further telephone call to Chairman Chung saying that the UK Prime Minister was in cahoots with Recovery Island and that he would leak information that would thwart the Federation and, therefore, the Peoples' Republic of China. The proof he offered the chairman was that he had irrefutable evidence and photographs proving that Creswell had made illicit visits to the Island while pretending to be on holiday. Chairman Chung instructed Wilson to travel immediately to China in order to work with the Chinese military and assist in drawing up plans to occupy Recovery Island. Wilson congratulated himself on furthering his own plans through the clodhopping Chinese military machine; it did not occur to him that he was committing treason. Even if he had considered it he would have dismissed it out of hand.

*

The communications room on Recovery Island was now a hive of continuous activity. NRT initiated radar technology was working at full stretch, covering specific routes by bending the radar emissions around the earth's curvature in the direction of all the Federation air and sea bases in Europe, the USA, Canada, North Africa, Australia, Japan, the Philippines, and the South Pacific. In addition, they ran a sporadic programme of watching on all other possible locations around the globe.

Radar operators on the Island were still, after all this time, fascinated to see the holographic projections that illustrated to them, air, sea, and some sub-sea and overland movements. They were able to trace the progress of flights over and between Europe and Africa and America, manifested as aircraft hovering in hollospace above the surface of the hemisphere representing the globe. Large and small vessels were discernible on the ocean's surface and were travelling in real time across the Atlantic and around the coast lines, below the aircraft, on the surface of the hemisphere.

The Navy of the Federation suddenly became very active and a number of large warships began to converge on focussed areas of the North and South Atlantic. Aircraft were tracked, by long-range NRT radar, from air bases in China, the USA, and Canada to air bases on the eastern seaboard of the USA and the western fringes of Portugal and Norway. Recovery Island was being surrounded, although they had no way of knowing the actual numbers of troops and land equipment and vehicles, it was clear to them that an invasion of some kind was being prepared.

An extraordinary meeting of the ruling council was held when the picture of the potential aggression emerged; all members attended and there were no apologies for absence. Gilliland, Crook, and Pettit exposed the position to the members of the committee in unvarnished terms. It looked as though an invasion at worst or a tighter siege, at best, was being mounted. If either of those two scenarios were true the Island was in for a difficult time. Lives would be at risk, and the need to prevent occupation would undoubtedly lead to the Island needing to deploy its defences in aggressive mode.

They had no idea of the timing of the Federation plans, but it was decided to assume that an attack of some kind was imminent. Juilietta Gray, the director of personnel, who had represented the Island at the first, unsuccessful, meeting in the Azores with the Federation, took the floor and explained the plan in place for the evacuation of all but those essential for running the Island under siege. There were plans in place to evacuate 5,800 of the population of 9,787 which would leave enough specialists to run the Island in shut down mode for two years or even more at a pinch.

Information on the evacuation was relayed to the general population via information portals which, when sent to private and public screens, interrupted any programmes running and sounded a shrill alarm. The reaction from the Islanders was immediate and vehement, and the news received a resounding no from all of those identified as being selected for evacuation.

Gilliland decided to give a live broadcast to the Islanders to explain the situation to them. Gray involved herself in preparing for the broadcast with the suggestion that he should advise them that the plans for evacuation were in place and that in the event of an imminent invasion the plans would be implemented. Their wish to stay on the Island was acknowledged as being very patriotic, but in the event of the plan being implemented, it would ensure the safety of the evacuees and enable the Island to focus on rebuffing the attack without having to protect the whole population.

Those selected for evacuation all held dual passports that of their country of origin as well as of Recovery Island. The evacuees, together with their dependents, were to be transported by sea or by air to their countries of origin and would be furnished with sufficient funds to provide comfortable subsistence.

*

Trevor Coniston shuffled through the Connaught/Creswell file yet again, trying to identify why he found something about it to be out of line. The final piece that had been added was the report from Beijing that a mole in the Ministry of Information had uncovered a transaction that clearly showed that Coniston and Creswell were the same person and that the bank transfer of six million pounds had been sent by Creswell to Connaught and then transferred by Connaught to a Creswell offshore bank account from where it had since disappeared having, presumption indicated, been withdrawn by Creswell.

He should, he acknowledged to himself, have gone to the necessary authorities with the information to hand, but his uneasy feeling about it prevented him from doing so. In the loneliness of his position, he sought some sort of relief which could be achieved by bouncing some "hypothetical" scenarios off an authoritative but uninterested party. He considered talking to Sir Roland Clearman, whose integrity he could trust, but was aware from Creswell's file that he and Clearman went back a long way as indeed he did himself. He scrolled through the list of people who were not opponents, not in the cabinet and who would not appear to have an axe to grind; the name that came out was Sir Lionel Wentworth, head of the civil service—a man beyond reproach and a man of impeccable integrity.

"I need your complete confidence, Sir Lionel." Coniston swilled a brandy in its balloon glass as they sat in the library of Sir Lionel's club. "Something in one of my investigations is not gelling and if you're prepared to listen in absolute confidence, I'd like to discuss it with you."

"As long as you're not going to ask me to listen to something illegal, then I would be delighted to help." He squirmed inside at his own duplicity.

"Afraid I can't guarantee that it's not something illegal that's being done, but it is something of national importance."

"Very well, but if I tell you to stop before you have finished telling me your story, I want you to promise me that you will."

"You have provided me with documentation showing that a member of government has misappropriated six million pounds from government funds and has had it transferred to his own account in the newly formed Bank of Nuovostan at which point the trail goes cold. He did this by assuming a false identity."

"I can speak about information that has come to my attention but not about other issues." Wentworth was becoming very uncomfortable about being drawn further into this Wilson created quagmire, and he could see his involvement beginning to spiral out of control.

"You have provided me with copies of signed documents appropriating the six million pounds and that you witnessed the PM signing those documents records of both money transfers." Coniston looked intently at Wentworth and by his demeanour invited Wentworth to respond.

"I received the signed documents from the PM's office in a batch of other documents which I dealt with and filed accordingly."

"So you didn't actually see the PM sign these documents?"

"No, but the documents went into his office unsigned and came out signed. Ergo, I assume that he signed them." Wentworth had stumbled on to a way of extracting himself from the fraught situation without consequences. He satisfied Wilson's requirements of implicating the PM but divorced himself from being a physical witness by not confessing to be present at the actual signing.

"We also have a report from China, linking the person concerned to one John Connaught. There is also information linking the person concerned to the Chinese Ministry of Intelligence and a record of the passing on of classified information only known to senior cabinet members." Coniston once more invited a response.

"I can't comment on these other issues, they are beyond my purview as I have said, but it all sounds pretty damning to me. Why are you having difficulty in handing the matter over to the police?" Wentworth's fear began to mount; he recognised Coniston as a person of acute intelligence and integrity and wondered why such an open and shut case should be giving him pause to reflect. He was relieved that he had not personally identified the PM as Wilson's target just that the document had been signed and that the funds had been misappropriated by an unidentified cabinet member.

"I suppose I don't think of it as open and shut case because everything is just a bit too pat. The pieces fell into place just a bit too easily."

"And have you confronted the person you have presumably identified with this information?"

"Except for definitely linking the person to John Connaught, yes, I have."

"And what did this person have to say for him . . . or her . . . self?"

"The whole thing was denied."

"Do you believe this denial?"

"I want to but I have nothing other than an unsubstantiated denial to counter the evidence."

"Very well . . . so who is the author of this information?"

"Each piece of information came from a different source, including you, but as I said it is too convenient that each piece compounds the previous pieces in such a way that it appears to have been orchestrated."

"In that case, you have only one course of action. You must find the identity of the conspirator who has orchestrated this movement and ascertain what that person has to gain by such a course of action. Do you have any idea who it might be?" It occurred to him that here was an opportunity for him to escape from Wilson's stranglehold, if only he could find a way of implicating him without exposing himself to Wilson's destructive wrath.

"The accused person has given me a lead but cannot give me any proof of his accusation, in fact, he didn't reveal to me who the person was, although I have my own ideas about that."

Wentworth was left feeling decidedly uncomfortable at the culmination of the meeting. He felt he had handled it very badly and perhaps missed an opportunity to rescue himself from this nightmare.

Seventeen

*T*he men grouped around the radar table were all staring intently at the sweep multi-level, holographic beams. The projected distance of the surveillance was one hundred miles. There were a series of echoes around Recovery at between forty and eighty miles; successive projections showed most of these to be stationary, and these would be Federation vessels. The few that tracked on slowly across the map bed would be normal merchantmen plying between Europe and the Americas.

Pettit joined the group of ghostly-green lit figures and stared with them at the holographic images. Their concentration was interrupted when Gilliland and Crook joined them. The operators were used to Pettit being in the control centre but not the other big cheeses; their concentration was further eroded when Caine stepped into the room. The watching men drifted apart to allow Caine to approach and observe.

"What do we have?" she asked nobody in particular.

"Looks like we continue to attract the interest of the Federation," Mark Lawson offered his opinion.

She turned to him and her face showed recognition. "Don't tell me . . ." she frowned. "Mark Lawson of the China drilling team. We met briefly on your return from the ordeal."

"That's right, Ms Caine, it seems like a lifetime ago, but it's only what . . . a year or so?" He smiled broadly thrilled not only that she remembered his name, but also what he had done. "It's a pleasure to see you again, Miss."

"It's my pleasure to see you, and I will be spending more time on the Island from now, so I'm sure we'll meet again."

"I do hope so, Miss." He swelled with pride and looked around in wonder at all the people who had heard their conversation.

"How long have they been stationary?" Pettit asked Lawson.

"Maybe thirty minutes, sir," he answered briskly.

"I want you to contact me personally if any of them move at all."

"Yes, sir."

"What about the UAVs?"

"They are circling at fifteen miles out."

"Same goes with the UAVs. If they make a move to or away from us, I need to know right away. Make sure you pass that request on to the next shift leader. I am to be contacted any time of day or night—understood?"

"Understood, sir."

"Carry on." The visitors exited en masse and left the room to settle down.

"What's our next move?" Caine enquired as they walked towards the administration block.

"I recommend we don't do anything yet," Pettit said with the authority borne of his military past. "Let them think we are not aware of their moves, and let's see how they handle it."

"And if the UAVs move in, what then?"

"What are they going to see?" Pettit said to her. "Our naval secrets? Our massed Air Force? Our regiments of armed troops?"

"They'll see nothing," she said with and a slow smile spread itself across her face.

"Exactly, they'll see absolutely nothing of interest, and then what will they do?"

"Anybody's guess?"

"Absolutely anybody's."

"And now we wait," Gilliland looked at them levelly. "We wait like the proverbial mouse to see just what the cat will do."

*

Pettit was woken by the buzzing of his telephone. He looked blearily at the clock on his bedside table; Juilietta Gray stirred beside him, then buried her head under the bedclothes. The caller advised him that the UAVs had broken formation and that two of them would over fly the Island within ten minutes. He slid out of bed, kissed the top of Gray's head—the only visible part of her—and made his way to the control room.

Ten minutes later, he stood at the HMT bed once more. The naval vessels were still in about the positions he remembered from earlier; a second hologram layer showed the circling UAVs and the two which had broken formation heading north towards the Island. He watched as they flew their straight course to the south coast, and then as they split to circle the Island in opposite directions.

The defences had been shut off at his insistence during the initial telephone conversation, leaving the UAVs free to over fly the Island at will. The operatives looked puzzled at the decision to allow the UAVs access which had been denied before.

"We don't want to be second guessed, do we?" he addressed them all. "Let them fly, they'll be taking infra red photographs of us, and all we'll be doing is sleeping. They will also be wondering why we are allowing them to do so when we destroyed their last UAV."

He watched the two vehicles as they quartered the Island, paying special attention to the airfield and the docks. After half an hour, they joined forces and flew south back to their home ship.

Over breakfast on the following morning, Pettit told his three companions about the overnight activities, and how he had held off retaliating against the provocation. "We really are peaceable people." He was surprised by his own statement. "Without actually being pacifists, so we will not resort to assassination. That would make us as unprincipled as Wilson, but we do need to bring him down so that he can never again get up. Our intention is to have him sent to the one place he doesn't want to go—obscurity."

Eighteen

The Federation fleet made a move two days later and began to close in on the Island. The largest of the vessels the aircraft carrier HMS *Foxhound* moved to a point just five miles outside their twelve-mile limit where she dropped anchor and waited. Still Recovery Island made no sign of having detected the presence of the fleet. On-board the *Foxhound*, Wilson was in the war room, talking to the captain, Geoffrey Latimer.

"Any signs of activity yet?"

"No," Latimer said stiffly. He resented Wilson's presence on-board and resented even more that he was the emissary of Chairman Chung Ho Chen.

"Do you know I think I've got it, the reason they didn't detect the UAVs is that they don't keep watch at night. It could also be that their radar this NRT stuff needs daylight to operate."

"You're a bit premature," Latimer said tersely. "We only over flew once. That's not enough of a test to be able to draw that conclusion."

"That's the trouble with you military types," Wilson said viciously "You all procrastinate too much. You've got no sense of 'let's get on with it'."

"Fools rush in where angels fear to tread," Latimer countered. "I will not put my ship or my men in harm's way, based on a half-baked ill thought out plan."

"We'll see who's half baked. I'll make sure you get your orders, and you'd better carry them out damn quick, or you'll be in trouble."

"Until I get orders from those in a position to order. Get off the bridge, civilians are not permitted on the bridge at any time but especially when we're on standby."

Wilson stamped off the bridge, slamming the door behind him.

Later, on the same day, as his discussion with Wilson, Latimer received instructions from the Admiralty to proceed with Operation Overture and test the defences of the Island in respect of both sea and air penetration. It was also to reconnoitre the coast line for amphibious troop landings. His orders were to carry out the necessary sorties under the cover of night and that the operation should be completed over the next three nights. Based on his submitted report, the admiralty would issue further instructions concerning actions and personnel landings in the immediate future under Wilson's directions.

Latimer called a briefing for the UAV management team and outlined to them the orders received, and the tactical officer took over and began the briefing proper. He was aware as he spoke that Wilson had entered the conference room and included himself in the audience. He walked towards Wilson and with the inclination of his head indicated that they should both leave the room. Wilson followed him out and accompanied him to a separate but empty briefing room.

"I thought you would understand that civilians are not allowed into briefings especially during the course of military engagement," Latimer said frostily.

"I am the DDP, and as such senior in rank to you. If I choose to listen in to a briefing, I will do so." He grinned with no warmth at all. "Didn't

I tell you that we should carry out our task overnight when they would not be watching? And your orders are to do what?"

"My standing orders," Latimer said frostily, "are not to divulge my orders other than to the personnel needed to carry out the requirements."

"Smart ale," Wilson hissed and then quoted the orders that Latimer had been given verbatim, including that the landings would be under Wilson's command.

"Oh, you don't have to prove that you have the contacts to influence the orders given to me. Your hand in them is obvious and clear. The order is ill conceived and will be ineffectual. Carrying it out will waste valuable resources and will alert the Island to the nature of our presence."

"Orders are orders. You don't have to like them, but you do have to follow them, so be a good boy and get on with it. When you're through, I'll want a report from you that I can verify and pass on to the Federation."

"When my report is ready it will be sent through the usual channels, and they will decide who else can have access to the information."

"Don't cross me, Latimer. I make a bad enemy."

"Oh, really, well, I certainly don't want you as a friend—so enemy will just have to do. You are dismissed." He watched as Wilson left the room, and for the second time, in their short acquaintance, heard the angry slam of the door.

While he was still contemplating the door, the telephone on the conference table rang. He picked it up and announced himself. His caller was the Fleet Commander.

"Captain Latimer, it's Fleet here. I'm having my ear bent by Admiralty, seems you've upset the DDP by being uncooperative. In fact, they said you were downright rude."

"Not rude, Fleet, just dismissive. He really has no useful part to play in this exercise, and he rides roughshod through both protocol and security. He seems to think *Foxhound* is his personal property."

"Word to the wise," Fleet paused as he composed his wisdom revelation. "Don't antagonise him. I've been running a few checks on this character, and there's something not quite kosher about him. The checks are whiter than white according to the records, but the people with whom he has had contact are to say the least uneasy about being questioned."

"Thank you for the information, Fleet. You can pass on that you have admonished me, but not that I apologise—and just so that you're prepared I just put another flea in his ear about him interfering in military matters. No doubt it will come back to you."

"Forewarned is forearmed." Fleet laughed. "It's a good thing this is a secured line."

Nineteen

enelope Delaney continued her discrete uncovering of information, and she was acutely aware that the longer she stayed the greater the likelihood of discovery and the ties between the UK and the USA were not, since the formulation of the Federation of Nations, as strong as they had been. Should she be discovered spying on a senior government advisor, she had no illusions about the embarrassment it would cause, not the least for the Secretary of State who was not aware of the true nature of her mission but was still close enough to her family to go along unquestionably with her use of an alias.

Nevertheless, her fact finding was a long and slow process which she had to pursue at a measured pace. The process was slowed even further by the unexpected early return of Wilson to his office which she had occupied, with his blessing during his absence. He told her to continue using the second desk in his office and that his return was brief and that he would be returning to the Federation fleet as soon as he had made some important arrangement that she should "not be worried about".

He clearly liked the idea of sharing his office with a pretty post-graduate student, and it was obvious to him that she was in awe of him. Wanting to show off his trophy to all and sundry, he held meetings in his office with his staff and others, saying to them as they entered the office, "This is Ms Penelope Delaney. She's here doing research work for the American Secretary of State to learn how a department should be managed. My department was chosen naturally."

She smiled secretly at the spin he put on her presence and his self-aggrandisement and carried on appearing to work industriously while actually listening to the conversations that took place. Most of the content was innocuous, and she ignored it, but occasionally, there were some interesting titbits of which she took note. She was also intrigued by his side of some of his telephone conversations.

During one of the conversations with his office manager, he gave an instruction to investigate Captain Geoffrey Latimer of HMS *Foxhound* and to go into more than the usual depth and to do it immediately using any government department that was required to get the low down. The office manager promised to get the information by the middle of the next day. Towards the end of the conversation, she was aware that both men were looking in her direction, perhaps trying to judge whether she had been listening to them, suddenly aware that her continued presence in the office made them forget her and perhaps they had been indiscreet.

She kept looking at the monitor in front of her with her tongue sticking out and a frown of concentration. Absent-mindedly, she inserted her hand into the open neck of her blouse and pushed it down the sleeve to pull up and adjust her bra strap while mouthing an expletive at the screen. Both men looked away satisfied that she had not been listening.

She congratulated herself at her diversionary tactics; they had obviously thought that a sweet, innocent graduate like her would be mortified at the thought of them seeing her attend to her underwear and of her using immoderate language so she couldn't possibly have been listening.

One reference came up that jolted her to the point where she gasped and almost gave herself away. Wilson took a telephone call from Sir Lionel Wentworth, and in the course of the conversation, they discussed document signatures. Wentworth was told to be sure and stick to the agreed story and that it should be made known to Coniston via the usual discrete route anonymously. He finished the conversation and looked towards her again suddenly remembering she was there and wondering if he had let anything confidential slip. She looked up as though suddenly aware of his gaze and smiled disarmingly.

"I'm gonna get a soda," she said, overemphasising a deep south accent to distract him. "Can I git y'all anything?"

"No, that's okay." He was, as she had hoped, distracted by her accent into displacing any notions he had about her having overheard anything incriminating. "You sound different."

"Sorry." She looked bashful. "I guess I go back to my roots when I'm distracted, and I'm having a lot of trouble with the computer."

"What sort of soft drink . . . er . . . soda would you like? I'm going to order tea, and I'll get somebody to bring it in for you."

"That's okay, thanks. I want the powder room, and I'll pick a soda up from the machine on the way back." She left the office before he could respond and breathed a sigh of relief once she was outside. She hoped that this second diversionary tactic was as successful as the first.

She reported the information about Wentworth and the signatures to Gilliland during their customary secured satellite call that evening. He updated her about the Federation moves and that they were experiencing another wave of UAVs from *Foxhound* for the second night in succession. She was about to end the call when a thought occurred to her; the name *Foxhound* rang a bell.

"Foxhound has a captain," she paused as she tried to recollect the conversation. "Captain George Latimer, I think." She paused again "No, not George, Captain Geoffrey Latimer. He must be in trouble because Wilson is having a rush background done on him."

She reflected on the character of Wilson. She had previously imagined him to be an evil spider at the centre of a web of corruption, which reached out to ensnare the unwary. Since her original thoughts, he had matured, and the spider analogy was replaced with that of an octopus, the tentacles of which were far-reaching, tenacious, unwanted and deadly, tearing the life out of his unsuspecting prey.

*

Wilson sipped brown ale as he waited, in one of his favourite low drinking dives, for Sir Lionel Wentworth. He was feeling unusually mellow as he thought, with relish, through the destruction of Creswell which he was about to finalise. He was also confident that on the following morning he would have the background on Latimer that would enable him to commence destroying his newly acquired adversary too. These achievements, however, paled into significance when he savoured the actions that would lead to the overthrow of the Island's administration. Wentworth was pivotal to all of this, although he didn't realise the part that he was playing.

Wentworth arrived and joined Wilson's table in a dim corner of the dive. He sat down wordlessly, wrinkling his nose in distaste at his surroundings. He ignored Wilson's pointed look at his watch.

"You're late," he said sternly.

"Yes, I am." Wentworth made no apology. "I had a brief meeting with Coniston but it overran a little."

"To discuss the signatures?" he enquired gruffly. "I thought I told you to do it through an intermediary."

"There wasn't time. Your deadline was too short, and anyway, I didn't want to involve another party. The more people who know the more difficult the confidentiality."

"What did you tell him?"

"Simply that I could testify to the signatures." He did not add that he had neglected to implicate the PM.

"And he accepted it just like that?"

"Why shouldn't he? I'm the head of the civil service. What axe could I possibly have to grind?" He looked miserable, and his face was ashen as further thoughts of his betrayal washed over him.

"And what does he intend to do with this information?"

"He will confront Creswell, and if he doesn't receive verified assurance that the signatures were not his, he will advise the police, and they will set up an inquiry."

"When?"

"If he hasn't already done so, he will in the next few days. He has the proofs, such as they are, in place."

"Excellent, Lionel, you have done well," Wilson said uncharacteristically and looked very pleased with himself. On that very afternoon, he had made an anonymous donation, to MI5, of timed photographs and a brief report detailing Creswell's covert visits to the Island. "All in all a good day's work. I will hand over the incriminating evidence against you as soon as Creswell falls."

Sir Lionel left Wilson's dive with some relief but also with his head down. This was for him the ultimate humiliation. He had betrayed a good friend, and he had perjured himself and still Wilson had the damning evidence against him. He was still what Wilson called "on the hook". He was so preoccupied that he didn't notice a wraith-like figure following him. Normally, he would have taken a taxi back to his apartment but decided this time to walk, to think, and to try to clear his head. His follower tracked him through the West End on to the embankment and on towards his apartment.

She took care not to be obvious, in following him, but she need not have bothered; he was so wrapped up in his thoughts as to be oblivious to everything. When it became clear that he was heading back to his apartment, she left the Embankment and overtook Sir Lionel on a parallel street. When he finally reached his apartment, he was still deep in tortured thought and paid no heed to the woman standing in his way at the entrance to the apartment block. She stopped his progress, and he looked up startled; she saw that his face was streaked with tears, and he looked haggard beyond his considerable years.

"What . . . ? Oh . . ." He looked startled and confused. "Its Ms Delaney, isn't it?" He peered at her. "What are you doing here?"

"Sir Lionel, forgive me for intruding on your grief, but you and I should have a serious talk. It is in your interest, and dare I say, the interest of your country."

He opened the door, using a key card and held it open for her. She preceded him into the reception area where a concierge gave them an old-fashioned look. "Good evening, sir. Good evening, madam?" His brow furrowed, and he looked puzzled as they walked towards the lift. *Wentworth with a woman?*

Twenty

The control rooms on both *Foxhound* and the Island were on full alert. On the third night of the surveillance operation, there were five UAVs in operation. They were flying at just two thousand feet, and as far as Foxhound was concerned were not encountering any opposition or reaction of any kind from the Island's defence systems. Latimer looked at the infrared video transmissions on the bank of display screens in his operation's room. He was puzzled by the lack of any response and wondered if Wilson had actually been right in his assertions that the defence system needed daylight to operate. If they did, it was a serious even fatal weakness that would make his job of taking the Island so much easier. He almost wished that it was not so; the thought of Wilson being right and himself as a military man being wrong was anathema. In Wilson's temporary but welcome absence, he had returned to his Whitehall office on departmental affairs, and Latimer thought it wise to continue the aerial probing that had been part of Wilson's curious and undisciplined plan.

"This is the third consecutive night of UAV saturation. What do you think they're up to?" Caine asked Pettit as they stood in the glow of the HMT.

"My guess is that they are testing us to get a reaction and, at the same time, photographing us to find out about our defence systems."

"Why would they be photographing us? They most certainly have satellite images that are good enough for military purposes."

"It doesn't feel to me like a military move. Militarily one would not want to risk wasting time and resources for no justifiable reason and risking detection, so I'm guessing again that the politicians are involved."

"I suspect you think that's bad."

"Potentially very bad. Politicians are unpredictable and almost without exception they make a complete hash of the military matters in which they interfere." He stopped talking and watched the holographic radar images as the UAVs and retreated back to the *Foxhound*. The vessels at sea had maintained the same position surrounding the Island and were effectively forming a blockade, although they had not endeavoured to test it. The UAVs converged on the carrier, and their echoes disappeared from the screen when they merged as they landed on *Foxhound's* flight deck.

Latimer watched the last of the UAVs land and saw it swallowed up as it disappeared below to the hangar deck. He re-ran some of the night's video in the forlorn hope of seeing something of interest. There was nothing to see. There was no port or airfield activity save for splashes of brightness from the operating lights. The only vessel on the water was their strange coastal boat that had done so much damage to the Chairman Hi, the Federation MTB, during an earlier abortive incursion. There was one aircraft on the airfield apron which looked like the Island's only known form of air transport, the Apache Chieftain long-distance executive jet; neither of these caused any concern. He looked at more of the footage on fast forward and discovered nothing of interest. While waiting for the UAV team to analyse the tapes, he decided to begin writing the report for the Admiralty. There was little that he could say that they didn't already know, and the exercise had revealed nothing new. This view was confirmed by the management team who, after the first night, treated the manoeuvre as a training exercise during which they tested control programme modifications.

On the fourth night, no UAVs appeared, but the Island's control room did not stand down; they continued to scan sea and air approaches. The night was completely quiet except for the merchant vessels plying their trade between the Americas and eastwards to the rest of the Western world. The merchant vessels stayed clear of the Island by at least fifty miles.

Much to the surprise of the control room personnel, Pettit doubled up the observers and switched back on the Island's single dome defence system, which at four miles diameter gave a maximum dome height of around ten and a half thousand feet. Any craft, or creature, flying over at less than that level would be converted to finings if they endeavoured to fly through the dome. The observers were given the task of ensuring that no innocent craft or flock of birds detected by radar would be harmed.

There was no activity of any kind that night, and as the new day dawned, the Island began to come alive. Maintenance crews converged on the desalination plants, the geothermal power stations, the water pumping stations, the field irrigation plants, and the manufacturing complexes. It was, to the Islanders, just another day; the maintenance crews started at 5.30 a.m. and finished at 9 a.m. when the operators began their working day.

Gilliland was awake at the time that this was happening, and he stood at the window in the administration complex, watching some of the crews as they started their day's work. He was fascinated at how the Islanders in a very short time had adopted what was a completely alien way of life. They chose the work they wanted to do and were not asked to undertake more than they could accomplish. If any one person fell behind or was unable for whatever reason to complete a task, all they had to do was to let it be known to a facilitator, and "floating crews" would be drafted in to complete whatever the task entailed. The crews came from a pool of labourers, the members of which committed themselves to two or three hours per day for the purpose of filling in where required. When they weren't required, as crew members, they spent their time, tending in the agricultural area or working in the cafes and restaurants, or if they wished spending time at the gym or on the sports fields, or simply relaxing. Such a life was idyllic, and he and most of the Islanders wondered why the rest of the world did not have the sense to share it with them.

He looked down from the fourth floor window and felt a tug of disappointment. Their idyllic way of life was under continuous threat, and in the main, the population were ignorant of the full situation. They had all refused the offer of safe transport from the Island, when told of the threat, because they had absolute faith in the protection of Island society. He only hoped that their faith in the ability of the system was justified. He sighed deeply; it had never been the founders' intention that they should have to defend themselves against attack. The whole society was based on peace and security. The freedoms they had intended to engender were being challenged by forces much bigger than themselves; forces which had little by way of conscience or integrity.

His satellite phone rang softly but sounded loud in the empty, hollow room.

"Chez?" Caine's voice came through loud and clear.

"Morning, Penny," his voice was upbeat at hearing hers. "Making progress?"

"Some, and I'll tell you about it this afternoon when I come back."

"Were you able to talk to Wentworth?"

"Yes, and more than that, I had a meeting with Trevor Coniston of MI5. I'll tell you about it later. I called to make sure that the plane will be here in time to collect me."

"From memory it's expected in to Bessingford at around 1100, and it's due to take off for the return journey at 1330 Zulu."

"Good, but I think this will be my last journey incognito. I can't hold my cover much longer now that somebody else knows I'm not who they thought I was. In a way I'll be glad not to have to play-act, although it has been fun for a while."

"Okay, I'll catch up with this later." He looked up as the door opened to admit the first of the Ruling Council. "We're having a war meeting in about fifteen minutes, so I'd better go."

Caine's flight arrived thirty-eight minutes early, thanks to the less brisk than usual head wind. She went straight to Gilliland's office, where he sat wrapped deep in thought which lifted as she came through the door. He stood up and they embraced long and gently each savouring the familiar yet exciting tactility. After a pause, by some unspoken understanding, they parted with a chaste kiss and sat down side by side at his occasional table.

She apprised him of her discussions with Wentworth and Coniston and a little about Wilson but not too much because he always became agitated when Wilson's name was raised. He was happy with the progress she had made and congratulated her on her subterfuge. The meeting with Coniston had been at his invitation, and she found it puzzling. He had asked her in a skilful, seemingly innocent way, questions about Creswell, Wentworth, and Wilson in such an offhand way that it was obvious that he was unaware of her deceptions. She trusted him implicitly even though his questioning had been vague and did not see him as a threat.

A little hesitantly, she said, "I'm going to make a suggestion that you will initially reject, but after you think about it, you will see the advantages it will bring and will ultimately flatten your nemesis."

"Nemesis flattening is good." He looked at her inquiringly. "That is a statement not a question."

"I propose," she said, pausing for effect, "that we invite Wilson to the Island for a meeting about giving access to the technology." She said the single sentence very quickly so that he would not have time to protest before she had finished. She watched the emotions travelling across his face—he went from rejection to consideration to enquiry.

He thought for thirty seconds. "I'll take some convincing and so will he. If we invite him here, he won't come. He'll smell a rat," he paused again, "anyway, why the hell should we invite that rat here?"

"We need him on our territory, and we need to be able to isolate him to get his undivided attention. If we can sit him down in the same room as James, an unfamiliar environment, we can do a head-to-head confrontation, and maybe get James out of his fix and perhaps some pay back from us."

"How do we get him to come here? If we invite him, he will definitely shy away."

"Oh, just leave that to me, I've got a foolproof way." She winked conspiratorially.

Twenty-One

*J*ames Creswell was still in his office, burning the midnight oil. He sent an electro-message, instigated by Caine, to the ad hoc committee which had been set up to discuss possible access to the Island's technology, telling them that progress was possible. He invited the US president, the Federation president, and the French president to join him in the discussions. He sent, essentially, the same message to each but ended the message slightly differently in each case as he had been advised by Caine.

He slept badly and was back in his office by 7.30, the next morning; he activated his computer and scanned the electro-messages. He received a reply from each of the three people he had invited and an additional one from Wilson:

> *I have rearranged my diary to attend the access meeting on Recovery Island. It is imperative that we secure access without delay. My recent discussions with the Chinese government have a significant bearing on the flexibility issues.*
>
> *Under no circumstances will the Federation accept findings that do not take account of the Federations wishes. I will represent these at the meeting.*
>
> *Wilson.*

Creswell smiled to himself. How right Caine had been about the invitations being leaked to Wilson and his insistence that he should attend the meeting to which he had not been invited. The way Wilson's message was worded told him that the information had been leaked to Wilson by Van der Linde, as he thought it might be. Caine being a psychology major, he mused, clearly had its moments of value.

The Federation committee attending the meeting, including Wilson, sat in the comfort of the Apache Chieftain executive jet, bearing the Island's silhouette insignia on the tail fin. They each had a comfortable leather recliner chair set in an L-shaped table to the front and side of the chair. All the major international daily papers and an assortment of magazines were in slots set into the side table and a linen cloth had been laid on the front portion of the table.

Two cabin crew, one male and one female, served canapés and drinks from a top slung service trolley which could be raised at the touch of a switch when the central gangway was required to access the forward flight deck or the bathroom facilities in the rear.

Wilson chose Champagne to accompany the canapés that were offered. When the stewardess had poured a glass and placed it on his table, he grasped the bottle that she held.

"You can leave this with me. It'll save me having to wait until you come back." He did not recognise or react in any way to her look of abject distaste.

Creswell had made this flight enough times to have become familiar with the flight and the cabin crew and talked to them easily. Wilson watched Creswell and stored the familiarity away in his mind for future reference. He looked across the centre aisle at Pierre Savollard, Kurt Klastheim, and Jan van der Linde, who were deep in conversation while jointly inspecting the negotiation file in which were set out the trade-off they decided to tender in exchange for access to the technology.

Wilson looked out eagerly as they circled the airfield preparatory to landing. Although he had seen aerial photographs of the Island, he was surprised by the smooth contours of the Island, its sea wall defences and the rounded, timeless, pueblo-like architecture. If everything went the way he expected, he would soon be in charge of the Island as the first of many moves, and the Island's administrators would soon be behind bars. And if he could make treason stick, there was always the possibility of execution; especially if they stood trial in China, a thought which gave him a sudden surge of pleasure. Set against that background the deposing of Creswell dimmed into insignificance but would, nevertheless, be pursued with all the vindictive vigour he could muster.

Any need for diplomacy, as far as Wilson was concerned, could now be ignored. He had made private agreements with the Chinese administration which would lead to their supporting him in his direct approach to the required acquisition. He had no need to "pussy foot" around the problem; he could be blunt and straightforward as he felt necessary.

The military might of the Chinese Republic would ensure that he would be able to achieve his aims, and after their meeting when he had no further use for any of the meeting attendees, he would abandon them and their aspirations to the fates he had planned for them. Indeed, once he had secured the technology, he had no further use for the Chinese; something he had neglected to share with them.

The journey from the airfield to the administration centre by TC was an eye-opener for Wilson; the ride was smooth and silent. He asked one of the Islander escorts what the motive power was and was told that each TC was propelled by a linear motor fuelled by thermal power with pneumatic tyre fail-safe back-up. He also learned that each TC had a powerful enclosed opposing magnet collision prevention system which backed up an infrared anti-collision separator all of which was backed up by the inclusion of powerful brakes via the pneumatic wheels which would engage if the linear motors failed.

His interest was further fuelled when they alighted from the TC inside the administration building, and he looked up at the four-storey interior from the single four-storey high atrium. The walls and floor were smooth and seam free, as was the ceiling, as if they had been cast using a giant mould, using a technique he had not seen before.

His whole demeanour changed when he saw that the Island's negotiating team comprised of Gilliland, Crook, and Pettit. They looked at the four visitors with detachment simple saying good afternoon to them as if meeting for the first time.

"You don't much look like dead men to me." Wilson said without preamble, but he was still unable to process the fact that they were still alive and that they had fooled him. Neither the Islanders nor the rest of the negotiating team reacted to his jibe and Van der Linde interceded rapidly to prevent an acrimonious start to what was going to be a difficult discussion.

"May I suggest that we start the meeting without delay," He shuffled the papers on the desk before him. "Perhaps you would like to begin." He looked over his reading glasses at the three-man Islander team.

"Let's get down to the nitty-gritty." Wilson responded before any of the others had a chance.

"Really, Mr Wilson, we should give our hosts the right to propose terms first." Van der Linde looked aghast at Wilson.

"This meeting could go on forever if we let them have the floor," he said dismissively. "Let's get on with it. I am empowered by the Federation to demand the immediate release of NRT or BA, or whatever you call it now, to the Federation without let or hindrance. We will have free access to it and all the research papers . . ."

"Wilson," shouted Creswell in anger, "who the hell do you think you are? You report to me in the United Kingdom and to Van der Linde as a Federation representative? Have you suddenly become God?"

"As far as you lot are concerned I might as well be God." He laughed humourlessly. "I've been given the all-clear by the governing committee to state the view of the Federation. And that," he faced Van der Linde, "was the view of the committee after a vote taken in your absence, and it didn't even require a casting vote. It was unanimous."

Creswell waited for Van der Linde to tear a strip off Wilson for grossly exceeding his authority. When no such move was made, he once more stepped in, thinking as he did so that the reason there was no reaction was probably because Wilson had, he realised, the kind of hold over Van der Linde that he wanted over him.

"Wilson," Creswell said sternly, "shut up. You don't represent anybody but perhaps yourself. You report to me, and you certainly do not make unilateral decisions nor do you ever overrule the president of the Federation. Your presence at this meeting is no longer required." His face was white with anger. "You will apologise to our hosts and to the president of the Federation, and then you will leave this meeting. And I'll expect your resignation as DDP before we leave the Island."

The room fell silent. Creswell continued to look furious. Klastheim, Savollard, and Van der Linde looked shocked and uncomfortable, and their hosts looked impassive, and Wilson smirked and found the notion of his leaving the meeting slightly amusing.

"Gentlemen," Gilliland said softly in the otherwise eerily silent room. "may I suggest that we give the Prime Minister and his DDP a moment to consider their position? There is coffee and refreshment in the anteroom of which I suggest you avail yourselves."

Three of the Federation contingent filed out, looking relieved at being released from the stormy situation. For a few moments, the remaining group remained silent.

"You've got a big mouth, Creswell," Wilson said nastily, breaking the brief silence. "Now you're going to be in real trouble. I've got enough on you to bring you down and your lot," he looked at the three Islanders. "You are going to get your comeuppance for the traitors that you are." He laughed triumphantly. "This is going to be a red letter day for me."

To Wilson's surprise, the other delegates were summoned back to the meeting before he had properly completed his rant. Creswell nodded to Gilliland, and Gilliland reached forward to the controls of a video-conferencing machine and punched in an eleven-digit number. The large flat monitor screen sprang into life, and the crystal-clear image of a desk with a comfortable leather chair came into view. Trevor Coniston sat in the chair and looked at his own screen.

"Good afternoon, Gentlemen," the head of MI 5 said urbanely.

"What's going on here?" Wilson said suspiciously. "What's this all about, Coniston?"

"Damned if I know." Coniston looked mystified.

"What it's all about, Wilson, is that we have a need to clarify a few points concerning you, ourselves, the PM, and maybe a few more people," Gilliland said by way of introduction to the set up.

"What do you mean clarify?" Wilson assumed his nasty voice again. "What we have here are actually four traitors. These three." He indicated the Islanders, "are the traitors who stole MOD secrets—and a deserter. Creswell is a spy for a foreign power, and he's embezzled six million in funds from a government account. I told you." He swept his arm to encompass the other four. "Don't mess with me. See, I don't play by your 'let's keep it in the family' rules I call a spade a spade."

"And you substantiate this how?" Coniston asked calmly.

"Okay, let's start with the traitors. These two," he indicated Gilliland and Crook, "persuaded this traitor," he indicated Creswell, "that we should squander funds on a half-baked invention costing millions that they had no intention of completing in the interest of the government or the people." He waited for a response from Creswell but none was forthcoming. "And this one," he indicated Pettit, "is a deserter from His Majesty's armed services. He is AWOL."

"Second," he continued, "Creswell signed off six million from one of my accounts and paid it into his own bank in China and then had it transferred to an offshore account."

"I presume that you have something to back up these accusations?"

"You bet I do. I've got more than enough."

"Okay, so what else do you have?"

"That's enough to start with, and in case you silver-spoon mob try to gang up on me, there's more where that came from."

"And what do the others have to say about what's been said?"

"Should I start?" Pettit looked questioningly at his two colleagues. They nodded. "Mine is simple. I worked under the direction of the DDP on black ops, and I carried out missions, including disposing of people, in the nation's interest . . . or so I thought until I learned that I and my team were sent on a mission that was leaked and bound to get us killed. Some of my men were killed. I was lucky. I had left the group to reconnoitre and the mortar fire that was directed at us all missed me. The only man who knew what we were doing was Wilson. He was the one giving the orders. I didn't desert. Wilson gave orders to my men to assassinate Gilliland and Crook and to dispose of me."

"Now listen, Coniston . . . ," Wilson exploded. "This man tells lies. His people died because he is a useless soldier."

"Mr Wilson," Coniston said smoothly and evenly, "please allow these people to give their accounts uninterrupted in the same courteous way you were allowed to present your case."

"But that was all lies. They're trying to pull the wool over your eyes."

"Let me be the judge of that," he paused. "Messrs Gilliland and Crook, what do you have to say?"

"As joint principal designer of the NRT technology," Gilliland was the first to step in, "perhaps I should answer the accusations. Our experiments took place in a little over two years at a location on the Scilly Isles. We reported monthly to the then DDP and then to Wilson when he became DDP at the time of the governmental changes and kept them up to date with progress for the duration of the project. As we approached the culmination of the project, Wilson became less and less supportive until finally he was obstructive. Ultimately, he had the project shut down, and our facility was raided with the express purpose of taking our findings and completing the development by other means using his own team. What he and they didn't appreciate was that an anomaly discovered early on in the process was held back until we could explain it. Without knowledge of that anomaly, even Einstein couldn't have completed the project. Wilson has spent from then to now, trying to gain access to NRT, and for reasons, I will not go into we have resisted."

"It's all innuendo," Wilson snarled. "They have nothing against me. They are just trying to save their own skins. Ask them what proof they've got of this."

"Proof, if it exists, will come later. Gentlemen—please continue." Coniston said urbanely.

"My turn now," Creswell said, he was no longer white with fury but rather was icy calm. "I will try to take the accusations in turn. One that I am a traitor. I reject that unequivocally. With regard to the embezzlement of six million pounds, it is a pure fabrication. I have not knowingly signed release documents for this or any other sum of money for my own or anybody else's use."

"Unbelievable," Wilson snorted, "absolutely unbelievable."

"It, therefore, follows," Creswell ignored Wilson's distraction, "that if I did not appropriate this sum of money, then I couldn't have put it into a bank account, mine or anybody else's."

"What do you have to say about all of that, Mr Wilson?"

"What I say about that is that they don't have a shred of evidence to support their case, and there is nothing to support their lies." He looked smug again, "I on the other hand have proof, and if you'll all shut up, I'll tell you what it is." He waited for protests and receiving none, he continued, "As far as the deserter Pettit is concerned, he has no proof that I did what he said I did, and he's just covering up his desertion, so I dismiss him out of hand." He shrugged and turned the corners of his mouth down. "As far as the traitors, Gilliland and Crook, are concerned, I've got copies of their reports as they were sent to me, and I've got copies of the reports that are the true picture, which I got through electronic surveillance. I, of course, sent the copies of the report doctored by the two traitors to Creswell as MOD at the time who already had copies of the true reports from me, unknown to the traitors. He, Creswell, chose to support the duplicity of the traitors in return I presume for some kind of recompense. That is, of course, in addition to the six mill." Seeing the look of consternation on the faces of his foes, Wilson laughed. "That got you, didn't it? I'm guessing that you were going to say that I doctored the reports before I sent them to the minister." He laughed again. "There goes your story. They're as guilty as hell. Coniston you might as well hang them all now."

"Gentlemen," said Coniston dispassionately, "what do you have to say to Mr Wilson's assertion?"

The room was deathly quiet.

"What I say"—Gilliland broke the silence—"is that we only sent the true report out to Wilson and that he doctored it before sending it on to the minister, and this enabled him to persuade the minister to pull the plug."

"Weak as maiden's water." Wilson guffawed. "I hope you're not fooled by any of this, Coniston."

"It's not a question of me being fooled by either side. I'm looking for irrefutable proof, and so far neither side has given it." He sat back in his chair and looked directly at the screen. "All I'm getting is accusation and counter-accusation. What we have at the moment is stalemate. But let's carry on, Mr Wilson."

"Okay." Wilson sighed theatrically. "Creswell signed the money release documents for six million, and I've got a witness."

"That's unequivocal." Coniston said. "How do you react to that, Prime Minister?"

"I have no way of knowing who it is that claims to have witnessed me signing documents of release . . ."

"And I'm not going to tell you who it is so that you can intimidate the person concerned." Wilson interrupted yet again.

"But," Creswell ignored him again, "doesn't it strike you as being odd that if I were embezzling monies of that magnitude that I would allow my actions to be witnessed?"

"Even weaker than weak maiden's water." Wilson guffawed.

"Do you have anything *useful* to say?" Coniston snapped testily.

"I don't need to say anything." Wilson laughed. "This is all ridiculous."

"For your information," Creswell continued, "I had a meeting with Wilson in my day office at No.10, and he told me that his evidence was fabricated and that I would not be able to prove a thing because he had accessed and turned off the automatic recording device."

"Great!" Wilson was beside himself with staged mirth. "Now we're descending into the realms of total fantasy. There's no proof of any of this."

"Are you saying that this meeting did not take place, Mr Wilson?"

"Oh, I've had meetings in his office, but we never did have the kind of meeting he describes."

"Let us be clear about this," Coniston insisted. "You at no time had a meeting with the PM at which you discussed fabricated evidence."

"Absolutely not. Look, Coniston, let's end this farce right now. We'll ignore Pettit, he's a deserter and a traitor, and it's his word against mine. The other two traitors obviously doctored the reports they sent to me to put me off and gain sole access to the technology with Creswell's collusion, and I can give you copies of both reports as proof. I managed to acquire a copy of the undoctored reports by means of a ploy that I would not normally use. I stole them from the Prime Minister's desk because it was in the public interest. You've got copies of both reports, the originals and the doctored ones." He paused momentarily realising immediately that he had made a serious error. Having sent the reports anonymously, he was not supposed to know that Coniston had copies of both versions. Looking at Coniston on the screen and the faces of the Islanders across the table from him, he saw no signs that they had registered his faux pas, and he made sure of it by adding, "Clearly your investigations will have unearthed the duplicity of the two versions." Without further pause, he concluded, "Anyway, as far as Creswell is concerned, he stole the money, opened up an account in the name of John Connaught, and used that to gain access to the money."

"You can prove that?"

"Yes, I can, so let's ship them back to England for proper justice and get on with banging up these traitors and criminals like they deserve."

"Do any of you have anything else to say?" He received no response. "Very well, Gentlemen, thank you for your time. I will consider what you have said and get back to you with my findings. I must add that these accusations are very serious and, if substantiated, will lead to prosecution." The screen went blank when Coniston pressed the cancel switch.

Twenty-Two

The ever-vigilant watchers in the Island's control room began another night of endlessly scrutinising the HMTs. For so many nights now, there had been no activity and the watchers' became bored, and there was a danger that they would become inattentive. A single aerial blip on the screen escaped their attention until it was within twenty miles of the Island's coast; there was a stirring of alarm that dampened when they realised that the lone craft was flying low and slow, indicating that it was a UAV. As they had been ordered, they made contact with Pettit, and he ordered the single dome defence system to be switched on.

Pettit joined them in the control room and watched the progress of the UAV as it flew over the Island above the defence dome, which had been lowered in profile by advances in the BAM2 profiled projection technology which allowed them to change the shape of the dome and lower the zenith. The UAV retraced its steps back to *Foxhound*, and the screen showed that three smaller sea-level craft left the *Foxhound* and headed towards the Island. Assessing the speed of the vessels, Pettit predicted that they would make the journey in about an hour.

Gilliland and Crook joined them at the HMT's at Pettit's behest and were briefed on the progress of the three smaller vessels. Half an hour later, the vessels were some eighteen miles from the Island, and their speed was steady. Pettit made radio contact with *Foxhound* and warned them not to breach the twelve-mile exclusion zone. The response was slow and off hand and stated once more that the Federation did not recognise either the Island or the twelve-mile territorial limit and that any attempt to interfere with the progress of their craft would be taken as a hostile move and dealt with accordingly; the same old rhetoric, it was boringly predictable.

They allowed the three vessels to cross the twelve-mile limit. When they were clearly into the Island's territorial waters, they threw up an open-topped defence ring reaching one hundred feet into the air. Effectively, the three vessels were trapped between the Island's defence dome at a little over two miles from the centre, to accommodate the diagonal of the land mass of the Island and the twelve-mile limit truncated shield. The next communication with *Foxhound* was less laid back from the *Foxhound* perspective. The Federation spokesman warned that there would be significant retaliation unless they were allowed full and free access. The Federation were advised that the illegal sea craft would be allowed to leave the twelve-mile limit without hindrance but that they would not be allowed any nearer to the Island.

On board the *Foxhound*, Geoffrey Latimer was thoroughly peeved as Wilson and the quasi Federation negotiating team, after their unsatisfactory meeting on the Island, had been ferried to HMS *Foxhound*, where Wilson assumed the operational control of the invasion project, seeded to him by the Federation.

"Send in three bombers." Wilson spoke into his comm's system; he was still smarting at his dismissal from the Island after being, in his view, betrayed by Coniston.

"Belay that order," Latimer responded.

"Do as I say." Wilson looked at him in disbelief. "This is my show."

"These are my men and my aircraft, and I will not have them put at risk for no good strategic reason." Latimer was barely controlling his temper.

"I have the authorisation of the Federation Admiralty, and I have the authority to have you thrown in the brig and don't think I won't use it."

"You're a madman. There are three combat boats out there with sixty marines, and if you launch the planes, there'll be six aircrew, and you're putting them all at risk. You have no certain knowledge of the retaliatory capability of the Islanders under the threat your intended actions may engender."

"They're a bunch of idealistic wimps. They won't do anything when they see we mean business, and they'll fold."

"Like they did last time you mean," Latimer snorted. "They captured a ship's crew and disabled the Chairman Hi. We didn't exactly come out of that covered in glory."

"There you go again, typical military lack of resolve. If I left it to you, we'd never do anything. Tell you what." He jabbed Latimer in the chest with his extended forefinger. "Either get out of here, or I'll have you escorted out by my people. Don't forget my rank is superior to yours, and you're getting in my way."

Latimer left the room under protest and returned to the bridge to make radio contact with the Admiralty. Wilson repeated his orders to launch the three bombers, and they were ordered to disable the docks and the airfield. He listened in to the comms system as the pilots were briefed, two of the aircraft were assigned: one to the docks and one to the airfield. The third was to act as overlap in the event of either of the other two failing in their mission.

*

Pettit watched the three blips leave the *Foxhound*, and they covered the thirty miles to the Island in around two and a half minutes. It all happened so quickly that they had no time to react to the threat. Two of the incoming aircraft split between the north and south of the Island and the third took up a neutral position, circling over the coastline. The two released their bomb loads from above the zenith of the inner defence dome and made a fast exit; the third circled, taking photographs and digital movies as it went.

Radar showed the two aircraft streaking back home and the third circling. The bright flashes as the bombs encountered the dome were visible to the naked eye but did not show up on the scopes. The watchers were not aware of what had happened until they heard from the outside observers that the flashes had occurred. The third back up aircraft made a bombing run over the airfield before peeling off and returning to *Foxhound*.

In the debriefing, the aircrews expressed their disbelief at the outcome of their raid. They had all acquired the laser targets and followed standard bombing procedures and were at a loss to understand why they had not been successful. Latimer tried to put their minds at rest, but they were professional pilots who would not have their simple questions brushed aside.

"What I am about to tell you is classified," Latimer addressed the assembled crews.

"Shut up, Latimer," Wilson exploded. "Reveal any secrets, and you will regret it."

"Master at Arms," Latimer shouted firmly, "escort this civilian out of the briefing room and escort him to his cabin and don't let him out until I give the order. If he resists, throw him in the brig."

"You'll be court-martialled," Wilson shouted as he was bundled from the room.

"I've checked with your bosses. You had the right to direct the operation, but I am still master of this ship, and outside your allotted task, you have no authority on this carrier."

"Gentlemen"—Latimer turned to the aircrews after Wilson had left—"Wilson neglected to tell you before you embarked on your mission that the Island has a very powerful, top secret, defence system. I am not free to tell you anything about it, save for the fact that it can under certain circumstances be deadly. Wilson made the assumption that the Island's defence system would be inoperable because it doesn't work at night, but the Islanders outmanoeuvred him, and he fell to their superior tactics. We really don't have any idea how it works, but I think the best way to explain it is to show you the video footage that Tango Papa took on tonight's bombing raid."

He operated a remote control and an infrared image was shown on a large screen, and there were green-tinged splashes of light where the lights were switched on all over the Island as well as the docks and the airfield. A second screen showed the instruments in the two operational bombers and showed the bomb sights lined up on the laser markers. The released bombs followed the laser guidance and terminated in an instantaneous bright flash, but they did not explode. The main screen showed that the flashes made by the bombs, which to their surprise did not explode, were generated considerably above ground level and were nowhere near fierce enough to represent actual explosions; they simply disintegrated. The crews sat uncomprehendingly staring at the now empty screens.

"That, Gentlemen, is why you were unsuccessful. Their defence system will not allow any solid matter through, in this case your bombs." He held up his hand at the outbreak of murmuring among the crews. "I can't tell you more for two reasons: one, it is top secret, and two, I don't know any more."

"Was this known about before we took off?" the senior pilot spoke out.

"Wilson was aware of its capabilities by day but had assumed incorrectly that it wouldn't work at night or perhaps he had insufficient intelligence to realise that this was a possibility."

"What would have happened if we had decided to fly in lower?"

"Just use your imagination."

"I'd rather not, and I'd rather not take any more orders from that lunatic."

"I'll be giving the orders from now on, dismissed." But Latimer knew in his heart that he had expressed a hope rather than a fact.

Twenty-Three

"We're on full war footing now. This is no longer just a siege," Gilliland addressed the Ruling Council. "It is quite clear and has been for some time that the Federation, or at least a significant part of it, will stop at absolutely nothing to get hold of BAM2. We will not allow them access to the Island under any circumstances, but if our hand is forced, we will destroy all vestiges of the technology rather than use it as a weapon of war. We have enough provisions in the warehouses to last us for a considerable time, and we are, of course, energy and water sufficient. What we must now consider is to what lengths we will go to prevent occupation. We actually have the capability to destroy any aircraft or naval vessel which enters our space. One thing we will not do, however, is to take life irrespective of the provocation." He noted that Pettit looked disapprovingly at him after his remark. "I realise, Silas, that I am not doing the militarily correct thing in not using the deterrent under any conditions. BAM2 is not a weapon, it is a tool, and we will use it to work and defend but never to attack when there is risk to life and limb—theirs or ours."

"I understand your points, Chester," Pettit responded, "but we are dealing with people of low or no morals. They will stop at nothing to possess BAM2, and that includes sacrificing life of both their troops and us. If, as you suggest, we were to be overrun and you were to destroy the technology, they would have no conscience about disposing of us and covering it up."

"We will only ever use the technology for protecting ourselves and preserving peace. There will be no give in that respect and." He looked unflinchingly at the assembled councillors. "There will be no general discussions about this philosophy."

*

"We're all set then." Wilson said to the assembled officers and men. "I have decided that these renegade Islanders are too namby-pamby to actually harm us, so we're going in full strength, landing craft the lot."

He looked pointedly at Latimer and raised his eyebrows. "Care to share your thoughts with us, Captain? Not that I'm about to change my plan or my mind."

"You already know my thoughts." Latimer said tersely. "I would like to have another private conversation with you about the wisdom of your proposal."

"Make it public or keep it to yourself," Wilson said dismissively. "Okay, let's go." He didn't give Latimer a chance to respond.

The officers and men left the briefing room with obvious reluctance and dispersed to the appropriate parts of the *Foxhound* to undertake their appointed tasks. Within an hour, the first of the eight landing craft had departed, each carrying one hundred fully armed men. The Federation Probe class battleship, HMS *Javelin*, accompanied the landing craft on their journey to Recovery Island.

Their departure was witnessed in the Island's control room; the watch team were galvanised into action when they realised the size of the battle group heading towards them. They immediately alerted Pettit who in turn notified Gilliland, Crook, and Caine. Within minutes, the control room was a hive of cramped activity, and the HMTs were being scrutinised for both sea and air vessels; only the former were evident. At the other end of the control room, further localised HMTs indicated the activated positions of the defence domes.

The single Island defence dome was activated; other potential domes and defence walls were marked on the table screen but not illuminated, indicating that they had not yet been activated. As the advancing group neared the twelve-mile limit, Pettit made radio contact with *Foxhound* and warned them that they were entering Recovery Island territorial waters and that they should turn back.

The radio room on board *Foxhound* passed the message to Wilson in the ship's war room. He scanned the document and told the rating that the reply should be that they would continue their advance and that the Islanders should be ready to receive the Federation boarding party. He added as an afterthought that the signal should be signed by Latimer, Captain, *Foxhound*.

"Just you watch," Wilson turned to Latimer who had remained silent through the exchange, "when we cross the twelve-mile limit, it's obvious that we're not going to stop, they will allow us through because they are weak."

Latimer raised an eyebrow and looked askance at the alien creature before him. "If they do lift the defences, what do you intend to do, Wilson?"

"Nothing complicated. As soon as they lift the defences, and believe me, I know them well enough to know they will shell them using the whole of the fleet's arsenal of big guns. They'll be flattened within seconds."

"What about the civilians?" Latimer looked at him in disbelief.

"It's what you military types call collateral damage." Wilson dismissed the subject offhandedly.

"And what happens if they re-erect their defences closer to the Island. They will still stop you."

"This is where my Intel is so much better than yours. I have observed that from switch off to switch on takes about ten seconds, and that's more than enough to let our salvo of shells through and raise the place to the ground. Thirty ships can't fail."

As Wilson had predicted, the small armada crossed the limit without being challenged further but to make sure, the leading craft sprayed high-pressure water jets two hundred metres ahead and radioed back to *Foxhound* that the dome had been switched off. Following Wilson's orders, as soon as the information on switch off had been received, the message was sent out to all vessels to open fire. The sound of hundreds of guns erupted, and the Island was surrounded by a forty-mile circle of explosive light.

Together with Latimer, he watched the radarscope as the nine vessels crossed into the waters disputed by the Federation. They felt *Foxhound* shudder as her big guns opened up in cacophonic unison.

"So predictable," Wilson said gleefully, "they don't have the guts to really threaten the Federation. Unlike you military dinosaurs, I understand the weaknesses of the enemy. This is going to be, oh, so sweet."

"I give it two or three minutes until they hit you with a real broadside that you won't think to be so sweet. You have made one assumption too many, as a non-military man that is." Latimer looked steadily at Wilson.

"You're a bad loser, Latimer, and I'm going to make sure that you lose your commission over your dereliction of duty and your insubordination to me as your superior."

Through a view port in Wilson's stateroom, they were too distant to see the Island, but they were able to see at the horizon the devastating flash of multiple explosions which were less dramatic than Wilson had expected.

"What do you say to that, Latimer? Not bad for a non-military politician, isn't it?"

"Let's just wait and see. I think you've just made a big mistake. You walked straight into their tactical superiority just like the amateur you really are." Latimer said with a barely concealed smile.

"What do you mean their tactical superiority, we've just flattened them. Please try to keep up with me. They're all dust by now." Wilson dry washed his hands Uriah Heap fashion.

"Let's just wait and see. I think you'll find they are completely unscathed, like I said they've outmanoeuvred you."

"That's where you are wrong," Wilson taunted his adversary. "They may have anticipated me by lifting the bottom of the defence dome to let the ships through which means they were still defended by our long-range artillery, but my original plan is still in place. We are inside their defence ring, and they are at our mercy. All we have to do is shell them from the *Javelin*, and we've got them. What are they going to do? We are in their territorial waters inside their defence shield. We have them blockaded."

Wilson and Latimer went to the control room where Wilson personally insisted on issuing the order to the Captain of the *Javelin* to open fire on the Island, targeting the airport and the port. He smiled mirthlessly at Latimer. "That's how it's done. Game set and match."

"If I read them correctly, you are about to be given another lesson in basic military tactics." Latimer looked at Wilson with pity.

They remained in open radio contact with *Javelin* during the execution of Wilson's orders and were given a running commentary as the exercise was completed. They waited for the report of the outcome of the barrage. The radio remained silent for a long period; when the communication recommenced, the voice of the radio operator was flat and dispassionate.

"Five shells fired at the airfield and five at the port. Negative hits—I repeat negative hits."

Wilson looked stunned. "How can that be? They've still got the defence up at twelve miles? How come we made no hits?"

"I'm only a dense military man. But to me, it seems likely that they have multiple devices and can construct more than one barrier." Latimer was dismissive. "If you'd bothered to grasp that from what we've already seen of their capabilities, you wouldn't have made such an amateurish mistake." He laughed at his tit-for-tat remark. "Not only that, the whole of your force is hemmed in. They can't go to the Island because of the inner defences, and they can't come back here because of the outer defences." He turned to the radio operator. "Make a message to *Javelin*: *Heave to and wait for further instructions from me, under no circumstance attempt to land on the Island or to exit the twelve-mile limit, and under no circumstances take orders from any other, repeat any other, source, Latimer.*" He turned to Wilson. "You are relieved of your task. You will no longer issue orders to naval personnel. I will negotiate with the Islanders and see if I can extricate our men and assets without resorting to anything dramatic. Please leave and confine yourself to non-strategic areas."

As Wilson left, with a face like thunder, he was unclipping his satellite phone from its belt holster. Latimer waited until he had left and shook his head as he looked at the radarscopes showing the location of the battleship and the eight landing craft. He took the comms' handset and nodded to the radio operator to connect with the Island.

"Foxhound *to Recovery Island, over.*" He waited for a reply, and when none was forthcoming, he repeated his message twice.

"*Foxhound, this is Recovery Island, we are receiving you, over.*" The reply was thin, made indistinct by static.

"*Recovery, this is Captain Geoffrey Latimer of the Federation Aircraft Carrier HMS* Foxhound, *I need to address the current situation by talking to your senior representative, over.*"

"This is the Island's Director of Security. I am empowered to arrange such a discussion. I will need time to assemble the necessary personnel in the comms room, over."

"Face-to-face would be better. I can come to you immediately by helicopter, over."

"I will arrange for the defences to be deactivated as soon as your helicopter approaches, providing you are alone and your machine is unarmed."

"I will radio you when I am to depart by helicopter, over."

"Very well, you will be cleared to land on the H pad at the western end of the airfield. Only you will be allowed to disembark, and, I repeat, you may not carry weapons of any sort nor should the helicopter be armed or in any way threatening, over and out."

The small two-seat fast response helicopter bearing the insignia of the *Foxhound* descended gracefully on to the helipad in the still of a breeze free summer evening. It was met by the tall, imposing figure of Silas Pettit resplendent in a black, slightly sinister, one-piece uniform the like of which Latimer had never before seen. Pettit was accompanied by two other less imposing men in similar one-piece uniforms, but this time in pale brown. There were no badges of rank but each man wore a name badge on his left breast.

"Director Pettit." Latimer saluted.

"Captain Latimer," rather than return the salute Pettit extended his hand, which was grasped firmly by Latimer. "Our two most senior directors are waiting to see you." He indicated the way to one of two electric buggies, normally used for pulling luggage trains, parked close by.

Pettit's two companions indicated to the pilot that he should disembark, which he did, and they made a precursory inspection of the helicopter to ensure that it posed no threat. Perceiving that it did not, one of the men led the pilot to one of the luggage buggies and was whisked away into the evening gloom. The second man joined Pettit and Latimer in the other buggy, and they drove slowly to the perimeter of the airport to a TC station where the two groups entered different cars and went separate ways.

Latimer entered the room ahead of Pettit and saw Gilliland and Crook seated at the small circular conference table, waiting for him. His discomfort with the meeting was further exacerbated by the blank expressions on the faces of the two seated men. He extended his hand to both of them, and they responded politely but without any enthusiasm as they introduced themselves by title.

"You represent the Federation in what capacity?" Gilliland said without preamble.

"I am the captain of the flagship HMS *Foxhound,* and in the absence of the C-in-C Fleet, I am in command of the Federation battle fleet."

"Why are you making such a hash of your job?" Pettit asked pointedly.

"A hash?"

"Yes, I don't know how else to describe it. You sent a detachment of the Federation's finest to annex an Island with a population of a few thousand and with no military personnel and you made basic—very basic—mistakes."

"Basic errors were made," he conceded, "but my presence here is to defuse the current situation without the threat of further military activity."

"Very laudable," Crook took up the conversation, "but look at it from our point of view. You attempted to make an illegal landing on our territory, and when it failed, you decide to negotiate the release of your armada without penalty."

"This whole episode was a mistake." Latimer stated coolly, but his underlying discomfort was obvious. "Lame as it may sound, I can only offer my apologies for the error we made and to see if there is some way we can make amends."

The three sat regarding Latimer and were clearly puzzled. Gilliland broke the silence. "Were you the author of the strategy used?"

"I am captain of the fleet, and as such, I am responsible for all fleet actions." Latimer responded swiftly.

"From your answer, I presume that you are taking responsibility for somebody else's bad judgement."

"I am responsible for the actions of the fleet." Latimer was unmoving in his reply.

"What Chester is trying to ascertain," Pettit said with some exasperation, "is whether we are negotiating with the boss or a fall guy. If we reach agreement with you, will the agreement have any veracity? If you were unable to control a doomed military strategy, how can anything you say here be taken at face value?"

They all looked at Latimer in expectation.

"Nothing in this life is certain. We have many masters, and they do not necessarily have the same goals." Latimer's expression was pained. "What I can say to you is that as Captain of this fleet, I can guarantee that we will withdraw from this confrontation, and I will do my best to make representations to the Federation leadership in your favour."

"That for the moment will have to suffice," Gilliland said slowly as though trying to convince himself, "but be aware of one thing—and you can pass this on to whomsoever you wish—we will not give in to bullying, and we will not be shepherded into military retaliation. Having said that, we will defend our position to the end, and I think you are aware of at least some of our capabilities."

"You make yourself abundantly clear, sir, and I will try to communicate your clarification to the necessary authorities."

"Good then, I think this meeting is at an end, and when you return to *Foxhound* please pass on a message from us to Wilson: Tell him that he should stay away from strategy and military matters and stick to what he can do well . . . whatever that might be."

Latimer was unable to stop from grinning and the other three laughed at his involuntary admission.

Wilson, as was his way, made the best of the bad situation that he had created by laying the blame for his failure at the feet of Latimer. He contacted Chung Ho Chen's office and told the president's aide that the intelligence provided by Latimer had been entirely wrong and that the matter would be referred to the British Navy board so that the necessary action could be taken. He actually had no intention of doing so because it would lead to Latimer defending himself and making life difficult for Wilson. Telling the Chinese that he would report him would mean that they, the Chinese, would not feel it necessary to take any action themselves.

Having ingratiated himself, he decided to take the opportunity to go one-step further and told the aide that he had a plan of campaign that could be implemented simply by using a branch of the Chinese Air Force without involving any other nation or resources. The aide undertook to inform the president of the Peoples' Republic of the proposal and let him know of the outcome.

Wilson was surprised when the aide called back just thirty-five minutes later to tell him that the president had expressed interest in his proposals and that he should discuss the details with Chung Yi of the Chinese diplomatic mission who was already on board *Foxhound*, carrying out Federation duties which included an overview of Wilson's activities. Wilson had had discussions with Chung Yi over the drilling incident when they had earlier tried to acquire a BAM2 device and knew the term *diplomat* to be a blatant euphemism.

Discussion with Chung Yi took place, and unusually for diplomats or bureaucrats, they reached a swift affirmative conclusion. The basis of Wilson's proposal was that he had observed that the laser guidance systems used by the Federation forces, in their recent attacks on the Island, had penetrated the defence dome even if the bombs dropped had been halted by it. This exposed a vulnerability hitherto unrealised.

The discussion developed, and Chung Yi decided that using lasers from an aircraft would render the aircraft and the crew open to harm. Wilson immediately bridled at the comment and prepared in his mind a diatribe similar to that with which he had barraged Latimer, about the reluctance of the military to act creatively.

His negative thoughts were interrupted, before they had fully formed, by Chung Yi who suggested that a Chinese military satellite with laser capabilities could be deployed. Wilson cut off what was going to be a rebuke and wholeheartedly supported the counter proposal, which he immediately adopted as his own. He congratulated Chung Yi on having reached the same conclusion that he had, himself, sometime before.

Twenty-Four

The four founders who remained in Gilliland's office, after Latimer had departed, were in limbo. They had repulsed an attack without bloodshed, not because of their strengths but because of their adversaries weaknesses, and had negotiated an uneasy settlement with Latimer whom they doubted had the power to make such an agreement stick. Whether it stuck or not, they had to decide on their next moves, but they were emotionally drained.

"Problem is," Caine said reflectively, "whatever we do will not necessarily enable us to promote our ideals into any form of reality? All we want to do is lead a peaceful life which will incidentally and with intent give benefit to others as well as our Islanders, but we are up against powerful alliances whose sole aim in life appears to be to secure their position of supremacy regardless of human cost." She shared her innermost thoughts as she spoke out loud to herself.

"Worse," Gilliland interrupted her thought processes, "the whole thing is escalating, and if the only way to promote our own peace is to entertain warlike retaliation, we become as bad as they are. We become yet another evil power, and we will have failed entirely in our aims."

"And yet", Pettit broke in puckishly, "every cloud has a silver lining. The Federation thinks, erroneously, they are all powerful enough to ban us from the outside world. What they don't realise is that we actually have the ability to travel the world with complete and protected freedom by air, sea, or land, even through the Federation territory, without physically harming them or putting ourselves in harm's way. This means we can still trade with that portion of the world not controlled or beholden to the Federation."

"How do you propose we manage the miracle of travel?" Crook enquired of Pettit.

"Don't forget we have done to the aircraft what we did for *Wallow 5*, and we do the same to all other forms of transport we intend to use, BAM2, provided we have access to a power source that can shield us against anything."

"Almost anything," Crook said quietly to himself and then so that they could all hear his words. "We can develop a more powerful energy resource using the high-powered, enhanced modified ceramic batteries that Ed Pickering has developed, which can be recharged in minutes or can be solar regenerated or a hybrid of both."

"Thank goodness, I am surrounded by optimists." Caine said lightly. "Whatever we do, we must stick to our original ideals of peaceful existence if not actual coexistence. However, we must also make sure that our defences are up while we develop the ability to move freely about the world, always assuming that the Federation will fail to see the error of their ways."

Their ad hoc discussion dissolved, and they went their separate ways. Pettit went to the control room where the HMT watchers had been reduced as the imminent attack had been averted. Heeding what Caine had said, he reconfigured the inner defence dome with instructions that it was to be kept in place at all times until new orders were received.

Shifts in the control room changed and fresh eyes watched the Federation fleet disappear, some to the south and some the east. The stratosphere was clear of threatening aircrafts and only the occasional transatlantic flight strayed anywhere near the Island's territorial waters. The control room relaxed and a green-tinged calm descended which always caused the occupants to talk in hushed tones.

Ten days later, the Island had returned to its former tranquillity and thoughts of any hostility dissolved, perhaps uneasily, into the background. Summer had reached its height, and bright sunlight shone down from a cloudless blue sky on the Islanders as their normal daily activities were minimised so that they could enjoy the freedom to do as they liked.

They could swim off the beach within the safety of the reef, which they had created, or they could sit outside the cafes in the shade of colourful umbrellas and sip their beverage of choice, or they could sit in the shade of the fast developing subtropical trees in the centres of the wide boulevards to read newspapers or books. In short, they could do as they wished; they could live the relaxed Island life which was synonymous with the Island's philosophy.

The interruption to their tranquillity was, under these relaxed circumstances, all the more shocking. There was a shrieking sound and a red beam descended from the sky from an unseen source and struck the north-west geothermal power plant's above-ground structure. Great gouts of super-heated steam shot up into the sky where they boiled and writhed lit with an incandescent red glow which dissipated when it reached the underside of the BAM2 shield. The great disappearing cloud was visible from all parts of the Island. There was a stunned silence that finally erupted into mass panic all over the Island.

Crook had a grandstand view of the spectacle from the balcony of his fourth-floor office, and he watched in dismay as the superstructure of the power plant began to crumble undermined as it was by a destructive force, which he correctly identified as a concentrated laser beam. He reached for his telephone to call Gilliland, but it rang before he had a chance to pick it up.

"My office now!" Gilliland's voice was high with emotion.

By the time Crook reached the office, Gilliland, Pettit, and Caine were already deep in agitated discussion.

"What the hell is happening?" Gilliland was extremely agitated.

"I'm guessing it's a laser." Crook said breathlessly. "Looks like they've worked out a weakness, and they're exploiting it."

"I've isolated the plant and switched to the alternative south-east plant." Pickering said as he entered the office at the run. "I've also isolated the geo source underground so as soon as the balancing tanks are empty the steam will stop."

"What do we do now?" Caine looked expectantly at the three men.

Before they could answer, Gilliland's satellite phone rang. "Yes," he said testily.

"Told you I'd get you, you traitor."

"Wilson!" Gilliland shouted in disgust.

The others in the room turned to look at him when they heard the name; they saw the look of hatred on Gilliland's face. Waving her hands up and down in the horizontal position, Caine indicated that they should remain calm and that Gilliland should put the call on speaker. She put her index finger to her lips to indicate that they should all remain silent.

On board *Foxhound*, Wilson was enjoying a moment of sweet revenge after what he considered to be an interminable wait to get the satellite into geo synchronous orbit over the Island. He now had the attention of the people he hated, and he had them where he wanted them: at his mercy. He could tell by the change in background noise that Gilliland had put the call on speaker, and it made him feel so much better to know that he had an audience to witness his great triumph. Not only did he have an audience on the Island, he also had an important visitor from the Chinese Government, Chung Yi, who would be there to witness his triumph.

"You all think you're so clever and safe on your little Island, but you didn't reckon with me. The loser, Latimer, passed on your message to me. You know the bit about doing what I do . . . Whatever that might be? Well, one of the things I do is make fools of all of you. Let me tell you what I'm going to do. First, I'm going to destroy the building we just hit, whatever it is. Then I'm going to pick off all the other buildings around the edge of the Island and one by one I'm going to destroy them." He turned to Chung Yi who stood next to him in the radio room and winked conspiratorially. Chung Yi remained impassive. He then turned his attention back to the handset he was holding. "Are you still with me, little people?" He beamed his most sickly grin as he spoke.

In reply, he received only static noise. His brow creased in annoyance. He wanted to enjoy their discomfort and hear them beg for a way out of their dilemma. The silence continued, and his triumphant look turned to one of annoyance.

"So you want to have something else to consider, do you? This is not enough for you?" The silence continued. "Okay," he said with exaggerated patience. "How about this for size? I'm going to deploy more satellites so that we can destroy more than one building at a time. In fact, I'll deploy as many as I like. You're finished, so why don't you give in before I destroy the whole of your little Island, and the people on it." His face took on a puzzled look as he became aware that they had disconnected the call without actually saying anything to him or acknowledging his triumph.

Twenty-Five

In Gilliland's office, they all looked momentarily at Caine's delicate manicured finger as it pressed down on the red button on the satellite phone. They all looked puzzled, as puzzled, as Wilson had been on board *Foxhound*.

"No doubt you're all wondering why I did what I did?" She looked at them all with her eyebrows raised in query. She responded to their nods of agreement. "My background, as you know, gives me some insight into the personality of characters like Wilson. It also helps that I spent some days working with him in my guise as a post-graduate student. He has low intellect, but he makes up for it by being extremely cunning. He craves plaudits and will go to any lengths to harvest them. He hates to have his presumed superiority questioned and is likely to fill silences in conversation by giving away what he considers to be impressive information—to regain his feelings of superiority. This is precisely what he just did."

"You're absolutely right," Pettit cut in. "He confirmed our thoughts that it is a laser causing the damage. He also told us that it came from a satellite rather than an aircraft and that he has access to more satellites."

"Why is that important?" Pickering joined in.

"Because," Pettit said with delight, "it gives us an opportunity to retaliate while still maintaining our own charter."

"Exactly." Caine said excitedly.

"And I know what we can do about it," Crook added.

*

Wilson's triumphant look returned when he was informed by a radio operator that he was wanted back in the radio room for a conversation with the Islanders. He hurried to the room, looking forward to their capitulation from which he would wring as much pain as possible. He arrived after both Latimer and Chung Yi, who watched him in silence, as he bustled self-importantly into the room.

"Come to see how it's done, have you, Latimer?" When Latimer made no reply, he continued unabashed, "Let's see how good they are at capitulating." He nodded to the radio operator, who patched the call from the Island through to the desk-mounted console. "This is Wilson."

"Wilson," Gilliland responded. "I asked to talk to the person in charge."

"You are talking to the person in charge," Wilson sounded delighted.

"What about Captain Latimer?"

"Latimer answers to me, and I'm not giving him a say in anything that matters. What do you want to talk to me about?"

"Who do you report to?"

"Nobody, I'm the boss here."

"You represent the British Government. Who represents the Federation?"

"I represent the Federation. I am Chung Yi," The Chinese diplomat forestalled Wilson's reply.

"Now we're getting somewhere. Do you realise what you're doing? Do you have any idea of the damage you are causing and will be expected to pay for?"

"Pay for?" Chung Yi presumed his understanding of English was at fault. "Do you mean for repairing the damage?"

"Oh no, I mean pay for in a much more broad sense. You have made the mistake of being duped by Wilson into taking this course of action, and what you're about to observe will form a fraction of the ultimate cost for you."

"What can you possibly do? You have no military forces and save for your limited defence capability, which you appear to be unwilling to use if it puts life in danger. You have no means of retaliation against the laser that is destroying your installation."

"Can you observe the damage that is being done?"

"We have a camera mounted on a drone, and we can see what's happening in real time."

"I suggest you look at the screen in real time and see our response."

"We are looking, but we see nothing."

"Look again." Gilliland once more disconnected the call.

The three men in the *Foxhound* radio room watched the video image being beamed from the drone. It showed clearly that the building they had targeted was being destroyed systematically by the laser beam. Suddenly, the red line of the laser beam disappeared, and the destruction ceased.

"I'm only a simple military man," Latimer said to nobody in particular. "But I am presuming they simply tracked back up the laser with their BAM2 or whatever it's called and blasted your satellite out of the sky, that's what any self-respecting military man would do."

Chung Yi spoke urgently in Mandarin into his telephone which was patched through to satellite control in Beijing. He stopped talking, and his face became drawn and pale. He slowly shut down the telephone and turned to Wilson.

"Our satellite has been destroyed. It simply ceased to exist—it has gone."

"What do you mean, gone?" Wilson looked appalled.

"*Gone* is a singularly clear word in the English language." He gave Wilson a hooded look. "The Chairman wants to see you in Beijing immediately. He is most displeased."

"But the satellite was your idea," Wilson protested. "You said it was better than aircraft. That's what I wanted to do."

"From your telephone discussions with the Chairman's office, the impression they gained was that it was your idea and your idea alone. They were very clear about that."

Latimer offered a solution to Chang Yi. "He can take second seat in one of our fighter aircraft. We can refuel it over India, and he could be in Beijing in no time." "Just so," Chang Yi said while demonstrating that it was possible for him to smile and smile broadly.

"You realise what we've done, don't you?" Pettit could hardly contain himself.

"We've wrecked Wilson's life." Crook observed.

"Yes, but we've done much more than that. We've actually beaten the Federation, just us few. There's nothing they can do to us now."

"Don't get carried away with what we've done. It could be that we've stirred up a hornet's nest. Don't underestimate the Federation and certainly don't underestimate Wilson. He's the comeback kid incarnate," Caine gave stern words of warning.

"Don't spoil it, Penny," Gilliland chided her. "Let us have a rare moment of satisfaction before we start dreaming up a strategy which will permanently contain both Wilson and the Federation."

They immediately began the task of repairing the damage to the power station and of devising a strategy to deal with Wilson and the Federation on a more permanent basis. The former would be completed quickly. Thanks to their revolutionary liquid lava building techniques using the controlled flow of magma to the surface, cooling it with pressurised sea water and the shaping of it with BAM2.

Having staved off the latest attack, the Island returned, gingerly this time, to a tenuous tranquillity. The Islanders had witnessed that their defences were not as vulnerable as they had for a short while feared and felt they could, with caution, resume their former life. After a few months as the autumn skies began to cloud over from the west to all intents and purposes, peace reigned.

Pickering undertook the agreed course of action of devising a BAM2 in miniature that could be located within a car or plane or boat with a power source that would sustain it for considerable periods of time, and as BAM2 allowed sunlight through unchanged, they could continue recharging the batteries with the BAM2 dome activated. The device comprised a 5.8164 inch diameter magnetised sphere into which was embedded a micro-chip and a solar battery; the sphere was studded with a grid of tiny clear diamonds and sat in an indentation at the top of a truncated pyramid inside which were a duplicated battery and a matching chip. When activated, the sphere was floated from the pyramid indentation by means of powerfully opposing magnetic fields.

The basis of the vehicle protection system was that the device would be set to give protection with semi spheres to protect above in the case of a road vehicle or above and below in the case of a boat or plane. The minimum throw of the device would be set so that it would not destroy the transportation being protected, and at the same time, the device was fitted with a self-destruct mechanism that would destroy the workings from the inside if there was ever a need to protect its integrity.

The Federation was reluctant to pursue further discussions with the Islanders and meaningful communications were stalled with no real expectation of the talks starting up again in the foreseeable future. They neither suggested a peaceful settlement nor did they make threatening noises. Rather than being reassured by the lack of any threat, the defence committee, headed up by Pettit, put in place an enhanced sea and sky watch and kept the inner defence dome activated except when it rained when they allowed the natural irrigation of their intensive crops which, otherwise, they received in moderated hydroponics form from the central mountain lake which was fed from beneath the earth's crust. While it rained, the sky watchers were particularly vigilant; when the rain stopped, the dome was reactivated and kept operative at all times.

Pettit was amused and then surprised by his feelings of support for the independent actions of the technicians monitoring the dome activity. When they first started using the defence, the inevitable happened; migrating birds and those seeking the sanctuary of the Island as a place of rest, as they journeyed across the Atlantic, disintegrated when they tried to fly through the dome. To ameliorate this, the technicians attached a sound signal to the carrier wave, which formed the dome which produced a danger cry, at the domes extremity, for the full range of species likely to be making the journey.

At the same time as the Island was being returned to safe sanctuary status, Wilson was pursuing his vendetta against Creswell during his unwanted journey to China. His manipulation of Creswell was, he perceived, entirely successful; he had kept his job as DDP and would continue to do so as long as Creswell remained under suspicion, and he had placated MI5 and the House of Lords Review Committee without entirely preventing a possible reactivation of his original intention.

With revenge in mind, he decided not to involve the Chinese administration in his quest to steal BAM2 technology. He turned instead to the former Soviet Union satellite countries. His choice of ally was the newly formed amalgamation of four previously separate regions now called Nuovostan, the temporary home of some of the money he had generated below the grid. It was a troubled country being short of capital and, therefore, generous in interest rates and was politically unstable; in all, it was his kind of country. He could not afford to be open about his negotiations with the Nuovostan Government, so he decided to use his man, Simon Queeze, who, he thought with a wry smile, he could trust absolutely and implicitly. Queeze would know exactly what was wanted to the last detail.

Twenty-Six

Wilson was still smarting after receiving a tongue-lashing from Chung Ho Chen, whom he irrationally considered to be his inferior, about the failure of his plan to occupy the Island and his part in the destruction of the satellite which had cost billions of Dollars. He attributed his downfall to the devious ways of Chung Yi and vowed to make amends by returning the admonishment with interest. He had returned from Beijing with his tail between his legs and made himself feel better by castigating all his staff for what he perceived, irrationally, to be their errant ways.

He had the basis of an idea which would finally scupper the Islanders while leaving the BAM2 technology completely unharmed. That it would lead to the death of all people on the Island was of no interest to him. The important thing was that he would have unfettered access to the most powerful weapon ever devised. He viewed BAM2 only as a weapon. Its peaceful qualities were of no consequence to him. In his position as Director of Defence Projects, with an almost limitless black operations budget, he could finance his aspirations, thanks to the lemmings like British taxpayers and a weak and ineffectual government.

Creswell was an obstacle to be overcome. As the Prime Minister, he could separate Wilson from his access to the necessary facilities and funding, except for the six million sterling he had salted away, together with other "cost savings" in his secret accounts in Nuovostan, but that was nowhere near enough. If Creswell were to go, would he be able to control the new man? If Creswell were to stay, he was controllable. But how could he, Wilson, be sure of keeping his position as DDP? The hold he had over Creswell was tenuous but enough to prevent immediate meltdown of his plans. He just needed to find more time to allow his intentions to mature.

His next move was one which only Wilson could have the arrogance to contemplate. He arranged a meeting with Creswell in Creswell's Whitehall office to discuss what he alluded to as matters of the greatest national importance. Creswell resisted the offer of a meeting but after a constant barrage of requests, he finally relented. Creswell prepared himself for another battery of lies and innuendo.

"First," Wilson opened their meeting, "I want to apologise to you about our misunderstanding."

"Misunderstanding?" Creswell said, bemused at the unexpected opening.

"Yes, I was very unfair to you, but I swear I had the country's best interests at heart. You see, I was given spurious information which was leaked to me from, what I now know to be, an unreliable source in China. Until now he has been the provider of good information, but he seems to have got this one wrong." He smiled inwardly at Creswell's bemusement. "I took him at his word about the missing money and the bank account and you being John Connaught and the witness to your signature. I really am sorry about that." He adopted a look of abject contrition. "When I realised from another much more reliable source that he had given me bad information, I thought I would come straight to you and tell you."

"I don't understand you!" Creswell shook his head. "At the meeting we had on the Island, with those you refer to as traitors, you were vehement about my guilt, and you said you had a witness to my signing transfer documents, and you were prepared to state this to Trevor Coniston and start up a massive MI5 investigation."

"Like I said, this was all because of bad intelligence, Prime Minister. I am very conscious of security especially when it comes to making sure that government confidentiality is paramount. Look, I am admitting I got it wrong and that I over reacted, I should have checked out the information before going public, but the fact is I didn't, and I want to make amends."

"The first thing you can do," Creswell said hesitantly, "is to go to all the people with whom you discussed this and undo the harm you have caused, and I want them to report back to me when you have done so." Creswell could hardly believe that he was saying this to Wilson and entrusting him with a task but a euphoric wave of relief was washing over him, which overcame his natural wariness.

When Wilson was gone, Creswell heaved a great sigh of relief. It was as though a great burden had been lifted from his shoulders. He suddenly realised that since the initial meeting with Wilson, he had been drawn as tight as a bowstring. He picked up his secure phone and made a call to Gilliland.

Gilliland listened with rapt attention as Creswell unburdened himself. He found the content of the conversation, alarming although he did not communicate this to Creswell who was clearly so relieved that his torment appeared to be over. He allowed him to ramble on and accelerate the process of healing and at the culmination of the conversation, congratulated Creswell on his ability to stay calm.

Later, he discussed the telephone conversation with Caine, who listened intently asking questions to improve her understanding of the perceived meanings of Wilson's actions.

"Stockholm syndrome variation," she said. "He actually wants to believe it's all over so he fails to see the obvious. Clearly, Wilson is up to something, and that has to be bad for somebody, but for whom, we don't know."

"How can James have forgotten about the doctored reports on our progress that Wilson passed on to him?"

"That's the syndrome again, but what we should not do is burst James's bubble by discussing this with him. We just need to be aware that Wilson has changed tack, and I for one don't think that he has lost sight of his main objective of getting his hands on BAM2. We will just have to wait and see what Wilson's next move is."

"Remind me again," Gilliland put his head on one side, "why are we helping James like this? We have enough problems of our own, and he is after all technically in the ranks of the enemy."

"It's because he's in the ranks of the enemy that we need to nurture him. He is the only one who shows any empathy with us. He could be our Trojan Horse."

Twenty-Seven

Simon Queeze surveyed the unfinished and uncared for terminal buildings of Nuovoskya Airport as he descended the mobile steps, which bore the barely legible legend AEROFLOT in Arabic and Cyrillic scripts. He was met by the driver of a rusting ex-military jeep, who picked up his bags wordlessly and threw them on to the scarred back seat. Queeze joined the driver and took the passenger seat for a hair-raising journey across the airport, crossing active runways with assumed impunity. They left the airport through a hole in the perimeter fence and bounced along an unlit unpaved road into Nuovoskya city.

His sense of smell was severely tested as they entered what turned out to be a ministry building, by a mixture of overcooked indescribable ingredients and what was akin to multi-storey car park lift shaft odours. The lift had a notice taped to it, indicating that it was out of order. He also observed that the tape affixing it to the partly open door was yellowed and peeling, indicating that it had been out of order, probably, since before the new country was formed. The driver shrugged resignedly and pointed to the unlit staircase, holding up three fingers of his other hand, he turned, again wordlessly, and disappeared.

Queeze made his way, by feel, to the third floor where the corridor was lit by underpowered incandescent bulbs half of which were out or flickering as though about to extinguish. He was met by a very elegant woman dressed in designer clothes. She was professionally coiffured, and her French perfume was obviously expensive and was overpowering, probably to counteract the evil smell of the building.

"I am Irena Pelochev. Please to following me to the office of Minister Yuri Kurakin," she said, turning on her heel and causing her skirt to swirl fetchingly. Her perfumed fragrance wafted towards him enticingly.

He followed her, mesmerised by the hip sway, through a dirty peeling door into a seductively lit office, and the contrast with the rest of the building was immediately evident. This outer office was clearly the domain of his guide. It was wood panelled and had a highly polished brown lino floor. There was a selection of gaudily coloured velvet upholstered guest chairs and an incongruously modern secretarial workstation.

"Wait here, please." She indicated the chairs and disappeared through an intricately carved hardwood door.

Queeze took in his surroundings which, unlike its occupant, were an expensive mismatch of styles chosen by more than one person with absolutely no taste. Queeze found this curiously appealing. She returned after a brief time and held the door open for him to enter the Minister's office.

Once again, the contrast with the rest of the building was obvious; even more obvious than that of the secretary. The floor covering was of exceptional quality. Its dove grey deep pile contrasting with the dark mahogany of the hand-carved furniture. The pale grey painted walls were decked with modern art, and the whole ensemble was bathed in soft illumination from discrete lighting set in the walls just below the ceiling.

The Minister stood before a drinks cabinet, and he nursed a double shot glass of clear liquid. He was a direct contrast to the modern room; he wore an old-fashioned double-breasted plain brown suit with a yellow shirt, the collar of which was too big, and a garish hand-painted tie and polished brown boots. He did not offer to shake hands with Queeze; he simply grunted to his secretary and inclined his head towards the bar. She walked to the bar and poured clear liquid to the rim of a shot glass and handed it without comment to Queeze. The Minister grunted again and raised his glass. Queeze repeated the performance but without the grunt.

"The Minister is wishing for me to welcoming you into our country and has a need that we can satisfy business." She said this in her own quaint brand English as she returned to the desk at which the two men sat, carrying two full bottles of the clear liquid that they were drinking.

"This is Vodka?" he asked her.

"Da Vodka," although she pronounced it "Wodka." "Hundred forty proof."

The discussion commenced, and it was soon obvious that apart from being the secretary and the interpreter, she was also the decision maker. Whenever Queeze asked a question, she would translate it for the Minister who would incline his head to one side or turn down his mouth at the corners or simply shrug. He did not speak the answer to the questions she translated to him; her replies, however, were complete and more technical than Queeze could readily understand. Clearly, she was in control of the situation, and the Minister merely a titular head, who played no real part in the negotiation. He was very old style Eastern Block.

Each question asked prompted another glass of Vodka, which she refilled as soon as they drained the glass. Each reply was celebrated in the same way. Very soon, Queeze was aware that the strong alcohol was playing havoc with his sobriety. He was conscious that his words were beginning to slur, and what was worse he had no way of telling if the Minister was affected likewise because he was not speaking.

Finally, Queeze had asked his last question and received his last satisfactory answer, and the room fell momentarily quiet. The Minister looked at the secretary and lifted his eyebrows then jerked his head upwards and backwards.

"I will leave now to allow negotiation with price of services," she said in her charmingly accented pseudo-English. She noted Queeze's look of puzzlement.

"Minister knows numbers in Engelski. Can negotiate to you." She left the room.

The Minister filled both glasses once more each from its own bottle, which by now were two-thirds empty, picked up his own glass and chinked against Queeze's which was still on the table. Some of the liquid spilled from the overfull glasses. The Minister drained his glass and casually flicked excess vodka from his fingers. He indicated that Queeze should do the same and recharge his glass, which he did with an unsteady hand.

"Six million cash." the minister said with a slight slur although he pronounced cash as "kesh."

Queeze looked at him through a vodka-induced haze and assumed wryly that the Minister knew that six million was the extent of the kitty in Wilson's main account in the National Bank of Nuovostan.

"One million." Queeze held up one finger.

"Nyet." the Minister scowled and insisted they both finished off the drinks and refilled them.

Both bottles were empty when they finally settled on four-and-a-half-million sterling. Neither man was able to stand steadily by the time the negotiation was over. The Minister crashed his clenched fist down on to the top of his desk and shouted. Shortly afterwards, the door opened and the secretary appeared wearing a street coat and carrying the Minister's. She helped the Minister into his coat and then led them to a door opposite the interconnecting door, opposite the door from her office, which opened on to a lift lobby. The bright new stainless steel German-built lift whisked them in soft comfort to an underground garage where a militarily uniformed chauffeur stood to attention beside the stretched Mercedes limousine and held the rear door open. Queeze noticed as he passed that his luggage had already been loaded into the boot of the limousine.

They settled into the seats, the Minister on one side and Queeze on the other side with the secretary between them. She opened up a cocktail cabinet and took out a bottle of chilled Champagne and three glasses.

"Bottoms out," she said.

"With any luck." Queeze chuckled drunkenly to himself at her charming faux pas.

By the time, they reached the official residence, at which he was to stay for one night, the Minister had passed out and was snoring sonorously with his head resting on Pelochev's shoulder. She frowned and said something angrily, which Queeze didn't understand. The chauffeur opened the door and, observing the problem, shouted through the open door of the residence for assistance. Two swarthy dark-suited men pulled the unconscious man from the limousine and between them dragged him into the hallway and on into the interior.

"Minister has hard day. Two meetings like this on one day. Too much Wodka."

"One meeting was enough for me. I couldn't take another one."

"You are for sleeping, yes?"

"Yes, but first I need a shower."

"Not showering, bathing it is in your sleep suite. I get bath for you. You prepare for bathing."

He was shown up to a bedroom which had a bathroom en suite. He unpacked a few belongings, undressed, and donned a bathrobe and some towelling slippers that had been left at the foot of his bed. The bathroom was steam filled, and the large sunken bath was full and topped with white bath foam. He removed his robe and slippers and walked gratefully into the hot suds; no sooner had he sat down than a door at the other side of the bathroom opened and the secretary in a pink bathrobe entered. She slid out of the robe and got into the bath with him. He was suddenly sober.

"We have bathings and I washing you all over. Then you washing me all over. After washings I dry you, dry me, then we finish all negotiations in sleeping."

He didn't argue. He also didn't do much sleeping.

Twenty-Eight

C reswell was on a soft cloud of euphoria. The great burden had been lifted from him and he decided to put the whole distasteful episode behind him. For a moment, he had considered investigating what had happened but dismissed it almost immediately fearing that such action might ignite the flames of destruction again; far better to let sleeping dogs lie.

With induced benevolence, he stated acceptance, to those few interested parties, that he may have misjudged Wilson and that Wilson's driving force was patriotism. Had Wilson not, after all, been his champion in his election as prime minister, and he had done so with no thought about recompense of any sort. On reflection, it appeared that Wilson was a valuable asset to the government, and his tireless strivings in the interest of government and country could lead, perhaps, to inclusion in the birthday honours list.

What of the Islanders though? They had helped him in what he saw as his moment of need, but had they actually done so? Perhaps their preoccupation with Wilson, rather than his, Creswell's, interests had led them to furthering their own aims. Maybe they had seen him as a catalyst for their own aspirations. He arranged a meeting with Sir Lionel Wentworth to discuss among other things the potential of rewarding Wilson with an honour.

His meeting with Sir Lionel did not go at all as he had expected. When he suggested honouring Wilson, Sir Lionel froze and looked incredulous.

"An honour for Wilson, Prime Minister. What can you be thinking?"

"He has been working in government circles for some time now," Creswell explained, "but is hardly known to the public. Honouring him would be seen as rewarding one who has worked tirelessly in the background in the interest of national good even if we are aware that some of the work he carries out is somewhat distasteful and the methods that his position forces him to employ can sometimes be unethical. It is a burden he has to bear, and he does so with fortitude."

"Prime Minister," Sir Lionel hesitated as if lost for words, "his character is somewhat tarnished. He has been linked with some very questionable activities as well as . . ."

"Anything proven?" Creswell interrupted.

"Well," Sir Lionel blustered, "not exactly proven. He is a very resourceful man, but there is no smoke without fire."

"I'm surprised at you, Sir Lionel. You of all people should know that in politics it's all smoke and mirrors in which case, there is smoke without fire. He comes into the firing line only because his unsung successes are envied."

"Think again, James. Remember your past dealings with him, and you will realise why he has no friends. He is a dangerous man—so dangerous in fact that if he knew of the conversation we are now having my professional life would be in grave jeopardy."

"Lionel, if I didn't know better, I would think that you were one of the people of envy I was just talking about."

"Beware, Wilson," Sir Lionel said dryly.

"I don't think I share your view. Wilson has proved ultimately to be a good and loyal friend to his country and the government."

"Think again, James." Sir Lionel stood up and brought the meeting to an end.

Creswell smiled secretly to himself after he left Wentworth's office. Knowing Wentworth as he did he realised that he had just stumbled on to something of great importance, but he wasn't quite sure what *it* was.

After Creswell had left the office, Wentworth slumped down in his chair and looked dejected. He had always considered James Creswell to be one of the rare politicians of stable and high integrity and one who would develop into a fine prime minister given the room and opportunity. Creswell's proposal of an award for Wilson had come as a complete surprise to him. Clearly, Wilson had done to Creswell what he did so well when he had an ulterior motive. He had completely hoodwinked James into drawing the wrong conclusions.

He thought that with some authority, after all had he not fallen into the similar trap of being coerced into thinking Wilson to be a man of integrity, in direct opposition to his first formed impression. He, Wentworth, had dropped his guard and had ultimately paid the price for his lack of judgement when he allowed Wilson enough access to his life for him to have taken the incriminating photographs which he so much wanted to destroy but which still stayed tantalisingly beyond his reach. He had been pushed into doing things, which he knew to be unprofessional in the hope of retrieving the incriminating evidence, but after so long he realised, with dejection, that Wilson would never truly release him from his clutches.

Trawling through his mind, he recalled the discussion he had with Penelope Delaney after the awful meeting in Wilson's club. She had been a good listener and had not commented on the fact that he was weeping uncontrollably as he unburdened himself. He was aware that she had actually been working in Wilson's department at the time of his conversation with Wilson. Only later, in the cold light of the next day, did he feel alarm at what he had done. Delaney could be reporting to Wilson right then as he sat in trepidation unable to eat the light breakfast before him. Having no reaction from Wilson over the next few days gave him some assurance that his confidences had not been betrayed. A subsequent meeting with Wilson confirmed that fact to him.

In his wide-ranging confessions, he had released from his pent-up soul other damaging facts, including the contents of the invaluable secret information which he held as an anchor against Wilson's whim to destroy him when his usefulness waned. He was also acutely aware that if he were to release the information, he would also be destroyed in the fallout.

She had advised him not to be so wrapped up in his fear of revelation that he overlooked obvious weaknesses in whatever it was that Wilson was holding against him. There is a tendency, she had told him, to exaggerate the affects of the release of the damning information and whether or not that he who released it might also suffer consequences. Her advice to him was to look at how people reacted to him and to elicit from that what those people perceived to be the essential him. For example, she had said for him to talk to the doorman who had greeted them on their arrival at his apartment building, saying that his insight into the issues which bothered Wentworth so much might allay his trepidations. He had not yet done so but vowed that he would when the opportunity presented itself.

*

Creswell attended the month-end meeting of the Federation council. His companion at the meeting was Wilson who was calm and charming and who, unusually for him, gave the Chinese delegation the cold shoulder. He also ignored Van der Linde who seemed agitated when several attempts to engage him in conversation failed. Van der Linde took

Creswell aside and complained about the lack of courtesy being shown to him by the DDP. Shrugging offhandedly, Creswell told him that Wilson was his own man and that if he chose not to have a conversation he was exercising his right. Van der Linde's suggestion that Creswell should order Wilson to meet was met with another shrug from Creswell who turned and walked away, his actions testifying wordlessly to his intent.

There followed animated discussions between Van der Linde and the Chinese which became very heated and was adjourned to a side room where they could battle in private. Creswell was surprised to be invited into the side room meeting by a member of the Chinese delegation. He was even more surprised when he entered the room to see the Chairman of the Chinese Peoples Republic engaged in the discussion.

"Prime Minister," the bland-faced Chairman spoke English with a slight American accent, "it seems that your man, Wilson, is being difficult to pin down. Mr Van der Linde is trying to illicit some information from him, to do with Federation business of course, but is unable to get a response from him. We cannot have minor officials holding up Federation business. Kindly tell him to arrange a meeting so that this matter can be resolved forthwith."

"As I have already indicated to the president of the Federation, Mr Wilson is an adviser to the British Government and as such is free to pursue what he considers to be the appropriate course of action. If he chooses to say nothing, I am sure he has his reasons, but what I will do is raise the questions that you have with him if you would care to tell me, what they are."

"We wish to discuss them only with him. It would be tiresome to relay questions and answers through an intermediary."

"I'm not an intermediary. I'm his superior, and you will just have to wait until he's ready to talk." He walked swiftly out of the room aware of the babble of angry raised voices behind him.

Wilson looked at him expectantly as he left the side room used by the now irate Chinese delegation. Creswell outlined the content of the meeting and saw Wilson's face cloud over momentarily.

"What is it they want to talk to you about?" Creswell asked casually.

"Well," Wilson hesitated before responding, "as you know I was seconded to the Federation to advise on matters of federal defence, which I have been doing for some time." He looked uneasy. "They want me to get involved with something which doesn't feel kosher to me. I don't know what it is, and I'm not going to ask them. And I don't want to get involved—I just don't trust them." He looked contrite.

"Maybe," Creswell said slowly and thoughtfully, "just maybe it would be a good idea to string them along and find out what it is they intend."

"I think it would be better if we left them to their own devices." Wilson said with unaccustomed reticence. He said it in a tone which ensured that the discussion was over.

Creswell watched him walk away and was amused by the uncharacteristic lack of enthusiasm from one who was normally rugged enough to enter any lion's den.

Twenty-Nine

*I*n the, otherwise, barren mountains to the northern extreme of Nuovostan is a single fertile valley sheltered from the cold northern and eastern winds of winter by a huge geological upheaval which formed an abrupt cliff face a hundred metres high. The valley, of which the fault was one side, was fenced off on the other three sides against unwanted visitors. The fences were patrolled twenty-four hours a day by armed guards and packs of attack guard dogs. In the centre of the valley, a group of featureless concrete buildings, which were built more for function than form, sprawled untidy and unloved across the uneven terrain.

In Cyrillic characters the sign at the entrance, which translates as, AGRICULTURAL RESEARCH CENTRE, remained a completely indecipherable jumble of meaningless shapes to Simon Queeze. The road from the gate to the buildings was littered with tractors and harvesters which were unrecognisable in their various stages of construction, decay, or demolition. It was difficult to tell which. Simon Queeze was ushered through the main entrance by the Nuovostani minister, Yuri Kurakin, and his secretary, Irena Pelochev. The Minister was agitated and seemed in a hurry to be elsewhere.

They entered a workshop fitted out with sturdy cast-iron-and-steel workbenches, each of which was occupied by a hazard-suited operator. The poorly constructed walls, which showed clearly the faulty formwork joints that had been used in casting them, were in stark contrast to the pristine specialist machinery which was dotted at intervals around the walls. The Minister spoke softly and urgently to his secretary and departed to one of the side offices.

"He has meetink," she said simply.

"Vodka?" asked Queeze.

"Da Wodka," she responded with a faint smile, "we go now in laboratory for looking." She walked through a doorway with a Cyrillic sign, which he assumed on entering said something like locker room. "Putting on clean keeping suits." She held up a white one-piece suit against him, discarding it as being too large and selected another which was more to her liking. She selected one for herself.

He started to put the suit on when she stopped him.

"Not on top," she said. "Taking off other clotheses first," she demonstrated by removing her dress. "But leaving on underneath britches". She stepped out of her shoes and now wearing only her "underneath britches" and silk stockings she stepped energetically into the one-piece suit and zipped it up very quickly.

Correctly clad with the addition of safety shoes and goggles together with a hooded head cover, they entered the laboratory. Technicians were huddled around a three-metre long one-metre diameter shiny stainless steel carcase, which had several inspection hatches open, revealing various pieces of machinery and tubing inside.

"Laboratory is with positive air pressure. This keeping out is the dust and 'unpurities' is, which harm function," she said.

"How much more work to be done?" he asked.

"Tovarich," she said to an older technician who turned to face her. His expression said that he was wondering what if anything, besides the white suit, she was wearing. She spoke to him at some length in what he presumed to be Russian or a derivative thereof.

"He thinks another two weeks and will be ready for run simulation testings."

"I would rather it was sooner than that," Queeze said, showing his disappointment.

"He say it not safe to hurrying. Maybe don't work if not properly considering," she added after a further discussion with the technician.

They joined the Minister in the office off the workshop where he was talking to the facility manager. The requisite two bottles of Vodka were on the table both half empty, a third bottle still full was added to the group together with a double-shot glass. Queeze sighed deeply when he realised that they were in for another alcohol-fuelled afternoon. The secretary poured, and he groaned inwardly.

He awoke the next morning with a vicious hangover and no recollection of events after they left the "Agricultural" buildings. He was back in the Minister's residence, the bed was a mess of tangled bedclothes and the room odour made him feel nauseous. His head and face itched. He had been wearing his disguise continuously, much longer that he normally would and the perspiration accumulating under his wig and beard were irritating his epidermis.

Dragging himself out of bed, he stumbled to the door and locked it from the inside, and to be sure that he wouldn't be disturbed, he jammed a chair under the doorknob. Satisfied that he was safe from unwanted intervention, he drew all the curtains which plunged the room into semi darkness. Now he was safe from prying eyes. He looked at his ravaged face in the bathroom mirror and was shocked at how bad he looked. There were bags under his eyes and his skin was sallow and drawn and his cheeks unhealthily puffy, even more so than was normal.

He peeled off the beard, wincing because his natural beard had grown through the extra strong adhesive so that it was acting like a depilatory wax strip. His eyes watered until he decided that it would be better to bite the bullet and take it off with a single devastating pull rather than slowly as he usually did.

Removal of the wig was slightly less painful being, as he was, follicly challenged, but it was still painful especially in the delicate state he found himself after another night of Vodka. It had been a favourite drink of his because on the breath it was odourless, but he felt that he could not face Vodka ever again.

He was suddenly aware of the cold feeling of perspiration trickling down his body front and back. He was convinced that he was exuding pure Vodka. He ran the bath and dropped gratefully into the hot, perfumed water, allowing it to wash away what Pelochev would have called the *unpurities* and to relax his knotted muscles. He finally felt relaxed when he thought of the success of his mission and the financial reward it would bring. He also thought to would be a good idea if Irena Pelochev were here with him.

"I will taking you to airport," she said as Queeze, disguise restored, entered the kitchen which boasted an open wood fire, providing soporific warmth, "we needing to going maybe one and half hour—extra time for snowing." She indicated the window, where heavy snow could be seen falling and settling with alarming rapidity.

"Breakfasts?" she enquired with a raised eyebrow.

"No breakfast just hot, black unsweetened coffee and maybe a little dry toast."

"Wodka illness," she said to herself, "stopping man performance last night."

He was too unwell to ask her if she meant, to his disappointment, what he thought she meant; but he had no memory of it.

*

Queeze slept uneasily for most of the flight from Nuovostan to Santiago in Chile. The second leg of his journey was by a chartered private helicopter. As it landed, he stood impatiently waiting to disembark as the rotors began their noisy wind-down. A platoon of black ops marine guards, who had exited just moments before him, stood to attention as he alighted and to a man were watchful of their surroundings. The mountains of Chile were snow-clad, but here to the north and down at sea level, the temperature was more acceptable.

The rotors stopped and hung limp and impotent, shuddering slightly, buffeted by a light breeze. Two of the marines escorted him to the personnel access door which formed part of the main hangar door, and the remaining marines stayed with the now silent helicopter. They stood around it with their backs to it, and their combat weapons at the ready. The pilot remained in his seat visible only when he drew on his illegal cigarette.

Inside the hangar, the light was stark and bright. The ancient Russian built bomber, formerly owned by the Chilean Air Force, was partly stripped down and mechanics were clustered around the two pairs of wing-mounted engines all busily performing their tasks. A further group of men were working under the centre of the fuselage halfway along its length. A third group, smaller than the rest, was working around the tail section. They were dressed differently and appeared not to interact with the other two teams.

Queeze strode over to the team at the rear of the aircraft and was saluted by one of their number. He spoke earnestly to them and tapped his wristwatch impatiently. The man saluted again and turned to his men to give them a pep talk. Then he visited each group in turn and this time spoke to them through an interpreter on each occasion he repeated the watch tapping.

The team under the fuselage had enlarged the bomb bay doors and had fitted a frame in which were mounted three sets of jaws which when closed were about a metre in diameter. The mechanism was attached to a generator, which rumbled steadily, hardly discernible over the hubbub of voices and the high-pitched rapid burping of pneumatic tools around other parts of the aircraft. One of the mechanics cleared everybody away by sounding a warning claxon. Silence descended in the hangar save for the generator; they all waited expectantly as a switch was thrown, and there was a loud snapping metallic sound and the fore and aft set of jaws sprung open with such ferocity that the whole air frame shook, and the centre jaws were only half open.

There was much consternation as the centre jaws were examined to discover the reason for the malfunction. Queeze strode over to the team and began to gesticulate and could be seen to be less than congratulatory at the lack of performance. Having castigated the team concerned, he turned on his heels and left the hangar closely followed by his bodyguards. In contrast to his demonstration of ill will at the failure of the test, he was jubilant inside, apart from the minor malfunction the aircraft would be ready ahead of schedule. Once completed, the seizure of Recovery Island would be one large step closer.

Thirty

*J*ames Creswell walked away from the cabinet room as soon as the brief cabinet meeting was over. He looked and was puzzled until a short while ago Wilson had been his enemy and Sir Lionel his friend. Now their roles were ostensibly reversed—Wilson was now his friend, and Sir Lionel was not exactly his enemy, but there was a definite cooling in their relationship, Trevor Coniston was, like Sir Lionel, distant.

Clearly, they did not share his expressed magnanimity over Wilson's integrity. He considered this situation during the short chauffeured drive back to his Whitehall office. It was a pleasant day for a short walk between the two, but as a Prime Minister, such pleasantries were beyond possibility for reasons of security as well as the pressure of time. He also reflected during the journey that Gilliland and Crook did not suffer from the same problem. They were free to roam wherever they pleased and could even stop off ad hoc at a cafe or restaurant for a relaxing interlude, a luxury he, unfortunately, did not enjoy.

As his thoughts turned to the Island, he resolved to contact them and try to heal the tragic gap between the Islanders or at least the four main protagonists with regard to the Federation. He thought back over their joint relationship, which had developed during his time of need, and wondered once more if their motivating force for assisting him had not been just to further their own agenda. Certainly, his recent discussions with Wilson had turned cold when their names had been mentioned. He had tried to heal the rift, but his overtures had been rebuffed by Wilson just as they had been by the Islanders.

Perhaps, he thought, he should turn his attention to the Federation's intentions towards the Island. The Federation hierarchy was being very secretive about their next moves after their might had been negated by the actions of the Islanders when the Federation had mounted their last attack. The defeat had been humiliating, although he was assured by Wilson that the errors made during the course of the exercise had been the fault of the Federation military specialists. They had completely misjudged the capability of the Island's technology and had proved to be inadequate tacticians. Wilson had his own ideas about how the Islanders could be persuaded to co-operate but wasn't yet prepared to reveal his thoughts even to Creswell until he had thought them through more. Criticism of the way in which the Federation was run was a constant thread running through the conversations of Pettit, Crook, and Creswell, and Creswell had no qualms about keeping secret the fact that Wilson was using his considerable expertise to solve the problem which up to now seemed to be beyond their reach. He was still curious about what it was that the Federation were planning to do about the dilemma but had been unable to extract any information from Van der Linde no matter how blatantly or subtly he tried.

In Beijing, Van der Linde was suffering a dressing-down from Chung Ho Chen, who was furious that their assault on the Island had, once more, failed and that the Islanders would now be on full alert in anticipation of a further attack. Van der Linde squirmed as he reported that the military tacticians had so far come up with nothing concrete. Chung looked at him with dead eyes, and it was not possible to fathom what he was thinking except that he, Van der Linde, or somebody was going to suffer over the failure to come up with an alternative plan.

At the conclusion of their meeting, Chung enquired what Wilson was doing about the failure. Van der Linde suffered more abuse when he explained that Wilson was disenchanted with the ability of the Federation military, specifically the Navy, to carry out any plan devised with any hope of success. He had said that he would pursue alternative courses of action that stood a high chance of success without the need to call on any Federation resources. Chung's usually bland face almost became animated at the criticism of the Federation which was, in Chung's mind, under the absolute control of the Peoples Republic of China. Chung's parting remark as Van der Linde turned to leave was that the fault lay not with the Federation but with His Majesty's Navy, they were the force that was found wanting and he would see to it that the appropriate disciplinary measures would be taken.

The monthly military activity report which ended up on the PM's desk contained a single paragraph stating that Captain G. Latimer had been disciplined and would not be permitted to be awarded promotion above his current rank. He was removed from the captaincy of HMS *Foxhound* and transferred to a land-based logistics unit. Creswell frowned as he read the account and immediately telephoned the Lord High Admiral to register his surprise and disapproval at the removal of one he considered to be a very able career naval officer.

The Lord High Admiral promised to look into it and responded by secured e-mail.

Latimer court-martialed in absentia by the Beijing Federation military court. Found guilty of dereliction of duty in that he placed men and materiel in jeopardy without regard to good practice. Has been stripped of his specific Federation rank and demoted.

The court martial was attended by a Royal Navy representative
who ensured that the court martial was full and fair and undertook
to carry out the sentence of the court as directed.

Communiqué ratified by the Lord High Admiral and signed by him.
The signed original copy reference FNC / JDA—21C: MT is held
in the secured vaults at the Admiralty Data Centre, Plymouth.

Receipt of the response led to another telephone call to ascertain the identity of the Royal Naval representative at the court martial. Creswell contacted him and interrogated him about the court martial and the representation on behalf of Captain Latimer. He learned that information concerning the actions of Captain Latimer was presented, in the main, by a member of British Intelligence who was present during the abortive raid. His evidence was given in camera to enable him to protect his anonymity.

"Norman, when did you put the Chinese in charge of Royal Navy promotions?"

"What are you talking about James?" The Lord High Admiral grasped his telephone so tightly that his knuckles gleamed white. "I've done no such thing."

"Then please tell me why Captain Latimer has been court-martialed in absentia, found guilty, stripped of Federation rank, and has had his promotion prospects in His Majesty's Navy stonewalled."

"I've read the transcript of the court martial, and it seems to me that all avenues were explored, and his culpability was demonstrated beyond any reasonable doubt. The sentencing was a matter for the court."

"Let me put it another way. The court was Chinese—not Federation. Evidence was given in camera by an anonymous covert agent in Chinese. Our representative, who doesn't speak Chinese, was given an interpreter appointed by the Chinese court."

"Are you suggesting that there was something underhanded going on, James? Because if you are, there could be very serious consequences. You must be aware that the Chinese administration is very sensitive about criticism and without their support we would have to significantly reduce our naval operations."

"So, Norman, you are quite happy to throw Latimer to the wolves to stop the Chinese from being upset?"

"It's not that black and white James, we have a delicate and difficult line to navigate in Anglo Chinese relations."

"Interesting, isn't it, that I appear to be doing your job, in at least trying to salvage the career of a very able naval officer while you are trying to do my job in placating the Chinese. As PM, I am advising you to protect your man with all the tools at your disposal and leave the politics to me." He ended the call abruptly.

After his telephone conversation with Sir Norman Lotts, Creswell mulled over the conversation he had just had, and he considered it in the context of recent discussions with Wilson and factored in his own recent feelings about Gilliland and Crook. "*Perhaps,*" he thought, "*Wilson was right and had seen through the Islanders zealous protection of their new order and had focused his own emerging view that perhaps they were idealists. Idealism, history tells us, is a form of fundamentalism, and fundamentalism is a toxic influence, be it political, religious, or social.*"

He decided to make it a telephone activity day and made two important calls, one to the Federation and one to the Island. He called Beijing first and failed to connect with Chairman Chung, who was "not in a position to come to the telephone". He was ultimately able to talk to Van der Linde, who quite by chance was in his office.

"I don't have much time, Creswell," Van der Linde said dismissively when the call was put through to him by his secretary. "What can I do for you?"

"Jan, you sound harassed," he paused and getting no response, he continued, "I don't want to interrupt your busy day, but I am mystified about what we are doing about Recovery Island. Apart from one of our Royal Navy vessels being involved recently, I have no news of the next moves."

"The tacticians are looking into it," he said curtly. "Naturally, if the solution has any bearing on the United Kingdom, or what is left of it," he added unnecessarily. "You will be informed."

"Which tacticians are looking into it?"

"The Chinese group in Beijing." He realised as soon as he said it that Creswell would explode at this decision, of which he obviously had no knowledge.

"China is not the Federation, and the Federation is not China. Europe and the USA have an input to decisions of this nature. Did it not occur to you that it might be truly democratic to give us all a chance to have some sort of input?"

"The USA, China, and Europe all agreed to let the Chinese tactical group come up with a choice of solutions, and it was backed up by the nominated president of the New European Union who can take decisions on behalf of the Union. That being a majority of the Federation's full voting members gives sanction to the course of action that is being taken." The unequivocal statement led to the abrupt cessation of the conversation and the call.

An irate conversation with the president of the European Union did nothing to calm Creswell's anger. His objections about the use of the tactical group without reference to the UK Government were dismissed out of hand. He was informed that the Chinese proposal was accepted after a straw poll of selected European nation members, and they were in general agreement. The United Kingdom was not included because they had displayed an obvious bias in favour of the Islanders, and it was better to poll only neutral countries.

On learning this, Creswell launched into a bitter invective about the manipulation of the European block vote in a dangerously undemocratic way. He then launched into a pet subject of his: about the way the European Parliament was unduly influenced by a small club of nations, which excluded democracy for the countries outside that club who were after all the majority. His protests once more fell on deaf ears, and Savollard and his selected cronies continued to hold sway by manipulating the voting system.

By contrast, his telephone conversation with Gilliland was most congenial. They exchanged pleasantries and caught up on news since their last conversation. Gilliland was patient and did not press Creswell for the real reason for the call. Ultimately, the conversation turned to the mistrust between the Federation and the Island. Creswell did his best to represent the Federation in a good light, trying to assuage the Islanders' mistrust of Federation's intentions, but no matter how hard he tried, he could not get Gilliland to soften his approach to denouement.

It was with a great sense of unease that he broached the subject of the potential next steps in the Federation's quest to pursue the capture of Island technology. He felt as though he were being traitorous by saying anything at all, but at the same time, he felt obliged to return the assistance they had given him even though in the end, he had not needed their assistance. He shared the information that Latimer had been found wanting in his handling of the last abortive mission and that he had been sidelined to a shore position as punishment for his failure to handle the situation with sufficient sensitivity. He insisted that this had been done in the interest of harmony between the two factions and that even now the Chinese specialists were considering ways of bringing both parties together in a mutually beneficial way.

Gilliland's response to the overture was disappointing; he clearly still took a jaundiced view of any approach by the Federation, and try as he might, Creswell was unable to promote any movement in what he now looked upon as an intransigent stance. They sparred a little more in a good-natured exchange, but it was obvious to them both that the gulf between their positions was actually a chasm. After failing in a further attempt to heal the rift between Gilliland and Wilson, Creswell ended the call and decided that discretion was the better part of valour.

Gilliland spoke with Caine soon after the call and gave her a precis of the conversation. She sounded glum and talked more about a modification of the Stockholm syndrome which, in her opinion, was still Creswell's problem with regard to Wilson. Clearly, his sudden and unexpected release from what could have been a spectacular if untrue revelation that would certainly have led to his impeachment had clouded his better judgement. He had completely overlooked the fact that the evidence against him was entirely manufactured and appeared to look upon Wilson as his saviour rather than, as was the truth, his destroyer.

Thirty-One

Nematasulu's approximately square land mass borders on the Atlantic to the west and is dissected by the, renamed, Otomolo River. Its other three borders are at right angles to each other, and each border was, since the aftermath of the global crash, a new self-governing African country. At sixteen hundred square miles, Nematasulu is small and but for the support of Recovery Island would have been vulnerable to seizure by the surrounding countries.

The Otomolo River, just thirty-five miles long, rises in the mountains at the eastern border and tumbles spectacularly down the mountainside to the lowland slopes and plains and ultimately to the sea. The fresh water flowing from the mountains meets the salt water of the Atlantic up to ten miles from the estuary. In Africa, water is at a premium, and the Nematasulu people are forced to defend themselves against the greater and better-equipped forces of their neighbours.

When Tembo Mbunani negotiated trade deals with Recovery Island, he had assumed that they would be provided protection by way of arms and related military paraphernalia. To his surprise, arms were not a part of the agreement, but Gilliland assuaged his fears by promising him a defence shield, which would not kill his enemies unless they wanted to commit suicide by trying to breach the defences.

Clearly, a forty-mile diameter BAM2 dome would reach up to twenty miles into the atmosphere and would leave the corners of the country unprotected, neither of which was palatable and each of which would infringe international liberty. Crook, as part of developing their technology, had modified a BAM2 projector by manipulating each of the minute diamond projector nodes so that its projected distance could be changed to enable the shape of the dome to be modified to suit the border configuration and to reduce its zenith to an acceptable height not to interfere with legitimate aviation. The shield was also fitted with the anti-bird system, developed by the Recovery Island engineers, to prevent what the development engineers had termed it "anti-birdicide."

Pickering was sent to Nematasulu to install the defence shield and to supervise the building of a perimeter defence to keep out animals and unwanted people alike. He decided that the task would be well served by boring a twenty-foot-wide ditch to follow the contours of the country's boundary around the outside of the shaped defence cover. The finings from the construction of the ditch were used, mixed with cement, to build the fifteen-foot high perimeter wall.

His first construction task was to fix the centre point of the defence dome using GPS. Having established the centre, an underground bunker was constructed to house the BAM2 projector with its solar power panels and a back-up power source. Bulldozers were used to clear the twenty-foot wide strip of land on which the ring ditch would be sited in order to prevent harm to the indigenous animal life contained within it.

The profile of the ditch was plotted relative to the level of the BAM2 projector and the segments of the projector were set to the correct heights to follow the uneven terrain from mountain down through the plains down to coast level. The projector was then set to the inside profile of the ditch and switched on so that the base of the protective cover was some five foot below the terrain level, and the cover was then moved outwards by twenty feet, and this created a ditch twenty-foot wide and five-foot deep.

The simplicity of the operation never ceased to amaze Pickering. BAM2 technology had produced the ditch template, after the clearance of the land, in something like five minutes. Building the wall would take significantly longer because they thought it prudent not to use BAM2 and magma but to use more old-fashioned lift and grunt technology. The one hundred plus mile wall took six months and a legion of labour, which was sourced from Nematasulu and its surrounding countries.

Warnings were sent out to all neighbouring countries as well as to the Federation and to all airlines, advising them when the defence system was to be activated, and that there was danger of death and destruction of all materials living or inert. There was an almost immediate negative response from the neighbouring countries and the Federation and a slower response from Russia and other remote countries that were not directly affected.

Pickering set about responding to some of the objections, specifically those from the immediate neighbours who expressed concern about their citizens and wildlife wandering across the border inadvertently. The Federation had an entirely different agenda; their objections were expressed with indignation as though they had been specifically insulted. Pickering constructed the replies, which were sent out by Tembo Mbunani in his capacity of Homeland Minister.

The responses to neighbouring countries, and those not directly affected outlined the precautions taken to protect people and wildlife. The twenty-foot wide by five-foot deep ditch would deter even the most uncomprehending visitor, human or otherwise, and flying beasts were warned off by the use of the sonic repellent which caused mild panic but little else. Response to the Federation was more specific; it was pointed out to the President of the Federation that what happened within the borders of Nematasulu was a matter for domestic consideration and that Nematasulu did not fall under the jurisdiction of the Federation.

Five days after the switch on of the new defence system, Pickering left the Island via the new airport located in the south-west of the country, which was outside the main defence cover and had its own separate and independent protective cover. Access to the airport was by a tunnel, which ran from under the dome and beneath the ring ditch to the terminal buildings. Although outside the main defence dome, the airfield had its own mini dome should the need ever arise to repel invaders.

Overtures were made by both neighbouring and distant countries, once they realised that Nematasulu was unilaterally independent, expressing a sudden interest and the newly autonomous country was bombarded with offers of material and materiel assistance of which, ironically, they no longer had a pressing need. All offers were repulsed by the government of Nematasulu, who relished their new-found popularity but were not deceived by the reasons behind the philanthropy suddenly shown by former detractors.

As the coast of Nematasulu disappeared behind the modified Apache Chieftain jetliner, Pickering relaxed with a generous glass of single malt, a case of which had been presented to him by the President of Nematasulu for services rendered. Modifications had been made to the previously sleek jetliner to safeguard against the devastating effects of the failure in flight of the plane's single tail-mounted engine. Ingenious engineering had gone into providing safety in the event of malfunction of the single engine in flight and additional moulded capsules had been added to the upper wing surfaces and the upper and lower fuselage. In the event of failure, the shaped capsules would open up away from the fuselage and wings, powered by hydraulic rams, and would deploy ram air parachute pockets, similar to those used by precision display parachutists. This would allow the disabled craft to glide back to earth with a degree of, somewhat inelegant, control by the pilot. Landing almost vertically at twenty miles an hour would prove too much for the airframe but would at least give the passengers a good chance of survival.

Working away from his Island home was not something Pickering enjoyed especially as his wife Bella had not accompanied him on this particular time extended trip. They talked daily by satellite phone, but it was not a substitute to being with his wife of twenty years. He leaned back in his comfortable seat and rolled his head to look out of the small oval window at the sparkling blue green Atlantic below.

Far below a tiny freighter ploughed its way westward, leaving behind a white wake tinged with green which slowly dissolved back into the ocean mass and was no more, it was as if it had never been. The ocean's self-healing power demonstrated, quite simply, how easily Mother Nature overcomes the puny efforts of man to disrupt the natural order of things.

Something flashed across Pickering's line of sight, and in an instant was gone; he shook his head as if to clear his vision of the fleeting apparition. Moments later, he saw a more lasting image of what was a Mirage Proteus Fedro-Fighter, the pride of the Federation Air Force, as it banked around behind the Apache, in line astern. Three other fighters appeared, two on one side and one on the other, and they too swung round behind the Apache and then spread out so that they had an escort of four fighters in V-formation with the Apache as the arrowhead. The sudden appearance of the Fedro-Fighters over the open Atlantic came as no surprise to Pickering. In fact, he was almost disappointed at the predictability of the Federation's actions. Adie Cox, the Apache's pilot, burst out of the flight deck, looking wild-eyed, and he ran breathlessly to where Pickering sat transfixed. "Ed, you have to come to the flight deck and listen to what these crazy people are saying."

Once he was on the cramped flight deck, Pickering listened through headphones to the instructions from one of the Federation pilots and was alarmed by the overt threats to their lives. Although the actions of the Federation had been anticipated, it had not been presumed that they intended the immediate use of lethal force. He did his best to delay their action by adopting a forceful response, but it was to no avail.

"*i . . . mmediately and descend to five thousand metres.*" The heavily accented oriental voice spoke in flat unfeeling tones. "*I repeat. You are in contravention of aviation laws and must return to the mainland. You will be escorted to the Federation airbase in Western Nigeria where all contraband freight will be confiscated. Follow the fighter escort and reduce your airspeed to four hundred kilometres per hour. You must do so immediately and descend to five thousand metres.*" This was said hesitantly as if the message were being read.

"*Who are you?*" Pickering shouted into the transmitter.

"*Federation Air Force.*" The response was staccato and flat.

"*You have no jurisdiction over us, and we are in international air space which you do not control.*" As he said this, he fully realised that he was completely out of his depth and that thought was frightening. How should he handle this? He had to make an instant decision, and he thought rapidly that he could handle it like Chester, with emotion powering his thought processes or maybe like Silas who was cold, calm, and logical. He took on the guise and persona of Silas Pettit.

"*This is air piracy! We will not comply with your wishes. It is our intention to continue on our lawful way.*"

"*The Federation not to recognise you rights.*" The Federation spokesman mangled his reply which had obviously not been rehearsed.

"*Our rights are international, and we will continue with our, peaceful, planned flight.*"

"To continuing is not possible to follow us is must. We have orders to shoot you down if you refuse to comply." This statement was clearly structured and had obviously been rehearsed at some length.

"This is a civilian aircraft, and we are unarmed. You have obviously mistaken us for somebody else. We are continuing on our journey—this is not a matter for discussion." Pickering continued with what he thought was a Pettit-like statement.

Thirty seconds later, the escorts peeled away to port and starboard and flew a convoluted pattern to bring two of the fighters to within a mile, one on either side, flying towards them. Simultaneously, the rockets under their wings ignited and headed for the Apache trailing plumes of dense white vapour.

Their carefully designed and tested Stratosphere Floatation System (SFS) was of no value in this situation. The SFS was only designed to recover the aircraft in the event of engine damage or failure. A direct hit from the missiles carried by the Fedro-Fighter would destroy the SFS, the airframe, and the passengers and the crew. The missiles were launched, and their fate was sealed.

They were thousands of miles away from home and hundreds of miles west of the African coast. They had no parachutes except the retro-fitted fuselage and wing floaters which would be useless when the missiles struck, and the Apache disintegrated. Beneath them, the ocean was deserted except for the lone freighter which would be too far away to be of any assistance even if they did manage to survive the missiles and the uncontrolled crash into the unyielding sea either or both of which would without doubt claim their lives.

"Oh my God," the co-pilot croaked, his face in a rictus of horror, "they're going to murder us."

The process of air intimidation was observed remotely in the Recovery Island's sophisticated radar control room in which they had watched their aircraft take off from Nematasulu and commence its journey home across the Atlantic. They had also observed the formation of smaller aircraft approach their aircraft and had heard the threatening language of the Federation aircraft, and they heard Adie Cox shout in alarm that they were being fired upon.

Acting in accordance with the procedure dictated by Pettit, they activated the remote self-defence mechanism (SDM). The instruction travelling along a carrier wave at the speed of light took a fraction of a second to reach the control processor on the Apache Chieftain. The processor activated the on-board security sealed BAM2 unit which immediately encapsulated the aircraft in a spherical force field a fraction of a second before the arrival of the missiles fired from the Fedro-Fighters.

Adie Cox and the co-pilot watched at first in horror and then in fascination as the smoke trail emitted by the missiles suddenly in a brief flash of light, stopped forming. The voice of the Recovery Island controller in his headphones told him what had happened. His relief was so all-consuming that he was for a moment unable to respond. When he did, his language was such that it was sure to feature on the bloopers tape which was produced for the Island's Christmas entertainment.

Pickering looked pale and drawn. He had made sure that the time of their take-off from Nematasulu had been transmitted to Recovery Island control and that they would be able to activate the remote SDM, should it be required. There were two unknowns to this back-up plan: that in the fraction of time between the firing of the missiles and their arrival at their intended target would give a radar observer time to activate the SDM and that there was actually a watcher who was actually looking during that split second of time. Further, even if the watcher watched, whether the signal would be successfully received by the on-board SDM—it had never been tested over such a distance.

With a hiss, Pickering released his breath, which he had subconsciously been holding during the supercharged seconds that the incident had taken place. Perspiration beaded on his forehead, and his shoulders slumped. He was, he thought wryly, not a man of action and was also not built for this kind of explosive tension; he felt drained and extremely thankful to the President of Nematasulu for the donation of single malt.

He had, of course, been aware of the SDM, having been instrumental in its conception, although it had been completed and installed by others. It was still a matter of absolute amazement to him that BAM2 actually worked the first time it had been used in anger. Its simplicity and unerring reliability flew in the face of all his considerable engineering experience, but he realised there was still work to be done. They would have to remove the human observation element from the equation: it was too risky. He felt a deep chill as he realised that their lives had rested on the ability of a single, obviously well trained, observer. His integrity had saved their lives.

Thirty-Two

*S*imon Queeze watched as the ancient ex-Aeroflot freight aircraft made an uncertain attempt at a glide path into the single runway of the disused military airfield in the Chilean Mountains. He felt nervous as he studied the approach because he perceived that they were too low and would undershoot the runway by a considerable distance. The aircraft followed its low trajectory, and now it appeared to be travelling so slowly that it must surely stall. It lumbered on barely making the leading end of the runway where it flopped like an ungainly brown pelican, its wings flapping up and down unsynchronised.

The night was filled with the banshee shrieking of the six propellers as they were feathered and then set into reverse. The brakes were applied and added their grinding and squealing to the cacophony of the propellers. It soon became obvious why the pilot was making such a performance of the landing as the lumbering beast trundled in slow motion towards the end of the runway which was obviously too short to comfortably accommodate an aircraft of this size and vintage. It shuddered to a halt barely two fuselage lengths from the end of the runway where it settled down in what looked like a terminal resting place. The crew descended from the belly of the aircraft, speaking loudly in Russian and smoking great

Churchillian cigars. They completely ignored the danger of the stench of kerosene that seemed to seep from the pores of the sagging aircraft.

The rear cargo door of the transporter was dropped opened by one of the boisterous crew members who had remained on board, and it hit the rough tarmac with a bone jarring clang. A tractor was run up the ramp and emerged minutes later with a four-wheeled bogie, carrying the large stainless steel cylinder that had been worked on at the Agricultural Centre in Nuovostan. It was hastily transported to the hangar containing the modified bomber, and the doors were closed firmly behind it.

One of the transporter's crew, who was slightly less disreputable than the rest, accompanied the bogie into the vast cavern of the hangar. He watched the mechanics manhandle the cylinder into the jaws projecting from the belly of the aircraft and saw them close around it with an audible snap. At a signal from the crew member, the jaws were disengaged, and they snapped open with enough force to make the aircraft rock on its undercarriage. He nodded his head in approval and signalled for the jaws to be locked again and when this was completed, the cylinder was lifted off the bogie, which was moved away by the mechanics.

The visiting crew member undid a panel at one end of the cylinder and opened an inspection hatch. He plugged in a portable computer tablet and entered a series of commands which he checked with Queeze at each stage. Queeze nodded his agreement. When the exercise was completed, Queeze was presented with a simple remote control device similar to that used for opening a garage door. He was given some instructions, which he had to repeat several times until the crew member was satisfied that Queeze understood the mechanics of its operation by rote.

Having completed his allotted task, the crew member rejoined his colleagues, and they all piled into what had once been a sleek people carrier which was driven by the air freighter captain. The vehicle left the airfield, weaving an erratic course between oil drums and other assorted debris, which littered the uneven ground. After they left, an almost unnatural silence descended over the hangar and its environs. The mechanics operated the electric hoists that lifted the cylinder into the aircraft, and the bay doors closed silently behind it. It was now ready for deadly action.

Thirty-Three

*T*he Ruling Council was aware that the lull in activity was not cause for celebration. It emulated what at the time of World War II was called the phoney war, and to the council, it was a time of great concern. For the people of the Island it was a time to turn a deaf ear to the dangers that lay ahead, a time in which the pace of life was artificially increased to compensate for the anxiety which, otherwise, would have prevailed. They stayed out later in the evenings and ate and drank more than they normally would. They craved comfort and a place to hide from their fears.

In contrast, the scientists, engineers, and researchers immersed themselves in projects for which the funds provided had been made virtually limitless. These were the groups of people who had been instrumental in the building and equipping of the Island and who for three years had worked to almost impossible deadlines. When their work was essentially completed, they had fallen into a vacuum and had slowed down to the generally relaxed pace of the Island. Now, during this unreal period, they were reactivated and threw themselves into their work and special projects with a new-found energy that was palpable.

One of the projects carried out by Dr Carlina Tanterelli, the study of body regeneration, started with the simple observation of how the body performs in healing itself when it has been damaged: repairs such as the knitting of broken bones and the closing and sealing of damaged skin and tissue. At the other end of the natural recovery scale was the ability of a damaged liver to repair itself even without medical intervention. The intention was, once the mechanism of healing had been identified, to apply the understanding to all degenerative ailments, perhaps even as far as the regrowing of lost limbs.

Such commendable research was not without its controversy. In the early days, animal testing was used incurring the wrath of a group of preservationists. The Ruling Council stayed out of the argument and allowed the protagonists and objectors to find a mutually satisfactory solution. They did so by agreeing that disposable stem cells, such as those discarded during the birthing process and those that could be made artificially, could be used to produce the tissue used in experimentation.

Stem cells produced in the Island Hospital Maternity Unit by natural process of birthing procedure were supplemented by a culturing programme which made up the shortfall. No cells were harvested from the newborn babies, but they were garnered from the birth residue which would otherwise have been discarded and lost. The council did intervene when this agreed move was challenged by a small group of zealots who tried to insist that cultured tissue constituted a living organism, which was based on humankind, and, therefore, could not be used.

All children born on the Island were by right Recovery Island Nationals (RINs). Parents of the children were encouraged to ensure that their children would claim and register the nationality or nationalities of their parents who were themselves naturalised RINs. The first Island-born child, that arrived very early in the Island's development, was celebrated by making the day of his birth a national holiday which was called First Citizen's Day. The child was given the name Primo by his Italian parents.

The continuing frenzy of therapeutic work led to all maintenance being ahead of schedule. The streets were squeaky clean, and the smell of fresh paint was everywhere. Grass verges were trimmed, the goods on the market shelves lined up with military precision, and the Transfer Cars and stations cleaned and repainted. When all of these things were complete, some were started again. Very soon, the work dried up and, apart from the scientists and engineers, the population threw itself into physical activities of all types. Ball games, rock climbing, running Island circuits, surfing, sail boarding, and weight lifting were pursued with an alien fanaticism.

Gilliland, Crook, and Caine toured the Island, taking stock of the mood of the population. Caine expressed concern at the wild-eyed energy with which the people of the Island were inventing and fulfilling tasks to fill their minds. Caine expressed concern that the population was running out of plausible distractions and that the overspill of nervous energy could lead to serious civil unrest.

*

The cockpit of the unmarked military aircraft was suffused in an unreal light that made ghouls of the five-man crew even though half their faces were covered by oxygen masks. They were all concentrating hard on the instruments before them, making sure that the airframe and the engines were up to the task of flying at forty-five thousand feet, considerably above the original design ceiling for the aircraft. At this altitude, the engine note sounded strange, and there were unfamiliar creaks and groans whispering through the shuddering airframe.

They concentrated to the exclusion of all other thoughts even the thought of what the American dollars that each man was being paid for the mission would buy for them; it represented the equivalent of five years of their normal wage—tax-free. Nothing could be seen in the darkness below as they traversed the Atlantic, and their target was so small that without the addition of the GPS screen to the otherwise antiquated navigation aids, their task would have been impossible.

Before they had taken off, they were briefed in detail by the strange, bearded, Englishman with scary dark eyes, who had addressed them through an interpreter in the interests of three of the crew who spoke no English. The coordinates of the target were keyed into the GPS, which comprised two windows, one giving their present location and the other the target location.

Taking off was simple if somewhat nerve-racking as the ancient, lumbering aircraft used the full length of the runway before finally inching its way into the air. It took four hours to gain the desired altitude and a further four hours to reach the predetermined destination. Airspeed was decreased, and the wind direction and speed together with the height were fed into a small but powerful processor. The current location window on the GPS screen rolled to an ever-updating set of coordinates which glowed green in the dim lighting. Careful manoeuvring of the controls by the pilot brought the current location window into line with the target location, which turned the current and target location figures blood-red.

The pilot smiled an evil humourless smile as he manoeuvred the aircraft beyond the target location until the red numerals turned to green again. He switched the voice transmitter on and said in heavily accented English. *"Project leader, we are over target and window of opportunity is two kilometres, permission for continuing over."* He listened intently to the response and nodded to himself and the crew.

Easing the aircraft into a long lazy arc, he straightened out and flew steady and level, watching the GPS screen intently as the two sets of numbers began to merge, the numerals once more turned red. They flew for one further kilometre, and the loadmaster, who sat in the cold and noisy fuselage, depressed the handheld button connected by umbilical to the cylinder held in the belly of the aircraft. With barely a moment of hesitation, the cylinder dropped into the inky darkness. The aircraft lurched upwards and was immediately manoeuvred into a tight one-hundred and eighty-degree turn, and at the same time, the nose was dropped and the aircraft went into a steep dive. Down below them the darkness was penetrated by four separate flashes of strobe light, which repeated three times and then ceased to function.

The pilot let out a noisy sigh, releasing the tension of the last few minutes; he activated his transmitter once more. *"Project leader, cargo is gone, and strobes confirm that all four parachutes are deployed. Mission is completed, and we returning to home."* The pilot listened to the response and then switched to intercom mode and announced to the crew in Russian, "Mission complete. We're on our way home. Open the vodka and let's celebrate." He winced at the excited shouts that crackled through his earphones.

Queeze's shoulders slumped in relief when he heard that the mission had been completed, and he grimaced at the excited shouts of the crew as they prepared to celebrate. He listened to their intercom chatter which, because they didn't know he was able to hear them, when they assumed that the radio transmitter was switched off, was in a mixture of Russian and Spanish.

They had been instructed to fly back at forty-five thousand feet to avoid, they were told, detection by the Islanders. Queeze sat smugly listening to them as he counted the seconds to their demise. What they also didn't know was that the hand switch that had released the cylinder also started a timer which was set to detonate an explosive charge, located in the tail section by Queeze's other hangar team, which would cause catastrophic frame failure that would rip the craft apart. He listened to the excited chatter over his headphones; there was a brief crack and then, save for white noise, silence.

Queeze removed his headphones; he looked at his wristwatch, counting down. "That's it," he said to the empty room. "It will have gone off by now. An air burst of a neutron bomb over the Island, which will have killed all the inhabitants and would leave the infrastructure intact. Job done, the Islanders are no more." He revelled in his success.

*

Wilson, having later analysed the intelligence reports, sat back in his chair and admired the subtleness of the plan which could not be traced back to him—unless, of course, he wanted it to; his plan was brilliant, he mused. The neutron bomb, which he had financed, had killed off the population without harming the infrastructure. He had also cleverly and anonymously orchestrated the blowing up of the delivery aircraft and its crew, effectively disposing of the evidence of his crime. None of what had happened could be traced back to him.

For good measure, he let it be known that the downing of the aircraft was caused by the aggressive action of the renegade Islanders. It would also be revealed that due to a catastrophic failure in their equipment when they blew up the aircraft the entire population had been killed by a powerful pulse of radiation. This cause of death would be verified by his specially selected task force who would land on and take over the Island.

He was in real-time communication with the two landing craft which were heading towards the Island. He ordered their mother ship to launch a UAV to fly at one thousand feet over the Island to make sure that the Island's defences were inactive. It flew over the Island at one thousand feet and then returned at five hundred feet completely unscathed. He ordered the thirty men on each landing craft to don their anti-radiation suits in readiness for occupying and securing the Island. The lead landing craft commander reported to Wilson that there were no signs of resistance, or in fact, any signs of life on the shore except for all the lights being on in the buildings and on the street which was strange because it was well past dawn, and the day was bright.

He gave a sigh of relief when he was informed that the UAV had confirmed the defences were down and that the two landing craft could take the Island unopposed. His plan had worked like a dream, and he would soon be master of the Island and all its technology. What passed for a grin flitted across his face, all the planning was paying off. He had neutralised the British Prime Minister, fooled the Chinese into thinking that he would share the technology with them, and most important of all he would have the Broken Arrow technology. He all but had his own form of the technology, and the only others who knew about BAM2 were now dead. The world and all it contained would soon be in his control.

Thirty-Four

At the same time that Wilson had been sitting and anticipating the outcome of the new cunning attack he had masterminded on the Island, the watchers in the Recovery Island's control room, still jittery from the previous attack from the Federation Air Force, were on adrenalin-heightened alert. Three of them sat looking intently at the HMTs, watching the progress of a lone aircraft approaching them from the west. It was a high flyer at forty-five thousand feet and was only of interest because it was flying so slowly and was not following a usual trans-Atlantic course. Their interest quickened as it began to manoeuvre from its course and described a wide arc, and they placed a marker on the holographic image to record its trajectory.

"Sir," the senior watcher called to Pettit, who was in conversation with the three relief watchers at a briefing table, "I think you should see this." He pointed at the HMT.

Pettit watched intently as a line trace initiated by the watcher showed the erratic course of the passing craft. "Increase the resolution," his voice was terse.

The section of the sky occupied by the aircraft was holographically magnified and high-resolution NRT was deployed automatically. The image of the aircraft became better defined as the magnification increased, and the path of the aircraft straightened out, and it flew true and level for a mile or more before peeling off to retrace its original route. The watcher reached forward to switch off the magnification.

"No," Pettit shouted, "leave it on. Look." He pointed to a secondary trace line which had split from the main line. It was much fainter than the aircraft trace, and it was losing height rapidly as if in free fall. "More resolution," he said urgently, "maximum and now."

"Fully cranked, sir."

They all watched the second trace of the smaller object and saw it fall rapidly from forty-five thousand feet to thirty thousand at which point its descent slowed dramatically and the shape of the object changed.

"What do you make of that?" Pettit muttered softly not really expecting an answer. He looked intently at the shape on the magnified screen. "At this resolution, what size do you think the object is?"

"Difficult to be exact at this distance without doing some calculations." The watcher was cautious.

"Okay, well . . . , be exact."

"My guess is that it's about ten foot long and five foot wide, give or take, but I have no idea what the four long spiky things sticking out of the ends are."

Pettit looked at the trace of the object and saw that its descent was now steady and that it had changed course and was drifting straight towards the Island. Alarm bells were ringing in his head as he watched the progress of the object in the sky, and it was drifting on the wind.

"I'll be damned," the watcher hissed and pointed to the back-up scope which was not magnified and where the dotted trace line of the departing aircraft had ceased abruptly in a splash of diffused light which slowed and spread as it lost altitude. "The aircraft—it's blown up!"

Pettit's alarm bells reached a crescendo as he absorbed the information. "The thing with four spikes is falling in a controlled manner." He screwed up his face in concentration and in his mind ran through a series of alternatives as to what the object could be. His thoughts were translated into words, "The spikes look like they are parachutes and four of them indicates that whatever it is must be heavy or at least precious. If it is heavy, at that volume, it must be machinery because people wouldn't have mass enough to require four parachutes of that size and, any way, it's not big enough to carry people. It's being carried towards us by the wind."

"That means," the watcher joined in with the solitary conversation, "given the direction of the jet stream pushing it towards us and its current rate of descent, it will pass directly over the Island at about fifteen thousand feet."

"Now why would anybody send something over the Island in the dead of night to pass over the top?"

"Maybe a leaflet drop?" The watcher was not convinced or convincing.

"Way too complicated to be that." Pettit's face was wooden. "Whatever it is, it can't be good news. And what about the aircraft that dropped it? Why the hell did it blow up?" He continued to watch the floating object. "How long do you think it will take to reach us?"

"At the current trajectory, I estimate probably six to eight minutes."

Five minutes later a radio operator walked towards Pettit with remote operation earphones "You'd better listen to this, Mr Pettit." He handed the earphones to him.

"*International terrorism.*" Pettit recognised the voice of Wilson immediately, even through the mushy static. "*It is regrettable that this self-appointed renegade community have perpetrated this gross act of murder because they cannot get their own way. The attack on an unarmed commercial freight plane is indefensible and will not go unpunished, the Federation of Nations' Grand Council have determined that the Island will be sequestered using whatever means are at our disposal, and that the perpetrators of this foul act will be brought to book. The next of kin of the aircrew are being advised of the murder of their family members. You will be kept up to date with the actions being taken and occupation of the Island is imminent.*"

Thirty-Five

*P*ettit removed the earphones and took one further look at the scope showing the descending object. He moved from the NRT radar desk to the BAM2 console adjacent to it. With deft strokes on the keyboard, he linked the two systems together and the trajectory of the object was mimicked by the BAM2 screen. The object was at twenty thousand feet and was about five miles to the north of the Island and travelling due south with an ETA over the Island of four minutes.

Pettit telephoned Gilliland. His call was not answered. He tried Crook, and the result was the same. He glanced at his watch, ETA was now three minutes, and taking a deep breath, he connected BAM2 to the NRT carrier wave and pressed the trace projection button.

The object disappeared immediately from the screen in a multi-coloured blaze, which was quite startling. Whatever it was, it was no longer a threat.

"What was that?" The watcher turned his startled face to Pettit.

"Not something I've ever seen before," Pettit responded while picking up the telephone again.

"Crook," his sleepy mumble whispered through the earpiece.

"Bruce, it's Silas," he paused to allow Crook to emerge more fully to wakefulness. Part-way through outlining the event, Crook stopped him and said that he and Gilliland would be in the control room as soon as possible.

Crook looked wild-eyed as he ran into the room and hurried over to the BAM2 console and began typing hastily. He accessed an executive programme and keyed in spectrum analysis on rerun. The screen jumped back to the aircraft trace shortly after the launch of the so far unidentified object. The image suddenly flared and broke up leaving a yellow and brown stain, which he froze on the screen. He isolated the flare and gave the command to analyse the multicoloured smudge, and as he did so, a visual spectrometer icon appeared on the screen together with a timing strip graduated from 0 to 100 per cent. As the strip crept slowly towards completion, Gilliland appeared looking, characteristically, calm and collected. He was apprised of the situation, and they all looked at the time strip as it reached 100 per cent and faded to be replaced by a histogram.

It fell upon Crook to interpret the findings of the spectrometer. He frowned in concentration. "I can't possibly identify the readings without using reference tables, but the histogram shows metal alloys, plastics, and natural things like wood and textiles. There's a lot of aviation fuel and, sadly, evidence of human debris all wrapped up in strong evidence of explosives, probably Semtex." He returned to the keyboard. "Now let's see what happened next." He repeated the previous search, but this time concentrated on the parachuted object. As before, he isolated the image at the time it was obliterated by Pettit's activation of a BAM2 beam and set the mass spectrometer searching.

Both Gilliland and Crook looked puzzled at the misty red stain that appeared. Neither of them could recognise the multicoloured pattern produced as representing any of the groups of elements that they had programmed exhaustively, they thought, into the machine.

"Oh, wow!" Crook expostulated as he studied the histogram produced and enlarged one of the elements to identify it against the periodic table.

"It's a bit like the other explosion, except for the human elements, but it has one scary difference. It has fissile material, and as far as I can tell, this was a nuclear device. Somebody was trying to kill us, and there's no prize for guessing who. That doesn't make any sense though if they blow us up, they'll get no technology." He scratched his head in puzzlement and then suddenly brightened. "That's it," he shouted. "It was an air detonated neutron bomb. It would kill the inhabitants by radiation pulse but leave the infrastructure intact but because we vapourised it before it was detonated there was no radiation pulse to harm us and the debris of the deconstructed bomb was taken away on the westerly air stream."

Pettit stepped forward and looked haunted. "Gentlemen, sad to say, but we are now, without a doubt, at all-out, fully committed war with the Federation of Nations." His face was grim in the eerie green glow of the scopes. "We must immediately open up all incoming communication avenues and close down all outgoing comms, except from the two senior executives." He looked to Gilliland and Crook, who nodded their concurrence. He crossed the room and opened up the defence computer, which controlled the total Island's defence package. No physical item could enter or leave the Island while the defence dome was activated. Much to the surprise of all those present, he deactivated the defences.

"Somebody will be presuming that we are all dead from catastrophic radiation exposure," Pettit shuddered as he said it. "They will also be assuming that they will be able to take the Island without opposition. I suggest we let them approach us to find out who they are, Federation, Wilson, or somebody else and take it from there."

Thirty-Six

*T*he Islanders were woken up before sunrise by a shrill warning alarm, and their information ports had been activated automatically. The message it gave was simple and to the point

We have repulsed an attack by the Federation, and our Island is now in lock down. There is no immediate danger of further attack. The news channel will be continuously updated as more information is to hand.

Until further notice, outgoing communications are blocked. The ruling council is in permanent session and will remain so until this matter is resolved.

Apart from the communication restrictions, you are required to stay indoors—no outside movement is to be undertaken and any exterior lights which are on are to be left on. All animals are to be kept indoors until further notice. These restrictions are most important, and no transgressions will be permitted on pain of permanent exclusion from the Island.

Please acknowledge the receipt of this message to return your information ports to normal usage.

An expectant quiet settled over the Island as the inhabitants read the instructions and acted accordingly. The restaurants, cafes, and bars were populated by those either finishing a late shift or starting an early one. Conversation was stilted and muted. The utilities and services were manned by maintenance crews who kept the Island's lifeblood circulating.

Incoming news picked up exclusively by the control office was frantic and contradictory, reporting at the same time that the Island had been invaded and taken over by the Special Federation Forces, (SFF), or that it had been bombarded by the Navy and Air Force to make way for an invasion by a landing craft. It was also reported that a stricken civilian aircraft had been brought down by a nuclear ground-to-air missile fired from the Island and that radiation had been detected in the atmosphere and was being carried towards northern Europe by the jet stream. There was a demand by the Federation for the plethora of non-aligned governments to support the Federation efforts by pledging their support in whatever action the Federation deemed necessary to ensure world stability.

The Russian President stated that the use of nuclear force against the Island would be considered as an act of war against an ally of Mother Russia and nuclear retaliation would ensue if such liberties continued. Russia also offered the might of their armed forces in defence of the Island and any Islanders against the colonial aspirations of the Federation, and that as a sign of good faith towards the Islanders, the Russian Navy would be carrying out manoeuvres in the North Atlantic in readiness to come to their assistance should it be necessary.

Wilson thought it satisfactory in the extreme that the Russians were coming to the aid of any survivors. It was an act which would be a distraction for the Federation and would leave the field for Wilson's invading force less likely to be interfered with by the Federation. He also revelled in the realisation that he had by fortunate circumstance given his own special forces such a head start that they would be occupying the Island before the Russian fleet had cleared their ports to engage with the distracted Federation. He had supplied his task force with radiation hazard suits for their protection when landing, telling them that the Islanders would not be armed but that he had information that they were using domestic nuclear material that was not being managed correctly. Once they had landed and had discovered the dead Islanders, he would advise the world that the Island's dictatorship had caused the death of their own nation by resorting to nuclear profligacy.

*

The watchers were now working in six four-hour shifts because of the concentration needed to interpret all sea and air movements which could be a danger to the Island. In the early morning hours after the night attack, which they presumed was the work of the Federation, a large naval vessel was detected disgorging two smaller vessels at some twelve miles from the Island.

Pettit, Gilliland, and Crook were summoned to the control room to observe the movements. The two detached vessels began moving towards the Island at a speed which the watcher estimated would mean an ETA of some forty minutes. Pettit ordered a crew of three to board and make ready *Wallow 5* fully shrouded for protection and to be battle-ready at a covert location in the protection of the harbour. They carried out the orders and waited.

The appearance of a UAV caused a moment of concern. At one thousand feet elevation, it would have been vapourised had the defensive dome been in active mode and would have alerted the incoming vessels had Pettit not had the operational forethought to disable it earlier. He observed that with such a small, undisguised force, it was obvious that the Federation force clearly expected no resistance. This on its own, he thought but did not say, indicated that the bomb they had sent was a neutron device and had been intended to kill the inhabitants without harming the infrastructure.

Crook sent out a repeat message to all information ports and personal telephones and public broadcasting systems that all internal communications on the Island should cease and that all signs of life on the Island were to be masked. All personnel and animals were to be kept indoors or under cover and that all visible night-time lights were to be left switched on.

*

The lead landing craft forged steadily ahead, and the commander of the vessel scanned the Island as they approached within one kilometre of the harbour wall. There were still no signs of life, and there appeared to be no indication of resistance; he reported his latest observations to Wilson. Used as he was to following orders without question, the commander could not help wondering what was going on. Eighty fully armed insurgency specialists were being sent to occupy the Island which, as far as he could tell, had no firearms to repel borders but which had a devastating defensive weapon which was not being deployed in the face of what was obviously a hostile landing.

Despite Wilson's assurances that the Islanders were incapacitated by a radiation accident, the commander exercised extreme caution as they entered the harbour. The flotilla entered the harbour unchallenged. A sweep of the binoculars showed no movement, and to his surprise, the Geiger counters registered only the low background radiation that would be expected of a volcanic Island. As he reached for his radio to report these unexpected findings to Wilson, the rusting hulk of *Wallow 5* rolled into view looking comically incongruous to the crews of their sturdy landing craft.

The commander froze as he saw that there was a circle of bright water around the ungainly boat and then there appeared a larger ring which encompassed the Federation vessels. He clutched the radio and shouted to Wilson that all was not well. He received no response other than the slushy background noise of a jammed signal, changing channels, and he endeavoured to contact the other landing craft but was unable to do so—they too were radio jammed. He was suddenly aware of instructions being given through a loud hailer that told the invaders to stay at close quarters and not under any circumstances to cross the outer ring.

Furious at the deception, the commander bellowed to the men with the heavier calibre guns to open fire and sink *Wallow 5*, and the cacophony was deafening as they followed his orders. The assault troops, who had no knowledge of the power of BAM2, stared in disbelief when they saw that their onslaught had no effect. They continued mindlessly firing until they were ordered to stop. The cessation of firing was uncoordinated because the gunners were unable to hear the orders being shouted over their self-generated cacophony.

An uncanny stillness settled over the scene, and the only discernible sound was that of the landing craft chafing against each other in the slight swell within the harbour. They all watched as the superfine mist of atomised and neutralised shells drifted down from the inner defence dome to the water below.

Further instructions were transmitted through the loud hailer and were listened to in total disbelief by the commander and his troops. They were told to throw all arms and ammunition over the side into the water and to turn the bows of their craft towards *Wallow 5* and drop the front personnel disembarkation ramps. The troops looked helplessly to the commander for guidance. With a slump of the shoulders, he acquiesced, and they started and completed the task within minutes. Upon further instructions, they were told to dispose of, in like manner, their side arms. After a further delay, they were instructed to strip naked and throw their clothes and any other loose items into the harbour. The soldiers in the second landing craft were then told to join their comrades in the first craft, which they did.

With the open front of the now empty craft pointed towards them, the crew of *Wallow 5* could see that the vessel was clear of guns and any other dangerous artefacts. They then issued the order for the men to transfer one at a time from craft one to craft two and to pirouette one at a time as they crossed over to ensure that there were no weapons being transferred. It was during this process that it became clear to the observers on *Wallow 5* that a third of the troopers were female.

Pettit, who had directed the handling of the Federation crews, headed up the reception committee as the naked and dejected troops disembarked. As each one stepped on to the dockside, they were issued with a one-piece Island suit in bright orange and a pair of equally garish green felt slippers. They slid into their garments hastily and with some embarrassment after which they were separated by sex into two lines.

First off had been the commander, a seasoned and hardened soldier who was comparatively unflustered. He began his protest as soon as he was dressed but fell silent when he saw Pettit. Pettit smiled easily. "Well, well, a face from the past—one of Wilson's men, we should have known he was behind this. You're still doing his dirty work, I see."

The commander remained silent. The last time he had seen Pettit was after the jungle patrol in which Pettit was supposed to die. the others had died, but Pettit had managed to escape. Wilson had been scathing about the commander's failure to dispose of Pettit whom he had been informed was a traitor and had since that time given him the worst kind of jobs like this one was supposed to be, but there hadn't been any radiation; he shuddered to think what Wilson would make of this debacle.

Thirty-Seven

The look of satisfaction on Wilson's face gave way to concern as he stared at the radio receiver, which was issuing only static noise. The commander had seemed confident enough as they had entered the harbour and then suddenly nothing. He radioed the task force support vessel, which had stayed outside the harbour and learned that they too had lost contact with the landing craft as soon as it entered Recovery Harbour. The were presuming that there was some kind of jamming, once the craft had entered the harbour, and in the absence of any other form of communication, they had despatched a reconnaissance UAV, which was approaching the Island as they spoke.

The communication's officer on *Foxhound* watched the video screen and updated Wilson as the picture unfolded. The flypast was going too fast to view in real time as it passed over the whole of the Island in less than four minutes; the slowed down version showed the Island to be deserted. The only activity was in the harbour itself, where the two landing craft could be seen to be stationery in the centre of the harbour.

Wilson's look of concern relaxed as the report unfolded. It seemed that their original thought of radio blocking was automatic and this was why they had lost contact. His relaxation faltered as the report after the second flyover showed a further craft in the harbour that had not been there before. His first thought was that the Russians had beaten them to it and that would be a disaster. His scrambled thoughts cleared when he realised that the Russian craft was very small and appeared to be an assault vessel, which meant that his forces still had the upper hand. He was confident that the commander was independent enough, with eighty armed specialist forces, to overcome any threat from a small, apparently unarmed, Russian force.

He authorised another flypast after a full Island survey revealed that nothing else was happening on the rest of the Island. Further dockside images were first described to him and then relayed directly to his computer; he stared in total disbelief and froze a frame. The fuzzy image showed scores of people lined up on the dock either wearing day glow suits or they were naked; the landing craft contained people of both sexes all of whom were naked and unarmed.

Pettit had the confused Federation troops march to the council assembly hall, that being the only building large enough to hold the numbers involved, and they were provided with beverages and snacks and folding chairs. Commander Thatcher was singled out for discussion by Pettit, and they moved to a side room for privacy.

"Colonel, I never thought I would see you again, not after your disagreement with Wilson. That usually spells the end of the road."

"Not Colonel any more, Thatcher, just plain old Silas Pettit," he paused and added with a distant smile. "This is yet another one of Wilson's failures—very embarrassing for you to be captured by a bunch of unarmed civilian pacifists."

"Not exactly unarmed." Thatcher defended his honour. "What you've got is more than just a weapon and, anyway, what makes you think this is anything to do with Wilson?"

"Oh, please—you're treating me like an idiot. Have you forgotten so soon that I used to be directed by him. This ill-conceived plan has his name stamped all over it." His voice had taken on a testy tone at the mention of Wilson.

"I'm here on Federation business. It has nothing to do with Wilson, and you're going to be in a whole load of trouble when this gets back to him."

"Him?" Pettit laughed out loud. "Him? Surely, you mean them? 'Them' means the Federation 'him' refers to Wilson?"

"You're putting words into my mouth."

"It's all immaterial any way. What are we going to do with you and your merry men and, as I observed on the dock, your merry women?"

"Whatever you do, you'll be in trouble internationally. You've blown up a civilian airliner, hijacked an international task force, and that's just for starters. If I were you, I would surrender to our peacekeeping force, and I'll put in a good word for you."

"Interesting, you've been with Wilson too long, and sadly, you appear to believe what he has influenced you to say. Take a long, hard look at what has happened. You were sent into an environment which was believed, incorrectly, to be non-threatening, you are very lightly armed and poorly constituted. You also happen to be equipped with anti-radiation suits, presumably because you were expecting to encounter nuclear radiation. We have no sources of such radiation on the Island, so it must have something to do with the nuclear device that the Federation or, more likely, Wilson had dropped on us. As you can see," he spread his arms wide, "it was a waste of your time and energy."

*

"You're suggesting what?" Crook looked at Pettit askance "You're suggesting that we send them back to the carrier in their landing craft and just let them go?" He had asked Pettit what he thought should be done about their captives and had not expected the answer he got.

"There is a method in my madness," Pettit observed with overt patience. "Thatcher will go back to Wilson and tell him that our defence dome does not let radiation through."

"Your point being?" Before he heard the response, he realised what the point actually was.

"They will be under the impression that we are shielded against radiation which, of course, we are not, but the important thing is that, they will not try any more nuclear tricks."

"Of course, brilliant," Cook shouted, rubbing his hands together gleefully "Thatcher will be our Trojan horse."

Thirty-Eight

On board the *Foxhound*, Wilson was furious, and he vented the full force of his fury on Thatcher, who stood before his desk, hands behind his back and shoulders overly squared like a professional soldier except for the lurid one-piece body suit and felt footwear. Looking like a dejected clown, he had briefed Wilson on the events of the failed Island invasion, trying as best he could to spin it in his own favour, but there were too many negatives for him to be able to recover the situation. Even had he been able to fully justify his actions, it was clear that Wilson was on the warpath and would accept no excuses. No matter how he twisted it, his task force had been fully outmanoeuvred by what Wilson referred to as a bunch of unarmed rank amateurs. Thatcher tried tentatively to push the onus for failure on to Wilson's inability to give them accurate information concerning the passivity of the Island's defences and the question of the radiation, or rather the lack of it. His attempts were frustrated by a rampaging Wilson, just as he knew they would be.

Brutally, Wilson told Thatcher that his career as a special force commander was over, and as such, his army career was also over. There would certainly be no glowing reference after his dismissal, and in all likelihood, his pension would be reviewed unfavourably. Thatcher noted with a flash of fear that Wilson had ceased being vindictive, having made his point, and his demeanour was totally dismissive. His fear was fuelled by his knowledge that others he had seen subjected to this treatment had disappeared from the face of the earth never to reappear.

After dismissing Thatcher summarily, Wilson sat thoughtfully staring—out of focus—straight ahead, while his mind wind milled around the facts of the debriefing. There was no doubt in his mind that he could lay the blame on Thatcher for the failure of the mission, and that Thatcher would not be in a position to disprove the spin that he, Wilson, was going to use to ensure that his own standing, with the powers that were of current use to him, would be enhanced hopefully to a greater rather than lesser extent.

He ruminated for a few more minutes before taking a deep breath, which preceded his reaching a conclusion. He sat up straight and began to assemble his devious thoughts. Two important points came out of the debriefing, one was that their defences were even more powerful than he had assumed and that the Islanders were prepared to exploit that power and that they were, he had been misdirected, '*impervious to radiation.*' The second thought refined his intention to claim without foundation that the Islanders were carrying out nuclear tests in absolute contravention of international law, and that in doing, so they destroyed the civilian airliner and its innocent crew.

This action would harden international feeling against the Islanders and, together with a siege of the Island to prevent any ingress or egress of materiel aid, would bring the Islanders to their knees without further military intervention and leave the way open for him to claim their technology. His justification to himself for doing this was that he had, after all, financed their research and the fruits of their labour should in all reasonableness, according to his twisted logic, fall to him alone. That the financing was the product of his illegal fund manipulation did not even cross his mind.

He set the ball rolling by calling a press conference to impart what he called breaking news of a most disturbing nature. Having done so, he retrospectively contacted James Creswell with the intention of simply telling him what it was he was going to tell the press, but as he went through the process he intended to employ, it occurred to him that he could make one further use of the PM, who was by now completely subservient. He outlined the nuclear test scenario and the destruction of the airliner and then added his *piece de resistance* by suggesting to Creswell that he should brief the press on this terrible series of events, which would bolster Creswell's standing in the international community. He didn't add that it would also protect Wilson against any negative repercussions that there might be, and if nothing negative transpired, Wilson would let it be known that Creswell had taken credit for something that was really instigated by Wilson.

*

Thatcher waited in trepidation for the axe, which would terminate his military career, to fall. A few days after his traumatic debrief with Wilson, he was contacted in the Officers Mess by a lieutenant in the intelligence section. He had feelings of deep dread as he was informed that he was wanted for an interview at the London offices of MI5, on the following day. It was more serious than he had thought possible if Wilson had involved the secret service in his dismissal. He could only expect the worst. Maybe, he thought irrationally, even a trumped up charge of treason.

Returning to his billet from the mess, he became aware that he was being followed. He confirmed this by driving off the base and then returning, and the vehicle behind him echoed his moves. He had very little sleep that night; the car that had followed him was parked close by his billet with no visible lights but illumination from a three-quarter moon, which meant he was able to make out that there were two occupants one of whom occasionally held both hands up to his face. Although Thatcher could not be certain, he was fairly sure that the hands up to the face held binoculars.

The office in the MI 5 Headquarters in which Thatcher sat, on the next day, waiting to be interviewed had been furnished by a rabid minimalist. Everything was functional. There were no frills, and no attempt had been made to provide creature comforts. He became more and more nervous as time passed. He had arrived on time and was expected. His interviewer was, however, not so timely, and thirty minutes passed before he was startled out of his reverie by the sudden and noisy opening of the door.

"Mr Coniston will see you now." The severely dressed woman said through pursed lips.

He followed her meekly along a dimly lit unfurnished corridor, which led to a set of double doors and in turn opened on to an entirely different world. The footsteps that had echoed down the dreary corridor were now muffled into almost complete submission by luxurious deep pile carpet. The lighting changed from dingy to soft and relaxing.

She opened a heavy security door, and as he passed through, he was aware that he was being scanned, and as the door closed, he saw that he was in an ante room which contained a desk with a view screen mounted on it, which was being scrutinised by a shrewd-eyed technician. He glimpsed the screen as he passed the desk and saw an image of himself in all his naked glory. The scanned image showed buttons and zips, and the contents of his pockets and the medal ribbons on his dress jacket as well as showing the most intimate details of his naked body. He blanched and looked at his woman escort; she was not looking at the screen but at the technician who after a pause, nodded to her. She returned the nod and opened a second door, which led into the office of the head of MI 5. Announcing him by name, she ushered him into the office and turned away, leaving him to enter and close the door behind him.

Wearing his dress uniform normally gave him an excess of confidence, but standing before Trevor Coniston, head of MI 5, who looked every inch a well-heeled, well-connected toff, caused his confidence to evaporate. He stood nervously like an errant schoolboy before a strict headmaster.

"Please be seated, Commander." Coniston leaned back in his chair and placed his elbows on its red leather arms. "Now before we start, shall we have coffee?" He didn't wait for a reply but pressed a button on his telephone, "Stella, coffee for two and a selection of biscuits and don't forget to include some fig newtons." He returned his gaze to Thatcher. "Biscuits all right for you?" He raised both eyebrows in enquiry.

"Ah . . . Oh . . . yes." Thatcher was thoroughly taken back by the polite reception and thoroughly confused by the friendly overtures. Nothing like what he would have expected from Wilson.

"While we wait for Stella to bring the refreshments, after which we'll get down to the reason for our meeting, why don't you tell me about your awful experiences on Recovery Island. I must say that I find the scandalous inaccuracy in the intelligence you were given about the situation on the Island is beyond belief."

"Well," Thatcher was dumbstruck by the tenor of the conversation and panicked by the implications, which might be attached to his response, and it showed on his face.

"Please don't read anything into my observations." Coniston smiled disarmingly, "Anything you say to me is between us and will not leave these four walls. Oh, and just remember that you are free to talk to me without fear of breaching security, after all I am the head of MI5, and I know secrets that would make your hair curl—which it won't because all secrets are safe with me, so you will never learn them." He smiled once more. "So why not tell me about your experiences?"

Thatcher naturally set out his stall in a way which would absolve him of all potential blame. Refreshments were brought in by the secretary and placed on a coffee table located in a broad bay window. Thatcher continued elucidating his story as they took seats on opposite sides of the table. Coniston stood up and opened a window, letting in a breath of fresh air as well as the sounds of the river and roads outside. As Coniston took charge of the coffee ceremony, he said in casual tones. "I took the liberty of having you watched last night just to make sure that you would not be approached by any undesirable elements before our meeting—but I dare say that a man of your experience noticed that." He did not let it be known that the watchers were aware that they had become the watched and that he wanted to give Thatcher some reassurance that the intentions were one of offering protection. His reassurances were half-true; the other half was to ensure that Thatcher received no complicating visitors or indeed decided to take a defensive moonlight flit. He also did not mention that Thatcher's telephones had been placed, illegally, under twenty-four hour listening surveillance.

Having had the nagging question of being watched and by whom answered, the meeting with Coniston, which to Thatcher's relief was more like a friendly conversation than an interview, took on a more relaxed and informative tenor. At the close of the meeting, he was shown to a waiting room where he was joined by an escort who would complete all necessary procedures and escort him out of the building. While he waited, he mulled over the meeting and why it should have been with the top man. His fear had evaporated as soon as it became clear that it had not been Coniston's intention to pillory him as had been the case with Wilson. He had told his story with enough truth in its basis to be plausible but in such a way that his actual shortcomings were subverted. He was somewhat more guarded concerning the question of Wilson's involvement, insisting that his orders had been issued by the UK Government and that Wilson was merely an intermediary. He had considered spilling the beans about Wilson, but at the last minute, decided against it just in case Coniston was a friend and confident of Wilson. That would do him no good at all. After nearly falling into the trap that he was now sure had been set for him, he introduced some praise for Wilson's patriotism but not so much that he over egged the pudding.

The escort took him from the waiting room along the plush corridor in the opposite direction to that by which he had arrived. As they approached the general reception area, the doors opened, and two men walked through towards them. Thatcher looked at the two men. They were vaguely familiar. One was a tall willowy European and the other was the exact opposite, small and obviously oriental.

"Good morning, Sir Lionel," the escort said brightly.

"Oh! Good morning." Sir Lionel peered myopically at him. "How are you today?"

"Well, thank you, sir." The escort laughed when they had passed. "That's Sir Lionel Wentworth, head of the Civil Service. He has terrible eyesight especially in this lighting, and if you greet him, he responds as if he knows you just in case he does. He's so vain he won't wear glasses. He seems to think it's a sign of weakness."

"Who was the man with him?"

"The Chinese fellow . . . ? I don't know . . . never seen him before."

But Thatcher did know. He had seen him in the offices of the Chinese information bureau in Beijing on more than one occasion when he had visited with Wilson during their many clandestine visits about which he had been sworn to absolute secrecy.

Thirty-Nine

*T*he regular early evening news bulletin was interrupted by a breaking news item which created disruption to the normally smooth running programme.

Reports of sabotage continue to come in from East Russia via state-controlled wire services. Russian authorities, who are not customarily open about incidents like this, are warning that such attacks will not go unpunished, and they are making an international appeal for assistance with the apprehension of the perpetrators. The latest acts reported include the disruption of underground fibre optic communications, which is causing great distress in fields of medicine and the emergency services and is putting the lives of Russian citizens at risk. We have an unconfirmed report that a Siberian retirement home was burnt to the ground, with many elderly deaths and casualties, when it was found impossible to contact the Fire Department by the normal fibre optic route. By the time radio communications had been established, the blaze had become unstoppable, and the home was razed to the ground. This and other incidents in the recent past, including the loss of two Air Force jets—the wreckage of which—have still not been located and the collapse of a rail

bridge with the loss of many lives. As yet there is no news of any
progress being made by the Russian Government in apprehending
the perpetrators of these acts of sabotage.

Library pictures of Russian jets were shown, together with repeat shots
of the freight train wreckage and new shots of the smouldering ruins of
what had been the retirement home were shown on the split screen. The
camera returned to the face of the newsreader.

Understandingly, Russian citizens are seriously concerned about
these events, and there have been demonstrations in Red Square,
demanding action from the members of the Presidium to protect
the citizens from harm.

Live television pictures were shown of the several hundred strong
demonstrators in the square, who carried placards, mostly in Cyrillic
text, but with some in English which read: "*Protect Russian Citizens* and
Bring the terrorists to justice," among others. The demonstrations, as they
watched, began to turn nasty, and the police surged forward to quell the
unrest, and the live pictures stopped abruptly.

We appear to have lost contact with Moscow, but it is clear that the
people of Russia are beginning to panic at the apparent inability
of the authorities to control this situation.

He paused and his tone changed.

Meanwhile, here in London, the League of Russian Friends has
delivered a petition to Downing Street, demanding intervention on
behalf of the beleaguered Russian people. The Prime Minister the

Right Honourable James Creswell has agreed to make a statement outside No. 10, Downing Street, in about two hours, at 8 p.m. Meanwhile, our Russian political correspondent Simon Schumann will give us an insight into the background of these terrorist attacks and the progress, or lack of it, that has been made.

Wilson, in the privacy of his personal communications cabin, flicked the off switch on the television remote before Schumann's appearance and leaned back in his chair with his eyes screwed up in concentration. He wondered how he could make use of this situation to further his own interests. There was no sympathy from him about the plight of the Russian people; he just wondered how he could identify the terrorists so that he could use them as potential promoters of his own causes. They were obviously skilled in the arts that were so dear to him, and like all people of their shallow persuasion, they would be swayed by money, which was no problem for him. He could, if necessary, raid the coffers of his government's black account with impunity.

By his very nature, Wilson was a loner, and there were so many things going on that he was close to overload. In addition to his covert Federation duties, he was fully embroiled in Creswell's political destruction, and, of course, there was the ever elusive, but so important, BAM2 taking up too much of his time. He sighed as he tussled with the priorities. There was nobody to whom he could turn for support without blackmail and threats which by their own nature required more effort from him and demanded time that was just not available. The voices in his head were not helping either, so he tried his best to ignore them. But it was a losing battle, and as time passed, they became ever more persistant.

Forty

The scientists on their remote Nuovostan island heeded Wilson's persistent telephone conference instructions and continued tirelessly to understand and unravel the secrets of BAM2. Despite being renegade aficionados, Wilson's scientists marvelled at the revolutionary techniques that the originators of the experimentation had employed so cunningly. They checked and rechecked the algorithms and the notes provided by Wilson; they transmitted greater and lesser distances but still their scopes and screens remained blank, refusing to record the images that they should have detected. The diamonds that Wilson had provided to construct the transmitters of the BAM2 waves were of inferior quality, although the scientists had calculated that the carrier waves would be patchy, they believed they would still work sufficiently for their purposes, after a fashion.

Progress came to a halt when they realised they were going round in circles, and the scientists were uncertain about what to do next. They still wanted to milk Wilson for all they could get and hid from him the fact that they were stumped. Wilson became edgy when progress slowed down, and the demand for increased funding continued to increase, his fragile mental state continued to deteriorate, and he was increasingly prone to moments of extreme elation or depression or paranoia.

An unscheduled conference call from Wilson took the scientists by surprise and led to a certain amount of panic. Panic in others was something that Wilson not only expected but that which he actively nurtured. He looked at a digital image of the transmitter that they had constructed which had been sent to his computer tablet and compared it with the images that his Chinese spy had taken, with a telephoto lens, during the earlier oil-drilling operation in China where the Islanders had used BAM2 technology to hasten drilling for oil, before the breakdown in relations with the Federation had rendered them incompatible. They looked the same and matched the original notes and sketches from his files.

At his insistence, they allowed him to observe their efforts online. Despite his frightening real-time observation of their efforts, the experiments yielded no results. They set the transmit distance to one hundred miles and received no returning image signal and then to one mile and still with the same negative results. He ranted and issued unequivocal instructions for them to succeed whatever the cost or face the consequences.

Later, languishing in his private suite on board *Foxhound*, Wilson read the latest batch of reports from his network of spies, paid for by an unknowing British Government and people and which were for the enlightenment of Wilson alone. The reports were wide ranging, covering industrial and political unrest, the emergence of any dissident groups around the world, and reports of any unusual happenings. One incident caught his eye: the report of the two missing Russian military jets. He read on and coupled this incident with the downed power lines, the severed gas and oil pipelines, and two totally unexpected volcanic eruptions in areas which had not been considered vulnerable. He cast his mind back to the earlier Russian TV news reports, which he had watched but not fully comprehended and realisation dawned. The answers had been with him for some time, but he had not realised it; with an uncontrolled jerk, he jumped up from his seat as though scalded. His shipboard aide, sitting in a cubbyhole outside his suite, looked at him in alarm and at a loss when his cabin door burst open to reveal a wild-eyed DDP, who was only a short step from frothing at the mouth.

"Get me a map of the Nuovostan area," he demanded.

The aide, chosen by him more for her generous cleavage rather than her abilities, rushed into the suite and pulled a world atlas from the well-stocked bookcase. She thrust the atlas towards him in desperate panic. "I don't know where Nuovo . . . whatever is." She whimpered in abject terror. He snatched the book from her and began frantically to wrench the pages open.

"Got it!" He danced with glee, much to the astonishment of the aide. "Champagne and lots of it. You can join me in my celebrations. I have found the Holy Grail."

She had no idea what he was talking about but was mightily relieved that he was, bafflingly, in good humour; an extremely rare occurrence. The chilled champagne was poured into crystal flutes and she took the opportunity to join in with the celebrations, whatever the reason. Wilson jigged around the cabin with her taking unabashed pleasure and extreme liberties with parts of her body, which should have been reserved for the chosen one.

It was so simple, he thought, once he had joined the dots; the reason for the disruptions and the lost aircraft was obvious. The experiment that his scientists were carrying out were not a failure, they were an unqualified success but not in a way which was initially obvious. The BAM2 they had built and were testing did not have a working radar element to it; emissions were pure energy and, obviously, were only active at the distance set from the transmitter. He deduced this in a rare moment of clarity. The map of Nuovostan showed that the exact centre from which the incidences radiated was the Island in the lake which housed his laboratory and team of scientists.

At last, his dream had come true as he knew it would if he persevered. He now had complete possession of BAM2 technology. It was his and would soon be his alone, once he got rid of the traitors. They did not worry him; they were idealists who did not have the courage to use the true power of the anomaly for other than peaceful means; more fool them. He, on the other hand, possessed the necessary courage to exploit the technology for broader political aims. Not the Federation or the Chinese or the Americans or the Europeans could be allowed to have any influence over his domain. He would make sure that they all paid dearly for the humiliations he believed he had so unjustly suffered at their hands. He would control them; totally, he enjoyed a rare moment of pure elation.

A further realisation came to him. The original notes that he had given his scientists and which had brought the success he so badly needed were those he had held back from Creswell. He now had the comfort of knowing that even if Creswell or the MOD tried to continue with experimentation, they would fail because of the missing sheets from the file in their possession.

He could now return to Nuovostan, dismiss the scientists and keep the technology that he felt was rightly his. He toyed with the idea of contacting his scientists to inform them that their services were no longer required but had second thoughts, and he decided against the radio communication. He could not be sure whether the message would lead to all sorts of complications, not least from the scientists themselves, who might decide to abscond. He bit his lip, in frustration, until it bled, but in his euphoria, he felt no pain. His destiny awaited him at last; he was hypereuphoric.

*

Within the Russian Government, there was a great deal of anger and confusion peppered with strident calls for retribution. Their oil, gas, and water pipelines were being disrupted, and it was a natural assumption that there was sabotage afoot there being no other reasonable explanation. The obvious perpetrators could have been any of the disaffected Russian satellite countries but was more likely to be the Chinese, who desperately wanted to destabilise the Russian alliance and gain access to their precious energy supplies.

Investigating the incidents proved difficult for the Russian authorities; the incidences were up to hundreds of kilometres apart and all seemed to happen at exactly the same time of the day in coordinated batches: sometimes daily but with gaps, usually at the weekend. What was so frustrating for them was that they had, what they thought to be, infallible and extremely high-tech active surveillance all along the Chinese border and there was no evidence of Chinese incursion nor from any other potential external enemies.

No home-grown terrorists groups were known of in the area, and the authorities were certain that they had frightened the local population with sufficiently draconian reprisals to prevent any likelihood of such groups being formed. Still the disruptions continued; no sooner had they repaired one batch of disruptions than another occurred in different locations. They were at a loss to know how to defend themselves from this wave of invisible terrorism. No demands were being made by the terrorists, and the incidents seemed pointless and, apart from timing, random.

The final straw came when two of their Air Force jets, in mid-communication with their ground controllers, were lost in the Russian heartland without warning and despite many searches of the barren hinterland, they were unable to locate the wreckage of either aircraft. Official warnings were sent from Moscow to Beijing, accusing them of aggression bordering on war. The Chinese denied any complicity, just as the Russians had expected.

Forty-One

There continued to be no indication to Wilson that his renegade scientists had any inkling that they had been successful in discovering the powerful secret. They were isolated in their lake Island laboratory, and it was unlikely that they had heard about the strange disruptive happenings that had led him to uncovering their actual success. Their lack of comprehension had brought a bright light into Wilson's darkly disturbed world, and he needed to make sure that they did not stumble on the truth.

Time had now become of the essence with the abject failure by Thatcher to take advantage of the Island's defences being momentarily disabled, and it was important that he should secure the BAM2 unit from the test site in Nuovostan, which would give him, he had deduced, the ability to counter the Island's defences. He was not, unlike the idealistic Islanders, afraid to use his BAM2 for the purpose of destruction. It was his intention to destroy as much of the Island and as many of its inhabitants and facilities as necessary to satisfy his objectives.

He used Queeze, who had become the main visible connection with Pelochev, to make radio contact with her with the promise of a substantial bribe, which he had no intention of honouring. He inveigled her into flying to the Island on the lake to dismiss the scientists with the promise of a generous pay off, which he would later renegotiate, and to sequester all of the experiment notes that they had prepared and to make sure that there were no copies made. Once having done as she was instructed, she was to courier the notes and equipment to him via the UK diplomatic mission in Mongolia where Wilson had one of his many moles. It had never been his intention to let any other person get their hands on the coveted technology, but he had little choice but to involve Pelochev. The stand-off with the Island needed his absolute attention and could not be orchestrated remotely. He was sure that he could rely on Pelochev's avaricious nature to carry out the task for the overly generous reward she had been promised.

Pelochev, as he had supposed, was anxious to comply with the instructions, not from any sense of friendship or duty, neither of which she comprehended, but was spurred on by quantity of US Dollars, she was anticipating for doing very little. Had she realised the value of the cargo she was to despatch to Wilson she would undoubtedly have negotiated a better deal or perhaps simply have absconded with the equipment and notes and found a more generous purchaser. However, she did not know of the value of the equipment or its function or to whom it would be of interest, so she went along with the generous deal she had been gifted.

Nervously, she paced the cabin in the aircraft which had been arranged and financed through an "off the radar" contact to ferry her from Moscow, where she was currently ensconced, to Nuovostan. The pilot had his instructions from her which had been sanctioned by his paymaster. He was to take the most direct route at top speed and ignore any instructions from whichever source which would delay them in any way—quoting if asked that they were on a mission sanctioned by the Federation of Nations and no interference would be brooked.

Darkness consumed the flight as the winter sun set on the distant horizon, heralding the end of a short bout of daylight. Pelochev could not contain her frustration at the time the flight was taking, seeing in her mind's eye that the scientists would do something which would prevent her from receiving her generous bonus. She castigated the crew for not anticipating her every whim and shouted at the captain at the least provocation. The captain pointed out that he had no contro. over the influence of stratospheric conditions on the progress of their flight. For his pains, he received a torrent of invectives, concluding that his employment as a pilot was under great jeopardy. She had immersed herself so deeply in the task that Wilson had given her that she had, momentarily, become him. They flew over the lake which surrounded the Island in the caverns under which the experiments were being carried out. She had, on Wilson's advice, instructed the pilot to take an unusually high approach over the lake on the approach to Nuovostan International Airport. She had no knowledge of his real reason for issuing this directive, which was to reduce the likelihood of their being inadvertently vapourised by the ongoing BAM2 experiment, should it be in progress. Pelochev peered out of the cabin window at the surface of the lake but at their "greater than usual" height was unable to pick out the Island.

As Wilson's ipso facto clone, Pelochev, continued to make a nuisance of herself when they arrived at the Nuovostan Airport, her home territory, where her short temper was a legend and had been thrown into a turmoil by having her Russian visit interrupted. She demanded personal transportation to the lake Island laboratory and would brook none of the usual delaying tactics. She further demanded the most skilful driver be made immediately available to the exclusion of all other tasks and that the police be told to facilitate the limousine's free passage without regard to speed limits or other highway infringements. She instructed that the rest of her team should follow immediately in suitable, but less important, vehicles.

The driver was whipped into frenzy by Pelochev who was apoplectic to the brink of total overload. Her eyes and neck veins bulged as she shrieked to the driver to hurry and to ignore the laws of the road. The driver obeyed the madwoman, endangering both their lives. The wishes of his passenger were very clear. Several hours later, they screeched to a halt, in a cloud of dust and grit, at the lake side, opposite the jetty to which an ancient ferry cruiser was hitched.

Gesticulating wildly to the driver, Pelochev indicated that the craft should be untied and all speed should be made to ferry them to the Island. The driver was inert, looking with puzzlement out over the lake in the direction which had been indicated. She followed the man's gaze and her shoulders and head drooped dejectedly.

The "My god," she mouthed, in Russian, had no religious connotation. There was a look of incomprehension on her face.

She made immediate contact with Wilson by satellite phone. He was shaken out of his sleepy response. Her hopes of great riches receded to zero.

Wilson let out a string of profanities when he learned from Pelochev that the Island was gone and the lake's waters had closed over where it had been. It was as though it had never existed. The scientists, the experiment and their notes, and Wilson's aspirations of domination were all gone.

"They discovered the secret all right," Wilson said bitterly, "and the fools destroyed themselves with it and everything else into the bargain." Wilson lamented over the telephone to a distraught Pelochev who could feel her rich rewards evaporating as they spoke.

Forty-Two

Wilson's plans to acquire the technology had stalled yet again, and he vented his fury on all of those around him. Once he had satisfied his all-consuming anger, his devious and fertile mind turned compulsively to other forms of acquisition. He could team up with another country or group of countries to mount an invasion now that he knew the strengths and weaknesses of the Islanders, or he could launch another group of rogue scientists and give them more explicit instructions so that they did not annihilate themselves. One bright point was that he had been able to dispense with the support of the Chinese who were turning out now to be more of a hindrance than a help. He had fooled James Creswell into thinking that he was safe from the web of deceit that had been woven for him but now it to was time to leak the misinformation, discretely of course, to bring about his downfall and whosoever replaced him was of no interest to Wilson whose ambitions had moved away from the United Kingdom, beyond Europe and beyond even China. His ambition was now global; Creswell's downfall and disgrace would just be an icing on the cake. His megalomania continued to grow, and it recognised no bounds. The voices in his head encouraged him all the way and goaded him into ever more heinous plots.

With a little more time at his disposal through the pause in his ambitious plan, he began the moves to finally bring down the other three nightmare people. They had frustrated his plans for the moment, and he intended to thwart theirs for good, and his intention was that it would happen in the near future. His method was simple: the three traitors had, by his intervention, been rendered persona non grata with the majority of the world—now it was time to complete their isolation even with the less influential countries.

Furtherance of his smears was a simple process. He would personally contact all countries which had so far not come out against the Islanders and buttress any seeds of doubt that might linger. He could weave any story he wished to persuade them that their opposition to the Island would be of interest and reward to them. All he had to say to them was that any assistance offered to them by the Recovery Islanders would make them dependent on the dictatorship which could, and would, eventually take over their whole country by dependency or attrition or both.

Dealing with the PM began immediately, his sidelining was no longer required now that his alternative plan was to be unleashed. It involved implanting a saboteur on the Island, and he knew just who that would be.

Simon Queeze was deployed to call a meeting with D. K. Valerie, who was to provide a discreet gateway into the establishment press, as would Juliet Hammond via the tabloids, at a separate meeting, to the ragged end of the tabloid press. He was able to demand cooperation from these two august journalists, as he had Sir Lionel Wentworth, because he continued to hold damaging information on them which could destroy their careers if he chose to reveal the skeletons in their closets. The journalists had proved to be useful in the past when they were planted into the band of newspaper people who had been the first "outsider" visitors to Recovery Island.

The leak, via broadsheet and red top papers, was simple; it hinted that all was not well in Whitehall and that there was a highly placed traitor who among other things was siphoning off large sums of money for personal use. It was intended that the leakage would be slow and, at first, low profile; later, the leak would be accelerated and broad hints dropped. The information was attributed to impeccable sources which could not be disclosed.

The two journalists were assured via a secured telephone conversation from Queeze that this was positively the last thing they would be required to do, and as a token of intent, part of the incriminating evidence he held against them would be returned to them. In the meantime, Wilson made a late night telephone call from his private quarters on *Foxhound* to Sir Lionel Wentworth with the same deal that had been offered to the two journalists by Queeze. The seal was set, and the fabricated story was leaked. There was no turning back once the news hit the dailies. In their hearts, the three used in the smear knew that the likelihood of Wilson relinquishing the information he had on them was remote in the extreme.

*

Federation meetings became more frequent and were increasingly acrimonious. Wilson was no longer acting as a mole for the Chinese, making it more difficult for them to force their decisions through with ease. The Chinese representative became petulant when the direction he pursued, at his president's bidding, was delayed, blocked, or questioned.

Ultimately, the Chinese decided on unilateral action, they stormed out of a scheduled meeting vowing not to discuss the matter of actions against the Island with other member countries. They had decided on another, this time more effective, blockade of the Island, unilaterally, using the Chinese Navy and Air Force, without the irksome need to bring the rest of the Federation's interfering administrations into line. The aim was total siege to starve them out no matter how long it took.

When the Chinese tactics reached him, Wilson was secretly delighted with the news; it would give him time and opportunity to implement his own plan without any rush. The blockade would keep the Chinese and the Islanders busy, and he would be able to use the asset that the Hammond woman had acquired for Queeze. Jacques Pantin, the exiled dissident Islander, who had been recruited by Juliet Hammond at the bidding of Simon Queeze, was currently being "looked after" in a black ops hostel in the wilds of the Scottish Highlands since his flight from Recovery Island via Lisbon. Much to his disappointment, Julia Hammond was not at the hostel, and the taciturn intelligence interrogators who pounded him with endless questions were no substitute for her company, which had been a big lure for his being there. The questions were pointless and boring and did nothing towards making his stay one of interest or pleasure. Only an endless supply of whiskey and tobacco gave him any respite.

When after a short time, he was brought back into play by being returned to the Island, which would be achieved by his pleading penitence and homesickness with the pretence that he had seen the error of his ways. To further consolidate his cooperation, he was promised that when the Island was liberated, he would be given the freedom of the Island and be able to travel to the fleshpots of the world at will. Once there, he was given the task of disabling the defence systems long enough for Wilson's task force to land and take control of the, otherwise, defenceless people.

Pantin succumbing to the lure of freedom to travel the world, agreed to carrying out Wilson's plans. He immediately made contact with the Island and pleaded his case saying that he understood that he had been totally wrong and did not fit into the off-Island society or in the way of life of those he now considered to be his captors and that he longed to return to the Island as soon as possible.

The not inconsiderable matter of how he could return to the Island had to be addressed and, under tutelage from Julia Hammond, he threw himself on the mercy of the Ruling Council to facilitate his transfer from England to the Island and the freedom it epitomised. He promised to earn his freedom by playing his part in supporting the welfare of the Island and Islanders in whatever way was considered beneficial. The council approved his return without serious second thoughts.

Pantin wrinkled his nose in momentary distaste as he stepped on to the tarmac at the Island airport. He was keen to get to work on the task in hand and couldn't wait to get to his accommodation and assemble the satellite phone which had been provided by Hammond. The customs check was cursory, and the phone components, which looked like electronic games, were ignored.

As soon as he had assembled the phone, he pressed the call button and waited as the ring tone sounded. The instrument had been constructed to make calls to one number only and had no dialling pad. Julia Hammond answered the phone, and he advised her of his arrival. She told him to unpack his hand baggage and remove the false bottom to reveal a small black box together with a hand controller.

His language became very ripe when he thought the device he had carried was an explosive. She calmed him telling him that he had not been told of the presence of the device in his baggage, which was not an explosive, to protect him in his passage through customs. He was somewhat calmer when she explained to him that the customs officers used an iris scanner to detect the minute changes in electrical activity in the body caused by lying which would have been the case had he known about its presence, and he had been asked a pertinent question. His not knowing was part of their plans, she told him, to protect him from harm; a further part of his protection was that if the device had been discovered, it would have been leaked to the council that the hand luggage had been provided by one of the ministries and that it was their intention to retrieve it to be used for subversion at some later date, without his knowledge.

Without delay, as soon as he had settled in, he volunteered to help the Island's defence effort, preferably in the front line. He assured them that he was a reformed character, and that his former tawdriness was now in the past and his sole wish was to make a positive contribution to the Island's safety in the face of the enemy. He was given the job of observer and with powerful binoculars for use in daylight hours and night vision glasses; he watched the western approaches to the Island from a vantage point at the pinnacle of one of the hundred-foot high observation towers. The job, which he undertook for eight hours a day, was tedious and boring. He endured it only because he was fortified by the promise Hammond had given him concerning their relationship. Given the opportunity, he would not be drinking to the point where he had no memory of "knowing" her as he was told had been the case during their first encounter. Without him realising it, their previous sexual relationship, which she had planted in his mind, after he had a particularly heavy drinking session, was pure fabrication. After he had passed out in an Island apartment, which Julia Hammond had been allocated during her brief stay on the Island during her work as a journalist, she had planted false evidence of a passionate liaison. That liaison had never actually taken place, but he was fixated that it had, and he wanted a repeat which he would remember and savour.

Weeks passed and the tedium increased. There was a sudden flurry of activity among the defence staff when it became apparent that the Federation, or the Chinese, had instituted a sea-and-air blockade of the Island with the obvious intention of starving the Islanders into submission. There was activity all around the Island, although it wasn't obvious to Pantin with the movements taking place over the horizon. Each night without fail when he came off duty, he would report to Julia Hammond.

Once the blockade was fully in place, Pantin's instructions via Julia Hammond were changed. He was told to get a job in the control room on the night shift. He undertook to do so willingly spurred on by the promise of "further" delights when he returned to Julia Hammond in England. He spoke to his supervisor about the possibility of working in the control room, saying that he had served his apprenticeship in the observation tower and wanted a task with more upfront activity.

A week or so later, he was given the opportunity to stand in for an assistant who was suffering from stress brought on by too many hours of peering at the radar scopes. He grasped the opportunity with both hands and threw himself headlong into the job. It became obvious that there were unpopular jobs in the control room about which the old hands grumbled incessantly. One such task was the keeping of the hand-prepared activity log which was a last resort back-up, should the computer generated system fail catastrophically. He volunteered for the task and offered to take the most unpopular graveyard shift from 8 p.m. to 4 a.m. His offer was snapped up by very grateful schedulers. The scene for his treachery was set, and now he waited for final instructions to carry out the deed.

*

Wilson rubbed his hands with glee; his brilliant plan was working exactly as he had intended. With Pantin in place and with ten high-speed combat launches each with a compliment of eight specially trained troops on board, it was now just a matter of timing.

He made contact with the Chinese, advising them that he had a plan to penetrate the Island's defences and that he required their cooperation in doing nothing to stop his attack group from gaining access to the Island.

As he knew they would, they procrastinated about giving him assurances of non-interference, and he took advantage of the delay to further his plans against Creswell.

He now no longer needed to hold back on the exposure of Creswell as a traitor and an embezzler. Now that Wilson had an alternative plan, which did not require the support of Creswell, his boss and benefactor, he could continue with his destruction of his enemy. His telephone call to Trevor Coniston was by a scrambler phone, and he feigned a nervousness that he did not feel. Reluctantly, he said that he had very disturbing news concerning the most senior man in the government which he had gleaned from contacts in Europe and Asia and in whom he had the greatest of faith and it related to, among other things, national security. He delayed making an imminent appointment with Coniston, saying that he awaited a last piece of damning evidence, which was not the case, but he wanted to set the ball rolling slowly enough to give him time to occupy the Island before finally dealing with Creswell. He intimated to Coniston that his initial feelings about Creswell were probably correct and that his willingness to accept from Creswell that he was innocent of the charges made against him was a weakness on his part. He had come to his senses and now thought it probable that Creswell was guilty of some misdemeanour but that he was not clear at this time what it was.

An unaccustomed calm settled over him, and he leaned back in his chair and linked his hands behind his head. He dreamed of occupying the Island and of being its head of state. Gilliland, Crook, and Pettit would be disposed of, figuratively, if not actually, leaving him free to achieve his goals. Although it had been his original intention to sell the Island technology to the highest bidder, this was no longer his intention. Realising, as he now did, the scope and power of BAM2, he had decided to keep it to himself and use its devastating defence capability to make himself invulnerable and its equally devastating attack capabilities to ensure his dominance.

Forty-Three

*P*antin received his penultimate instruction. He was to remove the electronic device from its hiding place and smuggle it into the control room. He had described to Julia Hammond the set up of the control room, giving her a description of the layout and the functions of the various pieces of equipment. He was told to place the black box in the cabinet containing the computer which controlled the defence and radar systems and that he should make sure that it was hidden from sight even though it had been disguised as what looked like a bona fide electronic component. He did so, and as also instructed, he switched the device to on and then de-activated it using the hand controller. He could now operate the jamming device from a remote location, within fifty feet, as soon as he was instructed to do so.

He had, over the weeks that he had been in the control room, become part of the furniture and nobody gave him a second look as he completed his implantation task and closed the cabinet doors, and returning to his desk, he continued with his task of updating the back-up events log. The prospect of his reward kept him focussed and gave him a warm glow. The warmth even made bearable the abject boredom of being back on the Island with its tedious rules and mindless regulations. Even though his access to alcohol and cigarettes had been restored, he took care not to abuse the rights. The end reward was too precious for him to jeopardise.

*

Trevor Coniston's office was a hive of activity. Casual observers could be forgiven for thinking that the meetings were as a result of the siege of the Island and that an intelligence war was waging. The meetings were attended by members of the UK Government Departments, by Russians, or at least Eastern Europeans, and last but not least by the Chinese. Each of the ethnic groups was seen independently, and as far as could be ascertained, apart from the Chinese delegate, who was accompanied by Sir Lionel Wentworth, the groups were not aware of each other. One of the attendees, a very rare visitor to the MI 5 offices, was Sir Grenville Westinghouse the head of MI6. There was speculation among the ranks as to what convoluted plan was being hatched to reinforce the siege and as to why MI5 and MI6 were involved rather than the Federation intelligence agencies.

The two spymasters did touch on the subject of the siege but that was not the reason for the meeting. After they had been in discussion for an hour or so, they were joined by Wilson who was ushered in by Coniston's secretary whose demeanour was stern and frosty. She did not appreciate being referred to as "girly" by Wilson, or by any other person for that matter but especially by him. Cursory introductions were made between Westinghouse and Wilson, and they got straight down to business.

"Look"—Wilson stared directly at Coniston—"I know I got ratty with you during our last conversation when I was on the Island but bear in mind I was being backed into a corner by everyone, including you."

"I don't recall backing you into a corner," Coniston responded evenly. "I was an independent arbiter during that conversation."

"What I mean is," Wilson blustered on, "I didn't present my case very well because they were all against me, and they didn't really give you a chance to consider the strength of evidence that I have since refined and verified and which supports my case absolutely."

"The floor is yours," Westinghouse offered in neutral tones, "provided that you have no objections, Trevor?"

"None at all."

"Well," Wilson once again feigned discomfort, "like I said to you before"—he nodded towards Coniston—"I really find this quite difficult. I put Creswell forward as the prime ministerial candidate, and now I find that he is only in the position for his own gain." He looked theatrically crestfallen. "I come here with the greatest reluctance to confirm that he is a traitor and to see how the matter can be taken care of with without causing a complete political upheaval, which could throw the country into economic chaos. I'm also aware that I withdrew my allegations concerning Creswell because his lies were so plausible, but further research shows that my first instincts were right."

"First things first." Coniston half raised his hand palm out. "Your sentiments are laudable and provided you have irrefutable evidence, the necessary actions will be taken in the interest of national stability. You are quite right to assume that as a nation, we cannot at this time afford to have the integrity of any national figure opened to suspicion of wrongdoing. Our place in the Federation of Nations is tenuous, as tenuous as our relationships with the EU, and any major disturbance could unseat us and place us in the stable of dependent nations." He paused to allow the full meaning of his words to sink in.

"My thoughts exactly." Wilson hesitated to give himself time to assimilate Coniston's words and use them to his own advantage. "I don't want to stir up a hornet's nest and cause damaging trouble. I would just like to make sure that the country is in safe hands and to ensure that Creswell is finished politically." In a flash, he realised that he could take full advantage of this situation by not insisting on an in-depth investigation into the manufactured evidence against Creswell when it was just possible that he had overlooked a small matter, which could undermine his fabrications. "I suggest that we just take the evidence as it stands, and my proof of his law breaking without involving the Justice Department and the police, and so on. Let us keep this low profile and handle it amongst ourselves." He sat back looking very satisfied with himself. He added as an afterthought, "We could perhaps persuade Creswell to resign and sweep the problem under the carpet along with the embarrassment." Without showing the gloating emotions, he felt he silently congratulated himself on this move which would not expose any failings in the chain of evidence he had put forward and would enable him to leak Creswell's criminal duplicity to the press. He gave a satisfied sigh.

Wilson produced his evidence in the form of signed documents, records of cash transfers, reports from contacts in the embassy in Beijing and from the Chinese Department of Information also in Beijing.

"You will appreciate," Wilson said after presenting his proof, "that the information I have gathered uses sources that will be required to be protected. Their names must never be revealed because they could never be used again and their future information would be invaluable. They are in fact irreplaceable."

"That is understood," Coniston said patiently. "We are here from MI5 and MI6, and I think we know something about secrecy."

"I didn't mean to imply . . ." Wilson interrupted.

"Please," Coniston continued, "I was about to say that we respect your position and that any identity revelations will be kept strictly between ourselves and not let out of these four walls, provided that is the wish of the people concerned."

"Very well then, let us name names and get down to the business of making our case."

Wilson put in a truly thespian presentation as he appeared to wriggle on the hook as they forced the contact names from him. Slowly and skilfully, they wheedled out of him the names Chung Yi of the Chinese diplomatic service and Cheng Tor, an employee, of the British Embassy in Beijing.

"Okay, Mr Wilson"—Coniston finished making handwritten notes—"the only remaining name is that of the person who witnessed the Prime Minister signing the documents of transfer of funds from your special account to his own."

Wilson blanched. "That is a confidence too far," he said peevishly. "Surely, the documents and names I have given are enough?"

"Perhaps, but the witness to the signatures must be a member of the British establishment, and he or she must be aware that it is a requirement under English law that they should report to us this unlawful action. Not to do so would render the person or persons concerned, and indeed yourself, technically, liable to prosecution as an accessory."

"Surely, not me. After all, I am the one reporting it to you."

"The signatures took place some time ago. So, yes, it may not apply to you, but the other person must be identified, or there is a high risk of prosecution."

"Let me think." Wilson frowned and pursed his lips. He thought rapidly. If he revealed that his source was the head of the Civil Service what would the repercussions be? Would he lose his hold over Wentworth? If he did, would it matter? Wentworth, he decided, would be the loser in all this. Once MI5 and MI6 knew of Wentworth holding back this information he would be finished? On balance, he decided that losing Wentworth as a tool didn't really matter. He had been milked just about dry, and of course, he still had the damning letters and photographs. They would keep him quiet for good. "Very well," he said grudgingly, "the witness is Sir Lionel Wentworth." He pretended to look deflated while secretly patting himself on the back; after all, Wentworth was no longer of use, and his ruination was of little or no consequence.

Wilson was shown back to the reception area by "girly", who did not respond to what he thought of as friendly banter, and she could not wait to be away from his presence. He was feeling very pleased with himself; it seemed that he had the ear of the two spymasters and that they would not dig too deeply into the veracity of his story and the Island boy, as he referred to Jacques Pantin, had placed the jamming device in readiness for the instruction to activate. He was, as was his intention, in absolute control of the situation and feeling very powerful.

Forty-Four

Trevor Coniston scanned the list of names written neatly on his scratch pad. They comprised those whom he wanted to attend the meeting which he had designated as Operation Closure. Neutral territory was to be used for the venue, and the one location which he would propose to them satisfied the requirements of neutrality was Recovery Island. It was a convenient location to which they had access and, which he would propose, gave none of the attendees any advantage over the others. That was the line he would give to those required to attend, although it was not the real reason at all.

The supporting cast was easy to deal with, but Creswell and Wilson would be more complex, and then there was the need to persuade Gilliland that it was not an attempt to infiltrate the Island defences, more a move to mend fences.

Contacting the Island was difficult because of the communications embargo; no communications traffic was leaving the Island, and as a result, it was impossible to ascertain that any ingoing communication was actually being received. There was no capability to deliver a message by sea or by air which left only electronic means: e-word, radio, text, and telephone. If they were able to communicate in some way, it would also be necessary to deliver a succinct message, which would offer to the Islanders something of significant benefit.

The means of communication came to him as he leafed idly through the intelligence file. There were grainy but detailed images of Creswell being driven away from the Angam Bessingford Airfield into which it was alleged he had been flown from Recovery Island. He presumed, reasonably, that Creswell would have the means to contact the Island, but in contacting him for the information, he would have to be sure not to let slip that the meeting was actually convened at Wilson's instigation with the aim potentially, of disqualifying him from being Prime Minister.

It was Creswell's presumption that Coniston wanted to make contact with Gilliland to ameliorate the situation regarding the siege, but he did not give the required number; instead he offered to contact Gilliland and suggest that he, if he chose to do so, would instigate a call to Coniston.

Contact was made by Gilliland almost immediately, and the ensuing conversation was listened to by him with high suspicion. Gilliland was uneasy about the Russian and Chinese delegates because he didn't know them. Wentworth and the two British spymasters were acceptable, but Wilson was not. At first Gilliland, would not be moved concerning Wilson's attendance, but as Coniston unfolded the potential that subsequent to the meeting, Wilson would have greater priorities than pursuit of the Island technology, he relented.

Coniston's next move was to contact all of the delegates to arrange a mutually acceptable time for the meeting. The two main characters were given the freedom to choose an acceptable date. Wilson fell over himself to be accommodating, saying that he would willingly rearrange his diary to suit, and Creswell suggested a number of dates, which would be acceptable to him.

A date was selected and transport arrangements were made to ferry the delegates to the Island from Lisbon, using the Island's passenger aircraft. For tactical reasons, there would be two flights: the first, would carry Wilson and the two spymasters, and the second, the remaining delegates. Wilson was being helpful and undertook to communicate to the Federation that the two flights should be allowed free passage for the purpose of furthering its interests. The Chinese, who were self-elected to be the voice of the Federation, agreed without delay, believing that the meeting could only assist their cause.

*

In the days leading up to the summit on the Island, Wilson further refined his plans to commandeer Recovery Island. He played the alternative scenarios over in his mind and settled on the most expedient. A telephone call via Julia Hammond to be passed on to Jacques Pantin would instruct him to await a telephone call during the course of the Operation Closure meeting which was due to start at 2 p.m. European Mean Time in three days. By this means, he would be instructed to remotely activate the jamming device he had placed in the control room. This action would disable the Island's defences, and it would at the same time disable the automatic back-up systems, leaving the Island at the mercy of his invading forces, which would overrun the Island unopposed.

He then advised the new leader of his Island task force to be ready to make maximum speed to the Island once he contacted them, which he would do as soon as the jamming had been confirmed. Their actions, once the task force had landed, were well rehearsed. Each small group was deployed to areas of importance, based on the aerial photographs that had been taken by the reconnaissance drones and reinforced by the interrogation of Jacques Pantin.

His rationale was simple: why not take advantage of being invited to the Island by being there when the "invasion" by his task force took place? It would speed up the process, and he would dispose of the delegates, excluding, of course, the Islanders, by having them shipped off the Island by sea on one of the assault vessels and delivered to the Chinese fleet for them to deal with. Then it would simply be a matter of bringing the defences back online by switching off the jamming device. Job done, he mused, they had played into his hands, and for them there was no way out.

Forty-Five

On the first of the two scheduled flights to the Island, Wilson and the spymasters accompanied by President Klastheim arrived at the Island on the day preceding the meeting. Wilson was tempted to bring the invasion forward now that he was in place, but decided that seeing Creswell, Gilliland, Crook, and Pettit destroyed on the same day would be an additional highlight on the first day of his new and glorious life. He would bide his time and savour the moment slowly and frequently.

Having been on the Island's only passenger aircraft before, Wilson showed off his familiarity during the flight from Lisbon by explaining to the other two where everything was and how long the flight would take. He called for Champagne and offered the other three drinks as though he were the host; unconsciously, he was anticipating his assuming the ownership of the Island and its assets in anticipation of the event.

Neither Coniston of MI5 nor Westinghouse of MI6 reacted to his assumed superiority, which was a source of irritation to Wilson. They accepted the drinks from the cabin attendant and retired to more distant seats to have a private conversation which specifically excluded Wilson and was even more of an irritation to him.

As they approached their destination, Wilson joined them without being invited and commenced once more to flaunt his familiarity by describing to them what would happen when they landed and how they would be transported to the meeting place. He explained to them that the Islanders would want the meeting to be recorded but that he would insist on the meeting being confidential and not recorded. The spymasters reminded him that they had called the meeting, and that he was invited by them to attend, and that it was their hosts who would dictate the terms of the meeting in pursuit of the specific agenda, which would recognise the sensibilities of their hosts. Wilson made a mental note of the rebuff and filed the information away for future retribution on his part.

Arrival and transportation was very much as Wilson had predicted, but his description did not prepare the spymasters for the smoothness of the transition, for the impact of the pristine cleanliness of the architecture, and for the infrastructure. Written reports, they had often observed in their discussions, did no justice to the impact of actuality.

They were greeted with courtesy by Gilliland, Crook, and Pettit who formally shook hands with Coniston and Westinghouse and Klastheim while merely nodding at Wilson who himself made no response. They passed through the main meeting room to get to a small side lounge where they could hold discussions in comfort.

Wilson observed that the room was set out with scratch pads, writing implements, and water carafes for more delegates than he had expected. He ran through the number of delegates as he had presumed it would be and counting the two spymasters, himself, and Creswell, there were places unaccounted for. He questioned who the extra places were for but received no response from the hosts or the spymasters. He glowered very much put out by his demands for explanations being ignored. His scowling was replaced by a sly grin when he comforted himself with the thought of how they were playing into his hands.

On the second of the two scheduled flights, Creswell was familiar with only two of the five people accompanying him; there was, of course, his old friend Sir Lionel Wentworth and Cheng Tor of the Embassy in Beijing, and the other two were unknown to him. One was a very strikingly beautiful and earthy woman who he presumed from her speech was Russian and her companion who was less elegantly dressed as he was in a brown suit worn with an inappropriately patterned tie and polished brown boots. The other Chinese, Chung Yi, he had never seen before. He wondered how the strangers related to his meeting, if they did.

Creswell and Wentworth shared a private area, which had two seats facing with a low table in between. They talked of many things but excluded the subject of the upcoming meeting on the Island. Each had their own differing reasons for doing so, and each respected the other's position; each also observed the other's nervousness about what was about to happen.

Wentworth, like the two spymasters on the flight before him, was awestruck by what they experienced after landing on the Island. He was captivated by the quiet dignity of the people and the impact of what they saw before, during, and after the transition to the official building. They too were greeted by Gilliland, Crook, and Pettit as had been the other delegates on the previous evening. A light lunch was provided for them at which the drinks provided were non-alcoholic, much to the disappointment of Yuri Kurakin, the Nuovostani delegate, who spoke rapidly to his companion, Irena Pelochev. She pointed out to him that he had consumed vast quantities of Vodka during the flight and that it was necessary for him to be sober during the course of the meeting. Neither Creswell nor Wentworth spoke Russian, but they both got the gist of the conversation and smiled conspiratorially.

At 2 p.m., the meeting commenced, and the chair was taken by Gilliland. Wilson's hackles rose when he realised the meeting would not only be attended by Gilliland, whom he considered to be inappropriate, but it would actually be administered by him. He protested and appealed to the two spymasters for a change of chairman, and his protest was discounted unilaterally, and Wilson was reminded that his attendance was as a participant rather than an instigator.

"As a neutral party, I will chair this exchange," Gilliland opened the proceedings. "The purpose of the meeting is to examine evidence presented to MI5 implicating the UK Prime Minister in activities which have been and remain contrary to the interest of the Crown, Parliament, and the United Kingdom as a whole." He paused and looked at the assembled persons one by one. Coniston and Westinghouse remained impassive, Wilson looked around tentatively unsure as to how to react.

"A number of exhibits have been offered in respect of the alleged misdeeds and each one will be presented in chronological order so that we may build a logically progressive picture of events and consequences."

"Are you both insane?" Wilson looked directly at the two spymasters. "You're going to allow a bunch of traitors to have access to some most secret information that even the cabinet doesn't know about and then make a judgement about the validity of the information presented by a minister . . . er . . . ," he corrected himself, "a technical advisor to the cabinet on matters of national security. What's more"—he stabbed the air with his rigid index finger—"these same traitors are personal friends of the accused and have probably already made up their minds that Creswell is innocent despite the facts against him that they have, no doubt, already seen."

Gilliland looked at the spymasters "Does he have a point?"

"Granted the approach we have made to this vexing problem is unorthodox," Westinghouse was placatory, "but I should point out to you, Mr Wilson that Dr Gilliland does not have the power of decision making in respect of the Prime Minister's innocence or guilt. His role is to administer the proceedings. Our role is to determine whether the evidence warrants further investigation or whether the police should be consulted with a view to prosecution. Do I make myself clear?"

"I don't like it." Wilson shook his head. "Why did we have to come here to have this investigation? We could have done this much more easily back in London."

"Sadly,"—Westinghouse paused reflectively, "we have found of late that confidential information discussed in London has a habit of landing on the desks of foreign powers within hours, sometimes minutes, of the discussions taking place, and I'm sure I don't have to remind you that this is a very sensitive issue, if leaked, would have a negative impact on our country's standing at a very difficult time. Particularly"—he paused as though searching for diplomatic words—"particularly, as we are going through another difficult phase with the Federation of Nations and a continuous state of unease with the Chinese."

"I'm still not happy," Wilson insisted. "This will be very far from a neutral meeting. It seems to be me against the rest."

"Can I suggest that we commence with the meeting without delay," Gilliland interrupted. "Meetings within meetings are not helpful or acceptable." He raised his palms with a shrug and looked at the other three.

"Sir Grenville and I are in favour of commencing," Coniston said firmly. "What about you?" He looked pointedly at Wilson.

Wilson did not answer immediately. He was weighing up the situation; he was not happy about several things, but he still wanted to destroy Creswell and then the three traitors. He also wanted to prepare for the Island's takeover. If he delayed the meeting and was then excluded from it, his control of the situation would be made more difficult.

"Well?" Coniston woke Wilson from his reverie. "What do you say?"

"I say . . ." Wilson made up his mind. "I say—that I want to register in the strongest possible terms that I disagree with the way this is being handled. But in the interests of the United Kingdom, I will go along with it as long as it is based on the irrefutable evidence that is presented and not on hearsay and innuendo that cannot be backed up."

"Very well," Gilliland said brightly, "then let us commence."

Forty-Six

The Chinese fleet had completely surrounded the Island by the time the meeting started and regular air patrols flying circuits outside the twelve-mile limit relayed back real-time video images of the interaction between sea's surface and the edge of the dome as it dipped into the uneven watery surface. They had observed that when the two flights that Wilson had advised them of were permitted to land, the outer truncated dome was still active, but the inner complete domes had been deactivated for long enough to permit the aircraft to descend or ascend unscathed. Russian "trawlers" intermingled with the Chinese craft made their own observations, which led to a vast amount of extra radio traffic with Moscow.

It had been a great disappointment to the Chinese to learn that the defence domes were impervious to radiation as had been demonstrated by the lack of success of the neutron bomb which they put down to Wilson's failures. They had allowed him the freedom of two flights in and out of the siege circle simply to see how the defences would be manipulated to allow the aircraft free passage.

Observations proved to be of little value; the disabling of the defences was too time limited to provide them with an opportunity to slip inside the defences or indeed to fire a high explosive shell into the unprotected Island. Conversations between the fleet and Chinese Intelligence agencies were terse and irritable. The fleet expected the intelligence services to come up with a workable strategy that they could implement, and the agencies expected the troops on the ground, so to speak, to seize the opportunity and launch an intuitive attack. The resultant inactivity caused extreme frustration among the Chinese ruling hierarchy, who simply demanded success from the use of their highly superior military capability pitted against an insignificant little Island that possessed one civilian aircraft, one rowing boat, some lumbering old freight planes, and no guns or missiles, and had a population which was not much more than the crews on either of their aircraft carriers.

The Chinese Fleet Commander decided to scare off the Russian trawlers to give his command something specific to do rather than just having them carrying out filler tasks. MTBs and battleships were deployed to shepherd the trawlers to points fifteen nautical miles outside the Chinese ring. Some of the trawlers deployed guns mounted in the stern and fired off a few warning shots in an attempt to prevent their being ejected but the obvious superior firepower of the Chinese craft showered the Russians with a large barrage of counter-warning shots. The Russian trawlers retreated, and the radio chatter increased considerably between the trawlers and the Russian Navy, which was steaming steadily towards the Island from their base in Murmansk.

In the control room, unaware of the device Jacques Pantin had planted in the control computer cabinet, observations were heightened because of the meeting taking place between the UK, the Federation, and the Islanders. More faces than usual were clustered around the scopes and each minute movement of sea craft was recorded in the data memory banks and by Pantin in the hand log. Pantin had volunteered to be in the control room for the duration of the meeting that was taking place in the council chambers.

There was evidence of larger craft in the Chinese fleet, probably aircraft carriers, moving up to the imposed limit. The number of aircraft circling the Island twelve to fifteen miles out doubled as the meeting on the Island continued. They were also aware of the incoming Russian fleet which was a match in numbers with the Chinese fleet and had similar firepower. The situation grew steadily more volatile as the distance between the two fleets diminished.

*

With the exception of Pettit who was kept in the loop by the control room via a discreet ear bug the rest of the meeting, unaware of the build-up of military activity, continued in ignorance. Wilson was permitted to outline his version of events as an executive summary which would be expanded as the meeting progressed. He alluded first to the reports on the Broken Arrow Project, which he had passed on to Creswell and having been warned at the earlier acrimonious meeting that he stood accused of tampering with the reports, he took the opportunity of doing what he called "setting the records straight". He insisted that he had passed the reports to Creswell in the form that they had been received, and that it was Creswell who had edited them—not as Creswell had proposed, Wilson. He was stopped—when he tried to plant the idea that Creswell had wanted the technology for his own ends and told to stick to the evidence and not to speculate.

He moved on chronologically to the misappropriation of large sums of money, saying that his evidence was simple documentation giving the times, dates, and sums of money which had been transferred out of the MOD account, and he had produced witness testimony to the signatures in the form of Sir Lionel Wentworth—head of the Civil Service.

Statements from the Simurai Bank in the name of John Connaught showed the payment of three sums of two million pounds each into the account and matched the documents signed by Creswell. A Chinese Intelligence report was produced to indicate that John Connaught was an alias used by a senior member of the British Government who was suspected of laundering funds through Beijing. The client signatures on the bank documents bore a strong resemblance to Creswell's handwriting—as though it had been disguised, Wilson pointed out. Once more, he was told to stick to the facts and not to speculate.

Wilson's testimony was short and, after he was restrained, to the point. The supporting documentation was concise and clear and on the face of it plausible. He was asked, if there was anything else, of substance, he wanted to add to his testimony. He declined and only commented that he had been hoodwinked by Creswell, and that his only concern was to serve the British public and to safeguard their interests.

Having declined to add anything further, Wilson was instructed to leave the meeting so that they could interview Creswell. Having not been told before that Creswell would be in attendance, Wilson protested that he should be allowed to stay and listen to what he called Creswell's fabrications and put them right. He was told to leave the meeting and to give Creswell the same opportunity as he himself had had to present his case without interference. He did so unwillingly, and as he left the room, he felt in his pocket for the telephone with which he would instruct both Pantin and the task force. Slowing down as he approached the lounge that had been placed at his disposal, he caught a fleeting glance of Creswell as he left the room where he had been waiting. The door to the other waiting room closed slowly enough for him to catch glance of the other occupants of the room and was disturbed to see Wentworth and others whom he glimpsed but had no time to recognise. His grip on the telephone tightened, and he withdrew it from his pocket.

Creswell entered the meeting room and nodded briefly to its occupants. He assumed his seat and noted that one of the positions at the table, which had been occupied, judging by the doodles on the scribble pad and an empty coffee cup, was now vacant.

The preamble, which had been given to Wilson, was repeated for the benefit of Creswell. He accepted the neutrality of the chair without comment and listened to the catalogue of evidence that had been presented, he presumed correctly, by Wilson, although he was not mentioned by name. He was disappointed by the revelation that his accuser was no other than Wilson, whom he had let it be known, was a staunch ally.

Although he was aware of the nature of the evidence, from previous conversations with Wilson, it was depressing for him to hear the full catalogue read out dispassionately, and it struck him as being even more damning than he had previously thought. He was given the opportunity to respond to the accusations made in his own time and in his own way.

He was comparatively ill prepared; the only evidence he produced was the amended reports showing how they had been doctored before being presented to him by Wilson. He also reaffirmed that he had no knowledge of how his signature had appeared on the transfer documents. Further, he had no knowledge of a bank account offshore and professed that he did not know anybody with the name of John Connaught.

In that there was no way to refute the allegations made; that is, he could not prove that he had not signed the documents, had not opened a bank account, and did not know John Connaught, and his evidence was simply his word.

The three who listened to his brief evidence waited patiently until he had finished and then ascertained that there was nothing left for him to say. He did add that he had had a meeting with Wilson at which threats were made, and there was an admission by Wilson that the information was fabricated, although he was unable to produce any evidence of this because Wilson had disabled the recording device.

At this conclusion, the two spymasters gave each other meaningful looks and excused him. Like Wilson, he left the room to await the rest of the proceedings and like Wilson, he was troubled by the meeting. The three observers had made no comments about his denial of all the things of which he was accused and even to him his denials were appallingly, perhaps even terminally, weak. He was also concerned about the looks that the spymasters had exchanged at the weakness of his position.

Wilson sat alone in the waiting lounge; he was indecisive about when to start his assault on the Island and in agitation flipped his telephone keyboard open and close. He was sorely tempted to give the go straightaway, but if he did, the destruction of Creswell would be interrupted, and he would have no further chance to meet that goal. He thought it better to wait until Creswell had been found guilty of all the charges at which time he could leak the information to the European Press International Agency (EPIA), and the Popular Press Agency (PPA), via his two secret weapons, the two journalists, DK and Hammond. They would have no choice but to report exactly what he told them to. Their words would destroy Creswell and the impending capture of Recovery Island would lead to the downfall of the trio of traitors. A good day at the office he thought with satisfaction.

The Island's usual one and a half hour meeting limit having been suspended for this occasion, both Wilson and Creswell were summoned back to the meeting room. Already waiting for them were Coniston and Westinghouse with Gilliland, the three original adjudicators, and they, much to Wilson's displeasure, had been joined by Crook and Pettit. The air in the room was electric as they all settled in for the final run.

"Gentlemen," Gilliland opened the proceedings, "you are probably aware that I am of the opinion that meetings over an hour long are less than efficient. To overcome this problem, this meeting has been broken into several segments each of which lasted for less than an hour, some for only ten minutes." He paused and looked at each delegate in turn as if wondering at what level he should pitch his summary. "It does not fall on me to reach any conclusions about the information and evidence presented. It is my task to summarise such evidence and make non-partisan observations about their validity. The accusation is that James Creswell, Prime Minister of the United Kingdom, has abused his position of trust by falsifying research reports for personal gain and by misappropriating funds, namely, six million pounds, for his own use. Documentary evidence against him has been inspected. Evidence presented by him in his defence has likewise been inspected. These evidences are in conflict and have been scrutinised by some of the best experts in the world, and their findings are inconclusive."

"Just a minute!" Wilson rose to his feet to protest the questioning of his documents, which he knew had been forged by the best in the world.

"Sit down, Wilson, and listen," Gilliland said sternly.

"Who the hell do you think you are?" he snarled.

"Mr Wilson," Coniston interrupted mildly, "Mr Gilliland is in the chair, and it would be in your interest to listen to him in his official and neutral capacity."

Gilliland continued as Wilson subsided, "In that the findings of the experts relative to the validity of these documents are inconclusive, we must look again at the accusations evidenced and the rebuttals offered. Accepting, for the moment, that the accuser and the accused are men of integrity, we must use some other means to measure veracity. The first documentary evidence relates to the reports sent from the research facility on the Isles of Scilly. Creswell proposes that the reports sent via Wilson were doctored by him before being passed on. Wilson, on the other hand, assures us that the original reports sent on to Creswell by him were later doctored by Creswell for his own purposes."

Creswell half rose from his chair to protest that Wilson had changed his tune from the original version at the earlier meeting on the Island. He stopped when he noticed that Gilliland shook his head almost imperceptibly. The vacuum he left was filled immediately by Wilson.

"It seems obvious to me that I have presented concrete proof, and Creswell has produced only denials backed up by nothing." He sat back looking self-satisfied.

"Perhaps so," Gilliland continued, "and then there is the matter of the documents of transfer purported to be signed by Prime Minister Creswell. As I have said, the experts cannot be sure one way or the other concerning the validity of the signature, but we have talked to the person who is identified as being witness to the documents being signed by the PM."

"And?" Wilson interrupted.

"And he verified that he had seen the documents signed."

Creswell again half rose to deny the allegations and was stopped by another imperceptible shake of the head and a frown.

Wilson stood up triumphantly. "There I told you so. None of you believed me, and there's the proof."

"Please sit down, Mr Wilson. I would like to finish my review," Gilliland said softly. "There are other issues that need to be considered. There is the matter of the account with the Simurai Bank in Beijing held by one John Connaught. The documentation is clear. The account exists—the money was paid in, and it was paid out again to an offshore account through a series of confusing transactions, the trail for which peters out somewhere in Eastern Europe. We also have documentation from a Chinese source which links the account to the PM, and we have interviewed the document provider and are satisfied with his account of the situation." He looked at Creswell and again indicated that he should not react. Turning to Wilson, he said, "What do you have to say before I hand the meeting over to Mr Coniston and Sir Grenville Westinghouse?"

"Like I said before, it gives me no pleasure to expose the man that I championed as a fraud, but he obviously is, and as such, he should stand down immediately and then be prosecuted with the full force of law."

Forty-Seven

Jacques Pantin was distracted; he also felt claustrophobic having been in the control room for more than five hours. He looked again for the fifth time in ten minutes at the special telephone that had been provided for him and wondered for the tenth time in ten minutes what was taking them so long to make contact. He had also made several visits to the computer cabinet to make sure that the device was still there and was still switched on waiting for him to activate it. It was in place where it could not easily be seen by a casual observer; he satisfied himself that all was as it should be.

At the same time, the commander of the task force sat, heaved to, in the lead assault vessel just outside the twelve-mile limit. He too checked his telephone as he waited impatiently. He instructed the men in his boat, and those in all the others to recheck their own communication devices as well as their weapons. The engineers on board each craft were instructed to check engine functions and fuel levels. This was one commander who did not intend to share the fate of the previous commanders who had failed miserably and ignominiously and would pay Wilson's price for that failure.

On board *Foxhound*, the Chinese C-in-C fleet watched the radarscopes and the real-time video and saw that Wilson's task force was getting ready for something. They would keep a watching brief and take whatever opportunity the changing situation offered. If Wilson had a plan which breached the defences, they would allow him to take the initial action to commandeer the Island and then with their superior forces and firepower take it from him. The C-in-C felt confident that whatever happened, they would be the winner; if Wilson succeeded, they would take it over, and if he failed, they would simply sit out the siege as had been their original intention.

It had been made clear to the C-in-C that Wilson was now persona non grata, as far as the Chinese were concerned, and that they would only offer to help him if there was an advantage for them, otherwise, he was of no value. He had chosen to stop cooperating with the Chinese Government and agencies and had become a liability; he was to all intents and purposes entirely expendable.

The C-in-C's attention was diverted by news from the communication room that a number of warships were converging on their position from all compass points. Initial intelligence indicated that the vessels were Russian and the coded messages passing between them were for the present unintelligible. He ordered aircraft to find and identify the Russian vessels, which were still too far away to be an immediate threat and to send back photo reconnaissance of them. They judged it unlikely that the Russians would resort to a missile attack so early in the engagement. At the same time, the Chinese officer envied the Islander's sole ownership of NRT radar, which would have made their intelligence information so much clearer.

The Island's control room was buzzing with excitement as their HMTs showed additional shipping and aircraft and the radio chatter became frantic. Pantin watched with some apprehension not knowing whether this should be happening or if he should report his observations. He left the control room and went into the men's room where he locked himself in a cubicle and pressed the single call button, which put him through to his contact. To his surprise, he was answered, not by Hammond, but by a man's voice and the man was testy, to say the least. Pantin asked what had happened to Julie. He was asked what he wanted to say to Julie, and he spilled out information about the increase in sea and air movements, and he didn't know what to do. He was told to get off and keep off the line until he was called and the telephone went dead.

Wilson closed his telephone angrily. The interruption had broken his concentration at the moment of his victory over Creswell. He determined that the Island boy and Juliet Hammond would rue the day they had broken the silence and tied up the phone, which was his only means of coordinating the sensitive time constraints for the attack to be perfect.

The spymasters had now taken over the meeting, and the three adjudicators who had been joined by Crook and Pettit, sat back in their chairs as the meeting entered its final sweet phase.

"Gentlemen," Sir Grenville Westinghouse took up the cudgels, "despite what Mr Gilliland has just said, there are underlying issues which need to be addressed. These issues are threefold in scope: one, the doctoring of the reports; two, the transfer of the monies; three, the true identity of John Connaught."

"One, the doctoring of the reports." he continued without waiting for comment, "It has been alleged that the reports were doctored by the PM, then the Minister of Defence, and in that respect, I am assured by the two authors that the report sent to Mr Wilson by them was the full report. There are two versions of the report: one is the original, and the other is abridged. The question is at what juncture the edited report was prepared. During the course of a later meeting between you two," he nodded to Wilson and Creswell, "the PM produced the abridged report that he claims was the report given to him by Wilson and that at the end of the meeting the papers had disappeared, it is assumed by the PM, into the briefcase of the DDP." He looked at Wilson expecting and getting a tirade.

"Well, he would say that, wouldn't he? It's just another of his lies to cover up his duplicity." Wilson was on well-prepared ground and was confident of victory.

"Perhaps," Westinghouse responded, "or perhaps the PM is being truthful and you, Mr Wilson, are the one who is fabricating."

"Typical," Wilson exploded, "his word against mine, and you are going along with his."

"Not at all. We're not siding with anybody. I simply made a valid observation. Why should we believe either version? In this respect, it is "you said and he said, and he said and you said". It is not clear to us why either one of you would want the project stopped when it was progressing so well and after so much expenditure."

Wilson blanched at this observation; it was one of the many small weaknesses in his story which he had hoped would be covered by his endeavouring to short-circuit the investigative process during the meeting at the MI5 offices with Coniston and Westinghouse.

"Two," Westinghouse continued with the issues, without leaving Wilson time to interrupt further, "the transfer of the monies. As I have said, the handwriting experts are undecided about the validity of the PM's signatures, but we have interrogated the witness to those signatures, and they are indeed genuinely those of the PM."

Creswell held his head in his hands and sighed deeply. Wilson smiled to himself and was satisfied that his deception had been a great success. All he now needed to do was to wait for the conclusion of the meeting, leak the results, and disable the Island's defences. He was all but home and dry.

"Issue number three, who is John Connaught?" Westinghouse held up three fingers of his right hand in a Boy Scout-like gesture. "As far as we can determine, he does not actually exist, except on paper. Through our contact in the Beijing Embassy, we have been able to trace that he is part of the upper echelon of Westminster Government, although we have not been able to identify him exactly, we have considerable circumstantial evidence as to his identity. In the process of investigating this operation, we have actually uncovered more and perhaps greater treachery in the form of leaked Federation information and disinformation being inserted in its place. For the record, we have today had meetings with and elicited information from Cheng Tor, a Chinese member of the British Embassy staff, and Chung Yi, a member of the Chinese "*diplomatic*" service, for the want of a more accurate description, and to the head of UK Civil Service Sir Lionel Wentworth. It is from these sources that we have determined what in, all probability, is the truth about Project Broken Arrow, the misappropriation of funds, the actual John Connaught, and the disseminator of leaked information and disinformation." He looked up gravely at Creswell.

Creswell closed his eyes and his shoulders slumped. He knew he was finished; it was unfair, but there was nothing he could do about it.***

Forty-Eight

The room became suddenly quiet. Creswell remained slumped as he sat, his face grey and worn, the three Islanders looked on the scene with disbelief, the spymasters looked impassive and Wilson looked jubilant.

"You will excuse me for a moment, Gentlemen." It was not a request. Wilson stood up quickly hitting the table and causing the water in the carafe before him to shimmer in agitated colliding circles. "I won't be a moment." He rushed from the room hastily withdrawing his satellite phone from his pocket.

He returned to the room less than five minutes later, looking happy. Being impatient, he had started the ball rolling with both of the press agencies, the EPIA and the PPA, anticipating his victory over his adversaries. On his return to the room, he realised immediately that something was wrong and the look of happiness was replaced by one of apprehension. Taking his seat, he scanned the faces around him; the spymasters remained impassive, and the Islanders looked slightly stunned and—much to Wilson's alarm—Creswell looked composed.

"What's going on?" Wilson asked tentatively.

"We hadn't quite finished when you left the room so precipitously, so I'll enlighten you about the conversation we had in your absence. In addition to those people previously mentioned, we spoke to Yuri Karakin and his assistant Irena Pelochev."

At the mention of these two names, Wilson frowned in concentration and scowled when the penny dropped, out of context and because Coniston had pronounced their names correctly rather than the way they were stored in his head. He had not immediately recognised the two names; he also thought of them in his mind as the factory manager and his insatiable assistant rather than important players in this game of his making. Loud alarm bells began to ring in Wilson's jangled mind; he settled in his seat and waited now with some trepidation for the meeting to unfold.

"We have decided several things," Coniston took up the discussion. "One is that, the documents signed by the PM were blanks slipped in among the many documents which daily had to be signed by him. We know this is so, but we cannot at this precise time identify exactly who was responsible for the sleight of hand, having said that, it seems a little unlikely that the PM would have done this to himself. This information is verified by the person to whom you guided us." He looked directly and meaningfully at Wilson. "That being so, the issue of the bank account and the real identity of John Connaught do not attach in any way to the PM. Therefore,"—he nodded towards Creswell—"it is our finding that the PM is not implicated in the offences described. He is, therefore, able to continue in the position of PM, unimpeded, with the blessing of the secret services."

Wilson was beside himself with apoplectic rage. His ploy to destroy Creswell had failed; he had just told the EPIA and the PPA, news agencies, that Creswell was about to be revealed as a traitor and a felon by the British Secret Service. "Just like I said earlier," he spluttered indignantly at the spymasters, "you're taking the words of traitors,"—he indicated the three Islanders and Creswell—"over those of a true patriot." He patted his own chest. "Well, it's not going to rest here. I will be reporting this biased meeting to the police and other interested legal authorities. I should have known that all you university boys would stick together. Well, let me tell you when I'm through with you all, will you be sticking together as you all go down the tubes together."

"Are you finished yet because I am not?" Westinghouse looked severe. "We have trailed the Broken Arrow documents through your office, and it is plain that you are the one who had the opportunity to doctor them. We also have a recording of the meeting that you said did not take place between yourself and the Prime Minister in his office." He placed a small tape recorder on the table and pressed play. The recording quality was poor, but the raised voices were recognisable as Creswell and Wilson.

"I'm not a damn servant." Wilson's voice hissed venomously *"If you want coffee, get it yourself".*

"No coffee?" Creswell's response was calm. *"Never mind, I'll get some later."*

"Enough, you're a dead man. I've got enough dirt on you to sink your miserable career forever."

Realisation dawned on Wilson as he listened to the tape; his face at first paled and then became even more apoplectic. How had this happened? He had personally disabled the recording system, yet here was a damning record of their shouting match. He tried desperately to remember what it was he had said at the meeting with Creswell, before which he knew without a doubt that he had disabled the recording device in the office, and he tried equally desperately to think of a way out of this disaster. Clearly, Creswell had not made the recording, so he tried with some panic to imagine who might have done it. The only other person who might have known of his intent to frame Creswell was Sir Lionel Wentworth; if it was him, it would be necessary to discredit him and, therefore, the recording. These thoughts were over in a flash and the recording continued to play.

"I called the meeting, so let's deal with my bit first, and once, we've done with that, I'll listen to what you have to say to put it mildly, as I probably indicated to you on board Foxhound. I am most disappointed with your attitude. Your interpersonal skills are somewhat lacking, and you seem to think that you are a free agent, and as such, you can do whatever you like. You also seem to be using the Dark Ops Ffund as a personal unaccounted expense account. That has to stop. You are as accountable as any other member of this team."

"My god, just listen to yourself. I'm telling you that your career is about to be destroyed, and your harping on about my not being overkind to idiots and moaning about my expenses. You're a damn dinosaur, an inbred upper-class misnomer. You have no idea what's going on around you. God knows why I chose to support you as Prime Minister. I don't make many mistakes, but in your case, I did. But now, I'm going to undo that mistake."

"Really, and how do you propose to do that?"

"I could have been soft and diplomatic about this. But you're so stupid, I don't think I'll bother. I have irrefutable evidence that you are a crook and that you've been duping the country and stealing money from a covert account to feather your own nest." There was a rustling as he extracted papers from his briefcase. There was a moment of silence during which Creswell was presumably reading the documents. "I have no knowledge of this particular document," Creswell said.

"I have back up authorisations with your signature." There was a further rustling as Wilson presumably threw more documents on to the desk.

"I have no knowledge of these documents. They are obviously forgeries." Creswell was dismissive.

"Not only are they not forgeries but I have a witness to your signing them'

"And who might that be?"

"*Never you mind, who it is. That person will be called at the appropriate time. Not so cocky now, are you?*"

"*Not being prepared to tell me who it is makes me think that the person is a figment of your imagination or that they are unreliable or have no credibility.*"

"*Wouldn't you just like to know?*"

"*Not really.*".

"*Not really! You think I'm some kind of novice or something.*"

"*No, I think you're something else. I think you're an idiot.*"

"*Idiot, idiot, I'll show, you idiot. Take a look at that.*" There was a further rustling as Wilson threw more paperwork on to the desk. "*This links the payments you made to Connaught, and it attaches Connaught to you. In fact, it shows that you are John Connaught, and you've been caught with your snout in the trough. Not bad for an idiot, huh?*"

"*You could have written this proof yourself. In fact, you probably did. It won't stand scrutiny without independent corroboration.*"

"*Okay, smart alec, I've got independent corroboration. This is a report from an agent in our embassy in Beijing, who got it from a mole in the Chinese Diplomatic Corps. It proves that you and Connaught are the same person in the pay of the Chinese.*"

"*None of this is true, but I must congratulate you on the skill with which you have compiled this tissue of lies.*"

"*You say its lies, and I say it isn't. You have enough enemies, in your position as PM, who will believe the worst of you, and I won't be the one to contradict them. Don't you see I am above reproach. Don't you remember I'm the one who championed your cause as PM as everybody knows. I am seen as your ally, so why would I try to do you down. My words against you will be another, and perhaps, the final, nail in your coffin.*"

"*Your words will condemn you.*"

"Please," Wilson said with a pained voice *"Do you take me for a complete fool. I look after security in this building. I disabled this sound system earlier today."*

"Just as I said before—I congratulate you on your skilful manipulation of this fabrication."

Six pairs of eyes were focussed on Wilson as silence descended after the tape came to an abrupt end. He gathered himself together and displayed an offhand confidence that he did not feel. With feigned laziness, he returned their gaze and laughed humourlessly. "Please, what do you take me for?" He looked at the tape recorder with disdain. "There is only one person who could have forged that recording, and if you take his word for anything, you're more stupid than, I thought. Let me tell you some home truths about Sir Lionel lah-di-dah Wentworth."

"Enough," Coniston stopped him in his tracks, "we know all about the hold you have over Sir Lionel, and we have persuaded him to put himself in our hands rather than spend the rest of his life being beholden to you."

"He is a disgusting pervert," Wilson said viciously, "once the press get to know about this he will be finished, you see," he added with a look of cunning. "I hold all the cards in respect of Wentworth and Creswell—it's just the word of a pervert and a traitor against that of mine, and I am seen by the British public to be a true patriot and defender of the country."

"All the bravado in the world is not going to save you from your own duplicity," Coniston said dispassionately. "We know from both Kurakin and Pelochev that you were involved in the procurement of a neutron bomb from their facility in Nuovostan."

"Nothing to do with me. You must be confusing me with somebody else."

"You mean the deal was sealed by Simon Queeze."

"What do you know about Queeze?" Wilson looked alarmed. "Who is he?" He corrected his oversight.

"Take a look at these." Coniston slid a small pile of black and white photographs across the table towards him.

Wilson picked up the photographs and spread them on the table before him. They showed several images of the bearded Simon Queeze reclining naked on a satin-covered bed in Kurakin's Dacha. Progressively, the photographs revealed the figure with the wig removed to show a bald pate and the beard when removed showed a clearly unconscious Wilson.

"Fakes!" Wilson said without any real conviction. He was desperate to gain some time to explain away the damning images. "Look at the pictures, I had obviously been drugged, and you're looking at them back to front, that's not me being revealed having been disguised as somebody else. That,"—he jabbed his fingers at the photographs—"that is me being disguised as somebody else—and I don't understand why?"

"Damn, but he is good," Creswell's voice was tinged with admiration.

"Maybe," Westinghouse said, "but we have the testimony of the two Nuovostani witnesses, whom I mentioned to you earlier, they took the photographs."

"From the political perspective, we are weak," Creswell said with sadness, "it's his word against two quasi Russian bomb manufacturers."

"Taken in isolation, I agree with you, but collectively what have we got?" Coniston began counting off on his fingers. "He can be shown by the testimony of the chief civil servant, at least circumstantially, to have doctored the original project documents. He can be implicated in the procurement of the PM's signature by the same civil servant. He can be linked to the setting up of the bank account by a known member of the Chinese Security Services. He can be shown to be complicit in the setting up of information linking the PM to the imaginary John Connaught by a Chinese member of the British Embassy."

"Let's look at this dispassionately." Wilson snorted derisively. "Testimony from Russian bomb makers, circumstantially doctoring document, implicated in getting signatures, linked to setting up a bogus bank account, and to inventing Connaught." He shook his head slowly. "And look at the credentials of the corroborating witnesses: Russian bomb makers, a member of the Chinese Secret Service, and a questionable Chinese who was a civilian member of the British Embassy. Not, to the general public, the most reliable of sources and it would be very damaging for any member of the Civil Service to be implicated in such blatant illegal activities."

The DDP relaxed and smiled at his adversaries. "Where do we go from here, Gentlemen?" He was back to being full of confidence.

"The question is not where we go, it's a question of where do you go?" Creswell looked at Wilson speculatively. "You've screwed up all the relationships which could be of value to you: with the Islanders, the Federation, the Chinese government, your own government, and secret services. There's nowhere for you to go where you will be welcome."

"I don't need welcome I just need controlling power and let me demonstrate to you how it can be done." He stood up and took out his telephone pressing one of the speed dial numbers. "Be ready and move up to the line." Disconnecting the call, he made another. "Press the button and get out of there." He finished the second call and sat down. "Now, plebs, we wait for the invasion and," he turned to the three Islanders, "get ready for the death sentence from your new ruler."

The only person sitting at the table who didn't look confused was Wilson. He was still furious that he had failed to finish off Creswell, but he was mollified to find that the accusations made against him, with the possible exception of Wentworth, were entirely circumstantial. If he absolutely needed to do, so he could still pull the rabbit out of the hat that would harm Wentworth enough to render his account of events unacceptable.

"Too cryptic for me." Gilliland raised an eyebrow as he looked at Wilson, "What did all of that mean?"

"Just wait and see. You will be getting a telephone call very soon that will stand your little world on its head." He turned to Creswell with a sickly grin. "I'll get you next time, and I'll make a point of it."

"You won't be doing it as DDP," Creswell said quietly, "you are no longer required as an adviser to His Majesty's Government, and I will do everything in my power to bring you to book over all this."

"Ooh, I've got the sack," he said derisively. "Your problem is you think too small, and you always have. That is why I championed you to be Prime Minister. I knew I could manipulate you, and do what I'm about to do at your and the traitors expense."

Their conversations were interrupted by the flickering of the lights and then a complete power loss and the strident wailing of what sounded like an antique World War II air raid siren. Emergency lighting flickered on and, at the same time, the telephone rang and was snatched up by Pettit who said simply, "We'll be there." He leapt from his chair and shouted to his two fellow Islanders, "With me—we have an extreme emergency."

They departed the room, leaving Wilson and the spymasters in attendance.

"No need to rush, Gentlemen," Wilson said to the closed door, "there's absolutely nothing you can do about it. This place and the rest of the world are now mine."

Forty-Nine

The three founders ran helter-skelter down the stairs, across the atrium, and out into the open piazza. Crossing the space between the administration buildings and the control centre at full speed, they were joined in their flight by Caine whose hair streamed out behind her as she ran. Bursting through the doors, they tumbled into the dimly lit control room where the radarscopes and the other monitors were blank.

"Update!" Shouted Pettit.

"Complete power loss!" Lawson who was shift leader informed him. "Sudden and catastrophic."

"What happened to the automatic back-up?"

"It didn't engage. I've got one of the techies working on it now."

"Good, the info screens are obviously down, so what about the physical back-up log."

"That's being kept by Jacques Pantin," He looked around the room. "I don't see him anywhere." He went to the desk where the log book was kept. "The last entry shows the small flotilla approaching the edge of the dome at high speed."

"With the dome and the radar disabled, we're defenceless and blind," Pettit said more to himself than those around him. Then he added with more volume, "We have to assume that the flotilla is on its way to us, and the only way to see it is by eye, so let's get a coast watch set up and give them binoculars and walkie-talkies—so that they can keep in touch."

Pettit joined the techie at the computer cabinet where he was attaching pulse meters to various parts of the mechanisms. "What gives?"

"Power is still being supplied from the geothermal stations, but it's not getting to the network. It's not something I've come across before so I don't really know where to start." He shrugged in reluctant resignation.

"Keep looking and get help. We need to be on top of this very soon, or we could be overrun." Pettit did his level best to keep his voice calm, but the facts were that Wilson had known about this disaster in advance and keeping calm was not easy.

The lookouts radioed in the reports as soon as the incoming flotilla of ten combat vessels was visible to the naked eye. All ten stayed together in close formation; they were obviously not concerned about the destructive force of the defence dome and were aware that the Island had no firepower to enable their own defence and did not feel the need to tread warily; their only concern was the possible deployment of the Island's one and only highly destructive combat vessel.

Warnings from the coastal watchers became urgent as the incoming forces came nearer and then became frantic as they entered the harbour. Nine of the craft headed to the dockside to disembark, and one veered off to board and commandeer *Wallow* 5 where she lay tied up in the maintenance dock.

With practiced precision, the troops disembarked and formed platoons on the dockside. Each platoon was lead by an NCO, who ensured that the troopers were correctly equipped and armed. Each had a short barrelled assault rifle and spare magazines of metal jacket bullets. They wore Special Forces uniform similar to that which had been worn by Pettit just a few years ago when he was under Wilson's patronage.

Pettit scrambled into his own Special Forces uniform and ran at the double to the dockside to confront the invading force. His appearance in one of their uniforms with its colonel insignia discretely on one shoulder caused significant confusion. He walked up to the commander and snapped a professional soldier's salute. The commander hesitated clearly confused by Pettit's appearance.

"Since when did you stop saluting a superior officer?" Pettit snapped. "Stand up straight man and salute properly."

The commander saluted without conviction and muttered "Sir." Clearly, not knowing how to handle this unexpected intervention.

"What are your orders? And who issued them?"

"We are under the command of the DDP, and we are to occupy this Island."

"Do you mean to tell me that you are under the orders of a civilian?" Pettit was trying desperate delaying tactics to give the techies time to find and fix the computer malfunction.

A wild lone figure came running towards Pettit and the troops waving his arms. "What the hell do you think you're doing? Commander, detain that man, he is a spy in a British uniform." Wilson was, again, enraged.

The commander hesitated clearly undecided about which of the two to acknowledge as rightfully senior. Wilson stopped before them, puffing and panting, trying hard to catch his breath and issue more orders. He spluttered and pointed his finger at Pettit. "Detain that man, Commander, he is not a member of our forces, and he has no right to wear this uniform. Take him now and restrain him."

Making up his mind, the commander indicated to two of his bulky platoon leaders to follow the command. They approached Pettit with arms extended.

"Lay a hand on me, and I'll kill both of you," he said quietly and dispassionately, "and then I'll kill Wilson."

They hesitated and looked at the commander who in turn looked at Wilson; Wilson's face had gone pale.

"He is a prisoner of war," Wilson said in a barely controlled voice. "Treat him like an officer and escort him to the buildings over there," he indicated with a wave of his arm the administration block. "I'll be there later to interrogate him."

Pettit, deciding that discretion was the best immediate course of action gave his name rank and number with a sardonic smile. Those who heard his name looked at each other knowingly; they knew of the legend of Pettit who was recognised as the only man ever to have bettered Wilson, and they knew that given the glimmering of an excuse, he would carry out his threat of killing.

Wilson saw the looks that passed between the troops and grew apoplectic once more. He resolved to show both Pettit and the troops who was boss.

With their defences circumvented, the Island fell anti-climactically to the invaders without a whimper. The architect of their downfall, Pantin, who bit the hand that had fed him, was jubilant. The few Islanders who had observed what took place were stunned that what they had believed to be invulnerable was just so much smoke and mirrors. A relatively small force of a few hundred troops, one civilian and an Island collaborator had begun the destruction of a force which had been intended to be used for the ultimate good of mankind but which could now be used for the aggrandisement of one man; one very unstable and dangerous man.

Fifty

ack Pantin was pleased with himself, and he felt justified in his treachery. *Why had they picked on him so many times without good reason? They actually punished him for getting a little bit drunk and, what he termed, banging up the place a little bit. After all what he did wasn't serious, nobody was actually hurt badly—well, not too badly anyway. What kind of democracy was it that did not allow him the freedom to enjoy himself a little in this godforsaken boring place?*

He really enjoyed the powerful feeling of revenge he felt when he was called into the control room together with the detested leaders of the Ruling Council, to show them how he could reactivate the control systems with the click of a button. The moment he did so, the defence and radar systems came back online immediately.

Close-view HMTs showed the circles of the domes that provided defence and showed that some of the ships of the Chinese Fleet and some of the Russian observation vessels had strayed inside the twelve-mile limit, in the hour or so since the switch off, and were now trapped between the inner and outer defence domes.

"This just gets better and better," Wilson was jubilant. "Chinese and Russian ships at my mercy. I must talk to them—how do I do that?" He turned to Craddock his senior military technical specialist.

Craddock approached the computer array and inspected the layout. Picking up a hand microphone, he keyed the digital readout until he reached the wavelength he required and handed the mike to Wilson. "Press to send and release to receive."

"Who is this?" Wilson released the button. There was a hiss of static and a pause before a tinny voice responded.

"This is the communications centre aboard the Federation of Nations vessel *Huni*. Who are you?"

"This is Wilson," he hesitated as he searched for unfamiliar words, "and I am the ruler of Recovery Island." He released the switch, looking very pleased with himself.

"What is the nature of your communication?"

"You and the Ruskies are inside my territorial waters, and you're caught between two shields, so don't move around, otherwise, it'll be curtains for you. Cross the shield lines, and you'll be vaporised, so make sure you don't." He paused and added, "Tell the Ruskies too, the same warning applies to them."

Wilson turned and looked at the assembled Ruling Council members some of whom had been called in to witness the switch on. Armed guards were situated at strategic points in the room to ensure that none of the equipment was interfered with. He noticed with a glow that Gilliland, Pettit, and Crook were in attendance. He looked at some of the other faces and stopped suddenly as his gaze fell on Caine.

"Penelope, what are you doing here?" He looked puzzled.

"Mr Wilson!" She paused to give herself some time to think and launched into a breathless but adoring explanation, "I'm err . . . Still preparing my err . . . paper on the err . . . Democratic process, and that's why I'm here." She winced when she realised that she sounded so unconvincing—after all why would she come to what the world thought of as a dictatorship to talk democracy?

"Well, my dear, your being here is my good fortune. We shall have dinner together tonight. Corporal," he waved over an NCO, "escort Ms Delaney to her living quarters and make sure she is comfortable. If she's not, move her to a better location, close to mine." He turned with an unattractive smile to Delaney. "You will be escorted to my suite at eight this evening for dinner. Be ready on time." It was a command not a request.

His attention turned once more to the HMT tables where the vessels between the two shields appeared to be stationary. Wilson's technical specialist was exploring the unfamiliar system to determine the extent and control of the radar scans. The controls were simple, and it showed overlaid matrices covering sea and aircraft with numbers attached to the aircraft in height layers. Further manipulation extended the range of the radar which, on the current setting, was operational up to one hundred miles from source.

"Fantastic," the operator shook his head in amazement, "this set actually bends the radar signal over the curvature of the earth in all directions of the compass. The enlarged field diminished the size of the image on the screen and the air, sea, and land activity could be seen as minute shapes moving across the domed holographic table surface. Wow, just look at that—the radar is actually bending around buildings and obstructions, located hundreds of miles away in the Azores, to show what's going on at ground level behind them." He was lost in total admiration.

"Very good," Wilson's tone was dismissive, "time to finish playing, it's not a toy, you know. Come on do your job, and get back to the Chinese and Russian fleets—that's what I'm interested in. You can play later on your own time, so don't waste mine. Your job is to find out how to control the defence system and how to switch it off, talk to these Islanders and find out how to do it from them."

"I tried that but the controllers here said they don't know how it works and that only two people do."

"I suppose that's Gilliland and Crook?" He received a nod of consent. "They won't volunteer anything. You're the comms and computer expert, sort it out for yourself and don't waste any time about it."

*

Gilliland, Crook, and Pettit were shepherded into one of the small waiting rooms within the administration block. There was an armed guard outside to ensure that they did not wander. Pettit had a face like thunder, and he paced restlessly in the confined space.

"Damn," he expostulated, "I've let you all down. I acted like an amateur. I should have considered an inside job as a possibility after we'd allowed the journalists on to the Island. Obviously, he, she, or they nobbled somebody." He stopped and slapped his forehead. "Of course, it must have been Jacques Pantin, you remember him, the one who went to England with the tabloid lady . . . What's her name?"

"Somebody Hammond," Gilliland volunteered, "and don't beat yourself to death over it. There was no way you could know that he'd been planted or that he'd have the ability to do whatever it was he did to the control system. The important thing for us now is to find some way out of this mess. Where do we go from here?"

"They'll want to be able to control the defences so that they can repel all-comers and ultimately get air and sea craft to and from the Island." Crook, the most calm of the three, continued thoughtfully, "I am presuming that Wilson is not going to share his booty with anybody, least of all the Chinese and by default the Federation, so he has to get control of everything very quickly. The good thing about knowing him so well is that his irrationality is, paradoxically, predictable." He paused as he thought through the events that he anticipated. "What he'll find out fairly quickly is that his people will not be able to master the control system and that he will have to speak to Chester or me to be able to do so." He turned to Pettit. "And it's thanks to you, Silas, only Chester and I know how to master it. Courtesy your security protocol. So like Chester said, don't beat yourself to death over it."

"You're all very understanding," Pettit said resignedly. "But the fact is I screwed up and left us vulnerable, and we're all paying for it. That being said, let's look at the situation under a cold hard light: One—Wilson has unrestricted command of the control room. Two—we are the only ones who can show him how to control the control room. Three—we are out of the loop at the moment and can't influence anything that's going on to our own advantage. Fourth . . ." He paused and frowned. "The first three are enough to be getting on with, so let's examine what we must do to redress the situation."

They started a brainstorming session which produced some bizarre scenarios for regaining control starting with overpowering their armed guards by some subterfuge and breaking out of the building in which they were confined and progressing to more esoteric scenarios. One by one the possibilities were abandoned as the freedom they gained gave them no real advantage; they were three unarmed men against scores of armed professional soldiers.

Ultimately, Pettit came up with a plan which, although it was sketchy and relied a lot on luck, was at least a possibility even if the possibility was remote.

*

Caine was collected from her apartment shortly before 8 p.m. and escorted to the administration building using one of the airport VIP passenger transport buggies rather than a TC. People on the boulevards were surprised to see transportation on the normally pedestrian only streets and a number of potentially fatal accidents were narrowly avoided.

The vehicle was driven up to the administration building and through the double doorway directly into the atrium. The lift took them to the third floor where she was shown into one of the small dining rooms.

"Welcome, my dear." Wilson was rubbing his hands together like a latter-day Uriah Heap. "At last, we can have a private dinner together. I've already ordered for us. We're having an Italian salad to start, followed by fillet steak, followed by apple pie and ice cream. I'm sure you will find the meal satisfactory. I thought that candlelight would be appropriate."

She took the seat that was pulled out for her by a stony-faced, mess-uniformed waiter who looked as though he was more accustomed to wearing combat fatigues than his natty military waiter's uniform. He picked up the folded napkin on the table before her and offered to spread it on her lap. Wilson was attended to likewise by a second uniformed waiter who looked equally ill at ease. Once they were both settled, and his choice of sickly sweet aperitif wine had been poured, he dismissed the attendants, saying that he would call them when they were required.

"Well, Penelope Delaney, what a pleasant surprise to see you here. I really am having a magnificent day. What is it, exactly, that brings you to this part of the world?"

"As I said earlier, I am continuing my study on humane business methods just as I was with you in London." She looked at him with apparent innocence.

"The Island is rather an odd choice, if you don't mind me saying so," Wilson said ingratiatingly. "I would have thought, as this Island is so isolated, that they could offer very little by way of useful information."

She took a long slow sip of wine to gain time to consider any incongruities that he may be uncovering. "This is delicious, a perfect choice." She held up the glass of disgustingly sweet wine and smiled disarmingly whilst cringing inside.

He basked in the glory of his choice thinking that it was not often that the ladies enjoyed his choice of wine; clearly, this was another good omen, and the night was still young. "You are most discerning."

"I suppose it must look a bit strange, my being here," she continued, having given herself enough time to plan a strategy. "Actually, I must agree with you that it is strange, but my being here was a direct request from the Secretary of State back home, you know, the one who is mentoring me. He told me it would be an unusual and valuable addition to my thesis but actually," she leaned towards him conspiratorially and whispered, "I think he just wanted to find out a bit more about the Island. Some of the questions he wanted me to ask were nothing to do with my subject".

"I see," Wilson said sagely while at the same time thinking to himself that the Secretary of State was a wily old fox to be using a young innocent as a spy and what's more an unpaid spy. "Don't worry about having told me about what the Secretary of State asked you to do. I am the soul of discretion—not a word will pass my lips." He smiled inwardly at the thought that he now had something to hold over her and maybe even the Secretary of State and that, he thought, could be extremely useful in times to come.

"Let us eat," he said with as much good humour as he possessed. "This is fine food and, of course, as ruler of the Island, I get only the best, and as my companion, you will also get the best."

The food was served immediately at the simple wave of his arm. The salad was good except that he had chosen the wrong dressing to go with the avocado, mozzarella, and tomato. The steak was good quality but had been ruined by being overcooked. The apple pie was good, but the raspberry ripple ice cream served with it was inappropriate. She ate it all with apparent gratitude and hung on his every word as he wolfed down the repast voraciously but with no apparent enjoyment.

"There," he said as he finished off the second bottle of rich, again overly sweet, red wine, "the advantage of being ruler is that I can have what I like when I like and as much as I like." He waved his arm again and ordered coffee and large brandies, without giving her a choice, to be served in the adjoining lounge.

She followed him into the lounge and was almost knocked off her feet as the door swung closed behind him. She stopped the swinging door with both palms forward; he turned around at the sound but made no comment or apology. Coffee and brandy were served, and the waiter was instructed to leave the brandy decanter on the table and then he was dismissed with a final wave of the hand.

Wilson rose from his seat across the table from her and walked around it to join her on the double settee which she occupied; he sat close so that they were touching from knee to shoulder. She shuddered but resisted the urge to move away giving him the impression that his clumsy advances were permissible.

"How did you come to know the Secretary of State?"

"My father and he went to the same university, so he's a sort of family friend."

"That could be useful. It could be an advantage for me to have a good contact in the USA."

"I don't understand what's going on," she said timorously. "How did you get to be the leader around here, and what about the others and the Ruling Council and what about all those important people who were with you in your meeting, you know, like the President of the USA and the Prime Minister of Great Britain and the others?"

"How do you know about them?" he asked suspiciously. "That meeting was supposed to be secret."

"Oh!" She appeared, and actually was, flustered. "I didn't know it was supposed to be secret, I was in the same room as Mr Gilliland and Mr Pettit when they were discussing it—I don't think they realised, I was there. Did I do wrong?" The last sentence was spoken in her best little girl lost voice. On reflection she thought she had done well given the lack of time she had to cover her second faux pas.

His look of suspicion dissolved as he saw her apparent look of contrition. "Don't worry, my dear, as I said before, your secrets are safe with me." He put his arm around her but failed to notice the shudder of revulsion that his move engendered. To add to the deception, she gave him an adoring look.

"You're not going to hurt them, are you?" she said in a tiny voice. "Mr Gilliland and Mr Crook and that nice Mr Pettit."

"There's nothing nice about Pettit," he said harshly. "The man is a traitor of the worst kind, and he's a murderer."

"Oh!" She looked frightened. "I didn't mean to upset you—it's just that I'm worried about them. They've been looking after me since I've been here, and I don't know anybody else, and I don't know how to leave the Island without their help."

"I'm all the help you need. When the time comes, I will see that you leave the Island safely, but in the meantime, I have a lovely apartment at my disposal, but nobody to share it with, nobody to give me comfort tonight. I'll get my batman to have your things moved into my apartment right away."

"Oh dear, what a shame," she looked crestfallen. "It's a lovely idea, but we can't . . . you know . . . do it . . . I'm sorry it's the wrong time of the month." She had assumed before joining him for dinner that he would make an immediate move when he had her cornered and had taken the opportunity to prepare an excuse.

"Damn, and I was so looking forward to us becoming closer in the interest of my good relations with the US administration."

"I'm sure we will be able to cement all sorts of relations, including with the Secretary of State, providing I can ask them the funny questions I told you about earlier. The sooner I do it, the sooner it will be over. Maybe you can arrange for me to talk to them now. I mean there's not much else I can do tonight, is there?" She glanced at him coquettishly. "Things being the way they are right now." Her opportunism was impressive, even to her.

"For you, my dear." He was patronising again. "I will arrange it right away as long as you remember it is I who can do this for you, and I will expect some little favours in return."

As he left the room, he instructed an NCO to escort her to the room in which the three were held. His thoughts were then very focussed on one of the nurses on his medical team. She would be ordered to his apartment to scratch the itch that Penelope Delaney had created in him. The nurse was just the right kind; a great body and absolutely no brains. He laughed to himself as he thought. *"Just like Penelope Delaney, great body but a complete airhead".*

Fifty-One

Caine was shown into the room in which the other three were held under armed guard. They looked crestfallen as she was ushered in thinking that she had been discovered and was being incarcerated with them and for their wild scheme to have even the remotest chance of success her freedom was imperative. She placed her index finger across her lips to indicate that they should remain silent until the accompanying guard had left the room.

"Well, you three certainly know how to make a girl feel welcome," she muttered after the guards had left.

"We were hoping that you would remain undiscovered so that we can try to do something about this mess," Gilliland said forlornly. "That's just it. I haven't been discovered yet, and as long as I can stay out of sight of the US President and everybody else keeps quiet, I'm a free agent." She outlined her discussions over and after dinner with Wilson.

"Talking of the President," Pettit enquired, "where are they? With the defences back on again, they won't be able to leave the Island, and I don't think Wilson will be disposed to disrupt the system again to let them off because it will also let the Chinese Fleet in."

"They have the freedom of the Island," Caine advised them. "They are as mad as a bucket of frogs, specially the Chinese, but what can they do?"

"You may recall," Pettit said, "that during our earlier discussions, I said that one of the components to our solution was luck." He looked at them, and they both nodded. "Penny being undiscovered and getting to see us here is a good omen, and the beginning of the luck we need to implement our plan."

"You do have a plan then?" Caine looked hopefully at them.

"Not so much of a plan as a hopeful idea," Crook replied without enthusiasm.

"Whatever we do, it has to be quick. Once Wilson learns who I really am, it's all over for me." Caine produced a watery smile. "He will learn of that there is no doubt. Klastheim and James know who I am, and although James is okay, I can't predict how Klastheim will react. He was elected for his unquestioning compliance rather than his intellect and any of the Islanders could let my identity slip in an unguarded moment. As I said, whatever we do we have to do it quickly."

They outlined the plan, such as it was, to Caine. She considered it for a while and shook her head slowly. "It's a terrible plan full of holes but, hey, I can't think of anything better, so what the hell let's go for it hook, line, and sinker."

The first stage of the three-part plan was for Caine to make contact with Mark Lawson whom they knew they could trust implicitly and to instruct him on how to access the control system and get him to reroute the system and transfer the final control capability to a secondary system in the research laboratory. To obfuscate the possibility of the discovery of their deception, it was necessary for the control of the system to be perceived as still being in the control room. This could be achieved by a key input transfer, making the research laboratory the actual control centre and using the control room as a remote data input port.

The second stage would be to get Ed Pickering on board *Wallow* 5, which was under guard in the harbour. Pickering was the only other person, apart from Gilliland and Crook, who could operate the BAM2 equipment on board. Once on board he would be able to fire up BAM2 and use it to destroy the ten assault craft moored at the dockside.

The third stage was to let Bill Wilkinson, the chief geologist, who was located in the research laboratory, know that the control had been handed to his station so that he could capture any commands issued by the control room and modify them to manage any catastrophic directives.

With the exception of Ed Pickering, the other two men, Lawson and Wilkinson, were chosen to carry out these tasks because their presence in the control room and the laboratory would not arouse suspicion.

*

Caine left the three under lock and key with an armed guard and headed out of the administration building. As she exited the building, she was aware of a sudden burst of conversation as a group of men stepped out of the lift just behind her. One of the loudest voices was that of the American President, who was blustering and complaining about their being detained, in essence being his usual belligerent self. She realised, as she beat a hasty retreat, that Pettit's caveat that they needed luck for their plan to work had received another boost; had she left just ten seconds earlier, she would have bumped into the President as they both left the lifts and her luck would have run out before they actually started the plan rolling.

Finding Mark Lawson was her first priority. She returned to her apartment and activated the Information Portal and using the latest census information she accessed his address. Checking the details of the address, revealed that he was single and living on his own. Rather than contacting him via the portal, which would be traceable as soon as Wilson's men learned how to access the messenger service, she decided to visit him. It was now past midnight, and travel across the Island at this time would surely alert the night patrols about, which Wilson had told her, while boasting of his Island conquest, would be instigated immediately to stop the peasants getting the wrong idea about who was in control of the occupation. She had no choice but to wait until the next day.

Early on the next morning, but not so early that she would arouse suspicion, she took a TC to Lawton's apartment. He answered the door, looking dishevelled and with a considerable dark beard growth and slightly puffy eyes.

"Oh," he said as he recognised her, "sorry, I wasn't expecting visitors. I'm in a mess. I did the graveyard shift last night, and I just got to bed." Standing aside, he let her in.

"Sorry, to call on you unannounced, but I need a confidential discussion with you, and it's important. No, it's more than important, it's critical." She closed the door behind her and followed him into the living quarters.

"What can I do for you?" Drawing his dressing gown chord tighter, he shook his head in an attempt to wake himself up.

"Let me make us some coffee," she offered. "It'll give you some time to gather yourself together. What I've got to say to you requires your mind to be very clear and focussed."

At the conclusion of their discussion, Lawson was completely awake, and there was an adrenalin-fuelled spring in his step. His first task was to use the Information Portal to contact Bill Wilkinson, the chief geologist, and to get him to contact Ed Pickering, the chief engineer, to get them to meet him at his apartment without delay.

They arrived later that morning within a few minutes of each other and were surprised to be greeted by Caine. Both Pickering and Wilkinson had agreed to change their intended morning tasks when they were told, via the IP, by Lawton, that there was a way to access the control system without having to use the services of Gilliland and Crook.

"What possessed you to use the IP to tell us about alternative access to the control system? Wilson's men have access to the messaging service, and they will know that you have, or at least think you have, access," Pickering asked in disbelief.

"Don't shoot the messenger Ed." Caine interrupted. "Mark only did what I asked him to. The idea is that they will find out about it and watch him when he works in the control room in order to jump him when he gets access. They will think they have the upper hand and allow him under supervision to work at the keyboard."

"I don't know what you intend to do, or how, but you've obviously got a plan to get us out of this unholy mess, so why don't we just sit down and listen to your explanation." Pickering had calmed down as soon he understood the reason for leaking the information on the IP.

"I need to get back to my apartment." Caine was pensive. "Wilson thinks I am an American research student working on a thesis. When he finds out who I am, and he surely will, I will not be in a position to use my freedom to further the cause, so I must keep out of the way. Here is basically what I would like you to do. Mark will use the codes I have given him to get into the system. Once in, he will switch off the defence shields and immediately transfer control of the system to the research lab. Then he will lock out the main controls so that they can't actually operate them from the control room, but they will think they can, and the reason they will think so is that Bill will see a mimic of the instructions they are entering and emulate them, providing they are not harmful, from his terminal. They will believe they have control, but actually we will."

"Ingenious," Wilkinson sounded impressed but had reservations, "but once we change the instructions, they are putting in, they will know that we have diverted control and will be able to locate the diversion and reverse it. Anybody know how long that will take?"

"Anything between three and four hours, depending on how good their techie is, but the main thing is that, we will only change their instructions if what they are proposing to do is detrimental, and we can do that by using what will appear to be safety protocols." She looked at her watch and pursed her lips. "I really must leave soon. Ed, you have a task to do, but it's nowhere near as planned as the system bit. You job is to get aboard *Wallow 5* and operate the BAM2 to destroy their combat boats. I don't know how you're going to do it, but we have to destroy them all for the plan to work, it's imperative. If you can't do that, the whole plan fails."

"No pressure then," Pickering said grimly. "I'll do what I can." His companions displayed a far greater faith in his capabilities than he felt.

Fifty-Two

Pickering, Stuart Finlay, one of his trusted senior engineers, and Beverly Olsen, a strikingly attractive analyst from his research department walked slowly and casually towards the dockside. The men wore the standard Island garb of a one-piece bodysuit, which in Pickering's case was supplemented by a hip length top to detract from his spreading girth. Olsen, the analyst, looked very fetching in the figure-hugging suit and only those who knew her well would have possibly detected that she was a little more bulky than usual because of the dry suit she wore beneath it.

They approached the dockside so that they were slightly forward of where *Wallow 5* was tied up and entered into an animated conversation of which the two on-board guards could not actually hear well enough to make any sense. One of the guards shouted to them to stay clear of the vessel, and they waved an acknowledgement and carried on with their supposed conversation which was becoming more strident.

Both guards moved towards the bows of *Wallow 5* to admire the attractive girl at closer quarters as she began to berate the two men who retreated beyond the stern flinging occasional insults as they moved away. They stopped and turned to face her laughing as she gesticulated towards her adversaries, waving her arms and wiggling her hips in a way which accentuated the litheness of her figure, much to the delight of the two squaddies who leaned on the forward rail to get as close to her as possible.

Her insults grew louder and more vehement as she spiralled out of control jigging with greater exaggeration. The squaddies continued to watch her and ignored the two men who were the subject of her invective. Both squaddies froze momentarily as they saw her backing towards the edge of the dock, and their warning shouts came too late as she windmilled her arms and fell backwards into the turgid grey waters. She disappeared from view, and the two squaddies strained forward over the bows in a desperate attempt to locate her. Coughing and spluttering, she surfaced some fifteen feet from the dockside, her arms flailing as she tried to stay afloat.

"Can't swim," she gurgled through a mouthful of seawater to the squaddies. She showed all the signs of acute distress distractedly windmilling her arms as she disappeared and reappeared, spluttering and panicking.

One of the squaddies threw a lifebelt to her but her flailing took her further and further from the dockside. Picking up a second lifebelt, the second of the squaddies threw down his steel helmet and leaped untidily into the water; his remaining companion leaned out over the bow, shouting words of encouragement to him.

Distracted by the rescue attempt, he failed to observe the remaining two Islanders who stepped off the dock on to the deck of *Wallow 5*. Pickering picked up the discarded rifle and his companion ran forward hitting the squaddie full in the back and sending him and his rifle flailing out over the bow into the sparkling blue water.

Without the aid of a lifebelt the second squadie, in combat uniform was in difficulties and was thrashing about in the water in an ineffectual attempt to keep afloat. He was rescued by the female in distress who, he observed with self-deprecating resignation, had miraculously learned to swim with great skill. She collected the free floating lifebelt and swam over to the threshing victim and handed it to him; he accepted the gift with wordless embarrassed thanks.

Pickering stepped into the tiny all-weather cabin and slid open a table top, the otherwise invisible BAM2 controls. The power unit showed inadequate battery strength to be operational. As the, now uncovered, unit had been shown the light of day, the solar cells began to trickle charge. He started the inboard motor, and staying clear of the three in the water, moved away from the dockside some fifty feet. His position was precarious, without the BAM2 defence in place he was highly vulnerable.

As he moved away, two of the adjacent combat craft erupted into life with armed soldiers tumbling on board as the vessels backed away from the dockside to swing round and engage *Wallow 5*. The gunners on board brought their handguns to bear and opened fire on the tiny defenceless craft; the bigger guns were not able to cope with the pitching as the vessels rolled in their self-induced wakes. Bullets slammed into the superstructure, ricocheting off the steel struts, thudding into the timberworks and drilling into the water leaving behind an effervescent trail as they plummeted ineffectually into the depths.

Pickering pushed the throttles fully forward and spun the wheel violently in both directions throwing up spray and making the target more difficult to hit. The clumsy craft with its ungainly superstructure lived up to its name by pitching erratically in the now turbulent water. The firepower of both vessels proved too much and Pickering was hit. He fell to the deck blood gushing from his head; the dead man's controls stopped *Wallow 5* dead in her tracks. Pickering's hands had slipped from the controls as he slid on to the deck where his blood, stark against the pallor of his skin, mixed with the bilge water and was diluted to a watery pink. Without taking command of *Wallow 5,* their whole plan would fail and the Island would become Wilson's plaything, and the world would become a much different place.

Fifty-Three

Caine was talking to Wilson who had summoned her to join him for morning coffee. She first established that he had not discovered her true identity, and having satisfied herself that he had not done so, she set the scene for Lawson to accomplish his part of the plan as a back-up to the leaked information on the Information Portals.

"I think I heard some talk yesterday that you are looking for a way to get control of the defence system and that it's frozen in a configuration that you don't want?"

"Where did you hear that?" Wilson snapped bad temperedly.

"Some of the Ruling Councillors were talking, and I don't think they knew I was there—it seems to happen to me often—they kind of got used to me being around over the last few days and ignored me. I do kind of melt into the background. I heard them say something about only the founders knowing how to get into the system, and they wouldn't be giving the secrets away. One of them, I don't know who he was, said that he thought that the shift chief could probably do it, and that they would need to pass the word on to him not to give the game away."

"Who is the shift chief?" He was suddenly animated.

"They did say a name, but I can't remember what it was."

"Think again, it's very important." He gripped her shoulders and shook her violently. "Think," he shouted aggressively.

"Oh." She looked frightened. "I only heard it once . . . I can't remember."

"Was it a man or a woman's name?" He shook her again; his unreasonable anger at her answer was plainly visible on his face.

"I think it was a man's name." She frowned and concentrated. "It was something like Martin or Mike . . . I think."

"Stay there while I make a phone call." He spoke urgently into the phone and scribbled rapidly on a sheet of paper. "Here," he said as he disconnected the call, "which of these names is it?"

She scanned the hastily written list of six names and screwed up her face in concentration. "Your writing is difficult," she said defensively, "I can't read some of the . . ." She paused and scrutinised the list again. "Maybe this one," pointing to one of the names, "yes, I think that's it Marty Lewis." She looked again and faltered. "Oh, I don't know. It might have been Mark Lawson . . . No, I think it was Marty Lewis. But I can't be sure."

"Damn." He picked up the telephone again and spoke to his operator in the control room. Finishing the call he turned to her. "My man tells me that he knows both the people you named and doubts that Lewis had the brains to master the required codes, but that Lawson definitely has."

"So you're going to force him to give you the access codes then?" she asked, apparently naively.

"Sweet," he looked at her indulgently, "no, I'm not going to force anything out of him. I'm going to give him access to the system, and when he unlocks, it we'll take over and reset it as we want."

"I don't get it." She looked puzzled. "Why would he want to unlock the system? It wouldn't be in his or the Islander's interest, would it?"

"Don't worry yourself about it, girly, leave the details to the experts." He shuffled the papers on his desk and began to pack his briefcase. "And now it's time for me to set the ball rolling. I'm too busy for the rest of the week to have dinner with you, so you'll just have to fend for yourself but make sure you stay where I can find you easily. You'd better let my office know where you are at all times in case I need you." He walked away, wondering just how he could get the Lawson fellow to access the system without having to resort to force which he felt could be counter productive. He was smarting because it had taken an air-headed girl to find a weakness in his off the cuff plan.

*

Lawson was sitting at one of the Holographic Map Tables when Wilson entered the control room. His deep concentration was interrupted by Wilson's intrusive voice.

"What's happening?"

"Nothing much." Lawson did not turn to look at Wilson and offered no further comment.

"What about the ships marooned between the two domes?"

"They're not doing anything."

Who are you?"

"Lawson, I'm shift supervisor, running a second consecutive shift and not feeling happy about unnecessary interruptions."

"Do you know who you're talking to?"

"Yes." Lawson turned around slowly and looked disdainfully at Wilson.

"Be very careful." Wilson assumed a dark threatening tone.

"Or what?" Lawson shrugged and turned back to the HMT.

"Corporal," Wilson shouted to an armed guard who lurked in the shadows at the entrance to the room, "get somebody else to man this, whatever they call it table . . . now"

Wilson grabbed Lawson by the upper arm and pulled him out of his chair. "You and I are going to have a little talk." He pulled him across the room and thrust him down into a seat at the main computer console. "I know you have access to the source codes so access them, and do not cross me, you would not like the consequences."

"Obviously, you've been reading computers for beginners. I do not have access to the source code, but I do have it to the machine code."

"Craddock," Wilson shouted to his computer specialist, who was rooting around in the computer cabinets and trying to trace a means of access. "Get yourself over here and talk to this geek about machine codes."

Craddock slumped into the seat beside Lawson's and shot Wilson a vitriolic glare when he knew he could not be seen. "What do you want me to do, boss?"

"I want you to take control of the system, and this man will help you to do it."

"This man will help you to do nothing," Lawson injected as much insolence into his tone as he could.

"These people are all so lightweight," Wilson spat out. "You will give us access to the system, or we will reactivate the jamming device and let the Chinese Fleet in. Your Island will then become Federation property, and you will all be rehoused or jailed or both. Federation law also allows the death penalty for treason, and I'm sure I can persuade them that you have committed treason."

"You are the one committing treason. You want the Island for yourself, and for one, I'd rather we were taken over by the Federation than by you."

"So naïve," Wilson snorted. "It won't be the Federation that takes over, it will be the Chinese, and believe me when I say that President Chung Ho Chen will be an infinitely harsher taskmaster than me or the Federation."

Lawson paused and looked at Wilson long and hard. He had to turn away and look at the blank terminal screen to prevent Wilson from seeing the smile he could not suppress. "You will lose out no matter what happens either the Chinese or the Federation will be the winners and you, Mr Wilson, will be the outright loser."

"More naivety." Wilson sighed deeply. "If I let either the Federation or the Chinese in, they will give me responsibility for the Island. and you would not like that. So if you want any kind of future you will give me control of the system. If you don't, you will suffer a regrettably fatal accident before the day is out."

With a look like thunder, which was caused by Wilson's mounting instability, Craddock lit up the screen and opened up the menu. As had happened after previous attempts, the programme failed to respond to the commands entered. He turned to Lawson and shrugged his shoulders resignedly, turning his palms upward. Lawson, with a great show of reluctance, entered a password and began to write a Kludge, a subroutine that would remove the system blockage.

Craddock looked on with interest and made notes as Lawson constructed the Kludge.

"What's he doing?" Wilson asked Craddock petulantly; he did not like to be beholden to anybody and felt uncomfortably at a disadvantage.

"He's writing a sniffer in a language that the machine can decipher to find a way to unlock the jam."

"Can he do that?"

"We'll find out soon enough." Craddock held up his hand to stop further conversation from Wilson. "He's nearly done."

Lawson made a definitive strike on the keyboard and sat back with a sigh. After a brief interlude, the screen dissolved and went blank.

Wilson leaped forward and pulled Lawson out of his chair, throwing him to the ground and kicking him viciously. "What have you done?" He screamed, completely out of control. "And you," he pointed to Craddock, "have just committed treason." "Guard," he shouted in a spray of spittle, "detain Craddock and slap him in detention. If he resists, shoot to kill." He turned his vitriolic gaze to Lawson. "Get this sorted out, or you will be executed."

Craddock who was being restrained by the guard said in an unnaturally quiet and controlled voice, "The screen has gone blank because the system is cleansing. Have patience, and it will come back online."

"If it doesn't, you will be joining him in front of the same firing squad," Wilson chuckled insanely.

Within thirty seconds, a cursor appeared on the screen and began pulsing. Craddock punched the return on the keyboard and a menu appeared:

1	Remove lock	x
2	Reinitiate	x
3	Locate	x
4	Change access codes	x
5	Lock	x
6	Exit	x

Craddock clicked on Remove lock and nothing happened.

"Well?" Wilson was exasperated.

"Well, I guess we still need Mr Lawson to make it work," Craddock's voice showed equal exasperation

"Make the damn thing work." Wilson gave a further kick to Lawson who still lay on the floor.

Standing up slowly and painfully, Lawson clutched the back of his chair to steady himself. He shook his head and breathed deeply in through his nose and out through his mouth. With a wince, he slid into his chair and stared at the screen, flexing his fingers as they hovered over the keyboard.

Taking a further deep breath, he began the process of unlocking the system's highlighting option one, and he typed in his PIN and pressed return. The x adjacent to option 1: Remove Lock, changed to a tick. He repeated the process for option 2: Reinitiate the x, which also changed to a tick. The next option was 3: Relocate, the x changed to a tick and a sub menu appeared.

A: Master Remote	x
B: Admin Centre	x
C: Control Room	x
D: Control Tower	x
E: Research Lab.	X
F: Security	x

Lawson scrolled down to F: Security and highlighted it; he paused aware that Wilson was looking over his shoulder. Although expected, the blow from Wilson still caused him to shout out in surprise and pain as he once more fell to the floor and was kicked.

"You must think I was born yesterday," Wilson sneered, "and you," he pointed to Craddock, "are worse than useless. Why didn't you try to stop him? He was obviously going to transfer control to Security, and I ordered you to make sure control was from here."

"Sorry, sir," Craddock was uncharacteristically subservient, "maybe you should make the transfer yourself."

"If you want it done properly, do it yourself," Wilson said pompously. "Here we go." He shifted the highlight up to C: Control Room and pressed return, the x turned to a tick. "What do I do now, Craddock?"

"Scroll down to exit and press return, and that will be that." Craddock was strangely unemotional.

"Let's check to make sure that we have control. Do whatever it is you have to do."

Craddock opened up the starting menu and searched through the options available. They were simple and in plain language; he easily selected the outer defence shield and chose to switch the defence off rather than change its distance. The mimic screen remained unchanged; still showing the dome in place.

"What's up now?" Wilson hissed in frustration. "Why isn't anything happening?"

"Patience," Craddock waved his hand up and down, "this is a very complex operation."

"They watched the mimic closely, and fifteen seconds later, the outer ring as shown on the mimic blinked off."

"Damn." Lawson's voice drifted up slowly from where he lay on the floor.

"Guard, take him and lock him up somewhere. I'll deal with him later."

Craddock bent down and helped Lawson to his feet, turning his back to Wilson as he did so and in a soft voice, he whispered to Lawson. "I saw you do something to the programme. I'll find out what it was and when I do, there could be a lot of trouble."

*

Creswell looked up from the desk at which he was seated in a small meeting room that had been allocated to the stranded politicians and other delegates. His attention was caught by the sight of Wilson walking down the corridor towards their temporary home.

"Here comes trouble,.." he said to nobody in particular.

Klastheim walked to the door to confront Wilson as he entered the room. "What the hell is going on here, Wilson? Do you have any idea how much trouble you're in by kidnapping two heads of state as well as secret service chiefs and Chinese nationals?"

"Please, gentlemen, this is not of my doing. The Island's administration has lost its mind. It is they who have locked you away behind their defences. I, on the other hand, have been working to free you from the detention they have imposed, and by my dedication, I have been able to thwart their efforts, and as we speak, I have assumed control of the defences, and I will be allowing your release before the end of the day."

Momentarily, the room fell silent.

"You will be allowing our release?" Creswell's indignation was obvious. "You will be allowing our release? Who the hell do you think you are? No, I'll tell you who you are—or rather were, the DDP for the British Government, and you report to me. Despite your attempts to discredit me, I am still Prime Minister. You report to me—not the other way around. Any political decision you are involved in will go through the normal channels. You will not act independently, and as for having taken control of an independent state, well, I'm lost for words."

"I never have and never will 'work for you' as you put it." The nasty side of Wilson re-emerged after its brief respite. "Unlike you, I have only the best interests of the British people at heart." Wilson assumed a pompous air. "I have taken over this Island which you should have done ages ago." He glared at Creswell. "As the head of a dissolute government, you don't have the spine to assert your authority, so it is left to me to pick up the reins of national interest. This technology was developed at UK tax payers expense by two British citizens in a British Research Facility. Clearly, as head of the UK Government, you have abdicated your rights to it. I have, therefore, decided to take over this Island, its people and its assets and put them to good use."

"What about the Federation?" Klastheim said darkly.

"The Federation can take a running jump. I don't trust them and haven't done so for a long time."

"You can't do that," Klastheim blazed. "You are a private citizen, and what's more you are unelected, and you owe allegiance not only to the government that employs you but to the Federation. Where is your loyalty?"

"I only give loyalty to those who give loyalty to me, neither the British Government nor the Federation have shown any loyalty to me, so I do not feel beholden to either of them."

"Wilson," Creswell cut in, "you will stop this behaviour, and do what is required by your superiors. What you will do is come to your senses, stop this egotistical nonsense and stop inhibiting our departure from the Island. You will also, on our return to the United Kingdom, give me your immediate written resignation as DDP, and you will stop interfering with the administration of this Island."

"You can all leave immediately. Get your things together, and I will arrange your flight. I will also contact the Chinese fleet and make sure that you leave unhindered. As for the rest," He turned to Creswell, "you bore me with your weak threats. And I find you," he turned the rest of the assembled dignitaries, "are extremely aggravating and irrelevant."

The room fell silent as he turned on his heel and left them. His off key chuckling was chilling.

Fifty-Four

eaving her office, Caine walked to the lifts from where she intended to go to the control room to establish the status of their retrieval plan. Walking the short distance from the administration block to the control room, across the courtyard, she was about to enter the control room when she caught sight of a group of men, headed by Wilson, as they alighted from one of the TCs to enter the control complex, heading towards where she stood. In the group, apart from Wilson, she recognised Creswell, Sir Lionel Wentworth, Trevor Coniston, and one other she knew as being a senior government official without being able to recall his name, bringing up the rear was the American President. She sheered away from the control room door, trying to avoid the attention of the President who knew her very well by sight and name being, as he was, an acquaintance of her family.

Klastheim frowned when he caught a glimpse of her and narrowed his eyes in an attempt to recall her identity, having only had a fleeting glance. She was not being seen by him in her usual context as part of the expensively dressed and coiffured Washington cocktail set. Wilson had, however, seen her and instructed one of his guards to catch her up and have her join him in the control room. She was aware that the guard was hurrying after her and hurried away from him as fast as she could without attracting undue attention. Her knowledge of the twists and turns of the corridors in the administration complex allowed her to lose him, and she ducked into a store cupboard when she had created enough of a distance in the twists of the corridors for him not to see her enter in to it.

She heard his footsteps pass by on the other side of the door, and a little later, they returned pausing outside but not entering as he presumably read the name plate on the door proclaiming it to be janitorial. Waiting for a few minutes in the darkness until she was sure he would not return, she gingerly opened the door and peered out into the corridor, it was empty. As she made her way back to her apartment, she was acutely aware that it would be almost impossible for her true identity to be kept secret even after Klastheim departed the Island. She was simply too well known.

Back in her apartment, she reviewed the situation. The three elements of the recovery plan were in motion, but she had no way of knowing if any or all had been completed there being no telephone communications available. For the plan to work, Lawson had to gain access to the control system and transfer it to the laboratory system, Wilkinson had to seize control of the defences and mimic the instructions generated by Wilson's men, and Pickering had to seize control of *Wallow 5* and disable the assault vessels at the harbour side.

The first two could only be ascertained as being successful by discussion with Lawson and Wilkinson. The success or failure of the third element would be obvious when it was discovered because of the furore it would cause among the invaders. With all satellite telephones confiscated, there was no way of contacting Pickering, except by going to the port; she could only wait and see. One thing was certain; all elements had to succeed for the plan to work. If any of them failed, all would be lost; she felt extremely uneasy about the fragile nature of their plan for which there was no back-up.

*

Wilson was showing off, to the stranded dignitaries, the control room of which he had now taken complete command. He indicated on the close radarscope the circles described by the defence domes which he now called the attack system. The HMTs showed the vessels trapped between the inner and outer zones; it also showed the airport and the dock and all the Island's features. All the watching dignitaries were obviously impressed by the sophistication of the HMTs showing land, sea, undersea, and air activities to exact scale and in coloured layers.

"Time to go." Wilson had soon tired of showing off his new possessions and turned to look disdainfully at them. "You will be escorted to the airport and put on board the aircraft in which you arrived. You will be accompanied by an armed guard to ensure your safety during the journey. Take everything with you. Anything you leave behind will stay behind. Be outside the administration block in thirty minutes. Anybody not there on time will remain here and will not be going home for a long time—if ever." He turned on his heel and left the room without waiting for a response.

*

Gilliland, Crook, and Pettit continued to be frustrated by their incarceration; the room was small, and there were no obvious means of communication with the outside world. Their planning conversations with Caine on the previous day had been short and had hardly been conclusive. The three elements relied on each other for the tactic to be successful; it was all or nothing.

They had tried second-guessing Wilson but had concluded that he was too unstable to be anticipated. One thing was certain, he could not be allowed access to BAM2 technology because of its phenomenal power, a power which they, as the inventors, had still not fully explored but which they had the imagination to project with a chill of dread and horror.

One thing they had made allowance for, to their immediate relief, was that all BAM2 units were set to self-destruct if any attempt was made to open and inspect the mechanism. This was of little comfort when they discussed what could be done with the ten units that were currently activated. The static units which formed the defence shields were set to ground level, that is they were hemispheres, and the bottom of the domes were set at sea level and could be accessed from underneath; something that would undoubtedly be discovered in the fullness of time. Access to the projecting unit controls could, therefore, be gained and, given time, the codes could be broken.

Breaking the codes would be catastrophic, adjusting the domes to complete spheres would be cataclysmic; to do so would mean that the BAM2 unit would fall through the ground driven by gravity and the automatic removal of physical barriers and would continue to fall atomising all terrestrial matter as it descended until it was either burned up by the heat of the magma or until the transportable power source was depleted.

The resultant holes in the earth's crust, depending on the number, size, and location, could release magma on a scale never seen since the formation of the earth. It could bring about extinction of all living things by what was the equivalent of a nuclear winter in which the stratosphere was laced with enough toxic debris to prevent sunlight penetration. At this point, they suspended speculation. The horror of their projections forced them to change tack and consider how they could stop the catastrophe from happening. This doomsday scenario was unlikely but at the same time frighteningly possible; even more so in the wrong hands.

Pettit sat as if in a trance, his face locked in a mask of mental pain. He suddenly straightened up and launched into a dialog. "If the original sketchy plan doesn't work, and there's every chance that it won't, we need to have a plan B. For any plan B to work for us, we have either to get out of here or get tactics out of here via another party. Penny is a possibility, but she can easily be compromised by the discovery of her true identity. So," he paused and grimaced, "we have to get out of here. Any ideas?"

No ideas were immediately forthcoming. The room in which they were held was small, barely large enough to accommodate three, especially when it came to sleeping, there being only two armchairs on which sleep was possible. Sanitary arrangements were basic and controlled, all three were escorted by armed guards to a three cubicle toilet on the same corridor as the room in which they were held and were given five minutes before being returned to their prison room. So far basic cold food and water had been supplied to them at random intervals. There were two armed guards outside the door at all times, and it seemed to them that there was no obvious avenue of escape; they would simply have to wait until a suitable opportunity arose and play it by ear.

At 11.30 a. m. on the second day of their imprisonment, the door opened unexpectedly, and Caine appeared through it accompanied by one of the guards. The guard closed the door and, frustratingly, remained inside the room.

"Mr Wilson has kindly allowed me to speak to you again about the humanitarian subject we discussed before." She turned to the guard, "You don't need to protect me, these people do not pose a threat, and our discussion will be very boring. No need to stay, I'll call you when I'm finished."

The guard thought about what she said and then shook his head. "My orders are to stay with you at all times."

Caine showed great restraint in the face of his disappointing reply and simply shrugged. "As you wish, but you will find this very boring. At least, outside you will have your companion to pass the time."

"Makes no difference to me, orders are orders, and anyway, you've only got fifteen minutes. Them's Mr Wilson's orders."

With a hostile audience of one, albeit probably unintelligent soldier, she asked a series of pointless questions to which she received pointless answers. After ten fruitless minutes, she shrugged and stood up from the armchair which she had occupied and repacked her briefcase. "I may need to ask you more questions at a later date," she said in a neutral voice.

"You'll need clearance from Mr Wilson first," the guard said as they exited the room.

"Damn!" Gilliland said vehemently after they had gone. "She didn't get the chance to pass any information to us although her visit would not have been sanctioned if our plan had worked. So, how do we progress from here?"

There was no immediate response from his two companions. He slumped down into the armchair which had been occupied by Caine and hung his arms dejectedly over the chair's arms, leaving his hands dangling. They each sat in silence, for over an hour, wrapped in their own thoughts but apparently not coming up with any practical solutions to their problems. They were dejected and at a loss to cobble together any semblance of a cohesive plan.

Gilliland suddenly sat up with a puzzled look and levered himself out of the chair with a sudden burst of energy. Pettit and Crook looked up in alarm as their dark reverie was shattered. Gilliland reached down between the cushion and the side of the chair which had briefly been occupied by Caine and extracted an army field telephone which was set to vibrate. Gilliland looked at the utilitarian keyboard and pressed the receive key.

Fifty-Five

inlay rushed forward to the small day cabin as soon as the firing began and saw Pickering fall to the deck where copious amounts of his blood mixed with the sea water slopping around in the bottom of the boat. Firing from the assault craft continued as he ran forward, and he thought that he was being protected by some divine force. In the fraction of time that it took him to get to the day cabin, he rationalised that the divine intervention was the solar battery having picked up enough power to operate the BAM2 unit and activate the defence shield automatically.

He turned Pickering over and was appalled by the quantity of blood that dripped from the side of his head. Pickering's eyes flickered open and took a few seconds to focus, he sat up and shook his head spraying blood as he did so.

"What the hell!" he stammered as he clasped his hand to his ear, the lobe of which had been partly removed by one of the rounds sprayed in his direction. He removed his hand and took out a handkerchief which he clasped to his wounded ear.

He appraised the situation rapidly. The two soldiers were still in the water one of them being supported by Olsen who was beginning to struggle with the panicking squaddie. The BAM2 force field was overlapping the dockside and had cut an arc which was widening as *Wallow*

5 rolled in the gentle dock swell. He was tempted to reduce the diameter of the dome but hesitated because of the potential hazard to the three in the water. The three in the water had been fortunate. The BAM dome had been set to a diameter higher that *Wallow*'s superstructure which threw the dome beyond where they were in the water.

He started up and manoeuvred *Wallow* away from the dockside to stop it being further damaged. To prevent damage, he had to switch off the BAM2 projector while he manoeuvred away from the dockside, and he breathed a sigh of relief when he was able to reactivate the dome. When they were close enough to Olsen, Finlay threw two lifebelts which landed near to the two soldiers. Olsen grabbed one of the belts and thrust it into the hands of the soldier she supported and pushed him away after which she struck out powerfully to the stern of *Wallow 5*.

Firing from the assault craft had ceased when they realised it was having no effect, and they had failed to realise in time that the defence dome had been switched off momentarily. Both craft undulated and rolled in the swell and stood off thirty yards apart. The commander of the assault vessel picked up a powered megaphone and hailed, Wallow 5, "*There is nowhere for you to go stand down and release my two men.*" The arm holding the megaphone dropped, and he waited for a response.

There was a pause while Pickering found his own simple megaphone which was not powered, and he had to shout his reply to be heard at that distance over the mingled cacophony of the sea and engines. "Do not approach us, we are surrounded by a defence shield which will damage your vessel and any personnel who endeavour to cross it." He lowered the megaphone which was smeared with the blood leaking from his ear.

Olsen boarded *Wallow 5* over the stern rail and stood dripping on the after part of the deck. The two soldiers clung to their lifebelts and trod water aimlessly not knowing what to do. She threw a line to them and secured it to the stern rail and told them to remain in the water and warned them about the devastating effects of the defence dome. She told them to remove their side arms, hold them aloft, and then throw them as far as they could, away from the boat. They were ordered to repeat the exercise but this time with their knives, one complied, the other refused. Finlay brought the assault rifle to his shoulder and fired a single shot into the water within inches of the reluctant soldier's head. His compliance was immediate.

"Stuart," Olsen said in some surprise. "I didn't know you could shoot so well."

"I can't," he said with a tremor. "I was actually aiming a good ten feet away from him." He had turned a sickly shade of green.

Pickering eased *Wallow 5* towards the assault craft and gave Finlay the megaphone. "Tell him," he said, clamping the bloodied handkerchief to his ear which was still bleeding freely, "to return to formation with the rest of his craft and tie up."

Finlay did as was requested, and there was no response from the lone vessel. Pickering eased forward again and watched the bright circle of the force field as it dipped in and out of the water, approaching the bows of the other craft. He stopped when it looked to him that the bright arc was only feet from its bow. The commander remained defiant and refused to back away; standing legs akimbo on the brief fore deck cover thrusting his chin out pugnaciously, assault rifle sloped across his chest. He fired an ineffective shot in their direction.

Pickering eased *Wallow* gingerly forward at minimum revs. He was acutely conscious that the commander was standing on the reinforced over deck only six foot from the extreme point of the bow. He threw *Wallow* into reverse as he saw the bright line approach the bow and then disappear as the swell pitched *Wallow 5* bows up before the gimbals could correct the trajectory. When it settled down again, Pickering reduced the dome diameter to thirty feet and inched closer to the assault craft.

The diameter being reduced also decreased the pitching of the bright ring perimeter and when he was close enough to talk to the commander without the use of a megaphone, he advised him to retreat or to suffer the consequences. Once more, the commander refused, and Pickering advanced slowly again until he saw the bright ring overlap the extreme point of the bow. The disintegration of the bow was accompanied by a brief high-pitched buzzing and two feet of it disappeared in a puff of finings, which spread out on the water's surface.

The commander leapt backwards as the bows vanished before his eyes and ended up in an untidy heap, scattering the men behind him as he fell. After disentangling himself from assorted men and equipment, he ordered the helmsman to reverse the craft back towards the dock. The bows remained afloat, although dipped in the water as the damaged forward floatation compartments filled with water and finings. He turned bows in when he reached the dockside and tied up.

All ten craft were tied up to the dockside side by side stern out and all the troops on board stood facing *Wallow 5,* which made a comical picture with the overly broad beam compared with her length and the hastily attached awkward gantry which carried the BAM2 transmitter rolling on the swell. There was a long moment of silence as the disproportionate forces faced each other.

The commander had decided not to advise Wilson of their situation, hoping that he would be able to rectify the stand off before it became irretrievable; the wrath of Wilson was not something he wished to invoke. He held the communication device in his hand, trying to convince himself that he did not have to use it. With great reluctance, he decided that he would have to let Wilson know so that the necessary recovery plan could be conceived. Pickering watched the indecisive commander raise the communication device to his lips and realised that if he did not stop this communication their plan could fail entirely.

*

Gilliland pressed the loud speaker button on the army phone he had recovered from the armchair and spoke into it quietly. They all listened with baited breath to the static noise which issued from it. "Hello." An indistinct voice distorted by the static said timorously.

"Penny," Gilliland recognised the voice immediately, "you're a genius, can you talk?"

"Only briefly," she said quietly. "I haven't been able to talk to Mark about how far along they are with their part of the plan, and I've got no way of getting to him or Bill Wilkinson to see if his part is in place. I'm in the upper part of the admin building, and I can see the dock. There seems to be a stand off at the moment. I can see *Wallow* out in the harbour, apparently holding the assault craft at bay, but I don't know what's going on. Must go, somebody's coming. Damn! It's Klastheim and Wilson." The line went dead.

As Wilson and Klastheim entered the room, the President's face lit up. "Why it's Penny Caine?" he said, in sudden recognition now that he was close to her, and he walked towards her and extended his hand.

She tried quietly and unsuccessfully to indicate that the President should not let Wilson know that he knew her by her real name. Klastheim failed to read her frantic signals and continued talking to her in familiar terms.

"You two know each other?" Wilson looked puzzled.

"No," Caine interjected hastily.

"Yes," Klastheim blustered self-importantly at the same time as her denial.

"Damn you for a bumbling idiot," Caine muttered almost inaudibly.

"How do you know Ms Delaney, Klastheim? Wilson's paranoia made him immediately suspicious.

"Delaney . . . but this is Penny Caine, daughter of the Caine family which owns Angam Oil in the States." Klastheim realised too late that he had said the wrong thing, although he didn't know why.

Wilson looked startled and called on two of his military entourage to capture and restrain her was about to question her when his field telephone shrilled. He pressed the receive button and listened for a moment. "Commander," he said testily, "calm down and talk to me sensibly." He listened intently as the boat commander told him that they had lost control of *Wallow 5* and needed help to reverse the situation. He snapped his radio phone close when the commander's voice suddenly fell silent and turned in fury to Caine, glaring at her with malevolence.

Caine closed her eyes and gave a deep sigh of resignation; there was no doubt that the game was up, whether or not Mark Lawton and Bill Wilkinson had succeeded, if Ed Pickering had not, then all was lost. The tension within her was so great that she felt like screaming and stamping her feet and shouting out to the world about the injustice of what Wilson was doing.

Craddock was in the control room, working on trying to understand the nuances of the control system as bidden by Wilson; his resentment of Wilson had assumed all encompassing proportions. He decided that he would do nothing to help the Wilson cause, and he was sorely tempted to sabotage it. Only strict military training prevented the realisation of his fantasy.

His reverie was interrupted by the radio call from Wilson, who curtly told him to report to the fourth floor of the administration block immediately and fully armed. He picked up his assault rifle and his side arm and checked them for readiness. Satisfied with their condition, he left the control room and crossed the intervening open space to the admin block at the double.

He reached the room which was occupied by Wilson and saw a shocked Klastheim and a stricken Penelope Delaney. Wilson was all but frothing from the mouth. "This, this, this . . . , woman," he spluttered pointing at Caine, "is not who she pretends to be. She is a spy, and I intend to have her shot as one." He was visibly shaking with barely suppressed anger. "Take her to the detention room with the other three and double the guard on the door. When you've done that, go down to the dock and sort out the idiot Islander, who is trying to make a name for himself. Then come back here with a firing squad, and we'll take care of the four traitors."

*

Caine's reappearance into the room in which the three were held was greeted with glee until they realised that this time the guard with her was actually her captor and that she was joining them in confinement. The guards said nothing but relatively gently pushed her into the room before closing the door behind her and locking it noisily.

"What happened?" Crook was the first to talk.

"That bumbling idiot of a president outed me," she fumed. "Dammit, he's being held prisoner by Wilson, and no matter how I tried to shush him, he insisted on bumbling on about how he knew me and my father and as soon as he mentioned Angam the penny dropped with Wilson. He went absolutely ballistic. I've never seen anybody lose it as much as he did. I thought he was going to have apoplexy. The upshot is he intends to have us all shot as traitors." She looked at them helplessly. "I don't know what we can do."

"Traitors to whom?" Pettit asked.

"Traitors to the Island."

"The Island?" Pettit frowned.

"Yes," Caine said in an unaccustomed voice laced with defeat. "he has proclaimed himself head of the Island and has determined that we are unjustly trying to depose him. He has clearly lost whatever little reason he had. He is, without question, certifiably insane and actually has been so for some time."

Fifty-Six

Pickering watched the commander talking into his radio for a few seconds and decided on the only course of action that was open to him. He advanced the defence force field, using the computer to control it while *Wallow 5* was stationary. The bright line reached the stern of the commander's craft and demolished the transom and sliced through the twin outboard engines, rendering them useless. He watched the commander drop his radio and yell a command to those on board. Without the need for a second bidding, they all ran to the damaged bow in total disarray and spilled out on to the dockside. *Wallow 5* was steered a course parallel to the dockside and moved along the line of the ten assault crafts, cutting off the stern and engines of each craft as it passed.

Very soon the dockside was populated by an army in total disarray, most of whom had left their rifles aboard the assault crafts, which were still afloat but floundering as the damaged buoyancy chambers filled tilting them over at an acute angle. The craft were fitted with craft-to-craft radio communications which could not be used to contact any other personnel. The commander had the only means of communicating with Wilson and he had dropped it, in mid call, in the scramble to vacate the damaged vessel.

He ordered a runner to deliver the information of the disablement of the task fleet to Wilson, not knowing how much of the message Wilson had received before the call was cut off. The runner was clearly not happy to be the bearer of bad tidings, being aware that Wilson had a very short fuse and was known to have those who gave him bad news thrown into the brig on a whim. Nevertheless, he was a professional soldier and carried out the order to the best of his ability. On his way to Wilson, he encountered Craddock coming in the other direction. The runner explained his mission and Craddock sent him back to the commander saying that he, Craddock, would deliver the message. The runner was mightily pleased by his good fortune.

Wilson had another bout of apoplexy when he was given the news that his assault fleet had been completely disabled. He looked as if he were about to strike Craddock when he gathered his thoughts, looked at Craddock and pointed to the chair at the control panel. "Fire that thing up and use one of the BAM2 to annihilate their damn boat and everybody in it."

"Two of our men are on board, sir," Craddock informed him.

"And your point is?" Wilson said archly. "Don't argue or tax yourself by actually thinking, just do it."

Craddock enabled the control panel and watched the screen come to life; the outer and inner main domes were still in place, trapping the Federation vessels. There was a dotted semicircle centred on one of the dock wing walls which covered the dock area. Craddock selected the line with the cursor and double clicked. The dotted line became a solid illuminated line and a simple menu appeared in a dialogue panel on the screen. One of the options was to increase the diameter of the force field.

"I want to do this." Wilson shoved his hip against Craddock almost unseating him. "What do I do?"

"Select increase." Craddock said noncommittally.

"Done; what next?"

"Select a rate of increase." Craddock pointed at a table of speeds upwards from one foot per minute. "Select five and watch what happens."

Wilson selected five and clicked. Nothing happened.

"What's all this?" He looked sharply at Craddock.

"Like I said before you have to give it time to select the necessary algorithm. Just give it a chance." Craddock's sharp response went unnoticed by Wilson whose complete attention was focussed on the image of the semi-circle on the screen waiting for it to expand towards *Wallow 5*.

After a twenty-second delay, the semicircular line began to creep out from the BAM2 projector, and it moved slowly towards the stationary screen image of *Wallow 5*. Wilson took great delight as he continued to watch the shimmering green line advance until it met and then crossed the line of the defence dome projected from *Wallow 5*. BAM2 was clearly unable to defend itself against itself Wilson mused. "You are about to see history made," he turned to Craddock. "I am personally going to destroy the pitiful naval capacity of this little Island and turn it into something great and powerful. History will record that I achieved this great victory with the loss of only two lowly privates and some unimportant Islanders." He sat back with a look of great satisfaction.

"With their vessel positioned where it is, you are going to destroy completely about half of our own disabled task vessels before you get to it and a large chunk of the dock," Craddock observed.

"It really doesn't matter," Wilson shrugged. "I'm bored—how do we make this thing go faster?"

The creep speed of the dome expansion was increased to an apparent maximum and the holographic table image showed the line reaching towards *Wallow*. For no apparent reason it stopped just short of the craft and nothing that Craddock could do made it progress. Wilson was winding himself up into another rage attack.

Craddock wrinkled his brow in concentration as he analysed the situation. "My guess is that there is a limit to the projection distance to prevent damage to the dock."

Wilson showed further signs of instability when a variety of emotions ran across his face, the last of which appeared comparatively rational and barked specific orders to be carried out immediately. Craddock left the control room with orders from Wilson to interrogate the traitors and find out as much as he could about the control system to Ginger up the process. He walked to the room where they were held and was deep in thought as the accompanying armed guard let him in. Pettit was still in his colonel's uniform and automatically, the guard squared his shoulders and gave a long way up short way down army salute; being hatless Pettit did not return the salute, he simply muttered, "Carry on, Private."

"My orders are not to leave the room, sir." The private said in a clipped military voice.

"I give the orders here," Craddock pointed to the WO1 insignia on his upper arm. "Carry on, Private. I'll let you know when I want to leave." Craddock looked at the three men and Caine with a neutral expression, neither hostile nor friendly. "I have some questions for you." This he directed at Pettit. "I need to get fuller access to the control system."

"Now why would we give you that kind of information . . . , Craddock?" Pettit peered with exaggeration at the name tag on the soldier's uniform. "You have invaded an independent country illegally, you have incarcerated us without giving a valid reason, and you have not observed our rights under the Geneva Convention, so I repeat—why would we help you?"

"Two reasons I can think of, sir." Craddock addressed Pettit once more, ignoring the others. "One is that I have been using the controls to manipulate the shields, but it's not doing exactly as I commanded, and if I get it wrong, it could do a lot of damage and potentially kill a lot of people. Second, if you don't help me, I believe it is Mr Wilson's intention to execute you by firing squad. Help me, and there may be something I can do to delay that situation."

There was a stunned silence at his words. The four Islanders looked at each other with alarm at the starkness of the statement while realising that Wilson was capable of carrying out the threat. Craddock turned and tapped on the door.

"You can let me out now," he shouted through the closed door. "I'll give you some time to consider what I've said to you," he uttered as the guard opened the door, "give it some careful thought." Then addressing the guard, "There's a problem down in the dock area I'm going to sort it out."

As soon as Craddock had gone Crook said angrily, "You were right, Penny. Wilson has finally lost it completely, what he intends is cold blooded assassination."

"Just think about it," Caine said with a sardonic smile, "that wasn't all bad news. He actually told us something very important. He said that the controls didn't do what he wanted."

"Which means what?" Pettit asked somewhat irritably. "The controls are quite complex, and they got it wrong and that's hardly surprising."

"Which means," she paused and gave a Madonna-like smile. "that he tried to do something harmful but was stopped by the system."

"For goodness' sake, Penny, spit it out. This is not a guessing game. What are you talking about?"

"You're taking all the fun out of it, Si." Caine suppressed a smile. "What it actually means is that he couldn't do what he wanted to because the controls were overridden by Bill Wilkinson in the Lab, and he was able to prevent any real damage being done."

"Do you think that was a slip of the tongue?"

"It could have been," Gilliland broke in thoughtfully, "except that he gave us some more information when he said he was going to the dock to sort out a problem." He stroked his chin thoughtfully. "That would be trouble caused by Ed Pickering. It probably means that Ed has fulfilled, or is at least engaged in, his part of the plan."

"Exactly," Caine said happily, "but we're still locked away in here, and we really need to be out there directing the next moves." Then she added more sombrely, "Before he carries out his threat of execution."

*

Wilson was less than happy when he was told by Craddock, when he returned to the control room, that the prisoners had refused to give him further information about the control system. He was also not happy that the destruction of *Wallow 5* had not happened, and he was positively thunderous that the task force vessels had all been disabled and that his finest assault troops were milling about aimlessly on the dockside.

He was slightly mollified by the thought that the aircraft which he had arranged to take the delegation to Lisbon would be back before the end of the day so that he would not be stranded on the Island if things turned sour, not that he expected them to. He had, through Craddock's supposed direct intervention, satisfactorily shut down the shield covering the airport to enable the aircraft to take off on its outward journey, and the same would apply when it returned, and its return was guaranteed by the armed presence on board.

The matter of destroying Creswell was temporarily on hold, so he had let him go with the others to face the music when he returned to England and reported complete failure. There would be plenty of opportunity to complete the final part of his plan when he had sorted out the current irritation of the traitors and the inability of his troops to carry out the simplest of tasks. He glanced at Craddock, who was on watch at the HMT; very soon Craddock's usefulness would be marginal. He now viewed Craddock, because of his non-cooperation and his disregard for Wilson's superiority, as the enemy within, and he would be dealt with accordingly at an appropriate time.

A quick review of the situation further calmed him. He had control of the shield weapons, and he had the only armed group on the Island; that was enough for the moment. That the task force vessels had been destroyed was no more than an irritation. He was still in control. Satisfied with that he decided to visit the prisoners to gloat.

Disappointment was his first feeling when the prisoners were accompanied into an anti-room by two armed guards. He had expected them to be dispirited and subservient; they were not. The four remained seated when he entered the anti-room, and he was somewhat perturbed by their relaxed postures and angered that none of them spoke to or looked at him.

"Stand when I enter," he said in a choked voice.

They made no move to do so, looking at him with bored defiance which was a Caine recommendation.

"You," he said to Caine, "I suppose you think you're clever, pretending to be somebody else. Well, that makes you a spy, and I will have you shot along with these three." He wrested a rifle from one of the guards and chambered a round. "Let's see how you all like a round in the leg just for starters." He took aim pointing at Caine. "You first, rich bitch." His knuckles whitened as he squeezed the trigger.

Fifty-Seven

Neither side could do anything definitive. Pickering watched the now largely disarmed, task force members on the dock, and they watched him standing legs akimbo on the aft section of *Wallow 5*. He was still mystified by the recent event when he had observed the bright water signature of a defence dome creeping towards him. It had already overlapped his defence dome by the time it stopped. The pause brought relief because the effectiveness of the dome force fields was not diminished when they passed through each other and had it continued, *Wallow* would have been destroyed, together with all on board as well as the two soldiers in the water.

Relief was replaced by puzzlement when he calmed down. The force field that had been sent to destroy him was not stopped by some automatic safety device; no such device had been fitted despite his suggestions to the contrary. His clinically logical mind sifted through the possibilities, and only one solution which he deduced would fit the scenario was that somebody had intervened to prevent the continuation which also meant that the transfer of the control system to the lab had probably been completed. He breathed a deep sigh of hopeful relief.

Signalling his success to his compatriots was a problem for him. Their communication devices had been confiscated, and he had no way of knowing where anybody was. Olsen and Finlay were watching over the two wet squaddies, who were now, having been allowed on board, sitting at the stern, looking sullen and ill at ease at being covered by one of their own guns in the hands of a woman.

Realising that he was too high a profile, Pickering decided to give the verbal communications task to Olsen. She was obviously a civilian, and even more obviously, a woman, and the attention she attracted would be because she was particularly attractive not because she was perceived as a threat. He told her the task to be carried out, and she accepted it commenting that being wet was going to make her more noticeable.

To the short-lived delight of the squadies, she unzipped her dry suit and struggled out of it to reveal a one-piece Island suit. The suit was revealing but not as revealing as they would have wished. She pulled her hair into a ponytail and secured it shaking her head vigorously to dislodge surplus water and bush out the tail.

Wallow's engine wound up from idle, and Pickering swung the wheel to turn away from the dockside. Living up to her name, *Wallow* turned sluggishly in a wide circle and headed to the western end of the dock. As they approached the dockside at the extreme western end, Pickering switched off the BAM2 unit, first making sure that the two captive squaddies were being held at gunpoint this time by Finlay. Olsen climbed the personnel ladder and jumped nimbly on to the dockside; she turned and gave them a comedy salute before trotting across the dock apron and disappearing between the wharf buildings.

Minutes later, after crossing the open piazza to the admin building, she went to the fourth floor and walked to Caine's office; it was empty. The next two offices were occupied by soldiers, the third was occupied by a clerk whom she vaguely recognised, she slipped through the door and closed it behind her. The clerk looked up and smiled at the wild-looking woman who stood before him, she was breathing heavily having been running for part of the way back. The deep breaths and the tight one-piece garment tantalised him.

"Hello," he said breathlessly. "What can I do for you?"

"I'm looking for Penny Caine," she said while rounding her shoulders in a futile effort to hide her fulsome front from his overt gaze.

"She's been taken," he whispered although there was nobody around to hear.

"Taken?" she repeated with a frown while looking at him with her head on one side.

"Wilson and the US President came to see her in her office, and there was a hell of a kafuffle and a lot of soldiers running around with guns. They took her away and I haven't seen her since."

"Where did they take her?"

"I have no idea." He looked crestfallen as she began to leave. "How about some coffee?"

"Some other time, I've got things to do that won't wait."

She walked towards the control room slowly so as not to arouse any curiosity. The entrance was guarded by two armed soldiers who were checking anybody entering the room. She paused and watched for a while observing that military personnel were allowed free access, but that the civilian Islanders were interrogated before being allowed to enter.

Returning to the breathless clerk's office she once more slid into the room much to his delight.

"Back so soon," he said with a broad smile.

"I need some help." She smiled at him disarmingly. "Do you have any really official files that I can borrow?"

"How do you mean *official?*"

"Something that looks official. Something that looks really important."

"Hum," he said thoughtfully, "I've got some stats that are very important but almost indecipherable. Hum," he thought again, "Let's see what I can do." He walked over to his computer and pulled up a publication tool screen. Typing the title of "Confidential information—Eyes only" he embellished it with a border of laurel leaves. Printing it off he trimmed it to shape and stuck it on to the front of a red card filing jacket and placed the stats in it. "That good enough for you?"

"Great, I owe you." She gave him another big smile.

"I will hold you to that." He returned her smile, "I really mean it."

She held the file in a prominent position as she approached the control room she gave an alluring and bright smile as she approached the guard and tapped her index finger on the lurid confidential label on the file.

"I have to get this information to Mr Lawson for the work he is doing for Mr Wilson."

The guard lifted the rifle that had been barring her way after glancing at the incomprehensive file and finding it innocuous, and allowed her through. She walked into the dimly lit room where several HMTs, of various ranges, glowed with multicoloured light shapes representing the sea and the land. The main display was showing the outline of the Island with the airport to the north and the dock in the south. The wrecked assault craft and the isolated image of *Wallow 5* showed up clearly as red images, and she was even able to trace the path she had taken between the dock buildings to get from the western end of the dock to her present position to the east.

A figure was sat hunched over a keyboard, his face looking sinister in the eerie colour changing light; he ignored her and concentrated on the task at hand.

"Mr Lawson," she interrupted his reverie. "I have the data file from Mr Pickering. He said to give it to you and to tell you that he's done his bit so everything is ready for the next stage."

Lawson paused and looked at her mystified. Realisation suddenly dawned, and he looked suddenly relieved and ten years younger. "Thank you, Ms . . ." He waited for her response.

"Olsen," she said, "Beverley Olsen." She held out her hand formally.

"Well, Beverley Olsen." He took her hand and shook it slowly and gently. "I'm Mark, and I am very glad to see you."

She smiled coyly impressed by what she saw as he turned his face away from the unflattering glow. He rose from his chair and stood close by facing her, dwarfing her five foot nine; he smiled down on her and reached out his hand to take the file. They were both almost bowled over by a caveman of a guard who snatched the file and passed it to a slightly less Neanderthal colleague. The colleague looked at the file and shook his head at the meaningless jumble of numbers and symbols; he put the file on top of a document storage locker and indicated with a grunt that Lawson should continue with his former task and that Olsen should leave.

"Thank you, Beverley, and thank Mr Pickering for me. Perhaps you would also tell him that the others are tied up at the moment, so we'll have to think of an alternative development plan." He looked pointedly at the guard to see if he had rumbled their poorly coded discussion. The guards looked bored and were more interested in looking at Olsen than listening to their boring conversation.

"It was good to meet you, Mark." She laid a hand gently on his shoulder. "I'll pass the message on and bring a reply back with any luck." She departed shaking her head in wonder that at a desperate time like this when they were all clearly in jeopardy she was trembling at the thought of meeting Mark Lawson again and was already engineering a way of doing so.

Fifty-Eight

Craddock grabbed the barrel of the rifle that Wilson had been pointing at Caine and twisted it so that it pointed at the ceiling.

"What the . . ." Wilson shouted in alarm and surprise.

"Just doing my job of protecting you, sir, had you pulled the trigger you might well have been killed by the ricochet along with any of the rest of us."

Wilson snorted and glared at Craddock. "Do that again," he said with an evil hiss, "and I'll have you court martialled and shot." He paused and smiled to himself. "But not necessarily in that order." His laugh was chillingly recognisable as that of an unhinged man.

"Sir," Craddock said in a deadpan voice his cold eyes fixed on Wilson. Wilson's threats had become so frequent and outlandish that he was no longer in awe of them.

The brittle silence was broken by a buzz from within Wilson's pocket.

"Wilson," he said tersely and listened briefly to the conversation. "Your stupidity will be suitably rewarded." His voice was full of spite. "You," he pointed at Craddock, "get back to the control room and sort out the mess that the commander has left us in. I want their damn rowing boat sunk with all on board. Do whatever it is you do with the controls

and get rid of it. I don't care about casualties theirs or ours just do it."
By the time he had finished his eyes were demon bright and there was
froth around his mouth.

"Sir," Craddock said in the same flat voice he had used previously.
"probably, best if you come back to the control room with me. Sir, I think
the situation needs your expert touch."

"I suppose you're right," he responded in a martyred voice. "As ever,
if I want something done properly, I'd better do it myself." With his
previous rage having abated he left the room, accompanied by the two
armed guards and Craddock, looking strangely neutral.

"Absolutely gaga," Crook said when they were alone and once again
locked in their small cell.

"Yes, he is," Caine said thoughtfully. "Seriously so, he is certifiable
and very dangerous. It's not possible right now to second guess him, he
is truly irrational."

"That's the bad news," Pettit volunteered. "The good news is that our
little plan to regain control has worked so far. We have remote control of
the defence systems and all his task force craft are disabled. We have the
beginnings of the upper hand. The next thing to do is to consolidate our
advantage and that means getting out of here."

Fifty-Nine

Shortly after Olsen left the control room, Craddock and Wilson entered. Wilson was back in full control mode for the moment. Lawson remained seated at his desk and did not acknowledge their arrival and gave no sign of the excitement he felt now that their plan to regain control was, so far, on track.

"Find some other way to get rid of their pathetic little boat," Wilson addressed Craddock. "If this person won't help you—get rid of him and then get rid of the boat. After that, get that useless commander up here. I want a special word with him about his pathetic failure." He paced the room, muttering to himself, "Then we can get the traitors down here and have them watch the destruction of their 'Navy' and then I'll dispose of them and get on with the job of running this Island, and I think I'll rename it and any of the Islanders who don't like it will be charged with treason." He nodded sagely to himself. In the ebb and flow of his emotions, reality had once more deserted him.

"Which of those things do you want done first?" Craddock said with an emotionless voice. "Find out how to sink the boat. Get Gilliland and Co here. Get the commander here or," he added with a straight face, "execute the traitors."

Wilson turned to him with a look of fury which evaporated as he watched Craddock's unreadable face. He tried to decide if he was being mocked or whether the enquiry was genuine. "Are you stupid or something? It's obvious, isn't it? Gilliland and his people first. Boat second. Commander third, and I'll ignore your stupid remark about the executions."

"Sir," Craddock gave a military turn and left the room to carry out the first order.

Cradock was deep in thought as he approached the room in which the four prisoners were held. Entering the room with two of the four guards, he stood indecisively for a moment waging an inner battle that showed on his face. The guards took up position on either side of the door with guns ported but ready for action should it be required.

"You two," he looked at the guards, "get the other two from outside and escort the prisoners to the control room."

The guard nodded and called in the other two guards and the four of them escorted the prisoners out of the room with admirable military precision.

The entry of a further eight people in the control room filled it almost completely and made manoeuvring in the restricted space very difficult. Wilson was by now surrounded by armed guards and was physically invulnerable. The guards surrounding him were the only soldiers empowered by Wilson to bring assault rifles to bear; the guards remaining with the prisoners and the rest of the control room personnel had their rifles loose slung on shoulder straps and their side arms unholstered.

Wilson started off his diatribe in an unaccustomed calm voice. "I have brought you four here to witness the demise of your pathetic little rowing boat. If you want to save the hides of your people on board, then I suggest you tell them to shut off their defences and surrender themselves to my troops." His statement elicited no response from the Islanders. "Very well, then we shall carry out the threat. Craddock, they have moved their rowing boat to the western end of the dock. Find an appropriate attack dome and annihilate them."

Caine watched Craddock as he undertook the task without comment. His relaxed actions surprised her; she was sure that he was a man of at least some integrity who, despite being a career military man, would not undertake such an inhuman action in such a relaxed fashion. He selected the central southern wall defence dome and activated it at ten feet per minute, and they watched as the semi circle of bright water line fanned out towards the stationery green blip of *Wallow 5*.

Craddock's face was completely relaxed as he watched the bright water approach the corner of the dock occupied by *Wallow 5*. It was clear that those on board the boat did not realise what was happening until it was too late; they were trapped as the arc of the dome approached the northern and western walls of the dock. As the force shield approached the walls, the angle of the arc was decreased so that the walls were not damaged. This "automatic" safety feature appeared to take Craddock by surprise as he watched the advance of the bright water towards *Wallow*.

The advance was suddenly halted when it was just short of the trapped vessel and Wilson's voice shattered the silence of the watchers with harsh demands made of Craddock to go for the kill.

He shrugged and turned to Wilson. "This is out of my hands, sir. There's nothing I can do until I learn to override the safety protocols."

"Enough is enough," Wilson said suddenly. "I am going to give the Chinese fleet an ultimatum and get them off my back. Either they go, or I annihilate them and I want these four traitors to see what I can do. Radio man, open up communications with the fleet commander." He turned to address Gilliland and the other three, "After that, you will be taken out from here to a public place of execution with the whole Island population in attendance, compulsorily." He took the hand microphone from the radio operator. "This is Wilson, who am I speaking to?" The response was in Chinese. "Don't be so damn childish, I know you speak English, just get your fleet the hell out of here, or I'll wipe it off the face of the seas. I'm having the outer shield switched off to release the vessels trapped between the two shields. They are to return to the fleet, and you are to go." He threw the hand mike back to the operator without signing off.

Sixty

Caine frowned as she whispered to her three companions. "He is now in a fantasy world of his own imagining. We need to be very careful about how we handle him. He has alienated just about everybody: us, the USA, the UK, Europe, the Federation, and China. There is nowhere for him to go now he has to make this takeover work. Problem is, I can't tell whether or not he realises that and if he actually does, whether he cares."

Craddock accessed the control panel and manipulated the menu. "Outer ring switched off," he said to Wilson. The screen, after its accustomed delay, converted the arc from a full line to dotted line, indicating that it had been deactivated but was still set at twelve miles. They all watched the screen avidly and saw the images of the trapped vessels begin to move out of territorial waters to the open sea and the rest of the fleet which was still peppered with Russian "observation" ships.

The rest of the fleet remained stationary and did not appear to be making any effort to regroup in order to leave as Wilson had ordered. The inactivity caused Wilson to fly into another rage, and he began jabbing his forefinger on to the HMT.

"Take out a few of their ships," he ordered Craddock. "Let's show them who is boss."

Craddock pulled down a menu on the screen and selected manual advance which allowed him to advance the force field at the speed of his choice. The circumference expanded rapidly heading towards the outlying vessels one of which appeared large enough to be an aircraft carrier.

They all watched with baited breath as the shield closed in on the stray vessels. Wilson stood bright-eyed, anticipating a demonstration of his power willing the line to travel faster. Just short of the first outlying vessel, the bright water line came to an abrupt halt.

"What are you doing, Craddock?" Wilson hissed. "Go for it, annihilate them—that's an order."

"I'm not in control of what's going on," Craddock responded without emotion. "I didn't stop it from happening. The defence protocols, as I have repeatedly told you are automatic, and I don't know how to override them."

"You four," he screamed irrationally, "fix it immediately. Do not cross me, I hold your future in my hands."

"Mr Wilson," Caine said in a placatory voice as though talking to a child. "What's happening cannot be fixed just like that. There are safety protocols which need to be overridden. Obviously, the inbuilt defaults protect against unauthorised or accidental activation." She was irrationally pleased with the smooth way in which she lied.

Gilliland and Crook looked at her with twin smiles of appreciation. They, of course, knew that no such protocols existed. She closed her eyes and shook her head imperceptibly. She now allowed herself the luxury of believing that what was happening was what they had actually, if somewhat tentatively, planned. Wilkinson was manipulating the system to mimic the parameters entered via the control room keyboard, to prevent or at least control any disasters. What she did not want to do was let Wilson know that they were actually in control, not him. Her reasoning was that, although they had control of the system, and they had disabled the assault fleet, Wilson still had control of the armed forces, and he still retained the capability of switching off the defence system, they were, at this point, in stalemate.

She continued to be confused about Craddock. He was, albeit marginally, an ethical man but seemed to be quite willing to carry out the orders of a madman while displaying no visible awareness of the obvious damage such orders could cause. Covertly, she watched him as he observed the screen with hooded eyes which, occasionally, flicked towards Wilson.

"Do something about it, Craddock, and do it now," Wilson said with quiet menace.

"What do you propose?"

"Well, if you don't know, and they won't tell you,"—he inclined his head towards Gilliland and Caine—"none of you are any use to me, and I have no intention of carrying excess baggage with me." He allowed the revelation of his intentions to peter out, and their conclusion being obvious. "We'll deal later with the Island's 'Navy'," he sniggered at his description of *Wallow 5*. "But first these four have to be dealt with. Craddock, take them outside and assemble the firing squad. I can't be bothered to get the rest of the miserable Islanders together to witness the carrying out of my sentence. I have tried them in absentia and found them guilty of treason. They will be summarily executed without delay."

Sixty-One

$\mathcal{P}$ickering was frustrated by the impasse. Olsen had returned from the control room and passed on the message that their compatriots were still incarcerated and were, therefore, out of the equation, meaning that Pickering and his team of two were going to have to act on their own. All but a handful of the troops were assembled on the dockside, some gazing dolefully at their disabled craft, obviously unsure of what to do next, rather like Pickering and his crew of two. The troops were armed with weapons of restraint as well as of killing; Pickering had at his disposal a weapon with no restraint capability—it was all or nothing.

Climbing the superstructure, boats binoculars slung around his neck Pickering was able to see the back of the control room and the front of the Administrative buildings with the open piazza in between. The area was deserted, the Island's indigenous population having decided to stay indoors and out of trouble. He swept the area surrounding the Piazza and saw no movement that was of any concern.

The superstructure had not been constructed to be used as an observation post and Pickering's arms soon tired of their task despite his changing arms when each grew tired. Finlay took his place and with the agility of youth, wrapped his legs and one arm around the vertical component of the structure and continued the observation.

Pickering stood at the base of the structure, rubbing his aching shoulders as he gazed up at Finlay. "Beverley, I'm too old to be doing this. After Stuart gets tired, you can take a turn at the observation post."

She nodded her assent and with a thoughtful look retreated to the stern to check the welfare of the two squaddies, who had been restrained using ship's rope, they were resigned to their fate and looked defeated. Satisfying herself that they posed no threat she opened up one of the after-locker boxes and searched among its contents. She returned to Pickering, dragging with her a coil of ship's rope. Pickering watched as she fashioned a fixed loop at one end of the rope and six feet further along fashioned a running slipknot. She shinned up one of the sloping spars to where Finlay was peering through the binoculars and slid the slip knot over the top of the structure and tugged it until it was taut. Tapping him on the leg she indicated that he should place his foot in the loop, he did so and visibly relaxed as it took his weight.

Later, as Olsen was preparing to take over from him, he shouted down in an excited voice. "There's something happening. There's a whole bunch of people coming out of the control room." He paused and peered intently. "There are four people each being controlled by a soldier on each arm. Three men and a woman—looks like it's Ms Caine, Mr Gilliland, Mr Crook, and Mr Pettit and a group of, maybe, a half-dozen armed soldiers and an officer and also a bald man—presumably Wilson, but I can't be sure at this distance."

"What are they doing?" Pickering sounded agitated.

"Our four appear to be having their hands tied behind their backs. Now they're being pushed down on to their knees, all four of them, and the armed soldiers are lining up ... My God, it looks like a firing squad." He looked appalled. "Wilson is standing there with his hand in the air. He's actually going to have them shot."

For a moment, Pickering was numb and inactive. He shook his head as if to clear his thoughts, squared his shoulders, and rushed into the day cabin where he coaxed the idling engines to full throttle, swinging the wheel as he did so to take them as close as possible to the east end of the dock, close to the Piazza in which the presumed execution was to take place.

The task force assembled on the dockside watched, passively as they moved from the west end of the dock, easterly, to a position near its eastern end where on full reverse they churned to a clumsy halt. During their brief journey from west to east, Pickering outlined his makeshift plan to Finley and Olsen. When they came to a clumsy halt, Pickering switched off BAM2, and he and Finley carrying the rifle and side arm that they had captured from the squaddies, jumped on to the dock once Olsen had manoeuvred close enough for them to do so. As soon as they were on the dockside, Olsen took *Wallow 5* away from the dockside and switched BAM2 back on.

The two men raced towards the Piazza at the speed dictated by Pickering's more advancing and somewhat sedentary years. With no regard for personal safety, they continued running helter-skelter across the Piazza where Wilson was shouting threateningly at Craddock while the firing squad, rifles at the ready, stood rigidly still.

Pickering approached them with his rifle at the ready pointing it with authority at Wilson; his authority was born of many years of big game hunting while working in the wildest parts of untamed Africa. Wilson was operating in his own fantasy world and seemed not to notice the advance of the two armed men and continued to harangue Craddock.

"I gave you an order!" he screamed at Craddock. "And when I give an order, I expect it to be carried out." He turned to the firing squad. "Fire immediately," he ordered.

"Hold that order," Craddock barked at the squad. The squad listened to their military leader rather than the politician but looked uncomfortable and uncertain, they were on the edge of uncertainty.

Wilson, seeing that his task force was considering revolt at last noticed one of the Islanders with a gun levelled at him he decided to turn the situation to as much an advantage as he could. He wheeled with surprising speed and ran towards the control room door half-way across the piazza, to the safety of his chosen bodyguards on whom he knew he could rely, at a price.

Craddock released the four Islanders who stood shakily as their bindings were removed. Caine smiled to herself and said to Gilliland, "Told you so, I knew Craddock was a good egg." She looked closely at the other three and marvelled at their composure considering, they had just been seconds from execution. Caine knew that a reaction to their situation would come later, and until that time, they were running on a crude excess of adrenalin.

"We'd better find out, what the madman is doing," Pettit said, looking at the others to see if they were okay.

Led by Pettit, the four former captives accompanied by Pickering and Finley with Craddock bringing up the rear, ran in Wilson's footsteps and spilled into the cramped control room. The only sound in the room once they had crashed in was the voice of Wilson from where he stood by the radio console, microphone in hand. They heard part of his message.

> *"Switch off, and you will have unhindered access to the Island. I have been able to escape from the Islanders, who have been holding me captive and who forced me to warn you off. I am now in control, and you can come and take possession of the Island and its technology. We will lose communication as soon as I disable the*

system, so I suggest you come in with helicopters and troops and
take over immediately. I will be holding it for you."

His uncontrolled laughter rang hollow as the control room was plunged into darkness and the computer powered down with a whining and mournful sigh.

Sixty-Two

Aboard *Huni*, the Chinese Aircraft Carrier, the Admiral of the day listened with some scepticism to the radio operator who relayed, verbatim, Wilson's message. Their own control room advised him that as far as they could tell visually, the defences of the Island had powered down just as Wilson had said they would. The helicopters watching from a safe distance, reported that the circle of bright water usually associated with the operation of the BAM2 defences was no longer visible. The Admiral was still undecided, a reaction which was engendered by his deep mistrust of Wilson who he knew to be, like themselves, predictably duplicitous. His aide was of the opinion that they should take whatever advantage they could of the situation but was also wary because of Wilson's track record of dealings with the Peoples Republic.

After a brief delay, they decided to make ready four of their assault helicopters each holding twelve operational commandos. Checking further, by blowing moisture saturated air towards where the defence dome would be, they saw that the defences were still down and an operator was assigned to make sure that if the defences were reactivated they would be warned.

Forty minutes after receiving the call from Wilson, the helicopters were loaded and ready to depart. Their rotors which had been idling wound up to a banshee pitch and all four wobbled unsteadily into the air as the cross breeze and their overlapping rotor wash caused dynamic instability. They lifted off the deck and hung nose down with their tail rotors pushing them around until they all faced towards the Island, which was discernable by the top of the central mountain breaking over the distant horizon. The rotor wash dispersed the water spray they were making to detect the dome and also flattened the surface of the sea into small angry ripples.

In blunt V-formation, they made their way to the Island, increasing their height as they also increased their speed. Both lead helicopters held specially trained insurgency troops and each contained officers capable of leading the battle contingent. The two following craft had extra arms and ammunition, and the troops on board these craft were engineers who specialised in, among other things, demolition and gaining access by means of explosive devices.

The helicopters split into twos, and they veered off in opposite directions to encircle the Island from both directions. They observed the airport at which there were no aircraft to the north and the port with a single small craft standing off from what appeared to be ten wrecked assault craft. Troops standing on the dockside adjacent to the damaged craft, waved to the passing helicopters. Each of the lead helicopters reported back to the Admiral what they had observed.

In the war room on board the *Huni*, the Admiral received the reports and wondered what they actually meant. Wilson had said that he had control of the Island, but the damaged vessels and the aimlessly grouped troops were puzzling. He delayed the landing of the airborne troops until he had time to digest what the mixed signals meant.

*

Wilson stood behind the radio desk, with Jack Patin standing defiantly at his side, behind the best four of his specially selected bodyguards, "best" indicated that they would kill without thought or question at Wilson's single command. They had been selected not for their military prowess, but for the fact that they had no morals and would do anything for the money he paid them. He was cunning enough to know that they would switch sides at the prospect of more money from a more generous master. He kept their "loyalty" simply by telling them that he would trump any other offer that may be made and pay a bonus on top.

"Mr Wilson," Caine said to him in soft placatory tones, "you don't really want to hand seizure of the Island over to the Chinese, do you?" She didn't wait for an answer. "I know that you are much too smart for that. You have another plan up your sleeve, don't you?" This time she did wait for an answer.

"I have," he said with self-satisfied overtones. "Of course, I have. But I'm damned if I'm going to tell you about it." He laughed humourlessly.

"I'm not so sure about that," Pettit said in the sudden realisation the she had a psychologically based displacement plan in mind. "You're obviously making this up as you go along. You don't have a plan at all. You're hoping that something will crop up which will allow you to take over the Island again."

"No, Silas," Caine broke in, "he has got a plan, but he is wondering how we managed to retake control of the system. Just like we're wondering how he managed to switch the system off without having the algorithms to do so. We thought we were clever, but he is cleverer than us."

"Never," Pettit said mockingly, "he doesn't have the intelligence to hack into the system and get to the base controls. Not in a month of Sundays."

"You're so mindless," Wilson snorted. "You really have no idea how I did it, do you?"

"I don't need to know how you did it. Okay, so you can switch the defences on and off, but you can't control them, only we can do that. You have an on off switch, we have control."

"When the Chinese land, they'll get the information out of you about the controls, and they will see that it was I who gave them the opening to do that. As a reward, they will give me governorship of the Island, and I will take it over from them in my own way and in my own good time." Wilson looked comfortable with his plans and gave a distant smile.

Sixty-Three

The bizarre situation in which the four Islanders found themselves had descended into an uneasy farce. Wilson had lost all vestiges of being in touch with reality and believed that anything he thought of would turn miraculously into reality. He had a degree of control over the system, which allowed him to switch it on and off, and the Islander's deception gave them remote control of system actions and enabled them to limit any damage Wilson might try to cause, but they were still unable to reactivate the system to their open advantage because he retained the ability to disable the whole of their control systems at will. Much to their frustration, Wilson retained the upper hand.

Helicopters from the Chinese fleet were circling the Island and could be observed through the windows of the control room. Once they landed, the situation for the Islanders was bleak; the Chinese had overwhelming numbers and could overrun the Island in a matter of hours, perhaps even minutes.

Caine's attempt at unnerving Wilson by appealing to his egotism had not had the desired effect; he had rationalised any shortcomings in his plan by inventing unlikely or unreal solutions. She looked at the young Islander standing next to Wilson and wondered about the connection between the two. She tried to recall his name, and why she knew him but the fringe memory remained on the fringe.

"Who is that?" she asked Pettit and indicated by nodding her head in the direction of Pantin. "I kind of know him, but I don't know why."

"Yes, you're right, you do know him." Pettit peered between two of the guards at the figure in the shadows. "That's . . ." He searched his memory for the name. "Porter, no not Porter—it's something like that. Perry? No, it's on the tip of my tongue." He screwed up his face in concentration. "Pantin, Jack Pantin, that's it. He's the one who left the Island and then came back a changed man."

"Yes, I remember," Caine said with a frown of concentration. "He was the career layabout who repented and came back to turn over a new leaf. Maybe he wasn't as changed as the repatriation group thought. How do you think he figures in this?"

"At a guess," Gilliland broke in to their whispered conversation, "I would say that, from where he's standing, he is a Wilson man through and through. He seems to be the only one on the Island who is." He paused and thought. "He must be the inside man who interrupted the system in the first place."

"If that is so," Pettit rejoined the conversation, "his presence here means that it is something he is doing that causes the shut down. As far as I know, he is not a computer specialist, so whatever it is he does needs little or no training. Now I'm stuck. Anybody else care to join in the thought process?"

"How about this?" Crook entered into the discussion. "To switch off the system usually means making an entry via the keyboard but that would be detected by Bill Wilkinson in the laboratory, and he would be able to switch it on again without being detected himself. He couldn't have simply switched off the power, otherwise, the automatic back-up system would have cut in. That leaves only one possibility."

"Yes, it certainly does," Gilliland hissed animatedly. "It means that he has control of a remotely jamming device or at least a trigger mechanism which operates a jammer which is probably in this room." He paused and concentrated. "Closer than that the jammer must be in the computer cabinet, and the switch must be in Wilson's or Pantin's pocket or at least within easy reach of either or both."

"Eureka," Caine hissed. "Now how do we get at it, bearing in mind that if the helicopters are allowed to land, and they will very soon, we're done for."

"Mr Wilson," Caine said above the mumble of other voices in the room, "I'm sure it has occurred to you that the Chinese military, once they take the Island at your invitation, will round up all invaders, including you, your troops—including your Islander friend, and you will all be imprisoned, and if history teaches anything, you will know that the new Chinese military does not take prisoners. Execution will be the order of the day."

The soldiers in the room began to look furtive and unsettled. They had worked with the Chinese and knew for certain that they exercised zero tolerance. When what she had said sunk into Pantin, he looked nervously at Wilson who gazed unseeing into the far distance.

"Mr Wilson," Pantin tapped Wilson's shoulder, "what she said is not right, is it? You won't let your friends come to any harm, and I have been very helpful to you."

Wilson remained locked in his own isolated world and made no response to the enquiry.

"You'll get no help there, Pantin," Caine said loud enough for the bodyguard and the other troops to hear. "He will drop you like a hot potato as he will all the troops that he brought along. You are all for the high jump."

The hush that had descended over the room was broken by noisy and indistinct static through which the voice of the sergeant in charge of the force on board the Island's civilian aircraft came in, indistinctly, over the military network. He said that they were on final approach and requested permission to land.

"Tell them to do it," Wilson had zoned back into reality, "and tell them to refuel and be ready for immediate take off and to stand by."

Craddock followed the orders given and made the necessary arrangements. As part of the arrangements, he advised the Chinese fleet that the aircraft was approaching and that it should be given safe passage. He further advised them that the aircraft was unarmed and posed no threat and that, in the interests of air safety, the encircling helicopters should be held off during the landing process. The bureaucracy within the Chinese administration was such that granting the request took time, and the aircraft had landed unhindered before any such undertaking was given. In the meantime, the aircraft was refuelled and made ready and the helicopters, for something to fill the time, continued circling and confirming that nothing else was happening visibly.

The tension in the control room was palpable. The Islanders were on edge not knowing what was going to happen; Pantin was clearly scared about his future prospects, and the troops were uncertain where their loyalties should lie. Wilson seemed to be in a trance, but he was not approached as he had in his hand a compact assault gun with a full clip.

"Jack, it's still not too late to make amends. Turn the computer back on, and we'll work something out," Caine said in a compulsive voice.

Pantin looked wildly around searching for a way out of his dilemma. The only friendly faces he saw were those of the Islanders; neither the troops nor Wilson gave any indication of succour.

Tangible tension in the room was broken when Adie Cox, the Island's chief pilot entered the crowded room. He froze when he saw so many guns and frightening-looking soldiers. Looking enquiringly at Gilliland, he slowly scanned the room, seeing Wilson and Pantin and a number of armed guards in one group and the Islanders in another, huddled together.

Wilson snapped out of his reverie, took a long step forward, and placed his left arm around Cox's neck from behind and at the same time pressing the short-barrelled assault weapon into the pilot's right side. "I need you to fly me somewhere, fly boy. Take it slowly, and you won't get hurt . . . yet." Turning to Pantin, he released his grip on the pilot but kept the gun pressed into his side. "You come with me, and mind you, don't cause me any trouble."

The co-pilot of the aircraft was making his external check in readiness for an unscheduled take off as he had been advised would be required. He saw seven people approaching: four were uniformed armed guards and the others comprised a young Islander from the radar room and a pasty looking bald man who held a gun to Adie Cox's back.

Four helicopters were clattering overhead seemingly aimlessly. The twin rotor wash as they passed over lifted debris into the air and scattered it over the apron temporarily blinding the mechanics, who had been attending the grounded aircraft.

Wilson ordered the guards to keep vigil at the bottom of the steps and then nudged Pantin ahead of him into the passenger cabin. Cox followed them and the four guards milled aimlessly at the bottom of the steps, looking lost, unsure of what to do next and confused. A few minutes later, he thrust his head out of the open door, propelled the guard contingent who were still on board from the previous flight which had carried the PM and the Presidents down the steps on to the apron and barked orders to the eight soldiers who stood in disorganised isolation. "Go back to the control room and keep everybody there under guard, including the other soldiers. Nobody is allowed to leave the control room until I say so,"

Wilson shouted to the disorientated soldiers. "I'll give you more orders later." He returned to the cabin where Cox stood at the entrance of the flight deck, looking bemusedly at Pantin, who was now handcuffed to the overhead rack.

"Don't just stand there, get us out of here." Wilson jabbed Cox in the chest with his extended forefinger.

"I'll need to file a flight plan."

"Do that after we take off."

"Where are we going?"

"Just fly east, and I'll tell you later."

"I really can't do that," Cox said testily. "There are procedures to follow."

Wilson drew back the curtain which led to the flight deck. "Get us out of here now, or your boss will be shot," he shouted at the co-pilot.

The co-pilot was terrified and looked to Cox for guidance. No guidance, only confused incomprehension was forthcoming. The small assault rifle pointed at him spoke volumes, and he went through the pre-flight procedures without a word being spoken. When the checks were hastily complete, they took off circling the Island once before heading east. He had already cleared the flight out of the Island with the Chinese as part of the evacuation of the dignitaries who had been attending the ill-fated meeting. So they had no interference from the Chinese Naval and Air Force, who were anyway still moribund by the bureaucracy of the Chinese Navy.

Persuaded by the gun, Cox had no choice but to allow himself to be shackled to the overhead rack in the same way as Pantin but on the opposite side of the aisle. The handcuffs used were too short to allow him to sit so he leaned against the back of a seat.

"I don't understand, Mr Wilson, why are we leaving the Island? And why did you shackle me? And where are we going?" Pantin asked fearfully.

"Questions, questions," Wilson was pained as he whispered to Pantin so that Cox could not hear. "I couldn't leave you behind because you know how the jammer works and where it is, and they could have got it out of you."

"I would never have told," Pantin said indignantly.

"Maybe and maybe not," Wilson looked as if his mind was far away. "As to why I held you at gunpoint. I didn't want to implicate you, so by making it look like I was holding you against your will there is a good chance they will not realise just how harmful you have been to their interests, and you could live to fight another day. That could be useful to me. You ask why we are leaving." He looked reflectively at nothing in particular. "The Chinese Navy are no longer friends of mine and given half a chance, they would scupper me, but the politicians see it quite differently. I can still negotiate with them and get the Island back. So where are we going? Well, I'm going a long way. You, however, are going to get off at our first refuelling point, and you will make your way to London where you can tie up with the Hammond woman and await my orders." He watched through hooded eyes as realisation dawned on Pantin's face that he was not being abandoned and that he would have a chance to complete unfinished business with Hammond. Wilson smiled to himself; the story he had spun for Pantin was marginally plausible but was, nevertheless, a tissue of lies. His real intention had been to keep the trigger away from the Islanders, and he wanted to keep Pantin in reserve in case he could be useful again.

Sixty-Four

*W*ith Wilson gone, the control room calmed down; Pettit tore open the doors of the computer cabinet which was in reality a small room and looked uncomprehendingly at the tangle of circuit boards and a plethora of unrecognisable components. One of the guards endeavoured to stop him, but Craddock intervened.

"As you were, Private." He placed his hand unthreateningly on the private's shoulder. "You're taking orders from me now that Wilson's gone, and I fancy we are not going to be seeing him again for a long, long time. Leave this gentleman be, and let him get on with trying to sort out this terrible mess." The soldier stood down.

"I haven't got a clue what I'm looking for. The whole room is just a mess of boxes and gizmos." Pettit emerged from the room, looking deflated, "Anybody else got any ideas?"

"I might be able to help." Pickering pushed forward through the bewildered and disorientated guards. "I was involved in this lot going in, and I might be able to spot something different." He entered the room and searched briefly before returning to the control room, shaking his head. "I don't see anything obvious."

"We've got to do something really fast." Pettit pointed out of the window. "Wilson's just taken off, and the Chinese will be with us any minute, and before they come in, they are probably going to hit us hard with shells and RPGs and what have you. Once they're here, if we survive the attack, our lives will not be worth living. They are a bunch of very angry sadistically motivated monsters."

"Gentlemen," Craddock pushed his way forward, "I actually made the device that is jamming the system, and I will certainly recognise it." He disappeared into the room and emerged a few minutes later with the black box jammer, which he had disguised as a complex circuit board. He placed it on the floor and stamped on it with the heel of his combat boot. The Wi-Fi device shattered and immediately there was a whining and rapid clicking sound that the computer made as it automatically rebooted.

The screens flickered back into life and the defence domes reactivated once more trapping several vessels between the inner and outer defences. It was fortunate that none of the domes were straddled by sea or aircrafts when they reactivated and none of the helicopters were fortuitously in positions of immediate danger. The over Island dome was deactivated to prevent catastrophic damage to the aircraft that hovered over the Island and could unknowingly drift into its clutches. The Apache Chieftain carrying Wilson was long gone and safe from immediate harm.

There was unimaginable relief in the control room once they had regained control of their defence systems. Domes and open-topped defence barriers were readjusted and absolute control of the Island's systems was transferred from its temporary home in the underground laboratory back to the main control room. Pettit made a mental note to have the controls reconfigured so that the nightmare of the last few days could not be repeated.

They set about the task of regaining control of their own destiny. To their surprise, the transition from hostage under sentence of death to regaining complete freedom of action was strangely low-key bordering on being surreal and had taken less than an hour. There was a moment of total silence in the control room as if they could not believe that the change was so dramatic and short-lived and final.

Almost in a daze, they arranged for the transportation of Wilson's troops away from the Island by allowing the besieging fleet to send in an unarmed seaborne personnel carrier with a minimum crew, all of whom were to be visible on deck on arrival. They also gave permission for the fleet helicopters which had carried the assault teams so hopefully to the Island, to return to their home carrier. Within a brief time, they were once more back in control of their immediate destiny.

Sixty-Five

Wilson gave the co-pilot a new heading, and they turned south-east towards the Mediterranean veering south over the straits of Gibraltar to a small private airport near Sidi bel Abbes in Northern Algeria. Pantin was dropped off with a significant sum in US Dollars, including enough for him to buy a new passport, and he was told to make his way to London under his own steam and contact Hammond while awaiting further instructions. The refuelled aircraft took off and headed slightly north of east to Baku on the Caspian Sea coast from where, after further refuelling, they flew directly into Nuovostan.

Adie Cox timed the final approach into Nuovostan Airport in daylight. It had not been possible for him to get permission for a night landing because of a lack of electricity to power the safety lighting. Landing instructions were basic and made in a mixture of English and Russian, mostly Russian, and comprised mainly "*Land when you can and be careful there may be other aircraft landing without authorisation.*"

Wilson disembarked with several heavy bags and boxes which had been loaded on board prior to the departure of the first flight which had taken the dignitaries back to Portugal. He had applied the last vestiges he possessed of reason in preparing a plan B in the event of the failure of his endeavours. His parting action, in an uncharacteristic humanitarian gesture, he threw the shackles key to Cox so that he could free the co-pilot from the overhead rack to which they had taken turns to be secured. Money exchanged hands and a ramshackle taxi was conjured up into which Wilson together with his luggage was squeezed. Both pilots watched the taxi disappear into the wasteland on which the airport was situated; they were suddenly alone.

Yuri Kurakin's office and the anti-room occupied by Irena Pelochev were exactly the same as his previous visits in the guise of Simon Queeze. Polchev looked shocked when she realised who he was and her hand flew to her mouth in shock; her other hand hovered over the telephone that would connect her to Kurakin.

"Don't be alarmed, Ms Pelochev, I mean you no harm." He gave an unconvincing smile. "I would like to talk to you and Mr Kurakin about things of mutual interest."

"But," she spluttered. "We have just returning from Recovery Island to give talkings about you. We think you are keeping on Island."

"I have a proposition for Mr Kurakin and you, which I think you will find interesting."

She picked up the telephone and spoke rapidly into it in Russian. Shrugging her shoulders, she replaced the phone and looked at him through narrowed eyes. "Mr Kurakin will seeing you but first must frisk to make sure no guns are."

"Frisk away." He smiled lecherously at her. "You frisk me, and I frisk you."

"Mr Wilson," she giggled, "you are naughty man. I frisk you now, and maybe later, you frisk me if we have useful agreements."

Kurakin sat behind the scrupulously clean desk in his sumptuous office; he looked up cautiously as Wilson entered and nodded his head imperceptibly towards a seat that faced the desk.

"I have a proposition which will make you very rich." Wilson launched directly into his pitch. "I need somewhere safe to stay, and I'm prepared to pay you one million US Dollars for it. Doing that is just the start. There are more millions for you, once I start implementing my plans, and for this, you have to do very little." He looked with concentration at Pelochev. "You, on the other hand, will have to do a few things to cement our relationship."

She smiled calculatingly and translated for Kurakin; he laughed out loud and spoke to her rapidly in Russian. "Mr Kurakin he say you are unusual man because we told to them things about you that get you into trouble, but you still want to dealing with us."

"I am talking to you because I know that you are motivated by money, and you have no morals. That means you are like me, and I understand people like me, and I can deal with them and you."

She translated Wilson's words and waited for the answer. "Mr Kurakin he says that it is good for us not trusting each other. We will do good partnership." She walked to the drinks cupboard and returned, predictably, with an unopened bottle of Vodka and three glasses. When she had poured three generous measures and distributed them, she held her glass up and said with gravitas. "Bottoms out," she said and tossed the measure down in one go. She watched Wilson do the same and filled his glass again. "Not too much Wodka, or we not cementing for relationships." She winked, and he felt the relief of at last being home.

Sixty-Six

egotiations between the Islanders and the Chinese fleet were taciturn and protracted and ill-tempered. Any proposals put forward by the Islanders were relayed from the fleet to the Peoples Republic in Beijing where they were considered at length before being rejected. The blockade of the Island, which had been so close to being successful and would have succeeded but for the unprincipled actions of Wilson, continued, and to the frustration of the Chinese and the Federation, remained ineffective and would continue to do so as long as the materials stockpiled in the warehouses to mitigate the effects of the siege were sufficient to maintain life and the Islanders continued to resist using their technology as a weapon.

Given that such a siege had been anticipated, there was enough food and other basics to last the population for two years. Fresh fruit and vegetables were provided by the intensive farming in the three thousand acre parcels of agricultural land around the slopes which lead up to central lake. Because the Island was warmed by the geothermal heat piped over the whole of the terrain, it was possible to produce several crops per year. A mixture of tiered agriculture and liquid and nutrients allowed a broad spectrum of fruits and vegetables, both temperate and tropical to be grown at the same time by using the slopes of the growing fields which faced the appropriate direction. Landscape areas which supported palm trees and fast-growing shrubs were also planted with sweet corn, peppers, courgettes, and potatoes to provide further sustenance which also gave the boulevards a lushness they had not formerly enjoyed.

The invaluable BAM2 protected the Apache Chieftain and enabled a limited amount of comfortable access to the rest of the less hostile areas of the world and was supplemented by their small fleet of ageing but robust cargo planes which could be protected remotely from the control room, also by BAM2. On returning to the Island, the Apache Chieftain had been subjected to desperate missile and fighter attacks by the Chinese which—had been frustrated by the BAM2 defence sphere capability as it continued to repel all efforts of destruction.

Negotiations, which were going nowhere to start with, went into reverse after the return of their air transport, and the Chinese, backed now by the coerced and coopted Federation, became even more aggressive, switching their tack by threatening to invade any country that had trading links with the Islanders and gave them succour.

Unreality reigned. The siege fleet, still being monitored by the Russian Navy, sat threateningly outside the force shields at the twelve-mile limit, waiting for an opportunity to pounce on any relaxation in the Island's defence capability. Islanders tried to live what to them was a natural life, but they were all very conscious of the threat over the horizon, and it could not be seen, but its ever-present threat was, nevertheless, real.

The tenor of the stalled negotiations changed when it fell to Creswell to make a last-ditch attempt to broker a deal. He was welcomed on to the Island as a lone negotiator representing the Federation. His return to the conference table where, only a short time ago, he had been defending his political life and fighting for his freedom gave him cause for optimism because he could use the language of moderation which was clearly the only way forward and was no longer under threat from Wilson.

Try as he might to win over the Island's leaders, his efforts were in vain, which came as no great surprise to him. The stumbling block was that BAM2 technology was still not negotiable as an asset to anybody other than the Islanders. The leaders refused point-blank to share what could be a fatally dangerous weapon in the hands of any other country. Specifically not with the Federation, which at the time of the negotiations was holding siege, and there were no current prospects of a withdrawal, even for the purposes of negotiation.

Creswell pleaded the case of the poorer nations which could benefit from the peaceful use of BAM2 in the furtherance of infrastructure, energy, and the health benefits that Island research was yielding. There was agreement by the Ruling Council to the sharing of any health benefits which had been developed and tested but not to the surrender of BAM2 which they knew, as a certainty, would be used for military purposes. Any use of BAM2 could only be countenanced if it were under the sole control of Island engineers and scientists, a situation which the Federation could not tolerate.

More in hope than expectation, Creswell shared the Islanders' proposals with the Federation and waited for a week to hear their response. When their views were finally expressed, they were an unexpected but, nevertheless, bitter disappointment to him. The well-trodden mantra of the Chinese, in the guise of the Federation, was trotted out. The Federation would only accept the release of the whole package of BAM2 without reservation and they, the Federation, would have responsible control of all the capabilities of the technology, naturally, they propounded, for the overall benefit of mankind.

The communication concluded that Recovery Island was denying the benefits of the technology originally financed by one of the Federation members and in doing so showed callous disregard for the human needs of poorer nations. This situation was intolerable to the Federation and would not be allowed to prevail.

"James," Gilliland said sadly as he finished reading the Federation's response, "it is just as we feared and expected. We have been very open in telling anybody who is prepared to listen that we will share the benefits with any country needing them, but we will not relinquish control. Certainly not to an active political entity or to a group which may become a political entity. We will give freely to poorer nations and offer considerable economic gain to those countries which are already more fortunate."

"What can I say?" Creswell said dejectedly. "There are none as blind as those who don't want to see, and I'm afraid the influencing bodies in the Federation are in that group."

No conclusion to the dilemma was reached, and ultimately, Creswell had to admit that his representations to the Federation would not bring mutual resolution. The Ruling Council met, and Creswell was permitted to attend. Doves and hawks alike were unanimous that under no circumstances would they approve the release of BAM2 and a statement was prepared for submission to the Federation. It basically stated what they had been proposing all along that the benefits of BAM2 and health research would be shared with poorer nations freely or by bartering for natural resources where they were available and required.

The statement was made in such a way that there was no room for manoeuvre, and the talks were abandoned before the receipt of comment from the Federation or any other country or organisation. It all ended in anticlimax and was disappointing for the Island's administration and thoroughly depressing for Creswell.

Once more the Island returned to an uneasy stalemate, and over time the unease of the stalemate would be replaced by an acceptance which diminished the effects of the external threat. One positive point that came out of the impasse was that the Islanders had a renewed and reinvigorated vision of their own identity; they were becoming a cohesive independent nation with an emerging identity.

Some three months after the breakdown of the negotiations, Gilliland received a telephone call from Crook who was located in the control room. "The Chinese are gone." He said with suppressed excitement. "Lock, stock, and barrel. All that's left are a few lonely looking Russian trawlers who appear not to know what to do."

The next meeting of the Ruling Council was brief and suffused with excited relief the enemy at the door was gone; they remained the enemy, but they were no longer at the door.

"Ladies and Gentlemen," Gilliland said in closing a brief overview of their situation. "We are again sole masters of our own fate. It is now up to us to try to bring peace and harmony to a fragmented world or to ignore it and reap the benefits of our good fortune by totally, and perhaps selfishly, isolating ourselves." He slowly took in all members of the Council and smiled benignly. "The next group session we have will address this question. I suggest you all go away and think about whether you support mankind with all its faults and evils or whether you want to insulate yourselves against the dangers that such an undertaking brings, by not getting involved." He turned to leave the Council Chamber. "Your deliberations 'yes or no' will be acted upon in a democratic vote." He left the room to a stunned silence.

The deliberations on the content of the discussion were considerably longer than the discussions themselves. Once more it was three of the female members of the Council, Penny Caine, Juilietta Gray, and Bell Pickering, who came up with a clear and definitive proposal about their future direction. Their proposal was simply that the Island should work with the only solution presently open to them, and that was to accept their isolation from the rest of the world and continue to develop and improve their society based on their own desires and wishes.

Their proposed decision was not, however, long-term isolationism; their intention was to continue to offer to the outside world, with no cost or strings attached, the medical and social innovations—with the exclusion of BAM2 technology—from which the Islanders were deriving benefit. By doing so, they hoped to lure the rest of the world into being more harmonious. They further proposed that their form of social management, government without political affiliations, should also be showcased. At the same time, they recognised that as long as a society was based on monetary exchange such changes to the structure of government would be fraught. Unanimously, the Council voted in favour of the simple proposal; this was overwhelmingly ratified by the Island's first Island-wide democratic referendum. Their nationhood was thereby firmly established.

Caine made an Island-wide presentation on the public and private Information Portals in which she stated the impressive numbers supporting the proposals. In closing, she was visibly emotional about the truly momentous steps that they were all taking. "Thank you, Islanders, for your support. We on the Council are thankful that you are with us in reaching for our collective dreams, without the stranglehold of corrupted politics. Your Council members are chosen for their ability to carry out their specialist tasks, not for any political leanings, right, left, or centre, moderate or extremist, which they are free to hold. We, of the Council, undertake to dedicate all of our efforts to ensuring that our collective freedoms are protected and that despite outside rejection, we will not abandon our fellow human beings, we will continue to nurture them."

Having concluded her broadcast, she turned and looked at her three founding companions and saw that they too were caught up in the emotion of the moment. It was only then that she was absolutely sure that, whatever happened as their plan unfolded, they had decided on the only right course of action for themselves, the Islanders, and yes, the rest of humanity.

"Well," she turned to her emotional companions, "we have made the great journey from irretrievably corrupt government to our own open and honest governance, if not for others we have at least done so for ourselves and those who have allied themselves to us. This part of the journey is complete, and there is no way back from it, nor would we want one. It is now for us to ensure that what we develop will reflect our aspirations and those of the people of the Island and of the generations to come. The initial journey is over for us, but the battle for opportunity will continue until we win. We must by all peaceful means work towards securing for ourselves and the rest of the world a legacy of which we can be justly proud."

After the decision had been reached and ratified, there was an overwhelming sense of relief and a firm belief that they could stop expending energy on defending themselves and concentrate on moving forward in developing their own interests. Plans were drawn up to improve their own lot and to divert energies towards the positive elements of improving their society by asking the Islanders to make a contribution to development ideas.

The Ruling Council was inundated with ideas from all parts of their society; they ranged from the sublime to the ridiculous, from mainstream to outlandish. One thing became clear if they were to pursue all the suggestions put forward, they would need to expand both population and land space. The process of weeding out the ideas presented was undertaken by a small group of four women: Penny Caine, Bell Pickering, Juilietta Gray, and Carlina Tanterelli.

They deliberated for some time but finally came up with a solution which they presented to a full meeting of the Ruling Council. Proposals put forward had been graded in order of excellence using an analytical points system. The outcome of the listing was that a large number of the suggestions came equal first and of the remaining suggestions only the most outlandish were not included in the list but they were not discarded, they were put on a "future consideration" list.

An announcement was made to the Islanders at the completion of the Ruling Council's findings, and it caused jubilation and celebration throughout the Island. The ladies had recommended that to meet with the wishes expressed by the population, it would be necessary for them to create more Islands to enable more leisure, farming, research, and other activities, a massive programme of improvement.

They had made the long journey from the initial idea of their new society to the present. They had not wavered in their resolve; they had a blossoming sense of identity which promised a safe and progressive future. They had arrived at a place which they could launch a new and fulfilling life. The journey had been completed, and ahead lay a future full of hope and fulfilment which was embraced by the whole Island.

Epilogue

Free from the threat of siege, the Islanders launched themselves with energy and gusto in to identifying and developing their own way of life in what they accepted was a new Genesis. But, as with the original concept of Genesis, from the good which was freely offered there emerged evil. The mythology of Garden of Eden teaches us that within even the most carefully constructed paradise, there is a serpent waiting to tempt with an apple of promise offering enticements which are difficult for mortals to resist.

There emerged from the Island's population a group of people who, knowing little or nothing of the outside world, wanted greater freedom to visit old homelands and to roam the world in general. Under the rules of the Island, they had the freedom to pursue the determination their own future, providing they did not use that freedom to unduly influence or coerce others. This proviso was to prove to be an influence which would split the Island population; it was the poisoned apple in their Island's Garden of Eden.

An underground movement for what was vaguely termed *greater freedom* gained impetus and covert moves were made to negotiate with the Federation or any other agency which could enable those of the Islanders who were dissident to move freely about the world by making concessions to Island's ideologies. The Ruling Council rejected any form of negotiation which might lead to the sharing of any technology; but still the movement clamoured for concessions.

The success of the new islands lent strength to those who favoured using their further journey towards self-sufficiency and independence. Self-sufficiency, while satisfying in itself, did not, however, give the Islanders the freedom to travel the world unhindered. This led, among some of the original inhabitants of the Island, to homesickness and general disquiet and newcomers picked up on the unrest and clamoured to have their views acted upon.

Detractors believed that isolationism would take several years to counter and even with the fullness of time, success was not assured. Fundamentalists in the movement formed by the detractors began to hold sway over the more moderate elements, and their proposed methods of achieving their aims took on a sinister undertone.

A small hard-core pulled away from the main body of the movement and began to set a more radical agenda. No matter how the movement, whether represented by the moderate or fundamental sections, approached the Ruling Council, there was no room for manoeuvre. The technology would not be shared in any way with a third party no matter what promises or assurances were received.

Moderate elements of the movement continued grumbling about the intransigence of the Ruling Council and continued to press for change, taking every opportunity to openly recruit support from as many incumbents as possible. The fundamentalists moved in a totally different direction, they withdrew into themselves and, as a reduced number, began to formulate their own version of positive coercion. They became a dissident sect calling themselves the Recovery Island Rebels, the RIR, which was populated in the main by militant activists. They formulated their own radical plans for reducing resistance to their reintegration with the world at large; finally their thoughts coalesced into the first simple act to further their cause.

Their answer was that they, as radicals, were determined to engineer the removal of the restrictive influence of the founders by fair means or foul. This would enable them to use BAM2 as a weapon of progress and allow them to move forward into a world full of unimaginable dark possibilities by releasing the full destructive potential of BAM2 technology. The radical Island group were not alone in wanting to achieve this objective; there were at least two other groups with the same aims. Although they were all too disparate to work together, they collectively reached one common and chilling conclusion: *the only way for them to access the technology would be to resort to wholesale assassination.*

Coming soon

Retrogenesis 3:
The Legacy

Prologue

The man on the control tower roof was virtually invisible; he wore dark patterned off Island clothes which blended in with the dappled shade of the overhang of the roof. Sixty foot below him and five hundred foot distant, four figures descended from an executive jet with its distinctive tail decoration showing the curiously regular silhouette of the Island superimposed on a blood-red setting sun.

From his elevated prone position, he pushed the long muzzle of his rifle through the safety railing and switched on the infrared range finder. Through the scope, he could see the three men and a dark-haired young woman quite clearly and could also see the red dot of the range finder in the centre of the chest of his target. There was a robotic buzz as the scope adjusted to raise the barrel, giving the correct trajectory for the distance calculated by the laser range finder. The light breeze which eddied around convoluted shapes of the towers superstructure ruffled the sleeves of his bomber jacket and his short hair but did not detract from his concentration to keep the red dot steady in the centre of the target's chest.

The rifle, which had been manufactured in Nuovostan, was a subsonic sniper's special or 4S as it was known to its few specialist users, was almost silent when fired; the specially modified projectile it fired travelled at less than the speed of sound and therefore, did not produce a sonic boom. The sniper rechecked his aim so that the dot was positioned exactly in the centre of the target's chest. Before squeezing the trigger, he switched on the vision and sound recording device which had been added to the rifle at the insistence of the sniper's paymaster.

Escaping gas hissed angrily through the barrel tip vents; a bullet leaving the muzzle and travelling at around seven hundred miles per hour would take less than a second to travel the distance from muzzle to target.

"*Bang!*" the sniper whispered softly, fractionally before he made the shot.

Through the scope, he saw blood blossom crimson on the chest of the target as he staggered backwards and fell. His three companions, after a shock-induced momentary pause, dragged the supine figure under the fuselage of the jet and out of further harm's way. Pressing the rewind button in the stock of the 4S, he looked at the full colour high definition record of the assassination. Satisfied that the images and sound were clear and definitive he began the task of dismantling the rifle.

With measured haste, he packed the rifle back into its snag-proof bag and descended the tower through the internal stairway down to ground level where he paused before carefully opening the personnel door which gave access to the smooth seamless surface of the apron. Within moments, he was inside warehouse 26C, which was situated on the western perimeter of the apron; he felt his way in the darkness of the closed up building and located his means of escape.

Even had the light been good, he would not have been able to see the outline of the door crafted into the side of the crate. He located the door by finding by touch a knothole in the centre of the top loop of the R in *freight* made discernible with the aid of a weak LED key-fob light. Once inside, he deposited the rifle in a lock box, which snapped shut and locked automatically, the next segment of his task would be boring in the extreme. He strapped himself into an airline style seat which had been secured to the base of the freight box. All he had to do now was to wait until morning when the crate would be loaded into the hold of the cargo plane which would take him to Madrid. He fell almost immediately into a deep sleep demonstrating that he was totally untroubled by the assassination he had just carried out.

He was awoken refreshed the next morning when the crate was lifted by fork lift and trundled across the apron and into the cavernous interior of a cargo plane. His task was complete and had been carried out nervelessly and with military precision. The period of boredom he had anticipated had been mitigated by his deep untroubled sleep, and he was now one million US Dollars richer and had the satisfaction of having achieved exactly what had been expected of him, to help rid the world of somebody who he had been told was a despotic dictator. He did not see how life could get better than this.

Lightning Source UK Ltd.
Milton Keynes UK
UKOW040613271112

202807UK00001B/1/P

9 781479 746996